Succubus Shadows

Richelle Mead

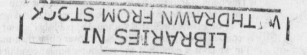

BANTAM BOOKS

LONDON • TORONTO • SYDNEY • AUCKLAND • JOHANNESBURG

TRANSWORLD PUBLISHERS
61–63 Uxbridge Road, London W5 5SA
A Random House Group Company
www.rbooks.co.uk

SUCCUBUS SHADOWS
A BANTAM BOOK: 9780553820317

Originally published in the United States of America by Kensington Books
First publication in Great Britain
Bantam edition published 2010

Addresses for Random House Group Ltd companies outside the UK
can be found at: www.randomhouse.co.uk
The Random House Group Ltd Reg. No. 954009

Penguin Random House is committed to a sustainable future for
our business, our readers and our planet. This book is made from
Forest Stewardship Council® certified paper.

MIX
Paper from
responsible sources
FSC® C018179

Typeset in Sabon
Printed in the UK by Clays Ltd, St Ives plc.

8 10 9 7

For my brother Scott, who always let his little sister
watch *Flash Gordon* and *Star Wars* with him

Chapter 1

I was drunk.

I wasn't entirely sure when it had happened, but I suspected it had occurred around the time my friend Doug had bet me I couldn't take down three vodka gimlets faster than he could. He'd promised to take my weekend shift at work if I won, and I was going to do his stock duty for a week if he won.

When we'd finished, it looked like I wasn't going to be working next weekend.

"How did you out-drink him?" my friend Hugh wanted to know. "He's twice your size."

Through the crowd of people crammed into my condo, I peered at the closed bathroom door, behind which Doug had disappeared. "He had stomach flu this week. I'm guessing that doesn't go so well with vodka."

Hugh raised an eyebrow. "Why the fuck would anyone take a bet like that after having the flu?"

I shrugged. "Because he's Doug."

Hoping Doug would be okay, I scanned the rest of my party with the pleased air of a queen sizing up her kingdom. I'd moved into this place back in July and had been long overdue for a housewarming party. When Halloween had finally rolled around, combining the two events had seemed like a pretty reasonable solution. Consequently, my guests tonight were clad in an array of costumes, everything from elaborate Renaissance fair quality garb to the slackers who'd simply thrown on a witch's hat.

Me, I was dressed as Little Bo Peep—well, that is, I was dressed the way Little Bo Peep would if she was a stripper and/or a shameless strumpet. My frilly blue skirt stopped just above the halfway point on my thighs, and my puff-sleeved white blouse was so low-cut that I had to be careful when leaning over. The crowning achievement—literally—was my curly mane of flaxen blond hair, neatly arranged into two pigtails tied with little blue bows. It looked perfect, absolutely indistinguishable from the real thing because . . . well, it *was* real.

Shape-shifting always came in handy as a succubus, but for Halloween, it was golden. I always had the best costumes because I really could turn into anything I wanted. Of course, I had to keep it within reason. Too much of a change would raise the suspicions of the humans around me. But for a hair change? Yeah. Shape-shifting was pretty convenient.

Someone touched my elbow. I turned, and my smug enthusiasm dimmed a little when I saw who it was: Roman, my sociopathic roommate.

"I think someone's getting sick in the bathroom," he told me. Roman was a nephilim, half-angel and half-human, with soft black hair and sea-green eyes. If not for the fact he occasionally went on immortal killing sprees and had me on his hit list, he would have been a pretty good catch.

"Yeah," I said. "It's Doug. He lost a vodka challenge."

Roman grimaced. He wore devil horns and a red cape. The irony wasn't lost on me. "Hope he's got good aim. I don't want to clean that up."

"What, you don't do housework either?" asked Hugh. He'd recently learned Roman wasn't paying me rent because he was "between jobs." "Seems like you should pull your weight around here somehow."

Roman gave Hugh a warning look. "Stay out of this, Spiro Agnew."

"I'm Calvin Coolidge!" exclaimed Hugh, highly offended. "This is the same suit he wore at his inauguration."

I sighed. "Hugh, nobody here remembers that." That was

one of the downsides of being immortal. Our memories became obsolete as more time passed. Hugh, an imp who bought souls for Hell, was much younger than Roman and me, but he had a lot more years than any human here.

Slipping away from Roman and Hugh's argument, I headed across the room to mingle with my guests. Some of my co-workers from the bookstore Doug and I worked at were huddled around the punch bowl, and I stopped to chat. Immediately, I was bombarded with compliments.

"Your hair is amazing!"

"Did you dye it?"

"It doesn't even look like a wig!"

I assured them it was a very good wig and dealt out praise for them in return. One person, however, earned a rueful head-shake from me.

"You have more creativity than all of us put together, and that's the best you could do?" I asked.

Best-selling author Seth Mortensen turned to look at me with one of his trademark, slightly scattered smiles. Even when I was dizzy with vodka, that smile never failed to make my heart speed up. Seth and I had dated for a while, plunging me into the depths of a love I'd never imagined possible. Part of being a succubus was an eternity of seducing men and stealing the energy of their souls—a real relationship had seemed out of the question. And in the end, it had been. Seth and I had broken up—twice—and while I usually accepted that he had moved on, I knew that I would love him forever. For me, forever was a serious matter.

"I can't waste it on a costume," he said. His amber-brown eyes regarded me fondly. I no longer knew if he loved me too; I only knew for sure that he still cared about me as a friend. I kept trying to portray the same image. "Gotta save it for the next book."

"Lame excuse," I said. His shirt depicted Freddy Krueger, which might have been acceptable if not for the fact I suspected he had owned it long before Halloween.

Seth shook his head. "Nobody cares what guys wear at

Halloween anyway. It's all about the women. Look around."
I did and saw that he was right. All the elaborate, sexy costumes were on my female guests. With a few exceptions, the
men's dulled by comparison.

"Peter's dressed up," I pointed out. Seth followed my gaze
to another of my immortal friends. Peter was a vampire, a
very fastidious and obsessive-compulsive one. He was clad in
pre-Revolutionary French garb, complete with brocade coat
and a powdered wig over what was normally thin brown hair.

"Peter doesn't count," said Seth.

Recalling how Peter had painstakingly stenciled swans
around his bathroom's baseboards last week, I couldn't help
but agree. "Fair point."

"What's Hugh supposed to be? Jimmy Carter?"

"Calvin Coolidge."

"How can you tell?"

I was saved from answering when Seth's fiancée—and one
of my best friends—Maddie Sato appeared. She was dressed
as a fairy, complete with wings and a gauzy dress nowhere
near as slutty as mine. Fake flowers wreathed black hair that
had been pulled into a bun. Her being with Seth was something else I'd more or less come to accept, though I suspected
the sting of it would never leave. Maddie didn't know Seth
and I had dated and had no clue about the discomfiture I felt
over their whole relationship.

I expected her to slip her arm around Seth, but it was me
she grabbed hold of and jerked away. I stumbled a bit. Five-
inch heels weren't normally a problem for me, but the vodka
complicated things a bit.

"Georgina," she exclaimed, once we were far enough away
from Seth. "I need your help." Reaching into her purse, she
pulled out two pages torn from magazines.

"With wha—oh." My stomach twisted uncomfortably, and
I hoped I wouldn't be joining Doug in the bathroom. The
pages showed photos of wedding dresses.

"I've almost narrowed it down," she explained. "What do
you think?"

Grudgingly accepting the man I loved was going to marry one of my best friends was one thing. Helping them plan their wedding was an entirely different matter. I swallowed.

"Oh, gee, Maddie. I'm not very good at this stuff."

Her dark eyes widened. "Are you kidding? You're the one who taught me how to dress right in the first place."

She apparently hadn't taken the lessons to heart. The dresses, while beautiful on the anorexic models wearing them, would look terrible on Maddie. "I don't know," I said lamely, dragging my eyes away. The dresses were conjuring mental images of Maddie and Seth walking down the aisle together.

"Come *on*," she entreated. "I know you have an opinion."

I did. A bad one. And honestly, if I were a good servant of Hell, I would have told her they both looked great. Or I would have endorsed the worst one. What she wore was no concern of mine, and maybe if she showed up at her wedding looking subpar, Seth would realize what he'd lost when we broke up.

And yet . . . I couldn't. Even after everything that had happened, I just couldn't let Maddie do it. She'd been a good friend, never suspecting what had occurred between Seth and me before *and* during their relationship. And as much as that petty, selfish part of me wanted it, I couldn't let her go forward in a bad dress.

"Neither are good," I said at last. "The full skirt on that one will make you look short. The flowers on top of that one will make you look fat."

She was taken aback. "Really? I never . . ." She studied the pictures, face falling. "Damn. I thought I had this stuff down now."

I can only assume my next words came from the liquor. "If you want, I'll go with you to some places this week. You can try some stuff on, and I'll tell you what works."

Maddie lit up. She wasn't gorgeous in the popular, magazine sort of way, but when she smiled, she was beautiful. "Really? Oh, thank you. And you can look for your dress too."

"My what?"

"Well . . ." Her smile turned sly. "You're going to be a bridesmaid, aren't you?"

At that moment, I reconsidered my earlier thoughts about nothing being more painful than helping plan her wedding. Being her bridesmaid pretty much blew that out of the water. Those who believed we made our own hells on earth must have had something like this in mind.

"Oh, well, I don't know . . ."

"You have to! There's no one else I'd rather have."

"I'm not really the bridesmaid type."

"Of course you are." Maddie's eyes suddenly looked at something beyond me. "Oh, hey. Doug's back. I'm going to go check on him. We'll talk about this later. You'll give in." Maddie scurried off to her brother, leaving me numb and speechless. I decided then it was worth risking illness to go get another drink. This party had taken a definite U-turn.

Yet, when I turned around, it wasn't toward the bar. It was toward my patio. One of the best features of this condo was its expansive balcony, one that looked out over Puget Sound and the Seattle skyline beyond. As I stood there, though, it wasn't the view that captivated me. It was . . . something else. Something I couldn't explain. But it was warm and wonderful and spoke to all my senses. I imagined I could see colored light on my balcony, kind of like the waves of an aurora. I could also hear a type of music that defied all human words and had nothing to do with the Pink Floyd blasting from my stereo.

The party faded into the background as I slowly moved toward the balcony. The door was open to air out the hot room, and my two cats, Aubrey and Godiva, lay near it to look outside. I stepped past them, drawn toward that which had no explanation or description. Warm autumn air engulfed me as I groped for what called me. It was all around me and yet out of my reach. It was summoning me, drawing me toward something right on the balcony's edge. I almost considered climbing on the ledge in my heels and looking over. I *had* to reach that beauty.

"Hey, Georgina."

Peter's voice jerked me out of the trance. I stared around, startled. There was no music, no color, no beckoning embrace. Only the night and the view and the patio furniture on my balcony. I turned around, meeting his eyes.

"We have a problem," he said.

"We have a lot of problems," I said, thinking of Maddie's wedding dress and the fact that I'd nearly walked off my own balcony. I shivered. I definitely was *not* going back for that next drink. Sick was one thing. Hallucinations were another. "What's wrong?"

Peter led me inside and pointed. "Cody's in love."

I looked over at our friend Cody, another vampire and Peter's apprentice. Cody was a young immortal, optimistic and endearing. He was dressed as an alien, with green antennae sticking out of his shaggy blond hair. The perfection of his silvery space suit made me think Peter had played a role. Right now, Cody was staring across the room, mouth open as he gazed at someone. He looked like I had felt just moments ago.

Her name was Gabrielle, and she'd just started working at the bookstore. She was tiny, almost pixie like, and wore black fishnets and a ripped black dress. Her spiky hair was also black, as was her lipstick. Easy coordination. Cody was staring at her like she was the most beautiful creature on earth.

"Huh," I said. Hugh dated all the time, but I'd never really thought of the vampires—particularly Peter—having any sort of romantic interactions.

"I think he likes that she's dressed as a vampire," said Peter.

I shook my head. "Actually, that's how she always dresses."

We walked over to Cody, and it took him several moments to notice us. He seemed excited to see me. "What's her name?" he breathed.

I tried to hide my smile. Cody being smitten was one of the cutest things I'd ever seen and a welcome distraction from the other drama tonight. "Gabrielle. She works at the store."

"Is she single?"

I looked back at her as she laughed at something Maddie had said. "I don't know. Want me to find out?"

Cody blushed—in as much as a pale vampire could. "No! I mean . . . unless you think it wouldn't be too obvious? I don't want you to go to any trouble."

"No trouble for me," I said, just as Doug walked by. "Hey." I caught hold of his sleeve. "Do me a favor, and I'll take my shift back."

Doug, whose Japanese-American skin was normally golden tan, could have also currently passed for an alien with his green hue. "I'd rather have my stomach back, Kincaid."

"Go investigate Gabrielle's romantic status. Cody's interested."

"Georgina!" exclaimed Cody, mortified.

Sick or not, Doug couldn't resist a little intrigue. "Sure thing."

He headed off across the room and pulled Gabrielle to him, leaning down so she could hear. At one point, he glanced over toward us, and Gabrielle looked as well. Cody nearly died.

"Oh God."

Doug returned five minutes later and shook his head. "Sorry, kid. She's single, but she doesn't think you're her type. She's into the Goth and vampire scene. You're too mainstream for her." I was sipping a glass of water and nearly choked on it.

"That," said Peter, as soon as Doug was gone, "is what we call irony."

"How is that possible?" exclaimed Cody. "I *am* a vampire. I should be exactly what she wants."

"Yeah, but you don't look like one," I said. If Gabrielle had been a Trekkie, he might have had a shot tonight.

"I look exactly like a vampire because I am one! What should I dress up as? Count Chocula?"

The party continued in force for another couple hours, and finally, people began trickling out. Roman and I, playing good hosts, smiled and bade each of them farewell. By the time everyone left, I was weary and more than happy for it all to be over. I'd refused to drink after the balcony incident and now had a headache as a pleasant reminder of my indulgences. Roman looked as exhausted as me as he scanned the messy condo.

"Funny, huh? You throw a housewarming party to show the place off, and then people trash it."

"It'll clean up fast," I said, studying all the bottles and paper plates with remnants of food. Aubrey was licking frosting off a half-eaten cupcake, and I hastily took it away from her. "But not tonight. Help me take care of the perishables, and we'll do the rest tomorrow."

"There's no 'we' in 'clean,'" Roman said.

"That doesn't even make sense," I said, covering up some salsa. "And Peter's right, you know. You really should do more around here."

"I provide good company. Besides, how can you get rid of me?"

"I'll get Jerome to," I warned, referring to his demon father, who also happened to be my boss.

"Sure. Run off and tell on me." Roman stifled a yawn, demonstrating just how worried he was about his father's wrath. The annoying part was, he had a point. I couldn't get rid of him on my own, and I doubted Jerome would really help. Still, I could hardly believe it when Roman did wander off to bed and leave me alone with the cleanup. I hadn't thought he'd go that far.

"Asshole!" I yelled after him, getting only a slammed door in response. He really wasn't that bad of a roommate, but our troubled past often made him want to annoy me. It worked.

Fuming, I finished the necessary tidying and dropped into bed a half-hour later. Aubrey and Godiva followed me, lying side by side at the end of the bed. They were a contrast in colors, like some piece of modern art. Aubrey was white with black specks on her head; Godiva was a riot of orange, brown, and black patches. All three of us drifted off to sleep immediately.

Sometime later, I woke to the sound of singing . . . or, well, that was the closest I could come to describing it. It was the same thing I'd felt earlier, an alluring, haunting pull that spoke to every part of me. Warm and bright and beautiful. It was everywhere and everything, and I longed to have more of it, to walk toward the light that shone with indescribable colors. It felt so, so good—like something I could melt into, if only I could reach it. I had the impression of an entrance, a door I simply had to push open and step through and—

Rough hands gripped my shoulders and jerked me around. "Wake up!"

Like before, the sensory overload vanished. I was left alone in a quiet, empty world. No more siren song. Roman stood in front of me, hands shaking me as his face stared down at me with worry. I looked around. We were in the kitchen. I had no memory of getting there.

"How—what happened?" I stammered.

The face that had taunted me earlier was now filled with concern, something that troubled a small part of me. Why should someone who wanted to kill me be worried about me?

"You tell me," he said, releasing his grip.

I rubbed my eyes, willing myself to recall what had happened. "I . . . I don't know. I must have sleepwalked. . . ."

His face was still drawn and anxious. "No . . . there was something here. . . ."

I shook my head. "No, it was a dream. Or a hallucination. I had it happen earlier. . . . I just drank too much."

"Didn't you just hear me?" There it was again, fear for me underneath the anger. "There was *something* here, some . . . force. I felt it. It woke me up. Don't you remember anything at all?"

I stared off, trying to summon up the light and haunting melody. I couldn't. "It was . . . it was exquisite. I wanted . . . I wanted to go to it . . . to be part of it . . ." There was a dreamy, wistful note in my voice.

Roman's expression grew dark. As a succubus, I was a lesser immortal, one who had once been human. Greater immortals, like angels and demons, had been created at the universe's beginning. Nephilim were born and fell somewhere in the middle. As such, their powers and senses were greater than mine. Roman could detect things I couldn't.

"Don't," he said. "You feel it again, you pull away. Don't let it draw you in. Under no circumstances should you go to it."

I looked back at him with a frown. "Why? Do you know what it is?"

"No," he said grimly. "And that's the problem."

Chapter 2

I tossed and turned the rest of the night. Being visited by a weird supernatural force will do that to you. Besides, I had never fully recovered from the time an über-powerful entity of chaos had merged with me in my sleep and sucked away my energy. Her name was Nyx, and last I'd heard, she was imprisoned. Still, what she'd done to me—and what she'd shown me—had left a lasting impression. The fact that Roman couldn't identify what had happened tonight was a little unnerving.

So, I woke up bleary-eyed, sporting a massive headache that was probably equal parts hangover and sleep deprivation. Succubi had the rapid healing that all immortals possessed, which meant I must have seriously screwed myself up to have these lingering effects. I knew the headache would pass soon, but I took some ibuprofen to help the process.

The condo was quiet when I shuffled into the kitchen, and despite my efforts to clean up the food last night, I was still surrounded in the tattered and worn-out feel that followed most parties. Godiva, curled up on the back of the couch, lifted her head at my arrival, but Aubrey continued sleeping undisturbed in her spot on an armchair. I started some coffee and then wandered over to my patio, staring out at the sunny day and the Seattle skyline on the other side of the gray-blue water stretching off before me.

A familiar sensation suddenly swept me, like brimstone and red-hot needles. I sighed.

"Kind of early for you, isn't it?" I asked, not needing to turn around to know Jerome, archdemon of the greater Seattle area and my hellish boss, stood behind me.

"It's noon, Georgie," he replied dryly. "The rest of the world is up and around."

"It's Saturday. The laws of time and space are different today. Noon qualifies as early."

I turned around at last, largely because I'd heard the coffeemaker finish. Jerome was leaning against my kitchen wall, immaculately dressed as always in a black designer suit. Also, like always, the demon looked exactly like a circa 1990s version of John Cusack. He could appear as anything or anyone he wanted in this world, but for reasons he kept vague, Mr. Cusack was his preferred shape. I'd gotten so used to it that whenever *Say Anything* or *Grosse Pointe Blank* came on TV, I always had to pause and ask myself, "What's Jerome doing in this movie?"

I poured a cup of coffee and held up the pot by way of invitation. Jerome shook his head. "I suppose," he said, "your roommate is also being a sloth and isn't actually out running errands?"

"That'd be my guess." I doused my coffee liberally with vanilla creamer. "I used to kind of hope that when he wasn't around, it meant he was out looking for a job. Turns out I was just setting myself up for disappointment."

Honestly, I was glad it was Roman that Jerome had come to see. When Jerome was looking for me, no good ever came of it. It always tended to result in some traumatic, world-threatening event in the immortal underground.

I trudged back across the living room, noting that the cats had disappeared upon Jerome's arrival. Coffee still in hand, I headed to Roman's room, knocking once before opening the door. I figured as landlady, I had that right. Also, I'd found Roman had a remarkable ability to ignore knocking for large amounts of time.

He was sprawled across his bed, wearing only a pair of navy blue boxers that gave me pause. As I'd noted before, he was terribly good-looking, despite the prickly attitude he'd had since moving in. Seeing him half-dressed always gave me a weird flashback to the one time we'd slept together. Then, I'd have to remind myself that he was probably plotting how to kill me. It went a long way to stifle any residual lust.

Roman's arm covered his eyes against the sunlight streaming through his window. He shifted, moving the arm slightly, and peered at me with one eye. "It's early," he said.

"Not according to your exalted sire."

A few seconds passed, and then he grimaced as he too sensed Jerome's immortal signature. With a sigh, Roman sat up, pausing to rub his eyes. He looked about as exhausted as I felt, but if there was one force in this world that could drag him out of bed after a late night, it was my boss—no matter Roman's bold claims from last night. He staggered to his feet and moved past me in the doorway.

"Aren't you going to get dressed?" I exclaimed.

Roman's only answer was a disinterested wave of his hand as he headed down the hall. I followed him back and discovered Jerome pouring himself a mug of some vodka leftover from last night. Well, it was five o'clock somewhere. He arched an eyebrow when he saw Roman's scantily clad state.

"Nice of you to dress up."

Roman made a beeline for the coffee. "Only the best for you, Pop. Besides, Georgina likes it."

A moment of heavy silence followed as Jerome's dark eyes studied Roman. I knew nothing about Roman's mother, but Jerome was the demon who had fathered him thousands of years ago. Technically, Jerome had been an angel at the time, but making the moves on a human had got him fired from Heaven and sent off to work for those down below. No severance package.

Roman occasionally made snide comments about their familial relationship, but Jerome never acknowledged it. In fact, according to both Heaven and Hell's rules, Jerome should have blasted Roman from the earth ages ago. Angels and demons considered nephilim unnatural and wrong and continually attempted to hunt them to extinction. It was kind of harsh, even with the sociopathic tendencies nephilim tended to have. Roman had been instrumental in saving Jerome recently, however, and the two had struck a deal that allowed Roman to live peacefully in Seattle—for now. If any of Jerome's colleagues found out about this illicit arrangement, there would literally be hell to pay—for all of us. A good succubus would have told on her rule-breaking boss.

"So what brings you here?" asked Roman, pulling up a chair. "Want to toss the old football around?"

Jerome's face remained impassive. "I have a job for you."

"Like one that pays the rent?" I asked hopefully.

"Like one that ensures I'll continue to allow him to live in the lifestyle he's accustomed to," replied Jerome.

Roman had an amused, devil-may-care smile on his face that was typical of him, but I wasn't fooled. He knew the threat Jerome represented and also knew that part of their deal involved Roman doing errands for his father. Still, Roman made a good show of acting like he was the one doing Jerome a favor. The nephilim gave an unconcerned shrug.

"Sure. I've got nothing else going on today. What's up?"

"We have a new immortal visitor in town," said Jerome. If Roman's attitude annoyed him, the demon was just as good at masking his feelings. "A succubus."

My removed, psychological study of father and son dynamics came to a screeching halt. "What?" I exclaimed, straightening up so quickly that I nearly spilled my coffee. "I thought we were set after Tawny."

I'd worked the succubus scene solo around here for years until Jerome had acquired another one several months ago. Her name was Tawny, and while she was annoying and pretty inept as succubi went, there was still something rather endearing about her. Fortunately, Jerome had sent her off to Bellingham, keeping her a comfortable hour-and-a-half drive from me.

"Not that it's any of your business, Georgie, but this one's not here to work. She's here . . . as a visitor. On vacation." Jerome's lips twisted with bitter amusement.

Roman and I exchanged looks. Immortals could certainly take personal vacations, but clearly, there was more to this.

"And?" asked Roman. "She's really here because . . . ?"

"Because I'm sure my superiors want to check up on me after the recent . . . incident."

His words were delicate, with a very subtle warning not to elaborate on said incident. It was the one Roman and I had rescued him from—a summoning that had imprisoned Jerome as part of a demonic power play. Letting yourself get summoned was embarrassing for a demon and could call his territorial control into question. Hell sending someone to survey the situation wasn't that crazy.

"You think she's spying to see if you can still run things?" asked Roman.

"I'm certain of it. I want you to follow her around and see who she reports back to. I'd do it myself, but it's better if I don't appear suspicious. So I need to stay visible."

"Lovely," said Roman, voice as dry as his father's. "There's nothing I want to do more than trail a succubus around."

"From what I hear, you're pretty good at it," I piped in. It was true. Roman had stalked me invisibly a number of times. Lesser immortals like me couldn't hide the telltale signature that wreathed all of us, but Roman had inherited that ability from Jerome, making him the perfect spy.

Roman shot me a wry look, then turned back to Jerome. "When do I start?"

"Immediately. Her name is Simone, and she's staying down at the Four Seasons. Go there and see what she does. Mei will relieve you off and on." Mei was Jerome's second-in-command demon.

"The Four Seasons?" I asked. "Is Hell paying for that? I mean, we're in a recession."

Jerome sighed. "Hell's *never* in a recession. And I didn't

think your droll commentary started until after you'd finished your coffee."

I showed him my cup. It was empty.

Jerome sighed again and then vanished without warning. He apparently had no doubts that Roman would follow his orders.

Roman and I stood there for several quiet seconds, during which both cats resurfaced. Aubrey rubbed against Roman's bare leg, and he scratched her head.

"Guess I should shower and get dressed," he said at last, rising to his feet.

"Don't trouble yourself," I said. "And won't you be invisible anyway?"

He turned his back to me and walked off down the hallway. "I was thinking of dropping off some job applications when Mei gives me a break."

"Liar," I said. I don't think he heard.

It wasn't until the shower kicked on that I realized I should have asked Jerome about that weird sensation last night. It was so odd; I didn't even know how to describe it. The more I pondered it, the more I wondered if it had been alcohol-induced. Admittedly, Roman claimed he'd sensed something, but he'd drank as much as me.

And speaking of jobs . . . my kitchen clock was telling me I needed to head off to mine. One thing about this condo was that the skyline view had come at the cost of work convenience. My old apartment had been in Queen Anne, the same neighborhood that Emerald City Books and Café resided in. I used to be able to walk to work, but that was impossible from West Seattle, meaning I had to allow commuting time.

Unlike Roman, I had no need to physically shower and change—not that I wouldn't have liked to. I found human routines comforting. A brief burst of succubus shape-shifting cleaned me up, putting me in a work-appropriate peach sundress and arranging my light brown hair into a loose bun. Roman didn't surface before I had to leave, so I grabbed another cup of coffee and left him a note asking if it would kill him to take out the garbage before he went off to play secret agent.

My headache and the last effects of the hangover were gone by the time I walked into the store. It was abuzz with late afternoon shoppers, people out running Saturday errands and tourists who had wandered over from the Space Needle and Seattle Center down the street. I dropped my purse off in my office and then did a managerial sweep of the store, satisfied that everything was running smoothly—until I noticed we had a line of eight people and only one cashier.

"Why are you alone?" I asked Beth. She was a long-time employee and a good one, answering my question without even looking up from her customer's order.

"Gabrielle's on break, and Doug isn't . . . feeling well."

Memories of the vodka competition came back to me. I grimaced, feeling both guilty and smug. "Where is he?"

"Over in erotica."

I felt my eyebrows rise but said nothing as I turned away and walked across the store. Our small erotica section was bizarrely stuffed in between automotive and animals (amphibians, to be precise). And crammed in between the two shelves of the erotica section was Doug, sitting on the floor with his head resting facedown on his knees. I knelt beside him.

"Hair of the dog time?" I asked.

He lifted his head and brushed black hair out of his face. His expression was miserable. "You cheated. You're like half my size. How are you not in a coma?"

"Older and wiser," I said. If only he knew just how old. I took hold of his arm and tugged it. "Come on. Let's go to the café and get you some water."

For a moment, he looked like he'd resist, but a valiant effort soon followed. He even managed not to stagger too much as I led him to the store's second floor, which was half books and half coffee shop.

I grabbed a bottle of water, told the barista I'd pay for it later, and started to drag Doug to a chair. As I scanned around,

I nearly came to a halt, causing poor Doug to stumble. Seth was sitting at a table, laptop spread open in front of him. This was his favorite place to write, which had been nice when we dated and now was . . . awkward. Maddie sat with him, purse in hand and light coat on. I recalled that we started at the same time today. She must have just arrived.

They waved us over, and she gave her brother a chastising look. "Serves you right."

Doug took a long gulp of water. "Whatever happened to sisterly love?"

"I still haven't forgiven you for the time you shaved my dachshund."

"That was like twenty years ago. And that little bastard had it coming."

I smiled out of habit. Doug and Maddie's bantering was usually must-see TV for me. Today, Seth held my attention. It had been easier to ignore him last night while in the throes of alcohol, easy to pretend I'd grudgingly accepted him moving on to Maddie. But now, in the cold light of sobriety, I felt that old ache stir within my chest. I swore I could smell the scent of his skin, his sweat mingled with the woodsy apple soap he used. Sunlight from the café's large windows infused his messy brown hair with copper, and I could perfectly recall what it had been like to stroke the lines of his face, the smooth skin of his upper cheek and stubble on his chin.

Looking up to his eyes, I was surprised to see his attention on me as the siblings continued their playful bickering. I'd almost convinced myself last night that he only thought of me as a friend, but now . . . now I wasn't so sure. There was something warm there, something considering. Something I knew shouldn't be there. I suddenly had a sneaking suspicion that he might be remembering the handful of times we'd had sex. I was thinking of it too. My powers had been shut off when Jerome disappeared, and Seth and I had been able to have "safe"—by which I meant, no succubus side effects—sex.

Except for one. He'd still been dating Maddie at the time,

and cheating on her had tainted his soul with sin. That was worse than if I'd sucked his energy away. As of this moment, Seth was a Hell-bound soul. He didn't realize that, but regret for betraying her was part of what had spurred him to a hasty engagement. He felt he owed her.

The guilt forced me to look away from him, and I noticed then that Maddie and Doug had stopped their arguing. Maddie was glancing over at the coffee counter, but Doug's eyes were on me. They were bloodshot and weary, with heavy dark circles. But in the midst of that miserable, hungover look . . . there was a glint of something puzzled and surprised.

"Work time," said Maddie cheerfully, standing up. She poked her brother's shoulder, making him wince and turn his attention from me. I was glad. "You going to survive your last couple hours?"

"Yeah," he muttered, drinking more water.

"Go count inventory in the back," I told him, standing as well. "I don't want customers thinking our staff can't hold their liquor. They'd be over at the chain stores so fast, it wouldn't even be funny."

Maddie's lips quirked into a smile as her brother wearily rose to his feet. "Hey, Georgina. Do you mind if Doug and I switch shifts on Tuesday? I need to go run some wedding errands during business hours."

Doug cut her a look. "When were you going to ask if I minded?"

"Sure," I said, trying not to wince at the word "wedding." "You can work the night shift with me."

"You want to come along?" she asked. "You said you would."

"I did?"

"Last night."

I frowned. God only knew how many promises I'd made and had now forgotten, thanks to vodka and weird magical forces. Vaguely, I recalled her showing me wedding pictures. "I think I have some errands of my own to run."

"One of the places is right around the corner from you," she urged.

"Maddie," said Seth hastily, clearly as uncomfortable with this change of topic as I was. "If she's busy—"

"You can't be busy all day," Maddie begged. "Please?"

I knew it was disastrous, knew it would be courting heartache and trouble. But Maddie was my friend, and the pleading look in her eyes did something to my insides. It was guilt, I realized. Guilt over how Seth and I had betrayed her. Her expression now was full of such faith and hope in me—me, the best friend she had in Seattle and the only one she believed could help her plan this wedding.

Which is why I found myself agreeing, just as I had last night. Only this time, I had no alcohol to blame. "Okay."

Guilt was probably the worst culprit of all when it came to stupid behavior.

Chapter 3

I worked until closing that night and didn't get home until around ten. To my surprise, I found Roman on the couch eating a bowl of cereal while the cats competed for who could take up the most attention on his lap. Honestly, they seemed to love him more than me lately. It was a betrayal of Caesarean proportions.

"What are you doing here?" I asked, sitting on the armchair opposite him. I noticed then that the last of the party untidiness had been cleaned. Somehow, I suspected mentioning that would result in him never cleaning again. "I figured you'd be out chasing Jerome's succubus."

Roman stifled a yawn and set the empty bowl on the coffee table. Immediately, both cats sprang off his lap to get to the residual milk. "I'm on break. Been following her all day, though."

"And?" My natural curiosity aside, I was uneasy about the idea of Jerome's authority being called into question. The archdemon might annoy me sometimes, but I had no desire for a new boss. We'd come dangerously close to a leadership change when he'd been summoned, and I hadn't been impressed with any of the candidates.

"And it was incredibly boring. You're much more fun to stalk. She went shopping for most of the day. I didn't even know stores would let you take that much shit into dressing rooms. Then, she picked up a guy at a bar, and, well, you can figure out the rest."

I rather liked the idea of Roman suffering while Simone had sex. "Figured your voyeuristic tendencies would be into that kind of pornographic display."

He made a face. "It wasn't good porn. It was like the nasty, kinky porn they keep in the back of the store. The kind of stuff that only really sick people go after."

"So no clandestine meetings to report to Jerome?"

"Nope."

"Makes sense, I guess." I stretched out and put my feet out on the table. With Doug incapacitated, I'd spent a rare day on registers, standing more than I usually did anymore. Unless I was mistaken, Roman's eyes lingered on my legs before returning to my face. "If she didn't see any immortal action today, she'd have nothing to tell on."

"Not until tonight, at least."

"Tonight?"

"How scattered are you? Peter and Cody are having one of their things tonight."

"Oh, man. I forgot." Peter loved to throw dinners and get-togethers and seemed unconcerned that I'd just had a major party of my own. As a nocturnal creature, his soirees always took place late at night. "And Simone's going?"

"Yup. Mei's with her now, and I'll relieve her at Peter's."

"So you'll be there in spirit, if not in person."

"Something like that." He smiled at my joke, and for the first time since he'd returned to town, I saw a genuinely amused sparkle in those teal eyes. It reminded me a bit of the witty, gallant guy I used to date. It also occurred to me that this was a rare non-antagonistic conversation for us. It was almost . . . normal. Misunderstanding my silence, he gave me a wary look. "You aren't thinking of wussing out, are you? Your day couldn't have been that hard."

I actually *had* been thinking of wussing out. After yesterday's drama and now my regret over yielding to Maddie, I wasn't sure I was up for my immortal friends' zany hijinks.

"Come on," Roman said. "Simone is *so* boring. And I

don't even mean her activities. She's just bland. If you're not there to entertain me, I don't know what I'll do."

"Are you saying the rest of my friends aren't entertaining?"

"They pale in comparison."

I finally agreed to go. Although, it wouldn't have surprised me if his interest in me making an appearance was just to bum a ride. Nonetheless, I was in a good mood as I headed over to Capitol Hill. It was a little weird having Roman with me and not with me. To continue his spying, he'd gone invisible and without signature. It was like having a ghost in my car.

As usual, I was one of the last to arrive. The Three Amigos—Peter, Cody, and Hugh—were there, dressed in their usual attire now, rather than historically accurate costumes. That meant a perfectly coordinated sweater vest and slacks for Peter, jeans and a T-shirt for Cody, and business casual for Hugh. I held the door open a little longer than usual, to facilitate Roman sweeping in after me. From there, I took it on faith that he was hanging out. As soon as he let us in, Peter scurried back to his kitchen without a word.

Simone was there too. She sat on the loveseat, long legs perfectly crossed and hands resting on her knees. Her body was slim with respectably sized breasts, clad in a black skirt and silvery silk blouse. Her hair was—unsurprisingly—long and blond. Most succubi seemed to think blond was a sure-fire way to get guys in bed. I considered that attitude a sign of inexperience. I'd been a brunette—albeit one with gold highlights—for a while and never had trouble scoring action.

Hugh sat next to her, wearing the flirtatious face that was standard for him when it came to wooing women into bed. Simone regarded him with a polite smile, one she turned on me when I entered. She stood up and held out her hand. Her immortal signature smelled like violets and put me in mind of moonlight and cello music.

"You must be Georgina," she said. "Nice to meet you."

She kept that same polite expression, and I could tell it

wasn't faked. It also wasn't mischievous or overly charming. Likewise, she bore none of the open hostility succubi had around each other, or even the sugar-coated passive aggressiveness that was also common among us. She was just averagely nice. She was . . . bland.

"You too," I said. I turned to Cody as I tried to identify the scents coming from the kitchen. "What's for dinner?"

"Shepherd's pie."

I waited for the joke, but none came. "That's not Peter's usual style." He was a great cook but tended to stray toward filet mignon or scallops.

Cody nodded. "He was watching a documentary on the British Isles earlier, and it inspired him."

"Well, I've got nothing against it," I said, sitting on the arm of the couch. "I guess we should just be grateful he didn't decide to make blood pudding."

"In Australia, they have a variant of shepherd's pie that has potatoes on the top and the bottom," Simone said out of nowhere. "They call it potato pie."

Several seconds of silence followed. Her comment wasn't entirely off-topic, but it was just odd—particularly since she didn't deliver it in a smug, know-it-all voice that you found among people who always won at Trivial Pursuit. It was just a statement of fact. It also wasn't very interesting.

"Huh," I said at last, voice deadpan. "Good to know the name's accurate. It'll avoid any embarrassing confusion that might occur at dinner. God only knows how many wacky mishaps have happened when people ordered sweetmeats."

Cody choked a little on his beer, but Hugh gave Simone a high-beam smile. "That's fascinating. Are you a cook?"

"No," she said. Nothing more.

Peter popped back in just then with a vodka gimlet for me. After last night's showdown with Doug, I'd vowed to lay off for a while—like, a few days. I suddenly decided I might need a drink after all.

Peter glanced around with a small frown. "This is it? I'd kind of hoped Jerome might come." Our boss used to hang out with us quite a bit but had been avoiding social events since his summoning.

"I think he's got some business to take care of," I said. I honestly had no clue, but I kind of hoped my vague allusion would trigger a reaction in Simone. It didn't.

Peter put on a good spread as always, his kitchen table immaculately set, along with cabernet sauvignon to complement the shepherd's pie. I noted that Guinness might be a better pairing, but he ignored me.

"Where are you from?" I asked Simone. "You're here on vacation, right?"

She nodded, delicately lifting her fork. She'd cut her pie into perfect one-inch-sized cubes. It was enough to rival Peter's obsessive compulsion. "I'm from Charleston," she said. "I'll probably stay for a week. Maybe two if my archdemon will let me. Seattle's nice."

"I've heard Charleston's nice too," said Hugh. He apparently hadn't given up on getting laid tonight.

"It was founded in 1670," she said by way of answer.

That weird silence followed again. "Were you there at the time?" I asked.

"No."

We ate without further conversation. At least, we did until dessert arrived and Cody turned his attention to me. "So, are you going to help me or not?"

I'd been pondering how Simone ever managed to score guys and if her use of adjectives expanded beyond "nice." Cody's question blindsided me. "What?"

"With Gabrielle. Remember? Last night?" Right. Bookstore Gabrielle who was only into Goth and vampire guys.

"I didn't promise you I would, did I?" I asked uneasily. There were too many memory gaps from that party.

"No, but if you were a friend, you would. Besides, aren't you some kind of love expert?"

"For myself."

"And if memory serves," said Hugh, "she's not even really good at that."

I shot him a glare.

"You have to give me something," said Cody. "I need to see her again . . . need something to talk to her about . . ."

I'd thought his infatuation with Gabrielle had been alcohol induced last night—seriously, was there anything alcohol couldn't be blamed for?—but that look of puppy dog love was still in his eyes. I'd known Cody a few years and had never seen this kind of reaction from him. I'd never seen it from Peter either, but my friends and I had secretly decided long ago that he was just asexual. If vampires had been capable of reproduction, he would have done it amoeba-style.

I racked my brain. "I saw her reading *The Seattle Sinner* the other day on her break."

"What's that?" Cody asked.

"It's our local industrial-Goth-fetish-horror-S&M-angst underground newspaper," said Peter.

We all turned and stared at him.

"So I've heard," he added hastily.

I glanced back at Cody with a shrug. "It's a start. We've got it in the store."

"Are you guys done with the boring love stuff?" a voice suddenly asked. "It's time to get onto the real action."

The new voice made me jump, and then I felt the familiar crystalline aura signaling an angel's presence. Carter materialized in the one empty chair at the table—Peter had set for six, hoping Jerome would show. Seattle's worst dressed angel sat back in the chair, arms crossed over his chest and expression typically sardonic. His jeans and flannel shirt looked like they'd gone through a wood chipper, but the cashmere knit hat resting on his shoulder-length blond hair was pristine. It had been a gift from me, and I couldn't help a smile. Carter's gray eyes glinted with amusement when he noticed me.

Hanging out with an angel might be weird in some hellish circles, but it had become pretty standard in our group. We were used to Carter's comings and goings, as well as his cryptic—and often infuriating—remarks. He was the closest Jerome had to a best friend and always had a particular interest in me and my love life. He'd let up a little since the recent debacle with Seth.

Carter might be commonplace to us—but not to Simone. Her blue eyes went wide when he appeared, her face completely transforming. She leaned over the table, and unless I was mistaken, her neckline had gotten a little lower since my arrival. She shook Carter's hand.

"I don't think we've met," she said. "I'm Simone."

"Carter," he replied, eyes still amused.

"Simone's visiting from Charleston," I said. "It was founded in 1670."

Carter's smile twitched a little. "So I've heard."

"You should visit," she said. "I'd love to show you around. It's very nice."

I exchanged astonished looks with Peter, Cody, and Hugh. Simone's bland demeanor hadn't lit up exactly, but she'd suddenly become 2 percent more interesting. She wasn't infatuated with Carter the way Cody was with Gabrielle. She was just trying to bag an angel. *Good luck with that,* I thought. That was ballsy for any succubus. Certainly angels fell because of love and sex—Jerome was living proof—and I'd even witnessed it once. But Carter? If ever there was a staunchly resistant being, it was him. Except when it came to chainsmoking and hard liquor, of course. Yes, things with Simone had definitely gotten more interesting.

"Sure," said Carter. "I bet you could show me all sorts of places off the beaten path."

"Absolutely," she replied. "You know, there's an inn there that George Washington had dinner at once."

I rolled my eyes. I doubted there was any part of Charleston she could show Carter that he didn't know about. Carter had been around to watch cities like Babylon and Troy rise and fall. For all I knew, he'd personally helped take down Sodom and Gomorrah.

"So what kind of action did you have in mind?" I asked Carter. As entertaining as Simone's pathetic flirtation might be, I wasn't sure I was up to American History 101 tonight. "I am *not* playing 'Have You Ever' again."

"Better," he said. Out of nowhere, Carter produced Pictionary. And when I say out of nowhere, I meant it.

"No," said Hugh. "I spent years perfecting my illegible doctor's signature. I've totally lost any artistic aptitude whatsoever."

"I *love* Pictionary," said Simone.

"I think I have some things to do," I added. I felt a shove on my shoulder and glanced around in surprise, seeing nothing. Then, I knew. Roman apparently still wanted me to entertain him. I sighed. "But I can stay for a little while."

"Great. That settles it," said Carter. He turned to Peter. "You got an easel?"

Of course Peter did. Why, I had no clue, but after he'd bought a Roomba and a Betamax player, I'd learned not to ask questions. We split into teams: me, Cody, and Hugh against the others.

I went first. The card I drew was "Watergate." "Oh, come *on*," I said. "This is ridiculous."

"Don't whine," said Carter, his grin annoyingly smug. "We all take a random chance here."

They started the timer. I drew some remedial waves that immediately got a "Water!" from Cody. That was promising. Then, I drew what I hoped looked like a wall with a door in it. Apparently, I did too good a job.

"Wall," said Hugh.

"Door," said Cody.

I added some vertical lines to the door to emphasize the gate aspect. After a moment's thought, I drew a plus sign between the water and wall to show their connection.

"Aqueduct," said Cody.

"A bridge over troubled water," guessed Hugh.

"Oh my *God*," I groaned.

Unsurprisingly, my time ran out before my teammates could figure it out, though not before they guessed "Hoover Dam" and "Hans Brinker." With a groan, I flounced onto the couch. The other team then got a shot at it.

"Watergate," said Carter right away.

Hugh turned on me, face incredulous. "Why didn't you just draw a gate?"

Simone went after me, and I hoped she'd get "Cuban Missile Crisis" or "Bohr's Law." The timer started, and she drew a circle with lines radiating out from it.

"Sun," said Peter immediately.

"Right!" she said.

I glared at Carter. "You. Are. Cheating."

"And you're a bad loser," he replied.

We played for another hour, but after my team got "Oncology," "The Devil and Daniel Webster," and "War of 1812," and theirs got "Heart," "Flower," and "Smile," I decided to go home. At the door, I heard a wistful sigh in my ear.

"You're on your own," I growled to Roman in an undertone.

I left amid protests about being a bad sport and considered myself lucky when Carter said they were going to play Jenga next.

The drive back to West Seattle was quiet this time of night, and after parking underneath my building, I was happy to see that today's unseasonable heat still hung in the air. Being so close to the water had cooled it slightly, bringing it to a perfect nighttime temperature. On impulse, I walked across the street to the beach, which was actually more like a park: grassy with only a few feet of sand. In Seattle, there were few places that offered much more.

Still, I loved the water and the soft sounds of waves against the shore. A light breeze stirred my hair, and those costly glittering lights shone in the distance. I'd moved here partially to get away from Queen Anne and its regular proximity to Seth, but also because the ocean always brought back memories of my mortal youth. Puget Sound was a far cry from the warm Mediterranean waters I'd grown up near, but it soothed something within me nonetheless. That comfort was bittersweet, of course, but it was an unfortunate tendency of mortals and immortals alike to gravitate toward things we knew would cause us pain.

The water was enchanting, glittering in both moonlight and street light. I stared off at a lit ferry moving toward Bainbridge Island, then returned my gaze to the lapping waves before me. They seemed to be choreographed into a dance, an alluring pattern that urged me to join in. I might not be able to draw, but dancing was an art I'd carried from my mortal days. The water beckoned, and I could almost hear the music it danced to. It was intoxicating, filled with warmth and love that promised to ease that constant dull ache in my chest, the ache I'd carried since losing Seth. . . .

It wasn't until I was calf-deep in water that I realized what I had done. My high heels were sinking into the sand, and warm day or no, the water was still at a low temperature, its icy touch seeping into my skin. The world, which had before seemed dreamy and hazy, now snapped into sharp relief, no longer an inviting dance that promised comfort and pleasure.

Fear sent my heart racing, and I hastily backed up, something that wasn't easy as the sand wrapped around my heels. I finally stepped out of them and reached down, pulling them up from the water and walking back to the shore barefoot. I stared out at the sound a few moments more, startled at how much it now scared me. How far would I have walked in? I didn't know and didn't want to think about it too hard.

I turned and hastily headed toward my condo, oblivious to the rough asphalt against my feet. It wasn't until I was safely back in my living room—having locked the door behind me—that I felt some measure of safety. Aubrey walked up to me, sniffing my ankles and then licking the salty water that still clung to them.

I'd had one drink almost two hours ago, a drink that had long metabolized out of my system. This had been no buzzed delusion—neither had last night's sleepwalking or near-balcony jump. I sat on my couch, arms wrapped around me. Everything around me seemed a threat.

"Roman?" I asked aloud. "Are you here?"

My only answer was silence. He was still out with Simone and probably wouldn't be back the rest of the night. I was astonished at how suddenly and desperately I wished he were here. My condo seemed lonely and ominous.

Water had splashed against my dress, and I changed out of it, swapping it for the soft comfort of pajamas. I decided then that I wouldn't sleep. I'd wait in the living room for Roman. I needed to tell him what had happened. I needed him to guard my sleep.

Yet, somewhere around four, my own fatigue overcame me. I stretched out along the couch, both cats curled against me, and gradually lost track of the infomercial on TV. When I woke, it was late morning, and sunlight warmed my skin. Roman was still gone. I hadn't been able to wait him out, but I *was* still on the couch. For now, that was the best I could hope for.

Chapter 4

I spent the whole morning waiting restlessly for Roman. Surely he had to come home at some point to sleep, right? Of course, being part greater immortal, he'd have a lot of the traits of his angelic parentage—and angels and demons never needed to sleep. Roman could likely get by on very little rest and simply chose to sleep in as often as he did for the fun of it.

I left a message on Jerome's cell phone, which was useless more often than not. I also kind of wished I hadn't parted from Carter so soon. Caught up in the Pictionary absurdity, I'd totally forgotten about my siren song encounters. Indeed, I'd nearly written them off until last night's repeat. But if Jerome was hard to get a hold of, Carter was impossible. He kept no cell phone and seemed to take personal pride in showing up at unexpected moments.

Left with no other options, I called my friend Erik. He was a human who ran a store specializing in esoteric and pagan goods. He was often my backup for bizarre supernatural situations, sometimes knowing more than my friends did. As I dialed his store's number, I couldn't help but marvel at the circles my life seemed to run on. I was repeating the same pattern over and over. Something weird would happen, I'd fruitlessly attempt to contact my superiors, and end up seeking Erik for help.

"Why the fuck does this keep happening to *me*?" I muttered as the phone rang. Cody never got stalked by paranormal forces. Neither did any of the others. It was like I was specifically being targeted. Or cursed. Or simply imbued with bad luck. Yes, my life was a never-ending spiral, doomed to repeat the same patterns of annoying immortal threats—and miserable romantic situations.

"Hello?"

"Erik? This is Georgina."

"Miss Kincaid," he said in his usual genteel voice. "A pleasure to hear from you."

"I need your help with something. Again. Are you around? I wanted to swing by before work."

There was a pause, and then I heard regret in his voice. "Unfortunately, I have to run errands and close the store today. I'll be back this evening. When do you finish work?"

"I'll probably be free at ten." Another evening shift.

"I can meet you then."

I felt bad. His store usually closed around five. "No, no . . . that's too late. We could try tomorrow. . . ."

"Miss Kincaid," he said gently, "I'm always happy to see you. It's no difficulty at all."

I still felt guilty when we disconnected. Erik was getting old. Shouldn't he be in bed by ten? Nine? There was nothing to be done for it now, though. He said he'd do it, and I'd seen him when he was obstinate. I had nothing to do but wait now and hope Roman would surface before I had to work. When he didn't, I simply left him a note saying I needed to talk to him immediately. It was the best I could do.

At work, no one was out or—best of all—hungover. I was caught up on my paperwork, which gave me a lot of free time. Whether that was good or bad, I couldn't say. It kept me from messing up my job but merely left me in a cycle of rumination.

It was nearly closing time when I noticed Seth at his usual station in the café. Maddie had worked the day shift, which meant I didn't have to face their cute couple antics. He caught my eye as I walked through, and against my better judgment, I sat down across from him.

"How goes it?" I asked. My usual romantic fixation with him was put on pause when I saw that he looked agitated.

He tapped the screen in annoyance. "Bad. I've been staring at this screen for two hours and haven't gotten anything done." He paused. "No, that's not quite true. I ordered a Wonder Twins T-shirt and watched some videos on YouTube."

I smiled and propped my chin up in my hand. "Doesn't sound like a bad day's work."

"It is when it's been going on all week. My muse is an ungrateful harlot who's abandoned me to actually come up with my own plots."

"That's a record for you," I observed. I'd seen him have fits of writer's block when we dated, but it never lasted more than a few days. "When's your deadline?"

"Not for a while, but still . . ." He sighed. "I don't like to be stalled out. I'm not really sure what to do with my days if I'm not writing."

I started to say that he must have wedding stuff to do but then thought better of it. I kept to lighter topics. "Maybe it's time to pick up a hobby. Fencing? Origami?"

That slightly bemused smile that was so characteristic for him crossed his lips. "I tried latch hook once."

"You did not."

"I did. Do you know how hard that is to do?"

"It's actually pretty easy," I said, trying to hide my laughter. "Kids do it, you know. Your nieces could probably do it."

"They can. And you're not making me feel better." But those beautiful brown eyes were amused. I studied them for a moment, loving the way they would sometimes turn amber. A moment later, I snapped myself out of my lovesick spell.

"There's always dancing," I said mischievously.

This made him laugh too. "I think we've proven how futile that is." I'd tried twice to teach him how to do it—swing and salsa—all with disastrous results. Seth's talents lay in his mind, not his body. Well, upon further consideration, I realized that wasn't entirely true.

"You haven't found the right kind," I said. I'd given up on hiding my grin.

"What's left? Riverdance? Square dancing? And do *not* even suggest jazz. I saw *Newsies* and was traumatized for, like, five years."

"Harsh," I said. "You could still probably wear your T-shirts with jazz dancing. I know you must have a 'Dancing Queen' shirt somewhere." His shirt today sported Chuck Norris. "Unless, of course, you wanted some variety. Square dancers have some pretty sweet costumes."

He shook his head in exasperation. "I'll leave the dancing getup to you. And no, no 'Dancing Queen' shirt yet—though I do have an Abba one. I think a 'Dancing Queen' shirt would be better for you anyway, not me." His eyes moved from my face to what he could see of my body at the table. "You look like you could go dancing right now."

I started to feel myself flush at his gaze and immediately utilized shape-shifting to nix it. The unseasonably warm weather lent itself to sundresses, and I had another on today. It was a cream-colored trapeze, sleeveless with a keyhole top that may or may not have been showing managerial-appropriate cleavage. He wasn't ogling me or anything, but I had learned long ago that Seth was good at keeping his emotions off of his face. I wondered what went through his mind. Simple aesthetic admiration? Lust? Disapproval of non-managerial cleavage?

"This old thing?" I asked breezily, uncomfortable for reasons I couldn't explain.

"You were wearing that color the first time we met." He suddenly seemed embarrassed. "Not sure why I remember that."

"You don't," I said. "I was wearing purple." Now I felt flustered to remember *that*.

He frowned in a way I found cute. "Were you? Oh, yeah. I guess you were. The violet top and flowered skirt."

Every detail. If he'd mentioned me wearing a snakeskin

jacket, I might have passed out. Yet, I had a feeling he did remember that. Probably my shoes and the way I'd styled my hair too. An awkward silence grew. I might have been keeping the flush off of my face, but there was warmth spreading through me. And only half of it was desire. The rest was something else . . . something sweeter and deeper.

I cleared my throat. "What's the book about? Cady and O'Neill, right?"

He nodded, looking grateful for the subject change. "The usual. Mystery and intrigue, sexual tension and life-threatening situations." He hesitated. "It's the last one."

"I—what?" I felt my jaw drop. Whatever romantic feelings that had been stirring in me immediately got pushed to the back burner. "You mean like . . . the end of the series?" Seth had written a lot of mysteries over his career, but Cady and O'Neill—his intrepid art and archaeology explorer duo—was his flagship series. "Why?"

He shrugged, eyes moving back to the laptop screen. "Because it's time."

"How . . . how will you make your living?"

His smile turned wry as he looked back up at me. "I've written other books that aren't about them, Georgina. Besides, you don't think my fans'll have enough faith to follow me to a new series?"

"True," I said softly. "We'll follow you anywhere." I'd meant to say "they'll," but it was too late.

"I hope so," he said, averting his eyes for a moment. When he looked back, I saw a spark of excitement. "But I'm actually into doing something new. I've got this idea—and it's really great. I just want to lose myself in it, you know?" I did know. I'd seen him forget parts of his real life plenty of times while caught up in a book. I wondered if this new project he was so enthusiastic about would intensify that zeal.

"So you've got the ending for Cady and O'Neill figured out?" I asked.

"No," he said with a sigh, glow dimming. "That's the problem. I don't know how this is going to end."

I suddenly wondered if he was still talking about the books. Our gazes met again, and whatever might have come next was interrupted when Beth appeared at my side. "Georgina? A friend of yours is here to see you."

My heart leapt. Roman. Roman had read my note. His advice on that eerie siren song was about the only thing that could have dragged me away from Seth. I sprang up from my seat, giving Seth an apologetic look. "I've got to go."

He nodded, some troubled emotion in his eyes that I couldn't identify. That troubled me in return. He might be good at keeping his emotions off of his face, but at one time, I'd been pretty good at figuring them out.

"No problem," he said. Wistfulness? Was that the mystery emotion?

I couldn't ponder it any longer. Roman was more important. I took the steps downstairs two at a time, anxious to see him. But when I reached the registers, where Beth had said my friend was waiting, it wasn't Roman I saw. It was Cody.

Or, well, I think it was.

It took me a moment to figure it out. He was dressed all in black—and not just jeans and a T-shirt. We were talking full regalia: a studded-leather jacket, steel-toed boots, and an—ugh—mesh shirt. His blond hair had black streaks in it, and heavy black eyeliner and lipstick over white foundation completed the look. I didn't know what to say, so I simply grabbed his arm and dragged him into my office before anyone else could see him.

"What the hell are you doing?" The sun had only just gone down, which meant he must have doubled the speed limit to make it here so quickly.

"I'm here to see Gabrielle," he explained, casting an anxious glance at my doorway. "Where is she? I wanted to get here before you guys closed."

"She's not working tonight." His face fell, but I couldn't help but add, "And honestly, I think that's a good thing."

"Why? Peter had a copy of *The Seattle Sinner,* and after

going through it, we thought this would be the way to get her attention. He helped dress me."

"Wait. Peter had a copy of—? Never mind. I don't want to know. Believe me, you would have gotten her attention. But I'm not sure it'd be the kind you want."

Cody gestured to his attire. "But she's into this scene. You said yourself that she dresses all in black."

"Yeah," I admitted. "But yours seems . . . I don't know. Overdone. People like her are always on the lookout for wannabes. You try too hard, and you'll just put her further off."

He sighed and slumped into my desk's chair, dejected. "Then what am I supposed to do? That newspaper was my only lead."

"Well, for starters, don't let Peter dress you again. Ever. As for the rest . . . I don't know. Let me ask around and see if I can get you more to go on. Just please don't wear this outfit again."

"Okay," he agreed.

Just then, Doug stuck his head in. It wasn't his night to work, so I was kind of surprised, but not nearly as surprised as he was.

"Hey, Kincaid, I had a question about the schedu—Jesus Fucking Christ! What *is* that?"

"It's Cody," I said.

Doug walked gingerly into the office and peered at Cody's face. "Well, I'll be damned. It is. I thought it was the ghost of Gene Simmons."

"Gene Simmons isn't dead," said Cody.

"Cody's trying to impress Gabrielle," I explained. Doug opened his mouth, no doubt to comment on the impossibility of that, but I held up a hand to stop him. "Yeah, yeah. I know. What did you need?"

Doug needed to switch some shifts, and without his lady-love around, Cody decided to leave. I let him out the back door, not wanting to cause a panic in the store. Once the schedule was set, Doug and I bantered about the Cody and

Gabrielle situation. Before long, I lost track of time, and closing announcements were being made on the intercom. Doug said his farewells—half afraid I'd put him to work if he stayed—and I set off to finish my own tasks. My meeting with Erik was getting closer, and I felt a mix of excitement and apprehension.

An hour after the doors were locked, staff began to go home. I made one last sweep of the store and found Seth still sitting in the café. No surprise. My coworkers could never bring themselves to kick him out when we closed. He'd actually gotten locked in once and accidentally set off the alarm. I walked over to his table, noting the enraptured look on his face as his fingers danced along the laptop's keys.

"Hey, Mortensen," I said. "You don't have to go home, but you can't stay here."

It took almost thirty seconds for him to look up, and even then, he seemed surprised to see me. "Oh. Hey."

I could feel a smile playing on my lips. This was picture perfect Seth behavior. "Hey, we're all closed down. Time to go."

He glanced around, noting the dark windows and lack of people in the store. "Oh, man. Sorry. I didn't even notice."

"I take it the muse came back?"

"She did."

"So you know how it's going to end now?"

"No. Not yet."

I walked Seth to the back door and armed the alarm before letting myself out. He told me good-bye, and if he'd had any dreamy affection for me earlier in the night, it was gone now. His characters now consumed his heart. It was something I'd had to accept when we were together, and watching him walk down the street, I decided that was how it should be. Seth's writing was too much of his being.

I let my own dreamy affection go and drove up north of the city to Erik's store. I still felt a little bad about him meeting me so late, but the lights in his windows gleamed out into the night. And inside, the usual music and incense were going strong, just as they would during business hours. Glancing around, I didn't see him right away. Then, I noticed him kneeling down in front of some palmistry books.

"Hey, Erik."

"Miss Kincaid."

He rose to his feet, but the motions were jerky and unsteady. And when he finally turned to face me, there was a gauntness in his dark-skinned face that hadn't been there the last time I saw him. My instinct was to rush over and support him, but I had a feeling he wouldn't welcome that. Still, I asked the obvious.

"Are you okay? Have you been sick?"

He gave me a gentle smile and began moving—slowly—toward the store's main counter. "A passing cold. They seem to last longer than they used to, but I'll be fine."

I wasn't so certain. I'd known Erik for a long time. . . . I'd lost track of the years, actually. It wasn't an uncommon thing with mortals, one that often blindsided me. One moment they'd seem young and healthy . . . the next, they were old and dying. It never hurt any less, either. Part of the reason Seth had broken up with me was to spare me the pain of that loss because I began growing overly paranoid about his well-being.

Now, watching Erik, I felt even worse for keeping him out so late. I also felt bad because I realized I never visited except when I needed something. When had I last seen him? Months ago, when Jerome had been summoned. I'd sought Erik's help then and hadn't been by since.

"Tea?" he offered, just like always.

"No, no. I don't want to delay you," I said. I leaned against the counter and felt relieved when he settled down on a stool. "I just wanted to ask you a couple things. Something weird happened." I almost laughed as the words left my mouth. That was such a typical opening statement for me. Again, that earlier thought returned: my life was one big circle, repeating and repeating.

I gave him the rundown on my weird encounters with the

unknown and—for the large part—indescribable force. He listened carefully, bushy gray eyebrows knit into a frown.

"I hate to tell you this," he said when I finished, "but there are probably a number of things that could describe."

"Surprise, surprise," I murmured. That was more a commentary on my life, not his abilities.

"The fact that your . . . uh, friend couldn't identify it is intriguing." Erik was one of the handful of people who knew Roman was in Seattle. Erik had no interest in Heaven and Hell's policies and wouldn't be tattling anytime soon. "Of course, he lacks the full skill set his relatives have. I don't suppose you've spoken to any greater immortals?"

I shook my head. "No. They're notoriously absent, as usual. I think I'll be seeing Jerome soon." He'd probably want to check in with Roman. "So we'll see then."

"I'm sorry I don't have any ready answers. I never seem to."

"Not in the beginning," I said. "But you always come through in the end. More patterns."

"Hmm?"

"Nothing," I said with a small sigh. "Sometimes I just feel like same things are happening to me over and over. Like, even this siren thing. Why me? In the last year, I've been targeted over and over. What are the odds? Why does this keep happening?"

Erik's eyes studied me for several moments. "There are some people around whom the powers and supernatural beings of the world will always circle. You appear to be one of them."

"But why?" I asked, surprised at the childish tone in my voice. "I'm just another succubus. There are tons of us out there. And why recently? Why only in the last year?" It had to be the cruelest joke in the world that all these paranormal mishaps had started happening right when my romantic ones had. Apparently, one source of pain just wasn't enough.

"I don't know," Erik admitted. "Things change. Forces move that we can't see." He paused and coughed, making me wince. How sick was he? "Again, I feel like I'm useless to you."

I reached out and gently squeezed his shoulder. "No, no. You're invaluable to me. I don't know how I would have gotten by all these years without you." This earned me a smile.

Wanting him to go to bed, I picked up my purse to leave. As I was heading to the door, he suddenly said, "Miss Kincaid?"

I glanced back. "Yeah?"

"Do you still talk to Mr. Mortensen?"

The question caught me by surprise. Erik had been intrigued when Seth and I were dating, marveling at the connection between a human and a succubus, though he didn't have the crazy obsession that Carter used to.

"Sure. Sometimes." My earlier conversation with Seth came back to me, the ease and warmth that had surrounded us.

"And things are amicable?"

"More or less." Aside from his impending marriage, of course.

"That's good. It doesn't always happen in these situations."

"Yeah, I know. Although—" I bit off my words.

Erik tilted his head, studying me curiously. "Although what?"

"It's amicable, except sometimes . . . sometimes this whole situation with him. It's like having my soul split in two."

"Understandable," he said. Those eyes burned with compassion, and I felt tears spring up in my own. "I'm sorry I brought it up. I was just curious."

I assured him it was okay and said good-bye again. The mention of Seth and the recollection of being with him earlier had made my mood go melancholy. I drove back to West Seattle, miserable that I'd be helping with his wedding tomorrow and worried over Erik's sickly state. As heavily as those thoughts weighed on me, they immediately flew from my mind as soon as I walked into my living room.

"Roman!"

He sat on the couch as he had last time, now eating a microwavable chicken pot pie. The TV was on, but he didn't seem to be watching it. When he looked up at me, he didn't wear that amused, teasing look. His expression was dark. Troubled, even.

"I've been waiting for you to get home," I exclaimed, tossing my purse and keys to the floor. "You won't believe what happened."

Roman sighed. "No, *you* won't believe what happened."

"Yeah, but this is—"

He held up a hand to interrupt me. "Let me get this out first. It's been driving me crazy."

I swallowed my impatience. "Okay. I'll bite. Does it have something to do with Simone?"

He nodded. "Yeah. I followed her tonight to this twenty-four-hour coffee shop called Bird of Paradise." He eyed me carefully. "Do you know it?"

Now I felt a frown creeping over my face. "Yeah . . . it's in Queen Anne, right around the corner from Emerald City. What was she doing there? I mean, aside from getting coffee?"

Roman's expression turned darker and—unless I was mistaken—sympathetic. "She was there hitting on a guy," he said. "Seth."

Chapter 5

I stared at him, and the world stood still for a moment. "Wait . . . Seth was meeting Simone there?"

Roman shook his head. "I wouldn't say that exactly. It was more like she sought him out. He looked like he'd been working there for a while when she showed up."

"And then?" My voice was very small.

"Then, she walked over to him and shyly introduced herself as a fan, saying she recognized him from his website. Picture perfect demure coquette."

"And *then?*"

"She said she wished she had a book with her to sign and asked if he'd sign a piece of paper instead. He said he would, and then she sat down, all apologetic for bothering him. She said she had a couple questions and hoped he wouldn't mind if she stayed for a few moments."

I noticed then that I was clenching my fists. With a deep breath, I released them. "Seth wouldn't strike up a conversation with a stranger like that. Not without being horribly uncomfortable."

"Yeah," Roman agreed. "He definitely had some of that social awkwardness." There was a wry note in Roman's voice that I didn't like. The two men had once been rivals for my affection, and apparently, Roman was still holding on to some bitterness—and a feeling of superiority. Roman could be quite charismatic when he wanted. "But she did a pretty good job at playing just as shy and nervous. I think it made him feel better."

"So she *did* sit down?"

"Yup . . . and stayed for about a half-hour."

"What?" I exclaimed. My volume made Godiva jerk her head up from a nap. "Did she try to seduce him?"

Roman's expression turned considering. "Not in the usual way. I mean, she wasn't as boring as usual. But she put him at ease enough that he relaxed and seemed to like talking to her. She wasn't overtly sexual, and he didn't look like he wanted to jump her. It was just . . . I don't know. A nice conversation. Although, it had a few of those annoying facts she likes to drop." He paused. "Oh, and she went brunette."

That bothered me more than it probably should have. "But he sent her away, right?"

"No, Maddie showed up, and he left with her—after telling Simone it was nice to meet her."

Oh, irony. Never, never would I have imagined I'd be so relieved to have Maddie show up and take Seth home. I also never thought I'd be glad his devotion to her would keep him from falling prey to another woman's charms.

I took a step toward Roman, my fists clenching again. I didn't blame him as messenger; I was simply driven by my own fury.

"What the hell?" I demanded. "What fucking game is she playing?"

He sighed. "I don't know. Maybe no game at all. She likes coffee. I've certainly seen her buy it before. She could have ended up there by coincidence and thought he looked like a good catch. God only knows why."

I ignored the barb. "Oh, come *on*, Roman. You're not that stupid. Do you honestly think that in a city like Seattle, out of all the men here, it's a coincidence that she shows up and starts hitting on *my* ex? You know as well as I do that there aren't many coincidences in our world."

"True," he admitted, setting the remnants of his dinner on the coffee table. The cats went for it.

"Will you stop doing that?" I demanded. "They're not supposed to be eating that kind of stuff."

"Don't take your bitchy attitude out on me." But he stood up and took the plate to the kitchen. When he returned, he crossed his arms over his chest and stood in front of me. "Look, you're right to a certain extent about coincidences. It is weird that she would hit on Seth. But think about this too: don't you think there are a few things around here a *little* more important than your ex-boyfriend? Jerome's theory makes the most sense, you know. Hell let him keep his job, but that doesn't mean they're letting the whole incident go. They're the ultimate grudge-holders. They'd want to assess the situation. That's why she's here."

"Except that she's not assessing anything! Unless you consider my friends' Pictionary skills."

"You should have seen them play Jenga."

"This isn't a joke. I need to figure out what her game is. You have to take me with you when you spy on her again."

He raised an eyebrow. "I think that's a terrible idea."

"I can go invisible."

"She'll still sense you."

"You can hide my signature. You told me before that you could. Was that a lie?"

Roman grimaced. Just before things had literally blown up between us, he'd asked me to run away with him, promising he could conceal me from the greater immortals.

"I can," he admitted. "But I just think you're asking for trouble."

"What am I risking?"

"A lot. Whether it's Seth or Jerome, there's obviously something going on. Get tangled up in that, and you could be risking your life. I won't let that happen to you."

"Since when do you care what happens to me?" I asked incredulously.

"Since you became my ticket to rent-free living."

And with that, he turned invisible, hiding his signature as well.

"Coward!" I cried. My only answer was the front door opening and then shutting. He was lost to me, and I realized I'd again missed my chance to bring up my weird encounters from these last couple days.

I tossed and turned again that night, but it had nothing to do with my fear of walking off the balcony or into Puget Sound. I was filled with rage, both at Simone for making the moves on Seth and at Roman for abandoning me. When I woke up in the morning, I took comfort in knowing I didn't need Roman to confront Simone. I could do that on my own.

Of course, there were a few complications there, the first being I didn't know where Simone was. Her hotel was probably the logical place to start, though most succubi—even a bland one like her—wouldn't spend a lot of time hanging out there. Well, unless she had company—and I didn't really want to walk into anything like that. And anyway, I had one tiny commitment to attend to before I could go bitch-hunting.

Maddie.

I'd regretted my decision to go shopping with her the moment the words had left my mouth. Yet, somehow, I'd totally blocked out those feelings yesterday when I'd been sitting with Seth. A brief thought about the wedding had flitted through my mind . . . and then it had been gone. I'd spent the rest of the time laughing and talking with him as though there was no Maddie in the world. But as I headed over to the bookstore, where she and I had agreed to meet, I had to accept reality once more. Seth was no longer mine.

He also wasn't Simone's. But I'd deal with that later.

Maddie was waiting for me downstairs, but I used the excuse of needing coffee before we left, in order to dash up to the café. I wanted to see if Simone was lurking. No matter her shape, I'd know if she was there. Yet, as I casually waited in line for my white chocolate mocha, I sensed nothing immortal. Seth was there, engrossed in his work, and never even saw me. Apparently, his muse was still going strong.

I let him be and joined Maddie downstairs again. She had a list of eight store names and addresses. Most were dress shops, and I was skeptical that we could make them all before we were due into work. She was more optimistic, but then, that was typical of her.

"No point in worrying right now," she said. "We'll just do them one at a time and see where that gets us. Besides, the last few are bakeries, and we wouldn't want to eat a bunch of cake before trying on dresses."

"Speak for yourself," I said, sliding into her passenger seat. "I'm not trying anything on."

She gave me a wry smile. "Aren't you? You're my bridesmaid, remember? We talked about it at the party."

"No," I said swiftly. "I said and did all sorts of crazy stuff that night, but I never agreed to it. *That* I do remember."

Maddie's expression was still light, but I thought I heard a little hurt in her voice when she spoke next. "What's the big deal? Why don't you want to be one? You know I'd never dress you in anything horrible."

Why? I pondered the answer as she pulled into traffic. *Because I'm in love with your future husband.* I could hardly tell her that, of course. As it was, I could see my continuing silence was making her feel worse. She was reading it as a slight to our friendship.

"I just . . . I just don't like all the, uh, fanfare that goes with weddings. There's so much planning and stressing about little details. I'd rather just sit back in the audience and watch you go down the aisle." Well, actually, that was one of the last things I wanted to do.

"Really?" Maddie frowned, but thankfully, it was more out of surprise than disappointment. "You're always so good at planning and little details. I thought you were into that."

That was a fair point. It was why I made such a good manager. "Yeah, kind of . . . but I mean, at the receptions, drunk guys always hit on the bridesmaids, you know? They think we're desperate because we're the ones not getting married." Also not entirely far from the truth in my case.

Maddie's smile returned. "Those are some pretty lame excuses."

They were indeed, but she said nothing more as we drove.

After Maddie's initial failure with picking flattering wedding dresses, she now threw her faith completely into me to lead her to fashion success. It wasn't the first time this had happened, and I found myself slipping into style-advisor role pretty easily. In fact, if I was able to preoccupy myself with the objective parts of this process—flattering fit, color, etc.—it was easy to block out the big picture of her and Seth.

The saleswomen working at the stores soon learned who was in charge here and backed off with their recommendations, simply fetching the dresses I indictated. I studied each one Maddie tried on, keeping my standards high. With so many stores to choose from, we could afford to be picky.

"That one's good," I said at our third store. It was corseted, narrowing her waist, and had a skirt that didn't flare. Those puffy ones always made the hips look bigger, though no one ever seemed to realize that. You had to be tall and thin to get away with that, not short and buxom like Maddie.

She admired herself in the mirror, a look of pleasant surprise on her face. She was still drawn to ones that I didn't think were good choices, and this was the first of my picks that she really liked. The eager saleswoman jotted down the style number, and then Maddie started to turn around and try on the rest waiting in her dressing room. As she did, a dress on a mannequin caught her eye.

"Oh, Georgina, I know what you said, but you *have* to try that on," Maddie begged.

I followed her gaze. The dress was slinky and sexy, floor-length violet charmeuse with straps that tied around the neck. *You were wearing that color the first time we met.*

I averted my eyes. "Not ugly enough to be a bridesmaid dress."

"It'd look great on you. *Everything* looks great on you," she added with a shake of her head. "Besides, you could wear that to other things. Parties and stuff."

It was true. It didn't scream bridesmaid. Not taffeta or bright orange. Before I could protest further, the saleswoman had already fetched one from the rack, guessing my size with that uncanny ability her kind had.

So, reluctantly, I tried the dress on while Maddie went to her next option. The size wasn't *perfect*, but a little shape-shifting neatened it up where it needed to be. Maddie was right. It did look good on me, and when I stepped out, she took it as a done deal that I'd buy it—no, *she* offered to buy it—and would be in her wedding. The saleswoman, seeing an opportunity, and possibly getting back at me for my tyranni-cal attitude, had "helpfully" fetched two more dresses for me to try while I waited for Maddie. Maddie claimed she couldn't stand the thought of me waiting around with nothing to do, so I reluctantly took them into the dressing room. They too looked good, but not as good as the violet.

I was returning them to the saleswoman when my eye caught something. It was a bridal dress. It was made of ivory duchess satin, the fabric wrapping around the waist and hal-ter top. The skirt was draped, pulled into little tiers. I stared. It would have been a disaster on Maddie, but on me . . .

"Want to try it?" asked the saleswoman slyly. Something told me that bridesmaids covertly trying on brides' dresses wasn't a rare phenomenon around here. The desperate and mournful not-getting-married attitude in action.

Before I knew it, I was back in the dressing room, wearing the ivory dress. *You were wearing that color the first time we met.* Seth had been wrong about that and corrected himself, but for some reason, the words came to me yet again. And the dress looked great. Really great. I wasn't overly tall but was slim enough that it didn't matter—and I filled out the top beautifully. I stared at myself in a way I hadn't with the other dresses, trying to imagine myself as a bride. There was some-thing about brides and weddings that instinctively spoke to so many women, and I shared the impulse as well, jaded suc-cubus or no. The grim statistics didn't matter: the divorce rates, the infidelity I'd witnessed so often . . .

Yes, there was something magical about brides, an image fixed into the collective subconscious. I could see myself with flowers in my hands and a veil on my head. There'd be well-wishers and joy, the giddy faith and hope of a beautiful life together. I'd been a bride once, so long ago. I'd had those dreams, and they'd blown away.

I sighed and took the dress off, afraid I might start crying. There would be no wedding for me. No bridal hopes. Not with Seth, not with anyone. Those things were lost to me forever. There was only an eternity alone, no lifelong lovers, only those I shared a night with. . . .

Unsurprisingly, I was kind of depressed for the rest of the day.

Maddie bought the violet dress for me, and I was too glum to protest—which she read as acceptance of my bridesmaid fate. We made it through the rest of our dress stops but didn't get to the bakeries. By the end of it all, we had four candidates for her dress, which I regarded as good progress.

My mood didn't abate at work. I holed up in my office as much as I could, seeking solitude and my own dark thoughts. When I finally made it home after that eternity-long day, I found the condo empty and was astonished at how much that hurt me. I wished with all my heart that Roman was around, and it wasn't even to talk about Simone or other immortal mysteries. I just wanted his company. I just wanted to talk to him and not be alone. He was an infuriating part of my life, but he was also turning into a fixed infuriating part of my life. With a gloomy eternity ahead, that meant something.

I knew better than to wait up for him . . . but found myself doing it anyway. I lounged on the couch with Grey Goose and the cats, taking some small sweetness from those warm, furry creatures that loved me. *Eternal Sunshine of the Spotless Mind* was on, which didn't cheer me up any. Like the masochist I was, I watched it anyway.

At least, I thought I was. Because suddenly, the loud shriek of a car horn blasted into my ears. I blinked and jerked my head around. I wasn't on the couch. There were no cats, no vodka. I sat on the railing of my balcony, precariously positioned. The horn had come from below, on the street. One car had nearly swiped another, and the near-victim had honked in his outrage.

I didn't exactly remember the trip out here. I did, however, remember the force that had drawn me—largely because it was still there. The light and the music—that feeling of comfort and rightness that was so hard to articulate hovered before me, off in the air. It was like a tunnel. No, it was like an embrace, arms waiting to welcome me home.

Come here, come here. Everything will be all right. You are safe. You are loved.

In spite of myself, one of my legs shifted on the railing. How easy would it be to step over, to walk into that sweet comfort? Would I fall? Would I simply hit the hard sidewalk below? It wouldn't kill me if I did. But maybe I wouldn't fall. Maybe I'd step into that light, into the bliss that could block out the pain that always seemed to surround me lately. . . .

"Are you out of your fucking mind?"

The driver that had nearly been hit had gotten out of his car and was yelling at the other. That driver got out and returned the insults, and a loud tirade began. One of my neighbors on the floor below opened his patio and shouted for them all to shut up.

The argument, that jarring noise, brought me back to myself. Once more, the siren song faded away, and for the first time, I almost felt . . . regret. Carefully, I climbed off the rail and back to the solidity of the balcony. A fall might not kill me, but good God, it would hurt.

I walked back into the condo, finding everything exactly as I'd left it. Even the cats hadn't moved, though they looked up at my arrival. I sat between them, absentmindedly petting Aubrey. I was scared again, scared and eerily attracted to what had just happened—and *that* scared me more.

Despite the vodka tonight, my last encounter had proven alcohol wasn't to blame. No connection. Yet . . . it occurred to me there had been a common link all three times. My mood. Each time, I'd been down . . . sad about my lot in life, seeking reassurance that wasn't to be found. And that's when this phenomenon would happen, offering a solution and the comfort I thought was beyond me.

That was bad news for me. Because if this thing was drawn to woe and unhappiness, I had plenty of it to go around.

Chapter 6

I awoke to the smell of eggs and bacon. For a moment, I had the strangest sense of déjà vu. When Seth and I were first getting to know each other, I'd crashed at his place after too much to drink. When I had woken up, I'd discovered a full breakfast spread in his kitchen.

A few moments later, reality sunk in. There was no desk or bulletin board of book notes, no teddy bear in a University of Chicago shirt. It was my own dresser that looked back at me, my own tangled pale blue sheets wrapped around my legs.

With a sigh, I clambered out of bed and walked out to the kitchen, wondering what was going on. To my astonishment, it was Roman playing chef at my stove, both cats sitting at his feet—no doubt hoping for a bit of dropped bacon.

"You cook?" I asked, pouring a cup of coffee.

"I cook all the time. You just don't notice."

"I notice you heating up a lot of frozen food. What's all this?"

He shrugged. "I'm starving. You don't get a lot of time to eat when you're on stalking duty."

I eyed the eggs, bacon, and pancakes. "Well, I think you'll be good to go for the rest of the day. Maybe the next two days. You sure did make a lot," I added hopefully.

"No need to be coy," he said, trying to hide a smile. "You can have some."

This was the best news I'd heard all day. Of course, I'd

only been up for five minutes. Then, last night's events came slamming into me. "Oh, shit."

Roman glanced up from where he was flipping a pancake. "Hmm?"

"A funny thing happened last night. . . ." I frowned. "Well, not so funny . . ."

I explained that mystery force's reappearance last night, as well as my unexpected swim from the other day. Roman listened quietly, the earlier levity rapidly disappearing from his face.

When I finished, he dumped his skillet of eggs into a bowl so hard that the bowl shattered. I took an uneasy step back. "Son of a bitch," he growled.

"Whoa, hey," I said. An angry nephilim was nothing I wanted around. "That's part of a matched set."

He glared at me, but I knew the anger wasn't toward me, exactly. "Three times, Georgina. This has happened three fucking times, and I wasn't around."

"Why should you be?" I asked in surprise. My surprise then took an odd turn into outrage. "You aren't my keeper."

"No, but some entity is invading my home." I decided not to point out that it was *my* home. "I should be dealing with that, not chasing some boring succubus for Jerome."

"Ask, and ye shall receive," a familiar voice suddenly said. Jerome's aura washed over us as he materialized by the kitchen table.

"About time," snapped Roman, that dark look still on his face. "I've been waiting forever for you to show up."

Jerome arched an eyebrow and lit a cigarette. "Forever, huh? It hasn't even been a week."

"Feels like it," said Roman. He handed me a plate of food, and I sat quietly at the table, deciding I should wait for this status report to unfold before delivering my latest problems to Jerome. "You guys should add following Simone to your list of punishments for the eternally damned."

Jerome smiled and flicked his ashes into a vase of gerbera daisies on my table. I wasn't thrilled about that, but at least it wasn't on my floor. "I take it you've seen no noteworthy activities? Mei reported the same thing."

Roman sat down beside me with his own food, setting the plate down with more force than he needed. I winced, but it didn't break. "She's done nothing but shop and take victims. Oh, and hit on Mortensen."

Both of Jerome's eyebrows rose this time. "Seth Mortensen?"

I started to ask how many Mortensens he knew, but Roman's next words cut me off. "Yeah, she's shown up a couple times, attempting some sort of lame seduction."

My anger started to kindle again and then—

"Wait. A *couple* times?" I exclaimed. "More than the coffee shop?"

Roman looked at me, a brief glint of apology showing through his angry expression. "Yeah, I didn't have a chance to tell you. She came to the bookstore while you were out with Maddie yesterday. Very nicely timed with your absence."

I slammed my fork down on my plate. Really, it was a wonder I had any dishes left. "Why the hell didn't you tell me?"

"Because I kind of didn't have the chance, seeing as we had bigger problems!"

Jerome had stiffened when Roman mentioned Simone attempting to seduce Seth. The reaction was weird, like he'd been caught by surprise. That was rare for a demon, rarer still for one to show it. Several moments later, he regained his composure, turning his attention to Roman's comment. "Bigger problems?"

"Georgina's being stalked," declared Roman.

"Georgina's always being stalked." Jerome sighed. "What is it this time?"

He kept his features neutral, but as we explained the situation, I saw something spark in his eyes . . . some sort of interest. At the very least, speculation.

Silence fell when Roman and I finished our story. I glanced at him, both of us waiting for my overlord to offer some sort of explanation.

"Your job with Simone is done," Jerome said at last.

"Thank God," said Roman.

"You're going to follow Georgie instead."

"What?" Roman and I exclaimed in unison.

"Same deal," added Jerome. "Invisible, no signature. Except when you're here, of course. Most know you two are roommates. It'd be odd if you disappeared off the face of the earth."

The last couple times that siren song had shown up, I'd desperately wanted Roman. I should have been glad to have him now, which is why the outrage that followed next was completely irrational.

"But he needs to follow Simone!"

"Oh?" asked Jerome. "Pray tell why? She's made no contact with anyone from Hell. Either she is here for innocent reasons, or she's too good at hiding her reports."

"But . . . but . . . she's following Seth. We need to figure out why!"

"I don't think it takes a genius to deduce why," said Jerome dryly.

"We have to stop her, though."

The demon snorted. "Georgina, do you have any idea how much I don't care about your ex-boyfriend? There's more in this universe than your absurd love life—or lack of one." I flinched. "Especially since he's sleeping with someone else now. If he's so in love with her now, Simone shouldn't be an issue. And don't glare at me like that," he added. "You already screwed his soul over when you fucked him last spring. Simone won't make any difference."

I gritted my teeth. "I still don't think—"

"No." Jerome's voice was hard, and he was using that tone you didn't argue with. He turned his attention to Roman. "You're done with Simone. You're with Georgie now. Understood?"

Roman nodded, not sharing my outrage. "Understood. Do you know what this is? What's happening to Georgina?"

"I've got a few ideas," Jerome growled. And like that, he vanished.

"Son of a bitch," I said.

Roman swallowed a bite of egg and looked remarkably relaxed, compared to his earlier state. "Was that a general statement of frustration or a slander on Jerome?"

"Both. Why do you look so pleased all of a sudden? You were ready to go on a rampage earlier."

"Because I'm done with Simone. And I get to chase better prey now."

"And because you don't care about Seth at all."

"That too."

I stared at my food without really seeing it. My appetite was gone. "I need to see him. I need to see *her* and find out if she's following him."

"No good can come of that," warned Roman.

I didn't answer. My mood had crashed. I was grateful for Roman's protection now, but in a lot of ways . . . well, I wanted to put Seth before myself. I wanted to defend him from . . . what? Having his life shortened by a succubus? Having his soul further darkened? Or were my motives more selfish . . . did I just not want him to sleep with another woman? Accepting him and Maddie was hard enough . . . and yet, if Simone did woo him, would that break up the impending marriage? No, I decided, Seth would stay true to Maddie. He wouldn't cheat on her. *Wouldn't he?* a nasty voice in my head asked. *He cheated with you. . . .*

"Damn it. I wish you wouldn't look like that."

I glanced up at Roman. "Huh?"

"That pathetic look on your face is killing me." He turned his gaze downward, moving eggs around his plate. With a sigh, he looked back up. "I know where Seth will be today. But I don't know if Simone will be there."

My eyes widened. "Where?"

Roman hesitated only a moment later. "The art museum. He mentioned it to Maddie yesterday. . . . Some exhibit he wanted to see that she doesn't. He was going to swing by there today. I'm not sure of the time, but Simone might have overheard. If so, it'd be the perfect time."

I stood up, and my appearance instantly shifted, ready to go. Hair styled long and wavy. Jeans and a T-shirt. Makeup perfect. "Well, let's go. We need to stake the place out."

"Whoa there, speedy. Some of us can't get ready that fast. *And* some of us aren't done eating."

I sat back down, not bothering to hide my impatience. He ate on, pointedly ignoring me and chewing every bite with care. A thought popped up. "Can you hide my signature? I'll go invisible. Lure her in."

Roman shook his head in exasperation. "I was hoping you wouldn't think of that."

I expected him to refuse me, but to my surprise, he did indeed hide my immortal signature when we finally set out to the museum. After shifting invisible, I was as incognito as he was by my side.

It was a pretty day to be out in downtown Seattle. The morning clouds had burned off, and the sun had nothing to hold it back. It was deceptive, though. The sky was a clear radiant blue, but fall's chill was starting to finally take its grip. So while the weather looked gorgeous through windows, a coat was required once outside.

The Seattle Art Museum—or, as it was affectionately know by locals, SAM—was massive, and its regular collection held exhibits from every place and period imaginable. Roman had told me the exhibit Seth wanted to see was a special one, only in town for a few weeks. It was a display of Late Antiquity jewelry, and I would have wagered good money that Seth was there to do research for Cady and O'Neill.

But when we arrived, there was no sign of Seth. Plenty of tourists—even on a weekday—filled the place, wandering aimlessly and pausing to study or read about the pieces. This period of time was near and dear to me, and I couldn't help feeling a little uneasy. It was the era I'd grown up in, the era

I'd spent my mortal days in. Seeing those items—rings, bracelets, and necklaces—was surreal. Many were from the Mediterranean region of the Roman Empire. Sometimes, when I thought about my past, it would make my heart burn. Other times, I felt removed, like I was watching a movie about someone else's life.

I'd been studying each piece in detail, intrigued at how some had been polished to brightness and others were corroded with time. A gentle nudge at my shoulder made me look up. I saw no one near me and realized it had been Roman. Turning around, I surveyed the gallery and found what—or rather who—he'd spotted. Seth stood on the opposite side of the room, face thoughtful and inquisitive as he studied one of the cases. A notebook and pen were in his hands. He'd come for research, as I suspected.

I studied him with equal fascination. As far as I was concerned, he was as rare and precious to me as any of the jewelry surrounding us. *Shit,* I thought. I was an idiot if I thought I was over him. Just standing there in the same room, I felt more drawn to him than ever.

I backed up to a wall near me, staying out of the way of patrons and simply keeping an eye on Seth, wondering if Simone would show her traitorous face. After a half-hour went by, my impatience grew. It was stupid, I knew. Seth would likely be here all afternoon, and she might arrive later. But . . . suddenly, talking to him seemed more important. I knew it was foolish, knew it was wrong . . . but, well, I'd done more idiotic things in the past.

I stepped out of the gallery and into a stairwell that was momentarily empty. It only took a second to go visible again. In my ear, I heard Roman's voice hiss, "Are you crazy?"

"Keep my signature hidden," I snapped back. "If she shows, we'll sense her before she sees me."

An elderly couple came down the stairs just as I finished my words, giving me an odd look. I smiled winningly and held the door open for them. They scurried through.

Seth was at a display of Byzantine diadems when I touched his arm. He flinched and turned around, though his shock immediately turned to pleasure when he saw me. *Shit,* I thought again. Far better if he'd looked dismayed.

"Let me guess," I said. "You're planning the perfect heist for Cady and O'Neill."

He smiled. "They're the good guys."

"They've been known to break the law," I pointed out.

"I like to think of it as bending the law. What are you doing here?"

I gestured around. "Revisiting my youth—or what's left of it. The sands of time bury most things, but a few remain."

"I never thought of that," said Seth, clearly intrigued. "This is your era. I should have been coming to you for research."

A vision of us having private study sessions came to mind. I immediately squashed it. "Better visual aids here. Anything catch your eye?"

He pointed at the case of diadems beside him. "I like these. It's a shame we don't wear stuff like this anymore."

I followed his gaze. "Not enough bling in the hair nowadays?"

He gave me one of those half-smiles. "No. There's just . . . I don't know. There's a beauty and skill we don't use. Look at that." He gestured toward one diadem, meant to resemble a crown of gold coins. Little strings of small gold circles hung down, draping through the hair. "Look at the imperfections. That was handmade, each one of those."

"Some would call that flawed." I loved it when Seth got caught up in these philosophical musings.

"That's what makes it great. And anyway, I kind of like the idea of adorning women in crowns and jewels. Call me sexist, but I think the fair sex should be worshipped." He paused. "And perfectly entitled to all the rights and opportunities of men."

I laughed and stepped away so that others could approach the case. "I think you're romantic, not sexist." A troubling thought came to me, recalling how Maddie had admired pearl tiaras and headbands at the bridal stores yesterday. Modern-day diadems. Would Seth like that?

"Call it what you want," he said, "but I just think our civilization has declined when scrunchies have become the prevalent form of hair ornamentation."

We wandered around the exhibits after that, commenting on and analyzing them. I tried not to overthink the situation. I didn't delude myself about whether we could be friends. I didn't wallow in guilt over carrying a torch. I just tried to enjoy the moment. During none of our time together did I feel Simone. Since Roman's senses were stronger, I had to assume he hadn't either. I also suspected he was rolling his eyes over my time with Seth.

Seth and I finally reached the last of the exhibit: Byzantine wedding rings. When I saw them, the warm, comfortable feelings that had wrapped around me suddenly turned to ice. I felt the change in Seth too. Most of the rings were of similar design, with a flat circle lying on top of the ring, the circle surface then engraved with some image. My troubled feelings had nothing to do with weddings or any other associations with Maddie.

Last Christmas, Seth had had a ring made for me in this style. He hadn't intended it as a wedding or engagement ring. He'd just done it as a gift, knowing the style was part of my past. It was beautiful, and I still had it. It was locked away in a box of treasures I'd kept over the centuries—items too precious to throw out and too painful to look at.

Neither of us said anything, and I wondered what he thought about. Was it just the awkward discomfort from memories of an ex-girlfriend? Was it stirring bittersweet feelings similar to the ones churning in me? When he and Maddie had gotten involved, I'd been convinced he'd moved on. Then, after our brief affair in the spring, I'd reconsidered. There were too many times now that he looked at me strangely, too many times that reminded me of when I was his girlfriend and the times he told me he loved me. But his wedding was still moving forward, with no sign of doubt on his part. I didn't know what to think.

I'm not sure how long we stood in silence, but Seth broke it. "Well . . . I guess that's it for the exhibit, huh?"

I glanced around as though attempting to determine if we'd seen it all. I already knew we had. "Yeah, I guess that's it."

He wouldn't meet my eyes, and his whole body radiated nervousness. "Thanks for the research help. I should get back to the store and put this to good use."

"Good luck."

His eyes lifted, and I offered a small smile that he returned. "Thanks."

We parted, and I left the museum, not sure where I was going—only that I had to go someplace where he wasn't. For an hour or so, I'd played make-believe with him, keeping that familiar depression away and allowing myself a small joy. Now, that darkness descended on me . . . and uneasily, I recalled how that mystery force always showed up when I was troubled. That was its lure: comfort when I felt desperate and alone.

Roman might be my offense, but I decided then to go for a good defense. I needed distraction. "You aren't going to like this," I murmured, assuming Roman was close enough to hear.

Distraction wasn't the only thing I needed. I needed a good energy fix. I was sleeping with enough men regularly that I had a pretty consistent supply of energy. Still, being at full power, so to speak, would keep my strength up—which hopefully would increase my mental resolve.

Not that sleeping with random men was always cheering. I was in no mood to go hunting for victims in a bar. I needed something slightly easier, something a little less sleazy. Normally those two were mutually exclusive, but I'd come up with an idea while driving home that might accomplish both.

There was a twentysomething guy named Gavin who lived in a condo down the hall from me. He was nice enough and had a serious crush on me. He never said or did anything overtly, but it was obvious. He alternated between nervousness and poorly done jokes whenever I was around. He always seemed unwilling to part when we ran into each other in the garage or lobby or whatever. His gaze also spent more time on my cleavage than my eyes.

The beauty of it all was that he also had a girlfriend. I didn't know if he'd cheated on her before or just wanted to. That wasn't important at the moment. What was important was that when I showed up at his door after the museum, his girlfriend wasn't around.

"Georgina," he said, taken aback. "How . . . how's it going?"

"Not great," I said, forcing distress into my voice. "I got locked out of my place and have to wait for my friend to show up with a spare set of keys. Can I wait here for her? I'm afraid if I go outside, it'll rain again."

It was then that Gavin seemed to notice my drenched state, particularly the now transparent white sundress I'd shapeshifted into without a bra.

His eyes bugged out, and then he glanced quickly behind him before turning back to the wet, clinging fabric encasing my breasts and their hardened nipples. "It . . . it rained? But it's so nice out." That brisk fall sunshine was pouring in through his windows.

"I know," I said glibly. "I was kind of surprised too. It was this really fast freak thing that came out of nowhere."

This was apparently so unbelievable that Gavin actually managed to tear himself away from me to once more scrutinize the brilliantly blue sky outside. Finally, deciding not to fight this, he beckoned for me to come in.

"Do you have a T-shirt or anything I can wear?" I asked sweetly. "I'm freezing in this."

His scrutiny had shifted from my breasts to the very noticeable black thong underneath the dress. I think changing out of the dress was a huge disappointment for him, but he wasn't so socially inept as to refuse me.

"Sure, come on."

I followed him to his bedroom where he dug out an oversized Seattle Mariners T-shirt and a pair of green flannel boxers. He handed them over.

"See if these work," he said, backing out of the room to give me privacy.

"Thanks," I said, giving him a winning smile.

He managed a nervous one in return just before shutting the door. I crossed my arms and waited a minute, during which an invisible Roman said: "This is ridiculous. You should have just shown up as a pizza delivery girl."

"Hey, the wet dress technique is tried and true. Works every time."

Roman sighed.

"Wait in the other room then," I said. "This shouldn't take long."

I opened the door and shouted down the hall, "Hey, Gavin? Can you come help me?"

He popped back in, and I couldn't help but notice his dark brown hair was a lot neater than it had been earlier. He'd probably dashed off to the bathroom in a quick grooming attempt to impress me.

"What's wrong?" he asked.

I turned around and pushed my hair over one shoulder, showing where the straps of my dress's halter top were tied behind my neck. "There's a knot here I can't get undone. Can you give it a shot?"

He hesitated for only a moment before moving forward to assist. I'd shape-shifted a pretty good knot, and it took him some time to work through it, during which I backed up against him as close as I could. At last, he managed to undo it, pulling the straps apart and releasing them so that I could grab them. I missed, of course, and as the straps fell, so did most of the dress. It went against the laws of physics, seeing as how clingy that wet fabric had been.

I caught the dress in a weak attempt at modesty, but not

before it almost entirely fell off. Nearby, I heard another ex-asperated sigh from Roman.

I turned to face Gavin, holding the dress against me in a way that completely exposed my chest. His eyes were natu-rally fixed on it, and I glanced down too, as though trying to figure out what he was looking at.

"Oh, man. I'm wet all over. Do you have a towel? I don't want to get the shirt wet."

"Uh . . . what? Yeah . . ."

In record speed, he raced to the bathroom and returned with a small hand towel. I decided then not to bother with any more convenient excuses and simply stepped forward, hoping he was smart enough to accept the invitation.

He was. Hesitant at first, he slowly ran the towel over my breasts, lingering when it was obvious they were dry. He moved down to my stomach—which he dried pretty quickly—and then to my hips and thighs. I'd long since let my soggy dress fall to the floor and helpfully pulled off my thong so that he could reach *every* part. He had to kneel to do my inner thighs, and I heard him mutter, "Oh my God." I wasn't sure if that was simply because of the situation he was in or because his girlfriend hadn't gone Brazilian.

"You have great hands," I purred.

"Th-thanks," he said inanely. He'd just finished my legs and stood up. I took the towel and tossed it on the bed. Catching hold of his hand, I gently stroked it and brought it between my thighs.

"Really great," I said in an even lower voice. "Long fin-gers . . ."

I guided a couple of those fingers into me, and I swear, he gasped louder than I did. After a little more urging, he no longer needed my assistance and began rapidly thrusting his fingers on his own. I pressed to him, moaning as though it were the most amazing experience of my life. I was wetter on the inside than out, and the only resistance he encountered was in how tight I'd made myself.

Reaching around his arm, I unfastened his pants and pulled them off in one motion. His erection pointed out at me long and hard and ready. It had probably been that way the moment I showed up at the door. Gripping his shirt I pulled him toward the bed.

"The rest," I gasped, spreading myself in front of him. "Let me see how the rest feels."

The hand that had been in me left as he laid himself on top of me. He pushed my thighs apart and thrust in with a force that contradicted his earlier shyness. In fact, his face showed no nervousness whatsoever anymore. He was all eagerness and desire, emitting small grunts each time he shoved himself into me.

"Harder," I told him, giving him big, passionate eyes. "I want it harder."

He obliged, increasing the speed and force. After about a minute of this, he shifted up so that he was kneeling. Holding my thighs just below my knees, he spread my legs far apart and leaned in. The new position allowed him to get deeper, and I exclaimed my approval, urging him again to do it harder and harder.

Steadily, I felt his life energy begin to flow into me. It was a decent amount, and it felt glorious, spreading through my being and reinvigorating me. With it came his thoughts and feelings, at which point I learned he never had actually cheated on his girlfriend before—but, oh, he'd wanted to plenty of times. She barely crossed his mind at the moment. He was too consumed by me to feel much guilt. The only brief concern he had was that he should have used a condom. That was a regret, but it wasn't strong enough for him to stop, not when I felt this good.

I let my cries escalate into small screams and felt him grow closer and closer to coming. My head was getting dangerously close to the headboard, but the roughness of it all was really turning him on. He'd never had the opportunity to just go so wild. Harder and harder he went, thrusting himself in all the way each time. The energy increased by leaps and bounds, and just before the big moment came, I decided to drive home the guilt a little. It made *me* feel some guilt in return, but at the end of the day, guilt marked the soul, and that was what Hell employed me for.

"Can she do this?" I panted. He was half a second from coming. "Can your girlfriend take it like this?"

The orgasm exploded—and so did he. He pulled out at the last second, not because of what I'd said but because this was his solution to the condom problem. Withdrawal was a horrible safe sex method, but whatever. His body spasmed and he came on my stomach. It was warm against my flesh, and he watched with a perverse fascination.

Yet, just before it had happened, I'd felt my dagger hit. He'd been so consumed by lust that he'd been able to block his girlfriend out earlier. My comment had pushed her to the forefront, but there had been no way he could stop what he was doing by that point. I'd felt the spike of guilt, just as the last burst of life energy sparkled through me.

He fell back against the covers, gasping and exhausted. Losing some of your life will do that to you. Whatever thoughts of guilt or satisfaction he felt now were his alone. The towel was still conveniently on the bed, and I used it to clean myself up. I stood up and walked over to the window while he still tried to catch his breath. He'd probably fall asleep in a few minutes.

"Oh, hey," I said cheerfully. "My friend's out there with the key." I picked up the sodden dress and headed for the door. "Thanks for letting me hang out."

Chapter 7

"**Y**ou're right," said Roman the next morning, ruminating over what had happened with Gavin. "I didn't like that."

I was standing in the bathroom, going over my hair with a flat iron. It was a pain in the ass compared to shape-shifting, but I liked the challenge. Plus, I could always fine-tune the frizziness away afterward.

"Not like it's the first time it's happened," I pointed out, my eyes on the mirror rather than where he leaned in the doorway. "You used to never mind."

"Didn't I?" he asked dryly.

"Well, being with him distracted me from wallowing in self-pity. Not that it made me feel that great either," I admitted. "But it kept my . . . whatever . . . away. And hey, it couldn't have been as nasty as what you saw Simone do."

"True, but now that guy's just going to come trolling around all the time. He'll be showing up to borrow cups of sugar in the hopes he can score some more action."

"I'll deal with him. I've got a little practice in pushing guys away."

"Don't I know it."

I paused to shoot him a glare. "Will you lay off the attitude this morning? You're starting to sound like you're jealous or something."

Roman snorted. "Hardly. Why in God's name would I be

jealous over the woman who got my sister killed and tried to unleash the forces of Heaven and Hell to destroy me?"

Fair point. "It's a little more complicated than that."

"Oh, yes, I'm sure." He crossed his arms and stared down at the floor. "But maybe the next time you're looking for distraction, we could rent a movie and microwave some popcorn instead of fucking the neighbors."

"You have horrible taste in movies," I mumbled. But that closed the conversation, and Roman wandered off. A few moments later, I heard the TV turn on.

I had to work today, but it was an afternoon shift. I was up and ready to go early because I wanted to visit Erik. I should have felt secure in Jerome's ability to figure out what was going on, as well as Roman's protection. But I'd had too much shit happen to me in the past to ever fully trust anyone. Erik had always proven a valuable resource.

Roman went with me, covertly, but it took a while for me to actually get some quality time with Erik. He had customers in the store—which was great for him, but I could hardly discuss immortal affairs with others around. When the people finally thinned out, Erik turned his attention to me, ready with his typical friendly smile. His color looked better, and his movements weren't as jerky. He was still weak, just not as weak.

"Your cold's cleared up," I said.

His smile grew. "Yes, I told you it was nothing. A mere cold isn't going to kill me off."

His voice was light, but I couldn't help a small frown. There had been something in his words—something I couldn't quite put my finger on—that made it sound like he *did* know what was going to kill him. A chill ran down my spine. I didn't like to think of those sorts of things.

I sat down at his little table with him but declined tea. "I just wanted to see if you'd learned anything else." It was a nervous impulse on my part. I knew he would have contacted me if he had discovered something.

"No, but as I said, the information we have is vague enough for it to be any number of things."

"That's what Jerome said."

Erik looked pleased. "I'm glad he knows. I've always said that your own people are more likely to know better than me."

I couldn't help a small laugh. "Debatable. I might have something to make it a little less vague." Briefly, I explained my recent encounter and how it had occurred to me that this force only visited when I was troubled and depressed. "It's like . . . it's like it's preying on my weakness. Trying to lure me in with promises of comfort."

"Then you must be careful not to give in."

If Roman had said that, I would have snapped at him for stating the obvious. "It's easy to say that now, in the cold light of logic, but when it happens . . . I don't know. I lose my grip on the world. Reason's gone. Hell, half the time I don't even know what's happening until afterward. It's like . . . sleeping. Sleepwalking. Whatever."

"And it always appears as a type of doorway?"

I pondered this for several seconds. "I don't know . . . kind of. I don't know how to describe it—and I know I keep saying that. And how useless it sounds. I'm not sure if it's a door, exactly, but it's definitely trying to pull me into something."

Erik had made himself tea and sat for almost a minute sipping it, his brow knit in thought. "I'll think about all of this. In the meantime, I'd just advise . . ." He hesitated. "Well, let me put it this way. You are a delight, Miss Kincaid, and I always enjoy my time with you. However, you are also—how can I say this—someone frequently given to darker moods."

"Is that your polite way of saying I'm always down?" I teased.

"No . . . not exactly. But if this thing is seeking out those in emotionally depressed states, then I'd say you are particularly susceptible. If it's at all possible, you should try to stay away from those moods."

I thought about it. One of my best friends was marrying

my ex—an ex whom I was starting to fall for all over again. An ex whose soul I had inadvertently damned to Hell and who was now being stalked by another succubus. My own soul had long since been Hell-bound, and I was committed to an eternity of sleeping with men whom I often didn't like. Oh, yeah. Let's not forget that my roommate was given to sociopathic tendencies and had me on his hit list.

"That might be easier said than done," I told Erik.

"I can imagine," he said ruefully. "But it may be the only way to protect yourself. That and your own willpower—the strength of which I firmly believe in."

Erik's faith in me warmed up a piece of my heart, even though the rest of today's insight hadn't been all that insightful. I thanked him for his time and headed off to work, grateful Roman offered no "witty" commentary during our drive.

At the bookstore, Seth worked alone in the café. Simone was nowhere in sight, which was one bonus. The fact that it was Maddie's day off also improved my mood. Maybe staying away from my usual glum state wouldn't be as hard as I thought.

"Yo, Kincaid."

Doug found me putting stickers on our rack of clearance books. They mostly consisted of out-of-print coffee-table books, things like *Stone Arches of Tuscany* and *The Complete Book of Bridal Cross-stitch*. I wasn't entirely sure what that last one was, but maybe it'd make a good wedding present for Seth and Maddie. The price was certainly a bargain. We'd reduced it three times now, and still no one wanted to buy it.

"What's up?" I asked.

"I've got news that's going to rock your world. And make you think I'm even awesomer than you already do."

"That's a bold statement."

He paused, apparently trying to decide if he'd been complimented or insulted. "I just found out that Gabrielle's a fan of Blue Satin Bra."

"She never struck me as that type. I figured all of her lingerie would be black."

Doug gave me a withering look. "No, Kincaid. I don't mean that she wears one. I mean that she likes the group. Haven't you heard of them?"

"There's a group called Blue Satin Bra?" I shook my head. "Sorry. I can't keep up with every new garage band in Seattle."

"They aren't a garage band! They're the hottest thing to hit the metal scene. They're going to make it big."

I tried to hide my skepticism. Doug himself was in a band called Nocturnal Admission, and whenever he spoke about local bands, it seemed like everyone was on the verge of making it big.

"What's this got to do with Gabrielle again?"

Doug was clearly growing frustrated with me. "She's a huge fan—and they've got a concert tomorrow night. Unfortunately, it's all sold out. She was pretty bummed about it."

Despite his annoyance with me, I could sense the smugness within him. "Here it comes. . . ."

Pride lit his features. "I'm friends with the bass player and managed to score some tickets. If your pal Cody approaches her with them . . ."

I paused in my stickering. "You're right. You *did* just get awesomer."

"You've got to go too, you know."

"I—what?" Me trailing along didn't sound romantic in the least.

Doug shrugged. "He can't just ask her out for an actual date. Not yet. He'll spook her."

"Then what exactly is he supposed to ask her out for?"

"I do the asking. I'll just be all like, 'Hey, Gabby, I got some extra tickets to the show. You want to go along with me and my friends?' Then she's off guard. She comes along, Cody's there, magic happens. . . ."

"Wow," I said. "Looks like you've got it all figured out. And I don't think she likes to be called Gabby."

"This is a good plan." He was clearly very pleased with

himself. "I've been around, Kincaid. When you get mad romantic skills like me, you'll understand."

I rolled my eyes. "We can only hope. So how many friends are going along exactly?"

"I scored four tickets. So: you, me, Cody, and Gabrielle."

"Sounds suspiciously like a double date. You trying your mad romantic skills on me?" It wouldn't be the first time.

"Hell no. Do I look suicidal? You're already claimed." For a minute, Seth came to mind, then Doug added: "I'm not getting on the bad side of that guy you're shacked up with. I mean, I can hold my own in a fight, but he looks like he could seriously fuck someone up."

"You have no idea," I muttered. No doubt Roman—lingering nearby invisibly—was loving this. "But we aren't involved. He's just my roommate."

"For now," said Doug ominously. He began a retreat. "I'll go invite Gabs. You tell Cody the deal and that you're going to be his wing-woman."

I shook my head after Doug left, wondering what I'd gotten myself into. His absurd comments about mad skills and wing-women aside, the whole casual group thing might be a gateway outing to get Gabrielle closer to Cody. I just hoped word of his Goth getup the other day hadn't gotten around to her. I also wondered what kind of experience I was getting myself into with Blue Satin Bra. Doug's bizarre industrial alternative music had grown on me over the years, but I had a feeling this concert would be a very different experience.

About an hour later, I was in my office when some unexpected guests popped their heads in. Well, one wasn't entirely unexpected. I'd found that even when Maddie wasn't working, there was never any real security. You couldn't count on her absence, not when her boyfriend and brother were often in the store. I could feel some safety when we didn't have the same shift, but I'd long accepted that Maddie could really show up at any moment.

No, the real surprise was that Maddie was in my office

with Brandy Mortensen, Seth's niece. He had five of them, and she was the oldest. When Seth and I had dated, I'd grown pretty attached to that brood. My longing for children and the girls' total adorableness made it easy for me to love them. They'd grown close to me too.

Of course, at fourteen, I suspected Brandy wouldn't appreciate being called "adorable." She stood with Maddie, who was holding a garment bag on a hanger. Brandy wore a surprisingly sullen teen expression. She seemed taller to me than when I'd last seen her. Just like with Erik, time was passing quickly for these humans.

"Hey, guys," I said, setting my paperwork aside. "What's up?"

"More wedding errands," said Maddie cheerfully. "We just came by to pick up Seth. We went back to that shop and got a dress for Brandy. She's a bridesmaid too."

Maddie lifted the edge of the bag, revealing the same dress Maddie had bought me the other day.

"How embarrassing," I told Brandy. "We're going to show up in the same outfit."

She gave me the ghost of a smile but stayed silent.

"We also went and talked to some florists but didn't really come up with any ideas on what to get. If I get something purple, will it be too monochromatic? And if I get a different color, will it look weird?"

"Hard questions," I said solemnly. Ones I didn't want to answer.

"Maybe you can come back with me and take a look at some of their books?" Maddie was giving me that hopeful, cheery smile that was so good at inspiring guilt in me.

"I don't know," I said vaguely. "Depends on my schedule."

"Well, let me know. Let me go grab Seth—maybe he has some ideas."

Good luck with that, I thought. Seth was notoriously awful at offering opinions, and he'd seemed particularly noncommittal about this wedding stuff, no pun intended. Maddie left Brandy with me, and I gave her a genuine smile.

"So how's it been going?" I asked. "Did you have fun shopping?"

Brandy crossed her arms over her chest and tossed her blond hair over one shoulder. She was wearing a formfitting *Rocky Horror Picture Show* T-shirt. Really, I thought. She was one step away from turning into her uncle.

"No," she said bluntly.

I arched an eyebrow in surprise. Last I'd known, shopping and having people buy you clothes was pretty sweet when you were a teenage girl. Maybe I was out of touch. "Why not?"

"Because," she said dramatically. "This wedding is a joke."

I cast an uneasy glance at the doorway. "Better not let them hear you say that."

Brandy looked unconcerned. She wasn't exactly scowling, but it was pretty close. "Uncle Seth isn't supposed to be marrying her."

"Why not? They've been dating for . . . well, a while." That was kind of true, guilt-induced engagement or no. "He proposed. She accepted. Easy as that."

"She's not the one," said Brandy stoutly. "He's supposed to be marrying *you*."

Yeah, I really wished the door was closed. "Brandy," I said, pitching my voice as low as I could. "Your uncle and I broke up. That's how it is. People move on."

"You two weren't supposed to. You guys were in *love*."

"He loves her too."

"It's not the same."

This was not a discussion I'd ever expected to have. I'd known Seth's nieces still liked me, but I'd hardly thought I'd left this sort of impression. "Do you not like Maddie or something?"

Brandy gave a half-hearted shrug and averted her eyes. "She's okay. But she's not you."

I didn't say anything for several moments. I wondered if

Brandy's resentment toward the wedding was because she had greater devotion to me than Maddie—or if it was part of some romantic ideal girls her age often had about love and soul mates.

"I'm sorry," I said. "Love in the real world doesn't usually work out the way stories make us think it should. We don't always get fairy-tale endings. People split up and move on. Just because you love someone doesn't mean you can't love someone else." I shivered. This was remarkably similar to a conversation Carter and I had once had, shortly after the (first) break-up with Seth.

"It's still not right," said Brandy obstinately.

Seth and Maddie retrieved her shortly thereafter, for which I was grateful. I really didn't want to have to play devil's advocate and defend a marriage that I was hardly thrilled about myself. I felt that sorrow that always seemed to plague me when I thought about them surface . . . and then remembered Erik's comments. Don't give in to it. Stay away from it—that was what kept leading me into trouble.

Easier said than done, just as I'd told him. Distraction seemed to be the key to it all, and I just didn't feel up to another liaison tonight. I certainly didn't need the energy.

"Distract me," I murmured when I was seated in my car. "Annoy me with your 'wit,' or just make me outright mad."

No physical evidence of Roman appeared—no signature, no physical appearance—but his voice answered me back just as softly. "Go see your friends. Aren't they going to that bar tonight? You need to tell Cody he's going on a double date."

"It's not a double date," I growled back.

But Roman had a point. I probably should let the young vampire know what was in store tomorrow. I was also kind of curious how Roman even knew about the bar outing. I'd received a voice mail message earlier today that one would think would have been out of Roman's hearing range. He'd either been standing really close, or nephilim just had superhuman hearing. And, well, seeing as they *were* superhuman, I supposed that wasn't too far off.

Another idea suddenly came to mind about tonight's social gathering, one that would most definitely provide a distraction—and possibly take care of a nuisance.

"The bar it is," I declared.

I drove down to Pioneer Square, Seattle's historic district, and sought out the Cellar, a dive of a bar located in a basement akin to its name. It was a favorite place for immortals—well, hellish immortals. Since most angels didn't drink—Carter being the exception—you didn't usually find them hanging out in bars. They were more likely to be found at upscale coffee shops. For inexplicable reasons, a number of them also liked to hang out at the restaurant on top of the Space Needle. Maybe they thought it was bringing them closer to Heaven.

And, indeed, as I walked down the stairs into the Cellar, I felt Carter's signature, along with those of my usual clique. Best of all, there was an additional signature I'd been hoping to find.

"Hot damn," I said, striding toward the table where Simone sat with my friends. She burned with the glow of energy that succubi stole from their victims. I hated to admit it, but hers was brighter than the one I still sported. I assured myself that it was just because she'd probably bagged someone today, rather than last night.

Hugh scooted to make room for me, and I pulled up a chair from a neighboring table. "Didn't think you'd show tonight."

I waved a waiter over and ordered a vodka gimlet. "You know I can't stay away from you guys."

"You're just in time," said Carter. His face was neutral, but I caught a mischievous glint in his eyes as he sipped his bourbon. "Simone was just regaling us with tales of the Underground Tour. Did you hear that Seattle burned to the ground and was rebuilt a century ago?"

"Only every time I take the tour," I replied. Which had

been about a dozen times. It was a tourist hotbed, and I'd taken friends and out-of-town victims on it often. I gave Simone a curious look. "Did you do that today?"

She nodded. "Figured I should take in the city while I'm here." She was still using that librarian voice, but I had to admit she looked more like a succubus than the last time I'd seen her. Her neckline was cut so low, it was a wonder her nipples didn't show. Her lips were fuck-me red, and unless I was mistaken, her hair was longer and more voluminous than before. I couldn't decide if she looked like an angel or a beach bunny.

And speaking of angels . . . Simone had her chair pushed right next to Carter's, so close that she couldn't help but brush her arm against his each time she reached for her drink. I suspected her leg was pressed up to his as well.

He glanced over, giving her a look that wasn't exactly romantic but filled with deep interest I felt certain was feigned.

"I find Seattle's history fascinating. I haven't been here that long, so it's great to keep learning new things."

Simone beamed. Across the table, Hugh choked a little on his drink. Carter had been in Seattle for a couple hundred years. True—not *that* long for an immortal like him, but he'd most certainly been here for the Seattle fire. Hell, considering how he'd once accidentally burned down my Christmas tree, he might have been the one who set the city ablaze, for all I knew.

My gimlet appeared, and I took a long drink of liquid courage. "From what I hear, you've been checking out some of our local celebrities too," I said sweetly.

Simone dragged her adoring gaze from Carter and fixed me with a frown. "I don't think I've run into many celebrities."

"Well," I said, still smiling like a fool. "I guess it depends on how you define 'celebrity.' I certainly consider best-selling authors celebrities. You've been chatting up one quite a bit."

Immediately, Cody, Hugh, and Peter eagerly snapped to attention. They could sniff female conflict a mile away and were undoubtedly bracing themselves for a cat fight.

"Oh, that," she said dismissively. "I thought you meant like an actor or something. Yeah, he's just someone on my radar. One of many. Pretty cute. Nice enough."

"And a friend of mine," I said. My voice was still cheerful, but I could see in her eyes that she was well aware of the escalating tension.

"Still, fair game," she replied with a shrug. "And what do you care? His soul's already tainted. He's not *that* good a catch. Not like I can do much more damage."

That wasn't true. Seth might currently be Hell-bound, but he wasn't beyond redemption—even though the odds of that were allegedly slim. If by some crazy chance Simone got him to cheat on Maddie again, his soul would grow darker and kill any lingering chances to save him. Plus, sin aside, Simone would shorten his life—which was something I was definitely against.

"So, he's just a random guy you scoped out?" I asked. The politeness was fading from me. It was disappearing from her too. So. Bland Simone wasn't quite as oblivious as she played. "The fact that he's a friend of mine *and* someone I used to date makes no difference?"

"You make it sound like I'm trying to get you back for something. I don't even *know* you. I'm just here on vacation. Getting guys is part of our life—and you don't have any territorial control like them." She nodded toward the vampires, who had very well-defined hunting grounds. "Unless," she added smugly, "you've got some kind of arrangement with Jerome."

I certainly didn't. In fact, my boss had made it extremely clear that he didn't care about what happened to Seth.

"No, but I'd think you'd do it as a courtesy when you're visiting someone else's city. It's the nice thing to do." My smile returned, filled with ice this time. "And it ensures that your visit stays nice too." Maybe using her favorite adjective would drive home my message.

Simone stiffened, attention totally on me now. "What is

this, some kind of warning that you'll come after me if I don't back off?"

I shrugged and finished my drink. "Just friendly advice."

She stood up and slung her purse over her shoulder with such force that it nearly hit Carter in the head. Apparently, he wasn't on the radar anymore. Well, at least for now. "I'm not going to stay and listen to thinly veiled threats. Especially ones over inconsequential men. If I want him, I'll get him."

"You'll be missed," I muttered as she stalked away.

"Oh," said Hugh brightly. "There is nothing I like better than when succubi fight. Puts *Dynasty* to shame. You could have cleaned the floor with Tawny, but Simone might give you a match."

"Hardly," I said. "And she'll have about as much luck with Seth as Carter."

Carter raised an eyebrow, apparently not agreeing with my statement.

"She's really hitting on Seth?" asked Cody.

"Yup. In a shy, starry-eyed fan girl kind of way."

"Isn't that how you won him over way back when?" asked Peter.

I shot him a glare. "It's irrelevant. It won't work."

"Then why worry?" asked Hugh slyly.

"Because an ounce of prevention—oh, never mind," I groaned. "I need another drink."

Hugh and the vampires were clearly amused by all this and weren't particularly concerned. I think they too believed Seth would prove immovable; they just liked the idea of me making another succubus irate. The sad part was that I'd probably just encouraged Simone to try even harder.

Two drinks later, I decided to head home. I was sufficiently angry that I didn't fear the siren song's comfort. Before leaving, I informed Cody about his impending date. Unsurprisingly, he freaked out.

"What? I . . . I can't. What will I say? What will I do?"

"Frankly, my dear . . ." began Hugh in an undertone.

"You'll be fine," I said. "Just stop stressing and be yourself."

"Sounds like a double date," said Peter. "I can get more black hair dye."

"No," I warned. "Do not even think about it." I could still see faint streaks that hadn't entirely washed out from Cody's blond mane. "Just dress like you are now. I'll meet you at the club."

I started to turn, and then a thought came to me. "Carter, can I talk to you?"

His lips twitched slightly. If that was his sign of surprise, I couldn't say. "Anything for you, Daughter of Lilith."

He followed me outside the bar, where we stood amid all the Pioneer Square partygoers. Once clear of the building's non-smoking interior, he promptly lit a cigarette.

"If you're jealous of my relationship with Simone," he said, "I can assure you, we're just friends."

"Oh, be quiet. You know that's not what this is about. Look, she was lying, right? About Seth being a coincidence?"

Carter took a long drag before answering. Angels could tell when others were lying. "Yep. But she seemed pretty sincere in the last comment about going after him regardless."

I grimaced. "Why? Why would she target Seth? Is it some kind of way to assert dominance over the local succubus?"

"Not sure. The ways of succubi—and all women—are a mystery to me."

"Jerome originally thought she'd come to spy. He had Roman follow her, but nothing came of it. She never reported in or anything. He pulled Roman from her—" I paused, suddenly turning over the events and analyzing them in a way I hadn't considered before. "But it wasn't until I told him Simone was hitting on Seth. It seemed like that was the moment Jerome pulled Roman. He seemed pretty adamant about leaving her alone."

"Did he now?" Carter inhaled on the cigarette again, but I could see thoughts churning behind his eyes.

"What?" I asked.

"Just a musing," he said. A half-truth, typical of angels. "Did Jerome do anything else after that?"

"Yeah, he put Roman on me."

This elicited surprise. "Why?"

Apparently, Jerome and Carter hadn't been hanging out recently. I gave Carter the rundown on my latest bizarre situation.

"That is weird," he admitted.

"Do you know what it could be?"

"Any number of things." He spoke flippantly, but I knew I'd piqued his curiosity—maybe even his concern.

I sighed. "I wish people would stop saying that. No one's really helping."

"I'll help you," he said, dropping the cigarette and stamping it out. "I'll follow Simone."

That was not at all what I had expected. "Why would you do that? Are you going to stop her from making the moves on Seth?"

This earned his amusement. "You know I can't interfere with that kind of thing. But I am curious about Simone's activities."

An uneasy feeling bubbled within me, one that had troubled me since I'd first met Seth, and Carter had begun taking an active role in my life. "Why? Why do you care so much about Seth? You've always been curious about what he does—and how we interact."

"I'm interested in the creative process of a great artist. It's fun to watch."

"Another half-truth." Like always, he answered the question without really answering it. I was astonished at the desperation in my voice when I spoke next. "I'm serious. Why, Carter? How does Seth—and me being with Seth—concern you?"

He chucked me on the chin. "You've got better things to do than worry about the goings-on of a curious angel. Besides, wouldn't you feel better if someone was reporting back to you on Simone?"

"Well, yeah," I admitted. "But—"

"Then it's settled. You're welcome."

He turned quickly away and disappeared into a crowd of partiers. I knew better than to go after him because he'd probably literally disappear once no one was paying attention. I sighed yet again.

Fucking angels.

Chapter 8

Knowing Carter was on the job with Simone made me feel mildly better, but there was something about him that always unnerved me when it came to Seth—and, well, my love life in general. He was too interested. I'd gotten used to an angel hanging out with my friends, but sometimes I wondered if I was being lulled into some kind of trick. Heaven had its own agenda, just as we did, and their motives were often harder to figure out.

I had a morning shift the next day. It passed by easily until Doug delivered some bad news to me about ten minutes before I was going to leave.

"Can't go with you tonight, Kincaid."

I looked up from my spreadsheet in disbelief. "What?"

He shrugged, hovering near the door to my office. He'd had the same shift as me today, and I had a feeling he was telling me at the end to save himself from hours of anger. Kind of like how people who get fired are told at the end of the day on Friday.

"There's this girl I met . . . and I can't really turn down the chance to go out with her. Oh, man. She's smokin'. She's got this body that—"

"I don't need the details," I interrupted. "Can't you just take her instead of me? Cody was starting to get into this idea . . . he'll be really down if it gets canceled."

"No need to cancel. Just go without me. I couldn't bring her instead of you—Cody needs you."

I groaned. "Yeah, but the safety of a group is gone, and I become the third wheel."

"Find someone else to go, then."

It was then that Maddie appeared beside her brother. She was relieving him for the next shift. "Go where?"

My next words made me cringe, but I did *not* want to go alone with Cody and Gabrielle. "Do you want to go to a, um, metal concert tonight?" At least having another woman along would kill the double date insinuations.

This clearly wasn't an invite that she'd been expecting. "Well . . . I would, except I've got to close, and then I'm supposed to meet a friend." I had serious doubts about the "I would" part and this so-called friend. Metal was not Maddie's scene. She suddenly brightened. "You know what? You should bring Seth."

"I . . . what?" I asked.

"Mortensen?" asked Doug, sounding as baffled as me.

"I don't think that's his thing," I said uneasily. I knew for a fact it wasn't.

"Yeah," agreed Doug. "Probably not a good idea."

I hid a frown at Doug's words. With as much as he wanted to get out of this and see his smokin' woman, I figured he'd be willing to push anyone off on me.

Maddie was oblivious. "No, really. He's been cooped up for weeks with the book, and I think it'd be good for him to go out. I think the wedding stuff is stressing him out."

Yeah, that made two of us. "Oh, I don't want to, um, push him outside of his comfort zone," I said lamely.

She laughed. "Like I said, it'd be good for him. I'll go ask him now."

She was gone before either Doug or I could protest. Several moments of silence hung between us. "Well," he said at last. "She can talk him into almost anything. I guess you're set."

"I guess so." He walked off, and I found it intriguing that neither of us was excited about this prospect. It drove home the double date thing even more and also made me feel guilty about Maddie's blind trust. On the bright side—kind of—I supposed it would take some balls for Simone to crash the concert and continue her "seduction" of Seth.

As Doug had predicted, Maddie did indeed convince Seth to go. It was a late show, and the four of us had agreed to meet outside the club around 10:30 so that I could distribute our tickets. Once we were all there, I glanced at the three faces before me, trying to decide whether it was all comical or pathetic. Seth was doing the averting-his-eyes thing, clearly uncomfortable that Maddie had pushed him into this. Cody was paler than usual for a vampire and looked ready to bolt at any moment. In fact, I wouldn't have been surprised if both men teamed up to formulate an escape plan. Gabrielle was the only one who looked excited to be there, her eyes alight and eager.

She was also the only one really dressed for the scene, all in black, with her hair spiked up and makeup done to dramatic levels. Cody and Seth wore their usual street clothes, and I'd dressed somewhere in the middle: black jeans and a black bustier top, adorned with heavy silver jewelry. It was clearly too designer for this place, however.

"Thanks so much for letting me come along with you guys," she said. "I didn't know any of you liked Blue Satin Bra."

"What's not to like?" asked Seth, face innocent.

I kept my eyes away from him because I had a feeling I'd start grinning. I handed out the tickets, and we headed inside, surrounded by a crowd that I decided I'd want on my side if I was ever in a street brawl.

We managed to snag a high-top table in the back. It meant standing the whole time, but at least we had a surface to put our glasses on. "Offer to buy her a drink," I hissed to Cody. The nice thing about playing Cyrano to a vampire was that his enhanced hearing meant I could keep my voice far below levels that Gabrielle could pick up. The noise in the room— even before the band started—also furthered the covert nature of all this.

Cody dutifully obeyed, and when Gabrielle started to dig

out cash, he assured her the first round was on him. The smile she gave him seemed to boost his confidence as he headed off.

Seth leaned toward my ear. He stood on the opposite side of me from Gabrielle, and she was too entranced by the sights to even notice us. "This might be crazy enough to work," he murmured.

"Don't get carried away," I responded back, trying not to think of his proximity. "The night is young. Any number of wacky mishaps might ensue."

He smiled. "Those are your specialty, aren't they?"

"Unfortunately, yes."

Cody returned with the drinks, earning more approval from Gabrielle. She wasn't showing any romantic attraction to him whatsoever, but at least she knew he was alive. While I still stood firm that he shouldn't overdo the vampire/Goth thing, I realized we were going to have to work hard to get past the "ordinary" facade she saw.

. "Talk to her," I told him. He'd slipped back to his place between me and Gabrielle. "Once they start, it's probably going to be impossible."

"What do I say?"

Seth, overhearing, leaned across me, and I wished I'd covered up more skin. His arm brushing up against me sent thrills through my body.

"Ask her if she's ever seen them live before," Seth said. "If she says no, tell her about this one time you saw them at . . . I don't know. A private party. If she says yes, ask her what she thought."

Cody gave an uneasy nod. He leaned toward her, and while I only caught bits and pieces of the conversation, she grew animated as she spoke. I leaned back to Seth.

"When did you become an expert in dating advice?" I asked incredulously.

"It's what O'Neill would do."

I scoffed. "You're using fiction to further Cody's love life?"

"Life imitates art, and art imitates life."

"That statement is ridiculous. And, you know, I've never really seen *you* utilize that advice."

"Well, that's O'Neill's advice. I have lots of characters I can draw from."

"Funny, I don't remember any introverted, stammering writers in your books."

"I don't stammer," he said defensively—though there was a smile under his words. "Besides, maybe there'll be someone like that *in the new series.*"

"Ooh," I said, mocking his melodrama. "What's with the 'maybe'? I thought you had the premise for this whole fantastic new thing figured out."

"I do. But it can always be improved along the way."

"Introvert authors improve everything."

"Damn straight."

Laughing, I remembered that I should have been helping Cody, but he was talking to Gabrielle on his own, which I took as a positive sign. I turned back to Seth. "So does this mean you've figured out the ending to Cady and O'Neill?"

"No." He still held his good humor, despite a small frown on his brow. "One of these days, I'll have to—"

His words were cut off when the eardrum-splitting screech of a guitar ripped through the room. Blue Satin Bra had come onstage while I was talking (flirting?) with Seth. I hated stereotypes, but truthfully: they looked like what you'd expect from an all-guy metal band. Black clothing, piercings, and hair that ran in extremes: shaved or super long. The one thing that differentiated them was, well, the fact that they were wearing blue satin demi bras over their clothes.

Even above the deafening music that followed, I could hear Gabrielle shrieking, "Oh my God!" Her face was ecstatic, and when Cody said something to her, she lit up further and nodded eagerly at the band. My guess was—whether it was true or not—he was reaffirming how awesome they were.

The music forced Seth and me to lean close in order to

talk. "You know," he said, "I'm pretty sure the bass player stuffed his bra."

"Nah," I teased back. "It's a push-up bra, so it just seems that way. They do amazing things for cleavage."

All things considered, Blue Satin Bra wasn't that bad. Metal might not be my favorite music, but I was still open to a lot of types. The setting and craziness that ensued throughout the night gave Seth and me lots of material to joke over. We were both in really good moods when the show finally ended and we walked out with Gabrielle and Cody.

"That was *awesome,*" she exclaimed. "Thank you so much for sharing the tickets."

"No problem," I said. My ears were ringing, and I wasn't sure if I was still shouting.

"I think that was the best show I've ever seen," said Cody nobly.

Gabrielle clutched his sleeve, and his eyes widened. "I know! Which was your favorite song?"

Silence.

"Mine was that one were they kept saying 'My Armageddon scales will burn your post office,'" said Seth deadpan.

"Oh, yeah. That's one of their greatest," she said. "It's called 'Plywood Fuck.'"

"That's my favorite too," said Cody. I somehow doubted he'd heard any of the music tonight. His senses were all on Gabrielle.

Perfectly in sync, Seth and I glanced at each other and exchanged secret smiles, both of us amused at Cody's love. I wasn't as far gone as he was, but when our group finally split up, I found myself walking on air too.

"Interesting night," Roman told me when we got home. He'd been along in spy mode. "I think Cody might actually have a chance."

"Maybe," I said. "He's clearly smitten, but she only seems mildly interested. In a friendly way, though."

Roman rummaged through the kitchen and poured himself a bowl of Lucky Charms. "He's not the only one who's smitten."

I sighed and collapsed onto the couch. "Let it go, okay? We all know I'm a long ways from getting over Seth."

Roman gave me a sly look. "I wasn't talking about you."

I stared at him for a moment, my vodka-addled brain trying to make sense of his words. "Wait . . . you're talking about Seth? He's over me."

"Oh my God, Georgina. Could you be any more delusional?"

"He's getting married."

"That means nothing. If it did, guys wouldn't catch chlamydia at their bachelor parties."

"But he *does* love Maddie. And no matter what you think about his feelings, he'll be out of my reach once they're married."

"The fact that they're dating means he should already be out of your reach—but past evidence shows that's not true."

I scowled and kicked off my shoes. "Don't bring that up. I feel bad enough—and so does he. If you're just going to taunt me, then I'm going to bed."

But to my surprise, Roman didn't wear that mocking look that had become so typical for him since returning to Seattle. His eyes were serious, his expression—almost—concerned. "I'm not trying to taunt you. I'm just stating the facts. No matter what happens, you and Seth can't seem to stay away from each other. You should put in a transfer request."

"What, out of Seattle?" I asked incredulously. "I love it here."

"You'll learn to love some other place. Honestly, it's the only way you're going to be able to move on—the only way either of you can move on. You're in a situation where you see him every day—tonight being a prime example. He broke up with you, and then you broke up with him for some 'greater good' kind of goal. But if you keep hanging around each other, it won't matter. You'll never heal. You're just going to get your heart ripped out every day."

I was so stunned that I couldn't even respond for several seconds. The old taunt danced in my head: circles and circles. "I . . . why do you say that? Why do you care?"

"Because I already see it happening every day. You *are* getting your heart ripped out over and over, and it kills me to watch it happen."

Again, I fell speechless for a moment. "I thought . . . I thought you hated me. I thought you wanted to destroy me."

He finished his cereal and set the bowl down. I didn't have the will to shoo the cats away. "I don't hate you, Georgina," he said wearily. "Am I upset about what happened to Helena? Absolutely. Am I upset about you lying about loving me? Yes. Do I want some kind of revenge? Maybe. Honestly, my feelings change from day to day. Some days I do want something awful to happen to you. Some days . . . well, I know you did what you did out of some misguided sense of . . . I don't know. You thought you were doing the right thing."

I wanted to tell him that I had loved him, in a way. But that probably wouldn't be useful right now. "Well, watching this Seth drama unfold is probably giving you lots of material when it comes to something awful happening to me."

"No," he said, with a weary head shake. "I don't like this. Like I said, I'd rather see you leave and start a new life. Every time I see you now, it's like . . . it's like watching you die. Over and over."

I stood up, suddenly wanting to sleep. "Yeah," I said softly. "That's kind of what it feels like." I hesitated. "Thanks for listening. And understanding."

"Anytime," he said.

This also caught me by surprise. Somewhere in these last few crazy months, I realized, Roman and I had become friends again. "I hate to ask you this, but, well, I'm not doing a very good job with keeping an upbeat mood tonight. Would you—"

He rose as well. "Yup. I'll watch you sleep. If you can handle the creepy factor."

"It's an acceptable trade," I said with a smile. "Thanks."

And maybe it was the vodka, but I stepped forward and

hugged him. He was stiff for a moment, clearly caught off guard, but then he relaxed and wrapped his arms around me. I rested my head against his chest, taking small comfort in someone warm and alive who wasn't a stranger. He smelled like I remembered, the clean, sharp scent of his cologne surrounding me in a way very different from Seth's woodsy smell.

I was just thinking I should pull away when a voice asked, "Am I interrupting anything?"

I jerked away from the embrace and found Carter standing in the living room, arms crossed and one eyebrow arched. Roman seemed equally flustered and took a few steps back as well, getting as far away from me as he could.

"Don't you ever knock?" I asked.

"Not sure you'd answer," said Carter good-naturedly. "Especially with the news I've got."

I groaned. "That was fast. Does it have to do with Simone?"

He nodded. "Afraid so. She met up with Seth again."

Chapter 9

"**S**he couldn't have!" I exclaimed. "He was with me all night."

"Not after the concert ended," pointed out Roman. "You know, I think that band might really be going somewhere." Whatever trace of sentiment he'd shown earlier with me had vanished in Carter's presence.

"Simone was hanging out in that twenty-four-hour coffee shop," Carter said. "Seth went there to work after—what was it you said? You were at a concert?"

"Yeah," I said. "Blue Satin Bra."

The angel gave Roman a nod of agreement. "Those guys *are* great."

"Hey, can we stick to the issue here?" I gave both of them glares. "What happened with Seth and Simone?"

Carter shrugged. "Same as usual. He came in and noticed her first, though. She had her head in a book—didn't even look up until he walked over."

"Well played," I said. "Forces him into the aggressive role."

"I don't think Seth's ever really in an aggressive role," mused Carter. "It just put him in a position to make the first move, if he wanted to be polite."

During our brief affair, Seth and I had made love so tenderly and so sweetly that poets would have wept at its beauty. Other times, things had been downright dirty, and I think Carter might have reconsidered his comment about Seth being aggressive, had the angel known.

"Then what?" I demanded.

"Like I said, the same. They talked about different things—a lot of topics interesting to Seth, really. I think she might have done some research on him."

"Fucking lovely." I collapsed onto the couch, and then I promptly shot back up. "I'm going over there—"

"Gone," interrupted Carter. "They went separate ways, and then she bagged some guy, and I decided it was time for me to fly away."

"Lucky bastard," grumbled Roman. "You have no idea what kind of shit I had to sit through."

The hint of a smile flickered on Carter's face before he turned back to me. I sighed and sat back down. "Confronting her's no good anyway. You already did it, and nothing came of it. I'm guessing this would just be a repeat."

Probably a good point. Being in a conflict with a succubus kind of sucked. I could punch Hugh or the vampires, and even with immortal healing, they'd still sport a black eye for a few hours—longer if I was really good. But with a succubus? I could smack her around, and she'd shape-shift the damage. And as for verbal fighting? Well, seeing as I had no real leverage, I'd probably just fuel her further and provide more cat fight entertainment for my friends.

"Well," I said to Roman. "I think I'm pissed off enough now that you don't have to go to bed with me."

Carter's eyebrow rose again.

"I mean, he doesn't have to watch me sleep," I explained. "I was kind of glum earlier, and we were worried my mystery . . . thing . . . might show up again."

"Why glum?" asked Carter. He attempted innocence, but I wasn't fooled. Even without being at the concert, he could easily figure out what had me down.

"Long story."

Those silvery gray eyes bored into me, and I shifted and looked away. I hated when he did that. It was like he could see into my soul. That was a place I didn't even want to look at—let alone have others do it. I attempted a change in subject.

"You know, I was thinking about this thing that's going on . . . this force or siren song or whatever. It's not like what happened with Nyx, but there's still a dreamlike quality to it, you know? I mean, it certainly seems like I'm sleepwalking. Do you think she could be back?"

"Nope," said Carter. "She's definitely still locked up. I checked myself."

"Really?"

"Really."

I didn't follow up with the obvious question. Had Carter done it for me? I mean, checking up on Nyx probably wasn't too hard for him. He probably just asked some angel buddy who asked another angel . . . etc. It still made me wonder about Carter's endgame. Why go to such trouble for me? Why look into this? Why track Simone?

His expression made me think he guessed my thoughts, something I hated. "Thanks," I said. "But I think I'm heading to bed now."

"And I," said Carter, "am going to get a drink."

"Done with Simone for good?" asked Roman.

Carter made a dismissive gesture. "At least for tonight. I'll find her in the morning."

"You're kind of a slacker spy," I pointed out, though I definitely understood his reasons for avoiding the other succubus' liaisons.

His only response was another smile before he vanished.

"Now what?" I wondered aloud.

"Now," said Roman, "you get your beauty sleep so that I can have another captivating day of listening to you give recommendations for people who enjoyed *The Da Vinci Code*."

"You know you love it," I said, walking off toward my bedroom.

"Sure you don't want company?"

I glanced back at him and studied his face, the lovely lines of it and blue-green eyes like the Mediterranean of my youth. His expression was speculative, wry humor twisting his lips. I couldn't entirely tell if he was joking. Or what his exact meaning was.

"Positive."

My words were a little bolder than I felt, but the night passed uneventfully, again furthering the idea that my blue moods were the target. Consequently, this put me in a good mood when I went to work the next day. I even wore yellow in an attempt at further cheeriness and greeted my coworkers with such enthusiasm that Doug wanted to know what drugs I was taking—and if he could have some.

All of that changed when, while headed for the science fiction section, I felt something totally unwelcome: an immortal signature. A *succubus* immortal signature. And I knew exactly which succubus it belonged to. I did a 180, took a few steps, and tried to pinpoint its direction. Fiction.

I headed straight over there, and sure enough, there was Simone—with Seth. She wore that guise I'd heard reports of, the bookish—yet sexy—brunette. They were standing by Seth's section, and she was holding up one of his paperbacks, *Idiosyncraso*. I knew she could feel my signature as I approached, but her eyes stayed on Seth, her conversation not missing a beat.

"You really wrote this in college?"

"Yup," he said. "It wasn't the first I had published, though. I shelved it for years before digging it out and revising it."

"Cool," she said, flipping through the pages. "I can't wait to read it. It'll give me something to do before your next one."

"Well, don't get your—oh, hey."

Seth had spotted me. I came to a stop beside them, and Simone turned toward me politely.

"How's it going?" I asked, voice harsher than I intended.

Seth, always sensitive to me, looked a little surprised at my tone but didn't acknowledge it. "Fine. Georgina, this is Kelly. Kelly, Georgina. Georgina's the manager here."

"Hi, *Kelly.*"

I shook her hand with a hardness she matched, and we both continued grinning at each other like Stepford Wives.

"I met Kelly at a coffee shop," said Seth mildly, not aware he was in succubus crossfire. "Told her she should see the store sometime."

"It's great," said Simone, all adorable innocence. "I'm a big reader. I love all things books. And meeting one of my favorite authors has given me great insight."

"Well," said Seth, a little embarrassed at the attention. "I don't know how much insight I'm really offering."

Simone laughed. "Lots. I feel like I'm getting something from you each time I see you."

"Have you seen each other a lot?" I asked.

"Kelly moved to Queen Anne," said Seth. "So we keep running into each other."

"It's a great area," I said. "Where do you live?"

Simone faltered. "Um, on Queen Anne."

"Street, Avenue, or Drive?"

Seth seemed surprised at the interrogative style of the question. Simone turned nervous. "Eh, Avenue."

Damn. Lucky guess. Queen Anne Street didn't exist.

"Nice place." Turning my back on her, I looked at Seth. "I came over because I heard someone say Maddie was looking for you." That wasn't true at all. Maddie wasn't even in for another hour. I gave Simone a casual glance. "Maddie's his fiancée."

"I didn't think she was in yet," said Seth.

Why, of all days, would his memory be up and running today? "Maybe I misheard," I said with a shrug. "But I figured you'd want to check."

"I will," he said, still a little puzzled. "I need to show Kelly one more book."

She shot me a triumphant look, but I knew she'd accomplished nothing with Seth. He had that expression he got when he was so focused on something—in this case, the history of books—that he was distracted from the world. "Kelly" was a pleasant coincidence. Simone was too overconfident to notice.

Seth turned back to the shelves, and me staying would have seemed awkward. With his attention elsewhere, I shot Simone a warning look. "Well, I'm sure I'll see you around."

"Oh," she said with a serene smile, "you will."

When I got home later that day, I was ready to break some furniture. "Did you see—"

"Yes, yes, I saw," said Roman, materializing beside me. "Calm down."

I let out a small cry of frustration, something primal with no real form. "I can't believe that bitch! Can't believe she'd actually do it *right in front of me!* She did it on purpose. She did it on purpose to taunt me."

Roman was the picture of tranquility as he leaned against the wall, a far cry from my frazzled, pacing state. "Of course she did. It's like mobsters who threaten their victims in a crowd—there's absolutely no way you could have fought back, not with that many witnesses."

"Nice analogy," I muttered. "Maybe there'll be a horse head in my bed next."

"I could leave one in hers, if it would help," he offered.

That almost made me smile. Almost. Except I wasn't entirely sure he was joking. "The really comical part is that Seth brought it about, you know? He was trying to stay away from me and walked right into this."

"The road to Hell is paved with good intentions."

I didn't dignify that with an answer.

"Look," he said in all seriousness, taking a few steps toward me. "It sucks that she's doing this, and we can definitely rule out coincidence. But if Seth's with Maddie while she's there, you know nothing's going to happen. And Carter will report back to us. No point in getting worked up over it."

"Easier said than done. Nothing's going to distract me from this."

He moved closer still and rested his hands on my upper arms. "Oh? When was the last time you went dancing?"

I blinked in surprise. The last time I'd been dancing? It had been a salsa lesson at the bookstore earlier this year, after which Seth and I had ripped each other's clothes off in my office.

"A while ago," I said evasively, thrown off by both the question and his fingertips on my skin. "Why?"

"Let's go out," he said. "There are a million places we can go. Any kind of dance you want. If memory serves, you're an okay dancer."

I narrowed my eyes. "I'm an *excellent* dancer, and you know it."

He leaned his face closer. "Then prove it."

"Irrelevant. I don't feel like going out."

Roman sighed and stepped away. I found I was a little disappointed to have him let go. "Man," he said. "I remember when you used to be fun. I'm glad I left town when I did." He walked over to my entertainment center and knelt down. "Well, if Muhammed won't come to the mountain . . ."

"Good grief. You're a wealth of religious proverbs tonight, aren't you?"

"Hey, just trying to—Jesus Christ. CDs? You do know the Dark Ages ended a long time ago." He pointed at my collection with disdain. "Everyone's gone digital now. You know, those little magical devices that store music? Or do you consider them some kind of witchcraft?"

"Technology changes every year. Jump on a fad, and you're obsolete before you know it."

"Honestly, it's a wonder you aren't cooking over a fire in the middle of your living room."

"You forget—I don't cook."

"I live here. I haven't forgotten."

By then, he'd put one of my "archaic" CDs in the player. I laughed. "You're one to talk about ancient history. This is old school."

"Nah." He rose and offered me his hands. "This is classic. Never goes out of style."

"Yeah," I said, as the music began playing. "All the kids

are doing foxtrot nowadays. Geez, it's even the slow style."
But I still let him take hold of my hands.

"Hey, you're the one who owns that CD."

We both fell into the steps effortlessly, gliding around the
living room and managing to dodge the furniture with some
grace. Roman had a long list of flaws, but one of his better
traits was that he was almost as good a dancer as me.

"Why do you dance so well?" I asked, stepping over Aubrey.
She didn't seem concerned at all about getting squashed and
had shown no signs of moving when we began to dance.

"What kind of a question is that? Why do *you* dance so
well?"

"Natural instinct, I guess. That's what I'm wondering.
Was it something you were born with? Or is it something you
can't help but perfect over the years? I mean, you've been
around for a while. I suppose if you put your mind to something that long, you can't help but master it."

He laughed. "To tell you the truth, I don't know. Maybe
it's in the blood."

"Oh, come on. I *cannot* picture Jerome out on the dance
floor."

"Not him. My mother. She was a dancer. A slave girl for
this king a long, long time ago . . ." Roman's gaze turned in-
ward. He didn't seem angry, so much as nostalgic. "Of course,
he was pretty pissed off when she got pregnant. That kind of
thing tends to ruin the chorus line."

"What happened to her?" I hadn't been around that long
ago, but certain things stayed the same through time. Slaves
who angered their masters got beaten or sold to someone
else. Or worse.

"I don't know. Jerome took her away, off to some village
where she could be a free woman."

I frowned. I still had trouble wrapping my mind around
the idea of my boss falling—romantically and divinely—for a
mortal. "Did he stay with her? He would have been a demon
by then. . . ."

"He never came back. First time I saw him was last year. My mother didn't hold a grudge, though. She would talk about him all the time . . . said he was beautiful. I don't know if she meant as an angel or a demon, though. Probably he looked the same, seeing as they're the same beings, really."

"I'm guessing he didn't look like John Cusack though."

"No." This made Roman laugh again. "Probably not. My mother took on mundane jobs whenever we moved villages— washing woman, field worker. But at least she was free. And she still danced sometimes. I saw her once, when I was really young . . . just before she was killed. There was a festival, and I remember her dancing in front of the fire, wearing this red dress." All mirth disappeared from him. "That image is burned into my mind. I can see how an angel would have fallen for her."

I didn't ask any questions about how she was killed. In those days, it could have been as simple as a raid or attack. They were commonplace. Or, more likely, she'd been killed in an attempt on Roman and his sister. He'd once mentioned that they were always on the run from angels and demons.

"So maybe you learned to dance as a subconscious tribute to her," I said, shifting to something lighter.

That half-smile returned. "Or maybe I just inherited my father's attraction to graceful, sensual women."

The song ended, and we stood there, frozen in time with our hands still entwined. Foxtrot was hardly the bumping and grinding seen in modern clubs, but our bodies were close, and I felt like I could sense the heat from his. Whether it was real or imagined, I couldn't say. But I did know there was something very seductive about dancing, about mirroring another's body, and somehow, I wasn't surprised when he leaned down and kissed me.

I *was* a little surprised that I kissed him back. But not for long. Because as our lips met, I realized how much I'd come to regard Roman as a comforting fixture in my life. We'd grown from adversaries to friends to . . . what? I didn't entirely know.

I did know that I liked having him around and that I'd never really shaken the attraction that had drawn me to him long ago. I also knew that I was lonely for the touch of someone I liked and that I had an automatic instinct to respond to this sort of thing.

His mouth pressed harder against mine, as hot and demanding as I recalled. His hands quickly moved from the formal orientation of foxtrot to something more intimate and eager, sliding down to my hips and somehow managing to push me against the wall while also shoving my shirt up. My own hands were around his neck, my lower body pressing against his as I felt all my nerves set on fire and lust coursing through me.

He managed to break away enough to pull my shirt off, and then his hands moved to my breasts, which were wrapped in a white lace bra. He glanced down and made a face as he pulled from our kiss. "Can't you make it a front hook?"

A small bit of shape-shifting made the bra disappear altogether. "Don't trouble yourself," I said.

He smiled and moved his lips to my neck while his hands cupped the curves of my breasts. It made it impossible for me to take his shirt off, but I slid my hands under it, loving the feel of his warm skin and taut muscles. I tipped my head back, letting him taste me and increase the intensity of his kissing.

And through it all, there were no voices in my head. I heard none of his thoughts, sensed none of his feelings. I was alone—alone with my own reactions, simply enjoying the way my body felt with no other interruptions. It was glorious.

I at last managed a break that let me pull his shirt off, and then my hands moved to his pants, putting us in a brief deadlock as he tried to move his lips to my nipples. I won and watched his pants fall to the floor. With that concession, he pulled me down as well and continued his efforts to kiss my breasts, almost kneeling before me as he did so. I ran my hands through his hair, gripping his head while his mouth sucked and teased. As he did, his eyes glanced up and met mine. I saw the desire in them and—something more.

Something I hadn't expected to see. There was . . . what? Love? Adoration? Affection? I couldn't quite pin it down, but I recognized the general category. It was a slap to the face. I hadn't anticipated it. Lust, I'd expected. A primitive instinct to throw me down and fuck me, in order to relieve his body's need. For so long, I'd operated on the assumption that he kind of liked me and kind of wanted to hate me. Yet, now, I realized those nice moments we'd had recently weren't coincidence. His sharp attitude had been a facade, meant to hide his feelings.

Roman still loved me.

I identified it for what it was. He wasn't doing this just because he wanted my body. He wanted *me*. This was more than just fulfilling a physical instinct for him, and suddenly . . . suddenly, I didn't know what to do. Because I realized then, I didn't know why *I* was doing this. There was a fair amount of lust on my part, and I'd grown closer to him since his return to Seattle. But the rest . . . ? I wasn't sure. There was so much going on right now: Maddie, Simone, Seth . . . Always Seth. Seth, who even now made my heart ache while I was wrapped in the arms of another man. My emotions were a tangle of confusion and hurt and desperation. I was with Roman as some sort of reaction, some attempt to fill the hole in my heart and seek false comfort. My feelings didn't match his. I couldn't do this with him. I didn't deserve to do this with him.

I pushed him away and jumped to my feet, backing off toward the hallway.

"No . . ." I said. "I can't . . . I can't. I'm sorry."

He stared up at me, understandably confused and a little hurt after the ardor I'd displayed seconds ago. "What are you talking about? What's wrong?"

I didn't know how to explain it, didn't know how I could even begin to articulate what I felt inside of me. I just shook my head and continued backing. "I'm sorry . . . I'm so sorry . . . I'm just not ready."

Roman sprang to his feet in one graceful motion. He took a step toward me. "Georgina . . ."

But I was already moving away, off to the safety of my bedroom. I slammed the door behind me—not from anger, but from a desperate need to stay away from him. From the hall, I heard him call my name and feared he'd come in anyway, despite my refusal to answer. I had no lock, and even if I did, it wouldn't stop him. He said my name a few more times, and then silence fell. I think he returned to the living room, backing off and giving me my space.

I flung myself onto the bed, gripping the sheets tightly and trying not to cry. That horrible despair that plagued me so often filled me now. It was an old friend, one that I would never be able to leave. All my relationships—friends and lovers—were a mess. I was either hurting them, or they were hurting me. There was no peace for me. There never would be, not for this servant of Hell.

And then, through that horrible, clenching pain inside me, I felt the lightest of touches. A whisper. A breath of music, of color, of light. I lifted my head up from where I'd buried it in my pillow and stared around. There was nothing tangible, not exactly, but I could sense it all around me: that warm, comforting siren song. It had no words, yet in my despair, I could hear it perfectly. It was telling me I was wrong, that I could have peace. And not just that—I could have comfort and love and so much more. It was like arms beckoning to me, a mother welcoming home a long-lost child.

I slowly rose from my bed, moving toward that which had no form. *Come, come.*

Outside my door, I heard Roman shout my name, but the tone was different from before. This wasn't confusion or pleading. It was frantic and concerned. The sound was grating to my ears as I stepped closer to that beautiful warmth. It was home. It was an invitation. All I had to do was accept.

"Georgina!" The door blew apart, and Roman stood there, blazing with power. "Georgina, stop—"

But it was too late. I had accepted.

All that joy and protection wrapped around me, taking me into its arms.

The world dissolved.

Chapter 10

I woke to blackness. Blackness and suffocation.

I was in a small room, a box really, crammed in so tightly that my arms wrapped around me and my knees were drawn to my chest. Weirdly, my limbs seemed too long. My whole body did, actually. My body changed all the time with shape-shifting, but this wasn't what I'd been wearing with Roman. This was different. For a moment, that horrible space seemed to close in around me. I couldn't breathe. With great effort, I tried to calm myself down. There was enough air. I *could* breathe. And even if I couldn't have, it wouldn't have mattered. The fear of suffocation was a human instinct.

Where was I? I didn't remember anything after the bedroom. I recalled the light and the music and Roman bursting in too late. I'd felt his power build up, like he was about to take action, but I hadn't seen the conclusion. And now, here I was.

Before my eyes, two identical luminescent forms suddenly appeared, like torches being lit in the darkness. They were tall and thin, with willowy, androgynous features. Black cloth wrapped around their bodies, seeming to glow with a light of its own, and long black hair flowed from their heads, blending in and losing itself in the cloth. Their eyes were a startling radioactive blue, too blue for any human, and seemed to bug out of those long, pale faces that were neither male nor female.

It was weird too because it was like they stood before me

in a large room, as though they were ten or so feet away from me. Yet, I was still crammed into the confines of my box and its unseen walls, barely able to move. Aside from them, everything else was pure, unfathomable blackness. I couldn't even see my own body or any other features of the room. My brain couldn't get a grip on this spatial hypocrisy. It was all too surreal.

"Who are you?" I demanded. "What am I doing here?" I saw no point in wasting time.

The duo didn't answer right away. Their eyes were cold and unreadable, but I saw a bit of smugness in their lips.

"Our succubus," one said. His—my brain decided to assign them a gender—voice was low and raspy, with a lisp that reminded me of a snake. "Our succubus at last."

"Harder to catch than we thought," added the other, voice identical. "We thought you would have succumbed long ago."

"Who are you?" I repeated, anger kindling. I squirmed in a futile attempt at escape. My confines were so tight that I didn't even have the space to beat my fists against the nonexistent walls.

"Mother will be pleased," the first one said.

"Very pleased," confirmed the other.

The way they alternated phrases reminded me of how Grace—Jerome's former lieutenant demoness—and Mei used to interact. That had had a charming, moderately creepy *The Shining* feel to it. This . . . this was something else. Something terrible and icy, burning my senses like nails on a chalkboard.

"Mother will reward us," the first said. I decided to call them One and Two for the ease of mental processing. "She will reward us when she is free, when she escapes the angels."

"Who's your mother?" I asked. A troubling suspicion was beginning to form.

"We will avenge her until she can do it herself," said Two. "You will suffer for betraying her."

"Nyx," I murmured. "Nyx is your mother. And you're . . . you're Oneroi."

They said nothing, which I took as affirmation. My head

reeled. Oneroi? How had this happened? Oneroi were a type of dream demon—but not demons like the ones I interacted with. Heaven and Hell were forces in the universe, but there were others, others that mingled with and often ran parallel to the system I existed in. Nyx was one such force, an entity of chaos from the beginning of time, when the world had been created from disorder.

And the Oneroi were her children.

I knew a few things about them but had never seen them—or ever expected to. They visited dreams, feeding on them. Nyx had done this too, but the manner had been a little different. She had manipulated people into seeing the future in their dreams—a twisted version that didn't unfold the way the dreamer expected. It had led to crazy actions that spawned chaos in the world, allowing her to grow stronger. She'd also fed on my energy directly, taking it in its purest form and distracting me with dreams of my own.

But Oneroi fed on the dreams themselves, deriving their power from the emotions and realities fueled by the dreamer. My understanding was that they also had the power to manipulate dreams but rarely had reason to. Humans provided plenty of hopes, dreams, and fears on their own. They needed no outside help.

That was the extent of my Oneroi knowledge, but it was enough. Feeling even a little informed about the situation empowered me. "That's what this is about? You took me because of Nyx? *I* wasn't the one who caught her. The angels did."

"You helped them," said One. "Led them to her."

"And then refused to save her," added Two.

With a pang, I remembered that horrible night, when Carter and his cronies had recaptured Nyx after her devastating free-for-all in Seattle. An angel had died that night. Another had fallen. And Nyx had promised to show me a future and family with a man I could love, if only I would give her the rest of my energy and let her break free.

"She was lying," I said. "She was trying to make a deal when she had nothing to offer."

"Mother always shows the truth," said One. "Dreams can be lies, but truth is truth."

I decided pointing out the redundancy of that statement was useless. "Well, I'm sure she'll appreciate the Mother's Day gift, but you're wasting your time. Jerome will come for me. My archdemon. He won't let me stay here."

"He won't find you," said Two. This time, I could definitely see smugness. "He *can't* find you. You no longer exist for him."

"You're wrong," I replied, with a bit of my own smugness. "There's no place in this world you can take me where he can't find me." That was, of course, assuming they hadn't managed to hide my immortal aura. To my knowledge, only greater immortals could do that. I wasn't sure where Oneroi fell in.

One actually smiled. It was not attractive. "You aren't in the world. Not the mortal world. This is the dream world."

"You're one of many dreams," Two said. "One dream among all the dreams of humanity. Your essence is here. Your soul. Lost in a sea of countless others."

My fear stopped me from offering commentary on his sudden shift into metaphor. The metaphysics of the universe and its layers and creation were beyond me. Even if someone had explained them to me, it was something past the comprehension of a mortal, lesser immortal, or any other being who was made-not-born. I had enough understanding, though, to recognize some truth in their words. There was a world of dreams, a world without form with nearly as much power as the physical one I lived in. Was it possible to trap my essence in it and hide me from Jerome? I was unsure enough that I couldn't write it off.

"So, what?" I asked, attempting haughtiness but mostly sounding as uneasy as I felt. "You'll just keep me in this mime box and feel better about yourselves?"

"No," said One. "You're in the world of dreams. You will dream."

The world dissolved again.

It was my wedding day.

I was fifteen years old, jailbait in the twenty-first century but more than old enough to be a wife in fourth-century Cyprus. And more than tall enough too. The Oneroi had sent me into a memory or a dream of a memory or something like that. It was a lot like the dreams Nyx had put me in. I was watching myself like a movie . . . yet at the same time, I was *in* myself, experiencing everything quite naturally.

It was a disorienting feeling, made worse by the fact that I had never wanted to see my human self again. Selling my soul had come with obvious downsides, but there had been perks too: the ability to shape-shift and never again have to wear the body that had committed such grievous sins in my mortal life.

Yet, there I was, and I was unable to look away. It was like being in *A Clockwork Orange*. My younger self had been about five feet ten inches tall by today's standards and a giant of a woman in an era where people had been shorter. When dancing, I'd been able to put that long body and all those limbs to good use, moving gracefully and effortlessly. In everyday life, though, I'd always been painfully conscious of my height, feeling awkward and unnatural.

Watching my old self walk now, from the outside, I was astonished to see I didn't appear as clumsy as I'd always believed. That didn't negate the revulsion I felt at seeing the thick, waist-long black hair or passably pretty face. Still, it was kind of a surprise to watch reality (if this was reality) and memory meshed.

It was just after dawn, and I was carrying a large amphora of oil out to a storage house beyond my family's home. My steps were light, careful not to spill any of it, and I again marveled at the way I moved. I set the vessel down beside others inside the shed and started to head back toward the house.

I'd barely taken two steps outside when Kyriakos, my husband-to-be, appeared. There was a covert expression on his face, one that instantly told me he had sneaked over here to find me and knew perfectly well that he shouldn't have. It was an uncharacteristically bold move for him, and I chastised him for the indiscretion.

"What are you doing? You're going to see me this afternoon . . . and then every day after that!"

"I had to give you these before the wedding." He held up a string of wooden beads, small and perfectly formed with tiny ankhs engraved on them. "They were my mother's. I want you to have them, to wear them today."

He leaned forward, placing the beads around my neck. As his fingers brushed my skin, I felt something warm and tingly run through my body. At the tender age of fifteen, I hadn't exactly understood such sensations, though I was eager to explore them. My wiser self today recognized them as the early stirrings of lust, and . . . well, there had been something else there too. Something else that I still didn't quite comprehend. An electric connection, a feeling that we were bound into something bigger than ourselves. That our being together was inevitable.

"There," he said, once the beads were secure and my hair brushed back into place. "Perfect."

He said nothing else after that. He didn't need to. His eyes told me all I needed to know, and I shivered. Until Kyriakos, no man had ever given me a second glance. I was Marthanes' too-tall daughter after all, the one with the sharp tongue who didn't think before speaking. But Kyriakos had always listened to me and watched me like I was someone more, someone tempting and desirable, like the beautiful priestesses of Aphrodite who still carried on their rituals away from the Christian priests.

I wanted him to touch me then, not realizing just how much until I caught his hand suddenly and unexpectedly. Taking it, I placed it around my waist and pulled him to me. His eyes widened in surprise but he didn't pull back. We were almost the same height, making it easy for his mouth to seek mine out in a crushing kiss. I leaned against the warm stone wall behind me so that I was pressed between it and him. I could feel every part of his body against mine, but we still weren't close enough. Not nearly enough.

Our kissing grew more ardent, as though our lips alone might close whatever aching distance lay between us. I moved his hand again, this time to push up my skirt along the side of one leg. His hand stroked the smooth flesh there and, without further urging, slid over to my inner thigh. I arched my lower body toward his, nearly writhing against him now, needing him to touch me everywhere.

"Letha? Where are you at?"

My sister's voice carried over the wind; she wasn't nearby but could no doubt show up if she sought me. Kyriakos and I broke apart, both gasping, pulses racing. He was looking at me like he'd never seen me before. Heat burned in his gaze.

"Have you ever been with anyone before?" he asked wonderingly.

I shook my head.

"How did you . . . I never imagined you doing that . . ."

"I learn fast."

We stood there, locked in time for a moment. Then, he pulled me back to him, his lips crushing mine once more. His hand returned to my dress, hiking it up over my waist. He held my bare hips firmly and pressed himself to my body. I felt him hard against me, felt my body respond to something that seemed both new and natural at the same time. The fingers of one hand slid over, feeling the wetness between my thighs. His touch felt like fire, and I moaned, wanting him to stroke me there more and more.

Instead, he turned me around so that I faced the wall. With one hand, he kept the skirt of my dress up, and with his other, I had the vague impression of him fumbling with his clothes. Then, a moment later, he pushed himself into me. It was a shock, like nothing I'd experienced before. I'd meant what I'd said earlier: that I'd never been with another man. And even wet with desire, it still hurt to have him inside me that first time. He seemed too big and me too small.

I cried out at the pain, an odd sort of pain that didn't diminish the fire that had been building within me. His thrusts were hard and urgent, no doubt fueled by feelings he'd long been holding back on. And after a while, the initial pain seemed irrelevant. Pleasure began to grow as he moved into me over and over, and I adjusted myself so that I bent over more and let him take me more deeply. He thrust more forcefully, and I again exclaimed in surprise and blissful pain. I heard a muffled groan, and then his body shuddered as he spent himself, his movements at last slowing down.

When he was done, he pulled out and turned me around. It was the first time I'd seen him naked in all of this. There was blood and semen on both of us, which I tried to clean off my thighs before finally just letting my dress fall back over me. I'd be bathing before the wedding anyway.

Kyriakos had just finished putting his clothes back on when we heard my name again. This time, it was my mother. He and I stared at each other in wonder, scarcely believing we'd just done what we had. I was aglow with love and the joy of sex and a whole host of new feelings I wanted to explore in more detail. Fear of my mother drove us apart.

Stepping back, he grinned and pressed my hand to his lips. "Tonight," he breathed. "Tonight we . . ."

"Tonight," I agreed. "We'll do it again. I love you."

He smiled at me, eyes smoldering, and then hurried off before we were caught. I watched him go, my heart filled with joy.

The rest of the day went by in a dreamy haze, partially because of the flurry of wedding activity and partially because of what had happened with Kyriakos. I'd had a vague idea of what would occur on our wedding night, but my imaginings had never come close to the real thing. I practically danced my way through the rest of the day, impatient to truly be Kyriakos' wife and make love again and again.

The wedding was taking place at our home, so there was

enough work (along with my own preparation) to *almost* keep me distracted. As the ceremony time grew nearer, I was bathed and dressed in my wedding gown: an ivory tunic of fine material, wrapped with a flame-red veil. I had to kneel a little for my mother to adequately adjust the veil, earning a number of jokes about my height from my sister.

It didn't matter. Nothing mattered except me and Kyriakos being together forever. Soon, guests began arriving, and my heart rate increased. Anticipation and the day's heat made me sweat, and I fretted about ruining the dress.

Someone called out that Kyriakos and his family were approaching. The excitement in the air grew palpable, shared by everyone now. Yet, when Kyriakos arrived, he barged right into the house, going against the traditional procession and stately ceremony that should have taken place. For half a second, some girlish part of me thought that Kyriakos—in his burning love for me—couldn't wait through the drawn out process of a ceremony. I was quickly enlightened.

With a face flushed with fury, he marched up to my father. "Marthanes," Kyriakos growled, finger in my father's face. "You insult me if you think I'm going through with this wedding."

My father was clearly taken aback—not an easy thing to accomplish. People chastised me for my sharp tongue, but that was largely because I was a woman. I wasn't half as bad as my father, and he'd intimidated a lot of men twice his size. (It was a sad irony that while I was tall for a woman, my father was short for a man.) A few moments later, my father recovered his usual bluster.

"Of course you are!" he exclaimed. "We've made the betrothal. We paid the dowry."

Kyriakos' father was there, and judging from his fine clothes and surprised expression, this was all news to him too. He set a hand on his son's shoulder. "Kyriakos, what's this all about?"

"Her," said Kyriakos, pointing his finger at me. His gaze swung to my face, and I flinched from its force, as though I'd been slapped. "I will not marry Marthanes' whore of a daughter!"

There were gasps and murmurs from those around us. My father's face turned bright red. "You're insulting me! All of my daughters are chaste. They're all virgins."

"Are they?" Kyriakos turned back to me. "Are *you?*"

All eyes turned to me, and I blanched. My tongue felt dry. I couldn't muster any words.

My father threw up his hands, clearly exasperated by this nonsense. "Tell them, Letha. Tell them so that we can end this and get our dowry back."

Kyriakos had a dangerous glint in his eyes as he studied me. "Yes, tell them so that we can end this. *Are you a virgin?*"

"No, but—"

Chaos erupted. Men shouted. My mother wailed. The guests were a mix of stunned shock and delight over a new scandal. Desperately, I tried to find my voice and shout above the din.

"It was only with Kyriakos!" I cried. "Today was the first time!"

Kyriakos turned away from where he'd been telling my father the dowry would *not* be returned. He glanced over at me. "It's true," he said. "We did it today. She spread herself as easily and knowingly as any whore, begging me to take her. There's no telling how many men she's offered her body up to—or how many she would even when married."

"No!" I exclaimed. "It's not true!"

But no one heard me. There was too much arguing now. Kyriakos' family was raging over the insult. My family was bristling against the name-calling, and my father was trying his best to do damage control, though he knew perfectly well that my own admission had damned us. Premarital sex was not so out of the ordinary for lower classes, but as a tradesman's family, we modeled a lot of our customs on our betters among the nobility—or pretended to. A girl's virtue was a sacred thing, one that reflected on her father and family as a whole. This disgraced all of them—and had serious repercussions for me. As Kyriakos well knew.

He had moved toward me so that I could hear him through the noise. "Now they all know," he said in a low voice. "They all know you for what you are."

"It's not true," I said through my tears. "You know it isn't."

"No one will have you now," he continued. "No one worth having. You'll spend the rest of your life on your back, spreading your legs for whoever comes along. And ultimately, you'll be alone. *No one will have you.*"

I squeezed my eyes shut to try to stop the tears, and when I opened them again, I was surrounded in blackness.

Well, not entirely in blackness.

Before me, the Oneroi glowed more brightly than before, lit from within by that eerie light.

"An interesting dream," said Two, with what I think passed for a smile. "One that gave us much to feed on."

"It's not true," I said. There were tears on my cheeks in waking, just as there had been in sleep. "That wasn't true. It was a lie. That wasn't how things happened."

The dream was muddling my brain, almost making me question myself, but my own memories soon won out. I remembered that day. I remembered kissing Kyriakos by the building and how we'd then gone separate ways, strengthened by the knowledge that we would soon be man and wife, making our wedding night that much sweeter. And it had been. It hadn't been rushed against a wall. We'd taken time to learn and explore each other's bodies. He'd been on top of me, staring into my eyes—not my back. He'd told me I was his life. He'd told me I was his world.

"It was a lie," I repeated more firmly, fixing the Oneroi with a glare. "That's not how it happened. That's not how it happened." I knew I was right, yet I felt the need to keep repeating it, to make sure the words were true.

One gave a small shrug, unconcerned. "It doesn't matter. I told you: Mother shows the truth. But dreams? Dreams are dreams. They can be truth or lies, and all provide food for us. And you?" He smiled a smile that was the mirror of his twin's. "You will dream . . . and dream . . . and dream . . ."

Chapter 11

I was in Seattle. Modern-day Seattle, thankfully. I wanted to
be nowhere near the fourth century, even though I dreaded
what awful vision the Oneroi would show me now.

Not only was I in Seattle, I was with Roman. He had just
parked on Cherry Street and was striding toward the heart of
Pioneer Square, which was buzzing today with tourists and
others enjoying the clear autumn night. This time, I wasn't in
the dream. I was an observer only, following along with him
like a ghost or maybe a documentary camera. I wanted to talk
to him, to communicate in some way, but I had no mouth
with which to speak. I had no form whatsoever, only my consciousness watching this vision.

His pace was brisk, and he pushed through the meander-
ing crowd with no concern for the dirty looks and occasional
comment. He was focused on his destination, one I recognized immediately: the Cellar. Our favorite immortal hang-
out was crowded with mortals tonight. Yet, for whatever
reason, no matter how busy the bar was, Jerome always managed to get the same corner table in the back. He sat there
now with Carter but didn't wear the usual unconcerned look
we often found him with while drinking. The demon's face
was filled with agitation, and he and Carter were arguing
about something.

Roman's signature was masked, so neither angel nor demon
noticed his approach. Jerome shot him a glare, no doubt thinking some human was bothering them. Jerome's expression

promptly changed when he saw who it was, and he opened his mouth to say something. He didn't get the chance because Roman spoke first.

"Where is she?" demanded Roman. He sat in a chair and jerked it toward Jerome so that father and son could look eye to eye. "Where the fuck is Georgina?"

The music and conversation covered most of his shouting, but a few nearby patrons gave him startled looks. Roman was oblivious. His attention was all on Jerome. Anger crackled around the nephilim like an aura itself.

Jerome had been clearly distressed about something when Roman had entered, but now, in the presence of an underling, the demon put on the cold, haughty expression that was so typical for him.

"Funny," said Jerome. "I was going to ask you the same thing."

Roman glowered. "How the hell would I know? She vanished right before my eyes! You're the one that's supposed to have some sort of divine connection to her."

Jerome's face didn't twitch, but his words were like a gut punch to both me and Roman. "I can't feel her anymore. She's disappeared for me too."

I might have had no physical form, but cold fear ran through me nonetheless. An archdemon was connected to his subordinates. He always knew where they were and could tell if they were in pain. When Jerome had been summoned, that connection had shattered, cutting us off from our hellish "gifts." Now, the opposite had happened. I had been summoned, so to speak, and torn from Jerome. The Oneroi's words came back to me: *He won't find you. He can't find you. You no longer exist for him.*

"That's impossible," growled Roman. "Unless . . ." A troubled look came over him. "Someone's hiding her signature?" It would be terribly ironic if the scheme he'd once planned came to be through someone else.

Jerome shook his head and gestured to a waiter for another round. "I wouldn't be able to find her if that happened, but the connection would be there. I'd know she still existed."

You no longer exist for him.

"Is she . . . is she dead?" Some of Roman's initial fury had dimmed a little.

It wasn't an unreasonable question, really. I kind of felt dead.

"No. Her soul would have shown up in Hell." Jerome took a sip of his new drink and narrowed his eyes at Roman. "But it's not your job to ask questions. What do *you* know? You said she disappeared. Literally?"

Roman's face was downright bleak now. He glanced between Jerome and a grim, thus far silent, Carter. "Yes. Literally. She's been having these . . . I don't know how to explain it. She couldn't even explain it."

"I was there," Jerome reminded him. "She told me. The music. The colors." The sneer in his voice made it clear that he regarded those types of things as nuisances.

"It was like this weird force pulling her, enchanting her. It wanted her to come to it." Roman was repeating known info, possibly to make Jerome take it more seriously. "She called it a siren song and kept sleepwalking, trying to get to it. And then . . . and then tonight, she went to it."

"Did you see it?" asked Carter. It was odd to see him so serious and . . . well, confused. The former emotion I'd seen only a handful of times. The latter I'd never seen on him.

"I saw her disappear. Like, vanish into thin air. But I didn't see it exactly. I felt it. I could sense whenever it was around."

"What did it feel like?" asked Jerome.

Roman shrugged. "I don't know. Just . . . a force. A power. Not an entity exactly. And not something I could identify. Not a greater immortal or anything."

"That," declared Jerome, "is absolutely useless information."

Roman's anger returned. "It's all I've got! If you'd listened to her more, this wouldn't have happened. You let this happen. You didn't take it seriously, and now she's gone!"

Yelling at Jerome. Not a good thing.

"Be careful, lest I revoke your invitation," hissed the demon, eyes boring into his son. "And I did listen. I set *you* to protect her. You, apparently, are the one who 'let' this happen."

Roman flushed. "I was in the other room when that thing showed up again. I hurried in as fast as I could, but it was too late. Georgina'd already given herself up, and honestly . . . I'm not sure I could have stopped it anyway."

It was a big concession for Roman. Nephilim could inherit anywhere from none to all of their immortal parent's power. Roman was very close to having as much strength as Jerome but still lagged behind just a little. Additionally, the types of power wielded by greater and lesser immortals differed. As a type of hybrid, Roman might not have been able to fight what Jerome could have.

Jerome didn't push that point further. "So, we still know nothing."

"We know that whatever did this isn't one of ours," said Carter quietly, speaking at last.

"Yes," snapped Jerome. "Which only leaves a billion other things it could be. Unless . . ."

He glanced over at one of the chairs at their table. One moment it was empty. The next, Simone sat there. Carter didn't seem surprised, but Roman and I certainly were. And she was especially surprised, as shown by her squeal of fear and befuddled expression. Being teleported by a greater immortal was not a pleasant experience.

She was blond today, dressed in a plain blouse and pair of jeans. It was a sign of her agitation that she didn't widen her neckline when she saw Carter. "What—what's going on?" she stammered.

"What'd you do to Georgina?" asked Jerome.

Her eyes went wide. He might still wear the guise of John Cusack, but as he stared her down, it was easy to see that he truly was a demon of Hell.

"Nothing!" cried Simone. She cowered back into her chair. "I don't know what you're talking about!"

Jerome was up and out of his chair so fast, he might have teleported himself. He jerked Simone up as well and shoved her against a nearby wall, hand on her throat. I'd been in a similar position with him before and felt pity for the other succubus. No one else in the bar noticed, so Jerome was either glamoring them or making him and Simone invisible.

"Do *not* lie to me!" he exclaimed. "What have you done? Who did you get to do this?"

I could see his line of reasoning now. What Roman had sensed might not be demon or angel, but it wasn't impossible that someone from our side could have worked with an unknown entity. It wouldn't be the first time. Roman had caught on as well and leapt up to stand beside his father.

"I swear, if you've hurt her even a little, I will rip you apart!"

Simone's fear was put on pause as she gave Roman a puzzled look. With his signature hidden, he only came across as a human to her. As far as she was probably concerned, he had no involvement in any of this—and no ability to back up his threat. Little did she know.

She turned back to Jerome, cringing when she saw his face once more. "Nothing," she said, her voice hard to understand with Jerome choking off her air. "I didn't do anything to her, I swear it!"

"You were trying to get Seth into bed," said Roman.

"That's all! I didn't do anything to her. *Anything.*" Simone's face turned pleading as she spoke to Jerome. "You have to know why I'm here. It's not to harm her."

Jerome's face was still filled with terrible fury, but there was also a flicker of consideration in his eyes. He said nothing, and it was Carter's voice that filled the tense silence.

"She's telling the truth," he said.

Jerome didn't break his hold on Simone, but that calculating look was still in his gaze. "Do you know anything about her disappearing? Anything at all?"

"No! No!"

Jerome glanced back at Carter, who gave a swift nod. With a disappointed sigh, Jerome released her and stepped back.

Roman looked doubtful, but he too had to know that if Carter vouched for her, it was gospel, so to speak. Jerome returned to his chair, downing his drink in one gulp. Roman joined him a moment later, but Simone remained standing, watching the whole group uncertainly as she rubbed her bruised throat.

"I don't know what's going on, but if there's anything—"

"I'm done with you," said Jerome harshly. He waved his hand in a type of dismissal, and Simone vanished as quickly as she'd arrived.

"That was mean," noted Carter, idly stirring his bourbon.

"I sent her back to her hotel," said Jerome. "Not to a desert island."

Roman's anger had cooled a little, and he wore a calm, considering expression that looked remarkably like his father's. "What did she mean when she said you knew why she was here? Why was I following her?"

"I can't report this," said Jerome. He was speaking to Carter, like Roman wasn't even there. "Not yet . . . not unless I have to. We can't let any higher authorities know."

"And I can't do anything at all," mused Carter. "This is technically your problem." He took a long drink, as though that would fix everything.

"But you will," said Roman boldly. "You'll try to find her?"

"Of course," said Carter. One of his trademark cynical smiles lit his lips, replacing the grim expression from earlier. I suspected it was a cover-up for how he truly felt. "This place would be too boring without her."

For a heartbeat, I kind of liked this invisible watcher thing. Carter had no sense that I was there, and for the first time, I was able to truly study him without him looking back. He might have that annoying levity on now, but he'd already shown concern for my well-being. And I really couldn't believe it was simply because he found me entertaining. What was his game? Those gray eyes revealed nothing.

"Yes," said Jerome dryly. "Who knows how we'll get by without her maudlin misadventures."

Carter started to protest, but again, Roman came forward with an interruption. "Oh. That's the other thing, what we talked to Erik about." He gave them a brief recap of Erik's observations and how I was only visited when I was depressed. Roman also described each of the incidents in as much detail as possible.

Jerome and Carter exchanged looks. "With as down as she usually is, that's not much to go on," noted the demon. "But it might be worth a visit to the old man."

"Jerome," said Carter in a warning voice.

The two locked eyes again and had some sort of silent communication. When Jerome finally looked away, it was to casually pick up his latest drink. "Don't worry. I won't scare him. Much."

I wondered if he'd go to Erik right then, but I didn't get a chance to find out. The world dissolved once more, and I found myself back in my prison. Aside from being terribly uncomfortable, I also felt exhausted. Studying the smiling, shining Oneroi, I could guess what had happened. In feeding off my dream, they'd taken some of my energy with it.

"Dream . . ." I murmured, suddenly confused. I'd braced myself for some terrible outcome, but it hadn't happened. "That wasn't a dream. That was real. You showed me what was really happening. What my friends are doing."

"Some dreams are true, and some are lies," said Two. I really wanted to slap him. "That one was true."

A story came back to me, the faintest memory from my childhood. Christian priests had long had a foothold in Cyprus when I was born, but old stories and rites had lingered. What were considered myths today had been held as fact back then. One such story said that dreams were sent to humans from one of two gates: one of ivory and one of horn. Those from the ivory gate were false; those from the horn gate were true. I didn't know if that was just a metaphor, but the outcome apparently had some validity to it.

"But why?" I asked. "Why show me true dreams? You'd torture me a lot more with another stupid nightmare." That nightmare hadn't been stupid. It had been agonizing, but I didn't want them to know that. What was stupid was me suggesting how they should torment me.

"Because you don't know," said One. "Soon you won't know truth from lies. You assume everything that causes pain must be a lie. But you won't know. Soon you won't trust anything at all."

"I'll know," I said adamantly. "I can tell the difference."

"You believe what you just saw was true?" asked Two.

"Yes. Absolutely."

"Good," said One. "Then you've also learned another truth: it's impossible for anyone to find you. You'll stay here forever."

Chapter 12

It occurred to me at some point that I wished the Oneroi would only send me false dreams. They hurt—no question—but there was a very, very small comfort afterward in knowing they hadn't really happened. Yet, my next few dreams were true ones, and I was forced to keep reliving the past.

One memory brought me back to fifteenth century Florence. At first, I felt a small blossoming of joy at repeating this. The Italian Renaissance had been a beautiful thing, and I'd been in awe watching the ingenuity of humans reawaken after the last few depressing centuries. Things were made that much more interesting because the Church was always pushing back against this artistic flourishing. That kind of conflict was what my kind thrived on.

Another succubus and I had shared a house, living luxuriously off of a textile business we ostensibly managed while our merchant uncle (an incubus who was never around) traveled. It was a good setup, and I—going by the name of Bianca—was the favorite child of our local demoness, Tavia, thanks to conquest after conquest.

It all started to go awry when I hired an eccentric and extremely good-looking painter named Niccolò to create a fresco for our home. He was flamboyant, funny, and intelligent—and had been attracted to me from the first day. Nonetheless, a sense of propriety and professional boundaries made him keep his distance. This was something I intended to change, and I frequently stayed with him while he worked on the wall, knowing it would only be a matter of time before he gave in to my charms.

"Ovid didn't know anything about love," I told him one day. I was lounging on a sofa, caught up in one of the literary discussions we so often stumbled into. His ability to engage in these talks added to his allure. He looked up at me with mock incredulity, pausing in his painting.

"Nothing about love? Woman, bite your tongue! He's the authority! He wrote books on it. Books that are still read and used today."

I sat up from my undignified repose. "They aren't relevant. They were written for a different time. He devotes pages to telling men where to meet women. But those places aren't around anymore. Women don't go to races or fights. We can't even linger in public areas anymore." This came out with more bitterness than I intended. The artistic culture of this time was wonderful, but it had come with a restriction of female roles that differed from those I'd grown used to in other places and eras.

"Perhaps," Niccolò agreed. "But the principles are still the same. As are the techniques."

"Techniques?" I repressed a snort. Honestly, what could a mere mortal know about seduction techniques? "They're nothing but superficial gestures. Give your ladylove compliments. Talk about things you have in common—like the weather. Help her fix her dress if it gets mussed. What does any of that have to do with love?"

"What does anything have to do with love anymore? If anything, those comments are particularly applicable now. Marriage is all about business." He tilted his head toward me in a speculative manner that was typical of him. "You've done something with your hair today that's extremely pretty, by the way."

I paused in return, thrown off by the compliment. "Thank

you. Anyway. You're right: marriage *is* business. But some of them are love matches. Or love can grow. And plenty of clandestine affairs, no matter how 'sinful,' are based on love."

"So your problem is that Ovid is ruining what love is still left?" His eyes drifted to the window, and he frowned. "Does it look like it'll rain out there?"

The zeal of this topic seized hold of me, making his abrupt interruptions that much more annoying. "Yes—what? I mean, no, it won't rain, and, yes, that's what he's doing. Love is already so rare. By approaching it like a game, he cheapens what little there is."

Niccolò abandoned his brushes and colors and sat down next to me on the couch. "You don't think love is a game?"

"Sometimes—all right, most of the time—yes, but that doesn't mean we shouldn't—" I stopped. His fingers had slid to the edge of my dress's neckline. "What are you doing?"

"This is crooked. I'm straightening it."

I stared and then started laughing as the ruse revealed itself. "You're doing it. You're following his advice."

"Is it working?"

I reached for him. "Yes."

He pulled back. This wasn't what he'd expected. He'd only intended to tease me, proving his point with a game. Averting his eyes, he began to rise.

"I should get back to work. . . ." He was rarely thrown off, and I'd disarmed him.

Gripping him with surprising strength, I jerked him back to me and pressed my lips to his. They were soft and sweet, and after a few stunned moments, he responded, his tongue moving eagerly into my mouth. Then, realizing what he was doing, he drew away once more.

"I'm sorry. I shouldn't have . . ."

I could see the longing in his eyes, the desire he'd held back since working for me. He wanted me, but even a roguish artistic type felt it was wrong to do this with an unmarried, upper-class woman—particularly one who'd employed him.

"You started it," I warned in a low voice. "You were trying to prove me wrong about Ovid. Looks like it worked."

I put my hand behind his neck, pulling his mouth back down to my own. He still initially resisted, but it didn't last. And when his hand began slowly pushing up the folds of my skirts, I knew I'd won and that it was time to retreat to the bedroom.

Once there, he abandoned any attempts at decorum. He pushed me down onto the bed, the fingers that so deftly painted walls now fumbling to release me from my complicated dress and its layers of rich fabrics.

When he had me stripped down to my thin chemise, I took charge, removing his clothing with a brisk efficiency and delighting in the way his skin felt under my fingertips as my hands explored his body. Straddling him, I lowered my face and let my tongue dance circles around his nipples. They hardened within my mouth, and I had the satisfaction of hearing him cry out softly when my teeth grazed their tender surface.

Moving downward, I trailed kisses along his stomach— down, down to where he stood hard and swollen. Delicately, I ran my tongue against his erection, from base to tip. He cried out again, that cry turning to a moan when I took him into my mouth. I felt him grow between my lips, becoming harder and larger, as I slowly moved up and down.

Without even realizing what he did, I think, he raked his hands through my hair, getting his fingers caught up in the elaborate pinning and carefully arranged curls. Sucking harder, I increased my pace, exalting in the feel of him filling up my mouth. The early twinges of his energy began seeping into me, like glittering streams of color and fire. While not physically pleasurable per se, it sparked me in a similar way, waking up my succubus hunger and igniting my flesh, making me long to touch him and be touched in return.

"Ah . . . Bianca, you shouldn't . . ."

I momentarily released him from my mouth, letting my

hand continue the work of stroking him closer to climax. "You want me to stop?"

"I . . . well, ah! No, but women like you don't . . . you aren't supposed to . . ."

I laughed, the sound low and dangerous in my throat. "You have no idea what kind of woman I am. I *want* to do this. I want to feel you in my mouth . . . taste you . . ."

"Oh God," he groaned, eyes closed and lips parted.

His muscles tensed, body arching slightly, and I just managed to return him to my mouth in time. He came, and I took it all in as his body continued to spasm. The life energy trickling into me spiked in intensity, and I nearly had a climax of my own. We'd only just started, and I was already getting more life from him than I'd expected. This would be a good night. When his shuddering body finally quieted, I shifted myself so that my hips wrapped around his. I ran my tongue over my lips.

"Oh God," he repeated, breathing labored and eyes wide. His hands traveled up my waist and rested under my breasts, earning my approval. "I thought . . . I thought only whores did that. . . ."

I arched an eyebrow. "Disappointed?"

"Oh, no. *No.*"

Leaning forward, I brushed my lips against his. "Then return the favor."

He was only too eager, despite his weariness. After pulling the chemise over my head, he ravaged my body with his mouth, his hands cradling my breasts while his lips sucked and teeth teased my nipples, just as I'd done to him. My desire grew, my instincts urging me to take more and more of his life and stoke my body's burning need. When he moved his mouth between my legs, parting my thighs, I jerked his head up.

"You said once that I think like a man," I hissed softly. "Then treat me like one. Get on your knees."

He blinked in surprise, taken aback, but I could tell something about the force of the command aroused him. An animal glint shone in his eyes as he sank to his knees on the floor, and I stood before him, my backside leaning against the bed.

Hands clutching my hips, he pressed his face against the soft patch of hair between my thighs, his tongue slipping between my lips and stroking the burning, swelling heart buried within. At that first touch, my whole body shuddered, and I arched my head back. Fueled by this reaction, he lapped eagerly, letting his tongue dance with a steady rhythm. Twining my hands in his hair, I pushed him closer to me, forcing him to taste more of me, to increase the pressure of his tongue upon me.

When the burning, delicious feeling in my lower body could take no more, it burst, like the sun exploding. Like fire and starlight coursing through me, setting every part of me tingling and screaming. Imitating what I'd done to him earlier, he didn't remove his mouth until my climax finally subsided, my body still twitching each time his tongue tauntingly darted out and teased that oh-so-sensitive area.

When he finally broke away, he looked up with a bemused smile. "I don't know what you are. Subservient . . . dominant . . . I don't know how to treat you."

I smiled back, my hands caressing the sides of his face. "I'm anything you want me to be. How do you want to treat me?"

He thought about it, finally speaking in a hesitant voice. "I want . . . I want to think of you like a goddess . . . and take you like a whore. . . ."

My smile increased. That about summed up my life, I thought.

"I'm anything you want me to be," I repeated.

Rising to his feet, he pushed me roughly against the bed, holding me down. He was ready again, though I could see the effort it took. Most men would have collapsed after that loss of life energy, but he was fighting through his exhaustion in order to take me again. I felt the hard press of him against me, and then he pushed—nearly shoved—himself into me, sliding almost effortlessly now that I was so wet.

Moaning, I shifted myself up so that he could get a better position and take me deeper. His hands clutched my hips as he moved with an almost primal aggression, and the sound of our bodies hitting each other filled the room. My body responded to his, loving the way he filled me up and drove into me. My cries grew louder, his thrusts harder.

And, oh, the life pouring into me. It was a river now, golden and scorching, renewing my own life and existence. Along with his energy, he yielded some of his emotions and thoughts, and I could literally feel his lust and affection for me.

That life force warred with my own physical pleasure, both consuming me and driving me mad, so that I could barely think or even separate one from the other. The feeling grew and grew within me, burning my core, building up in such intensity that I could barely contain it. I pressed my face against him, smothering my cries.

The fire within me swelled, and I made no more attempts to hold off my climax. It burst within me, exploding, enveloping my whole body in a terrible, wonderful ecstasy. Niccolò showed no mercy, never slowing as that pleasure wracked my body. I writhed against it, even as I screamed for more.

Doing this might make Niccolò immoral in the eyes of the Church, but at the heart of what mattered, he was a decent man. He was kind to others and had a strong character whose principles were not easily shaken. As a result, he had had a lot of goodness and a lot of life to give, life I absorbed without remorse. It spread into me as our bodies moved together, sweeter than any nectar. It burned in my veins, making me feel alive, making me into the goddess he kept murmuring that I was.

Unfortunately, the loss of such energy took its toll, and he lay immobile in my bed afterward, breathing shallow and face pale. Naked, I sat up and watched him, running a hand over his sweat-drenched forehead. He smiled.

"I was going to write a sonnet about you. . . . I don't think I can capture this with words." He struggled to sit up, the motion causing him pain. The fact that he'd managed all of this was pretty remarkable. "I need to go . . . the city's curfew . . ."

"Forget it. You can stay here for the night."

"But your servants—"

"—are well-paid for their discretion." I brushed my lips over his skin. "Besides, don't you want to . . . discuss more philosophy?"

He closed his eyes, but the smile stayed. "Yes, of course. But I . . . I'm sorry. I don't know what's wrong with me. I need to rest first. . . ."

I lay down beside him. "Then rest."

A pattern developed between us after that. He'd work on the fresco during the day—his progress slowing significantly—and spend his nights with me. That twang of guilt never left him, making the experience doubly exciting for me. My essence drank from his soul while my body enjoyed the skills of his.

One day, he left to run errands—and didn't come back. Two more days passed with no word from him, and my worry began to grow. When he showed up on the third night, there was an anxious, harried look to him. More concerned than ever, I hurried him inside, noting a bundle under his arm.

"Where have you been? What is that?"

Unwrapping his cloak, he revealed a stack of books. I sifted through them with the wonder I'd always had for such things. Boccaccio's *The Decameron*. Ovid's *Amores*. Countless others. Some I'd read. Some I'd longed to read. My heart gave a flutter, and my fingers itched to turn the pages.

"I've gathered these from some of my friends," he explained. "They're worried Savonarola's thugs will seize them."

I frowned at this reference to the city's most powerful priest. "Savonarola?"

"He's gathering up 'objects of sin' in order to destroy them. Will you hide these here? No one would force them away from someone like you."

The books practically shone to me, far more valuable than the jewelry I'd amassed. I wanted to drop everything and start reading. "Of course." I flipped through the pages of the Boccaccio. "I can't believe anyone would want to destroy these."

"These are dark days," he said, face hard. "If we aren't careful, all knowledge will be lost. The ignorant will crush the learned."

I knew he spoke the truth. I'd seen it, over and over. Knowledge destroyed, trampled by those too stupid to know what they did. Sometimes it happened through forceful, bloody invasions; sometimes it happened through less violent but equally insidious means, like those of Fra Savonarola. I'd grown so accustomed to it that I barely noticed anymore. For some reason, it hit me harder this time. Maybe it was because I was seeing it through his urgent eyes and not just observing it from a distance.

"Bianca?" Niccolò chuckled softly. "Are you even listening to me? I'd hoped to spend the night with you, but maybe you'd rather be with Boccaccio. . . ."

I dragged my eyes from the pages, feeling my lips quirk up into a half-smile. "Can't I have you both?"

Over the next few days, Niccolò continued to smuggle more and more goods to me. And not just books. Paintings accumulated in my home. Small sculptures. Even more superficial things like extravagant cloth and jewels, all deemed sinful.

I felt as though I'd been allowed to cross through the gates of heaven. Hours would pass as I studied paintings and sculptures, marveling at the ingenuity of humans, jealous of a creativity I had never possessed, either as a mortal or immortal. That art filled me up with an indescribable joy, exquisite and sweet, almost reminding me of when my soul had been my own.

And the books . . . oh, the books. My clerks and associates soon found their hands full of extra work as I neglected them.

Who cared about accounts and shipments with so much knowledge at my fingertips? I drank it up, savoring the words—words the Church condemned as heresy. A secret smugness filled me over the role I played, protecting these treasures. I would pass on humanity's knowledge and thwart Heaven's agenda. The light of genius and creativity would not fade from this world, and best of all, I would get to enjoy it along the way.

Things changed when Tavia showed up one day to check in. The demoness was pleased at the report of my conquests but puzzled when she noticed a small sculpture of Bacchus on a table. I hadn't yet had a chance to hide the statue with my horde.

Tavia demanded an explanation, and I told her about my role in protecting the contraband. As always, her response took a long time in coming, and when it did, my heart nearly stopped.

"You need to cease this immediately."

"I—what?"

"And you need to turn these items over to Father Betto."

I studied her incredulously, waiting for the joke to reveal itself. Father Betto was my local priest. "You can't . . . you can't mean that. This stuff can't be destroyed. We'd be supporting the Church. We're supposed to go against them."

Tavia raised a dark, pointed eyebrow. "We're supposed to further evil in the world, my darling, which may or may not go along with the Church's plans. In this case, it does."

"How?" I cried.

"Because there is no greater evil than ignorance and the destruction of genius. Ignorance has been responsible for more death, more bigotry, and more sin than any other force. It is the destroyer of mankind."

"But Eve sinned when she sought knowledge . . ."

The demoness smirked. "Are you sure? Do you truly know what is good and what is evil?"

"I . . . I don't know," I whispered. "They seem kind of indistinguishable from one another." It was the first time since becoming a succubus that the lines had really and truly grown so blurred for me. After the loss of my mortal life had darkened me, I'd thrown myself into being a succubus, never questioning Hell's role or the corrupting of men like Niccolò.

"Yes," she agreed. "Sometimes they are." Her smile vanished. "This isn't up for debate. You will yield your stash immediately. And maybe try to seduce Father Betto while you're at it. That'd be a nice perk."

"But I—" The word "can't" was on my lips, and I bit it off. Under the scrutiny of her stare and power, I felt very small and very weak. You don't cross demons. I swallowed. "Yes, Tavia."

The next time Niccolò and I made love, he managed a tired but happy attempt at conversation in his post-sex exhaustion. "Lenzo's going to bring me one of his paintings tomorrow. Wait until you see it. It shows Venus and Adonis—"

"No."

He lifted his head up. "Hmm?"

"No. Don't bring me any more." It was hard, oh God, it was so hard speaking to him in such a cold tone. I kept reminding myself of what I was and what I had to do.

A frown crossed his handsome face. "What are you talking about? You've already collected so much—"

"I don't have them anymore. I gave them up to Savonarola."

"You . . . you're joking."

I shook my head. "No. I contacted his Bands of Hope this morning. They came and took it all."

Niccolò struggled to sit up. "Stop it. This isn't funny."

"It's not a joke. They're all gone. They're going to the fire. They're objects of sin. They need to be destroyed."

"You're lying. Stop this, Bianca. You don't mean—"

My voice sharpened. "They're wrong and heretical. They're *gone*."

Our eyes locked, and as he studied my face, I could see that he was starting to realize that maybe, just maybe, I spoke the truth. And I did. Sort of. I was very good at making people—especially men—believe what I wanted them to.

We dressed, and I took him to the storage room I'd previously hidden the objects in. He stared at the empty space, face pale and disbelieving. I stood nearby, arms crossed, maintaining a stiff and disapproving stance.

Eyes wide, he turned to me. "How could you? How could you do this to me?"

"I told you—"

"I trusted you! You said you'd keep them safe!"

"I was wrong. Satan clouded my judgment."

He gripped my arm painfully and leaned close to me. "What have they done to you? Did they threaten you? You wouldn't do this. What are they holding against you? Is it that priest you're always visiting?"

"No one made me do this," I replied bleakly. "It's the right thing to do."

He pulled back, like he couldn't stand my touch, and my heart lurched painfully at the look in his eyes. "Do you know what you've done? Some of those can never be replaced."

"I know. But it's better this way."

Niccolò stared at me for several more seconds and then stumbled for the door, uncaring of the curfew or his weakened state. I watched him go, feeling dead inside. *He's just another man*, I thought. *Let him go*. I'd had so many in my life; I'd have so many more. What did he matter?

Swallowing tears, I crept downstairs to the lower level, careful not to wake the sleeping household. I'd made the same journey last night, painstakingly carrying part of the horde down here—a part that I didn't give to the Church's minions.

Splitting the art and books had been like choosing which of my children had to live or die. The silks and velvets had been mindless; all of them went to Fra Savonarola. But the rest . . . that had been difficult. I'd let most of Ovid go. His works were so widespread, I had to believe copies of them would survive—if not in Florence, then perhaps some other place untouched by this bigotry. Other authors, those whom I feared had a limited run, stayed with me.

The paintings and sculptures proved hardest of all. They were one of a kind. I couldn't hope that other copies might exist. But I'd known I couldn't keep them all either, not with Tavia checking in. And so, I'd chosen those which I thought most worth saving, protecting them from the Church. Niccolò couldn't know that, though.

I didn't see him for almost three weeks, until we ran into each other at Savonarola's great burning. History would later know it as the Bonfire of the Vanities. It was a great pyramid stuffed with fuel and sin. The zealous threw more and more items in as it blazed, seeming to have a never ending supply. I watched as Botticelli himself tossed one of his paintings in.

Niccolò's greeting was curt. "Bianca."

"Hello, Niccolò." I kept my voice cold and crisp. Uncaring.

He stood in front of me, gray eyes black in the flickering light. His face seemed to have aged since our last meeting. We both turned and silently observed the blaze again, watching as more and more of man's finest things were sacrificed.

"You have killed progress," Niccolò said at last. "You betrayed me."

"I've delayed progress. And I had no obligations to you. Except for this." Reaching into the folds of my dress, I handed over a purse heavy with florins. It was the last part in my plan. He took it, blinking at its weight.

"This is more than you owe me. And I won't finish the fresco."

"I know. It's all right. Take it. Go somewhere else, somewhere away from this. Paint. Write. Create something beautiful. Whatever it takes to make you happy. I don't really care."

He stared, and I feared he'd give the money back. "I still

don't understand. How can you not care about any of this? How can you be so cruel? Why did you do it?"

I studied the fire again. Humans, I realized idly, liked to burn things. Objects. Each other. "Because men cannot surpass the gods. Not yet anyway."

"Prometheus never intended his gift to be used like this."

I smiled without humor, remembering an old debate of ours about classical mythology, back during our sweeter days. "No. I suppose not."

We said nothing else. A moment later, he walked away, disappearing into the darkness. For a heartbeat, I considered telling him the truth, that much of his treasure was still safe. I'd paid well for it to be smuggled out of Florence, away from this mad destruction.

In fact, I'd actually sent the goods to an angel. I didn't like angels as a general rule, but this one was a scholar, one I'd met in England and tolerated. Heretical or no, the books and art would appeal to him as much as to me. He would keep them safe. How ironic, I thought, that I would turn to the enemy for help. Tavia had been right. Sometimes good and evil were impossible to distinguish from one another. And if she'd known what I had done, my existence would probably be over.

So I couldn't tell anyone. The secret had to stay with me and the angel, no matter how much I wished I could share it with Niccolò and comfort him. I had to live with the knowledge that I had taken his life, soul, and hope. He would hate me forever, and it was a sting I would likewise carry with me forever—one that would slowly make my existence more and more miserable.

My world dissolved into darkness. I was back in my box, still cramped and uncomfortable. As usual, I couldn't see anything, but my cheeks were wet with tears yet again. I felt exhausted, even a little disoriented, and my heart ached with a pain that I could never put into words. I didn't see the Oneroi, but something told me they were probably around.

"That was truth," I whispered. "That really happened."

As suspected, a voice answered me in the darkness, and I suddenly knew the real reason they kept showing me true dreams.

"Your truths are worse than your lies."

Chapter 13

I woke up next to Seth, and for the space of heartbeat, I thought I truly was *waking*—waking up from an awful, awful dream about the Oneroi and everything else that had happened since Seth and I had broken up. He lay asleep in bed with the sheets tangled around him, his light brown hair glinting reddish in the morning sun. He slept only in boxers, and his chest looked warm and smooth and perfect for cuddling against.

His breathing was even, his posture still and relaxed. I drank it all in, all the little Seth details I'd been missing for months. I swore that I could even smell him. Did dreams have smells? This one did, I was certain. That soft woodsy-apple scent wrapped around me like an embrace.

After a few moments, he began to stir and sleepily open his eyes. He squinted at the light and rolled onto his back, stifling a yawn. I wanted to roll right over to him and snuggle against his warmth, telling him all about the nightmares I'd been having.

Then, I realized there was no way I could go to him. I couldn't move. Well, that wasn't exactly true. There was more to it than that. I just didn't have a body. I was an observer only, like the invisible camera I'd been with Roman and Jerome. This apparently was not a dream I was active in, and the realization of that drove home the terrible truth: this *was* still an Oneroi dream. I hadn't imagined them. I hadn't imagined Seth and me breaking up.

He sat up in bed and rubbed his eyes. It was such a familiar, nostalgic sight. Getting up was always hard for him, largely because of the bizarre writing hours he kept. He glanced over at the clock, which was near the direction from which I was "watching." His eyes passed right over where I would have been. Yes. I was just a ghost in this. But what was "this" exactly? Truth or lie?

The time on the clock—nine in the morning—must have been motivation enough for him to drag himself out of bed. Still in boxers, he stumbled into the bathroom, miraculously not walking into anything in his sleepy state. While brushing his teeth, he noticed a note on the counter. I immediately recognized the writing because I saw it all the time at the bookstore.

> *Went in early today to get a few things done and*
> *should be done by six. Bring Brandy by, if you*
> *can, to try on those shoes.*
> *Love,*
> *Maddie*

Seeing Maddie's name jolted me out of the Seth Fantasyland I'd been living in as he went through his morning routine. Expanding my vision now, I saw changes to his bathroom—things that hadn't been there when we'd dated. Another toothbrush, for one thing. Makeup in the corner. A pink robe on the bathroom hook. On the books, Maddie was still sharing a place with Doug, but we all knew what the reality was. That pain that hadn't really left since my last dream grew tighter within my chest. She was all over this place. She had left her mark everywhere, everywhere in this space he and I had once shared together. I had been replaced.

Seth went through the rest of his routine, including a remarkably fast shower. He was notorious for staying in there forever while plotting some story line. I tried hard not to focus on the sight of him naked and wet and instead pondered where he might be going today. If it was just to write at the bookstore, he wouldn't have been moving so briskly.

He easily found clean boxers and jeans, but the hardest part of his day came next: what T-shirt to wear? When we'd been together, I'd loved watching this. I'd lie in bed—after all, I had no urgency to ever get ready—laughing while he deliberated and deliberated over his massive T-shirt collection. Each had its own hanger, displaying some bit of retro or pop culture novelty. Vanilla Ice. *ALF*. Mr. T cereal. He flipped through them all, studying each one carefully as his hand touched each sleeve.

Then, his fingers suddenly brushed against a sleeve longer than the others. His closet wasn't all T-shirts. There were a few sweaters and pullovers crammed into the sides. There was also a flannel shirt; it was what he'd stopped and noticed. Pushing the other shirts aside, he took the flannel off of its hanger and held it up, his motions almost reverent.

Even without physical form, I had the sensation of my heart going still. I knew this shirt. It was one he'd given me to wear a long time ago, the night I'd passed out at his place from too much alcohol. I'd met his family the next day, looking ridiculous with the flannel over my strappy party dress. Even while dating, I'd totally forgotten all about that shirt.

He held it there between his hands, and the look on his face . . . there was so much there, I didn't even know where to start. Seth was so good at keeping his expression neutral and could be extremely short-spoken when he chose. But here, alone, he was unguarded. There was sorrow on his face. Sorrow and regret. And when he held the shirt up and rested his head on it, I saw longing as well. The whole mood was rounded out with a sort of helpless resignation. He inhaled deeply and then hung the shirt back up. As he did, I caught the faintest whiff of tuberose blossoms—the leftover scent of my Michael Kors perfume. Seth had never worn or washed it again, I realized with a start. He'd just kept it like some sort of treasured artifact.

After that, he simply grabbed the first T-shirt his hand came across, without even looking. It was an old favorite of his, showing the Tasmanian Devil from *Looney Tunes*. Seth's mood had shifted considerably, down to something a little more solemn and thoughtful than when he'd gotten out of the shower. My observations didn't go into his head, though. I could only judge by outside signs.

His reason for getting up turned out to be a trip to his brother's house. Like always, the elder Mortensen's home was chaotic, with small adorable blond girls running around, many of them shrieking when they saw their favorite uncle. He'd barely stepped inside when Andrea, his sister-in-law, came out to greet him. She wore a corduroy jacket with her jeans and T-shirt, her blond hair slicked back into a neat ponytail. She gave Seth a startled look.

"You didn't bring your laptop?" Andrea was as cheerful as always but appeared tired.

He gestured over to where his twin nieces, McKenna and Morgan, were playing tug of war with a string of Christmas lights. It was odd because Christmas was over a month away and also because the lights were plugged in, which seemed like some sort of electrical risk to me. Apparently Seth felt the same way because he hastily intercepted them and removed the string of lights altogether, amid much protest.

"I don't think I'll get much work done with these guys," he said dryly.

"Yeah," she admitted. "I can see that." She glanced at her watch. "Okay, gotta go. I don't know how long this'll take."

"No problem," he said. "Do what you need to."

She scurried out the door. I wanted to ask where she was off to but had no means. Again, I was reminded how out of the loop I was from the Mortensen world now. Once I would have known every detail.

Kendall, a precocious nine-year-old, solemnly walked up to Seth. "Uncle Seth," she said, "will you play Loan with me?"

Seth arched an eyebrow. "Loan? What's that?"

"It's where I'm the mortgage broker, and you come to get

a loan for a house but don't have the money for a down payment." She paused. "We'll have to make a pretend income fax for you."

"Tax," he corrected. "And how about we go to the bookstore instead?"

She frowned. "I want to play Loan."

"They have real estate books there," he said. "I don't think we can play Loan without sufficient background."

"Okay," she conceded. "We can go."

Brandy strolled into the living room just then with her four-year-old sister in her arms. Kayla looked like she'd woken up from a nap and sleepily had her head against Brandy's shoulder. I loved all the girls, but something about Kayla always affected me more strongly.

"Go where?" asked Brandy, shifting Kayla's weight. Although she held her sister tenderly, Brandy had a dark cloud around her.

"To Emerald City."

Brandy sighed. "Don't you spend enough time there?"

"Maddie got a few pairs of shoes for the dress and needs you to try them on."

Brandy gave him a look that exquisitely expressed all of her feelings on that topic.

"Don't start," he warned, in as chastising a tone as I'd ever heard him use. Welcome to adolescence, Seth.

"Is Georgina working?" she asked.

Kendall looked up from where she'd been starting to color. In orange crayon, a blank piece of paper read "IRS."

"Yeah, can we see Georgina?" Kendall piped in.

Seth looked pained. "I don't know if she's there or not."

I didn't know either. I didn't know if this was a true or false dream. It felt true so far, but I didn't trust the Oneroi. Being an observer, I had to think I wouldn't be there. Certainly I wouldn't if this were true. I wondered what would happen at the store when I suddenly stopped showing up.

"I can just stay here while you're gone," Brandy said. "Mom doesn't mind if I'm alone."

"Then you can't try on the shoes. Which defeats the whole purpose."

After a carefully worded "discussion," in which Brandy suggested he just bring the shoes to her, she finally conceded. With the whole gang along, they had to take the Mortensen van, which Seth didn't seem overly thrilled about. But there was no other way to transport five girls, one of whom needed a car seat.

The troop arrived at Emerald City. Seth left the four younger ones in the kids' section, which was a wonderland of picture books, puzzles, and stuffed animals. Janice was working that area today and told him she'd keep an eye on the girls. Seth also put Kendall in charge of her sisters, with the bribe that he'd buy her some finance books.

That left him and Brandy to find Maddie, who was holed up in an office. Her face lit up when she saw them, and she practically flew from her seat to give him a quick kiss. Brandy scowled, and a troubled feeling burned within me. The love on Maddie's face was so obvious, so strong . . . anyone could see it. She made no attempts to hide it, even at work. I hated their relationship, but how could I resent her feelings? How could I resent her loving the man who meant the world to me?

"How's work?" he asked her, smiling fondly. Was that his way of showing love too? How had he looked around me? For some reason, I was certain he'd been different . . . hadn't he? I couldn't remember.

Maddie gestured to the desk she shared with Doug. "A little crazy. Yet strangely boring. I'm stuck on paperwork all day. Performance reviews."

"Hey, I'm stuck on paperwork every day."

She rolled her eyes. "Bad joke. And not the same at all."

"Try putting some sex and violence into the reviews, and they might go faster."

I was too disturbed by their banter to pay much attention to the fact that Maddie was doing my job. Brandy looked equally pained by the conversation. As Maddie and Seth spoke,

I studied him further, trying to read his feelings. Yes, there was affection . . . yet, it reminded me a little of the warm indulgence he showed his nieces.

At last, Maddie produced a shopping bag full of shoes. Brandy's dress was hanging in the office, and Maddie ordered Seth to leave while his niece changed.

Just before he was shooed out, Maddie remarked to Brandy, "I'm glad this color looks good on you. I decided to do everything purple because of how great it looked on Georgina. I found some awesome flowers that go with it all too."

Oh, fucking fantastic. I had influenced the color scheme for their wedding.

Seth left, and I went with him. He wandered through the store, browsing through books—an activity he never tired of. Several employees said hello to him as they passed by.

Including me.

Seeing as the Oneroi had put me in dreams a couple times now, I shouldn't have been surprised. Except, whenever I was a character in the theatre of these dreams, I'd always had awareness of it. I'd watched me and *felt* me. Now, I saw myself approach Seth exactly the same way I'd seen Maddie and Brandy approach him. I was still objective. No inner connection. Again, just like watching a movie. I didn't entirely understand it, but nothing the Oneroi did should really shock me anymore.

"Hey," I (she?) said, shelving a couple books. They were copies of *The Scarlet Letter*, and I'd set them in new releases.

"Hey," said Seth, a weird mix of shyness and familiarity in his manner. "How's it going?"

"Not bad," I said. "Quiet day. Mostly just putting away books."

"You've got Maddie doing reviews."

"Yeah, well, I thought she could handle it. Besides, this dress is new. It'd be a shame to keep it hidden."

My watching self had already noticed the dress because that was second nature to me. It was a great dress but not necessarily one to wear to work. It was a silk sheath that stopped high on the thigh, with straps tying around the neck and a scoop neckline that showed a considerable amount of cleavage. There was no bra anywhere. I looked like I should have been clubbing, not shelving. Seeing as this whole vision was no memory of mine, the dress only furthered the fact that this was one of the lies. I wasn't afraid to tart it up, but even I had boundaries at work.

Seth seemed surprised at the dress but not unappreciative. "You should be hand-selling," he said. "Go outside with a book, and I bet you could push it on anyone."

"This dress might not work on *everyone*," I pointed out.

He gave me one of those little smiles of his, and I wondered if the other Georgina melted like I did. "The dress is only half of it. You're charming enough to talk anyone into anything."

I gave him a smile in return, one that was both cheery and sly. "Anything?"

The innuendo didn't progress because Kayla suddenly pranced over and wrapped her arms around Seth's legs. He scooped her up and glanced around. "What happened to Kendall? No finance books for bad babysitters."

My alter ego peered over toward the magazines. "Is that her?" I sounded uncertain, which was odd because when Seth turned to see, it was perfectly obvious it was Kendall. She was reading *Forbes*.

Seth sighed and called her over. She brightened when she saw me. "Hi, Georgina! You're so pretty today."

"Thanks," I said, beaming.

"You were supposed to be in charge," said Seth. "Go get the twins. Hopefully they haven't wandered out into traffic."

Kendall shook her head. "They're playing with puzzles." But she raced off nonetheless.

Kayla was staring around the store in that distracted way children her age had, watching the people and sights. Seth gave her a slight nudge. "What about you? Aren't you going to say hi to Georgina?"

Kayla glanced in the direction he indicated, looked me

over, and then continued her survey of the store. It wasn't so much she shunned me or was repulsed by me; it was more like she was disinterested. I didn't stand out to her more than any other patron or even one of the shelves.

"One of her moods," said Seth apologetically.

Brandy surfaced, still annoyed by the shoes, but immensely happy to see me. The rest of the girls were rustled up, and after a bit more chatting, Seth and the nieces left me to my bad shelving. He'd continued holding Kayla in his arms, and she suddenly turned to him in all seriousness.

"When are you going to find Georgina?" she asked. Her voice was small and sweet. She rarely spoke, so I always loved the sound of it when she did.

He frowned, trying to open the van door with one hand. Brandy helped him. "We just saw Georgina," he said. "Inside."

"No, we didn't," said Kayla.

"We did. You snubbed her," he teased. "I told you to say hello."

"That wasn't Georgina. You have to find her."

"What have you been smoking?" Brandy asked, taking over to buckle Kayla into her booster. "That was Georgina."

Seth sighed. "Be careful with your choice of expressions."

The topic dropped after that, but as they drove back to Terry and Andrea's, a chill ran through me. Kayla knew. Kayla knew I was gone. This must be a true dream after all. We'd learned recently that she had the faintest stirring of psychic powers and the ability to perceive some things on the supernatural plane. She had a vague sense of my aura, and she'd realized that it wasn't me in the store. That's why she'd been so disinterested. It was also why I hadn't been inside that Georgina. It *wasn't* Georgina.

Then who was it?

With a sinking feeling, I immediately answered my own question. Who else would have an interest in looking like me *and* flirting with Seth?

Simone. Simone was impersonating me in my absence, I was certain of it. Son of a bitch. I couldn't feel her aura in this dream form, and no mortal could, period. Except for Kayla. Fuck. This was not what I needed.

The rest of Seth's day was uneventful, though he thankfully never ran into "me" again. Andrea returned, and it was then I learned she'd been at a doctor's appointment. She thanked Seth for his help, though it took a long time for him to leave, due to all the younger girls' good-byes.

Seth finally returned to his condo and spent the day writing, which was boring for me to watch. I didn't get why the Oneroi hadn't pulled me out yet. Sure, it had been disheartening to see that no mortal knew I was gone, but this dream hadn't had the devastating effects of the others.

Evening fell, and Maddie returned home. Seth, engrossed in his work, stayed at his desk until she found him and spun his chair around. She climbed onto his lap, wrapping her legs around him in a way very similar to what I used to do.

He smiled at her, wrapping his arms around her as well and returning her hello kiss.

"How was your paperwork?" he asked.

Maddie ran her fingers along the side of his face, that love radiating off of her. "Nonstop. Georgina left it all on me today. I don't know what was up with that."

"She said she thought you could handle it."

Maddie pulled a face. "More like she wanted to take the day off and prance around. Did you see that dress she was wearing? I mean, yeah, she can pull off anything she wants to wear, but that wasn't really work appropriate."

He laughed and pulled her closer. "I think Georgina thinks her wit and charm can let her get away with anything she wants."

"Yeah, well, she's not as funny as she always thinks she is," grumbled Maddie. "And all she got away with today was looking like she was trying to pick up some guy at the store."

"Wouldn't be the first time," said Seth with a shrug.

"What?"

"You didn't know? She sleeps with Warren all the time. Usually in his office."

I couldn't believe what I was hearing. Not only were the two of them mocking me, Seth had also told Maddie about my on-again off-again affair with the store's owner Warren. Doug had always had his suspicions, but other than Seth, no one else knew. I had never expected Seth to betray that secret.

"I had no idea," said Maddie. "And yet . . . I don't know. Maybe I did. I mean, everything she wears is kind of slutty."

"She sleeps around a lot. She'll pretty much go home with anyone." He paused. "She even tried it with me once."

"Really?" Maddie's eyes went wide. "What'd you do?"

"Nothing. I have no interest in *that*. I couldn't handle being with someone so easy. She'd probably sleep with all my friends while we were dating." He cupped Maddie's face in his hands. "Not that it matters. I have no reason to even go looking, not when I have the best thing right here."

He drew her to him, and they kissed again. It wasn't the earlier hello kiss either. It was deep and ardent, both of them eagerly trying to get as much of the other as they could. His hands gripped hold of the bottom of her tank top and jerked it over her head, revealing a black satin bra I was pretty sure I'd helped her pick out. Never breaking the kiss, his hands then went around her waist as he half-carried, half-stumbled out of the office and into the bedroom. They fell onto the covers, hands moving all over each other's bodies and kisses starting to spread beyond lips.

No, I thought, unsure if the Oneroi could hear me or not. *No. I don't want to see this. Take me back. Take me back to the box. Send me to another dream.*

But if they were there, they weren't listening. I had no eyes to close. I couldn't look away. There was no way to unsee what I was seeing. I'd experienced a lot of heart-wrenching things in my relationship with Seth, things that had hurt me so badly that I swore I wanted to die. But nothing, nothing could have prepared me for seeing him have sex with another woman. And it wasn't just watching the act itself, the way their naked bodies intertwined with one another and the cries of pleasure elicited in the height of orgasm.

It was the look on his face as he did it. There it was. The love I'd been searching for earlier. I'd thought before he only regarded her with a strong affection, similar to the fond love he had for his nieces. No. This was passion I saw on his face, the kind of love that burned so deeply, it connected two people's souls.

He was looking at her the way he'd once looked at me.

I had never thought it was possible. Somewhere, somehow, I'd been convinced that he loved her in a different way from me. Maybe their love was strong, but I'd felt certain it could never match what he felt for me. Ours was different. Yet, seeing them now, I saw that wasn't true. And when, at the end, he told her she was his world—just as he'd once told me—I knew that I really was nothing special. The love he had for me was gone.

And in the terrible, excruciating pain of that moment, I no longer wanted to die. There was no point because I was certain just then that I had died—because surely, surely, Hell couldn't be worse than this.

Chapter 14

I was never entirely sure how much of that dream was true and how much was a lie. That it was a mix, I felt certain. I couldn't think of any reason the Oneroi would show me Kayla noticing my absence when no one else did. That had to be true. Yet, I also couldn't imagine Seth and Maddie slandering me so much. I especially couldn't imagine him breaking a confidence. Surely that was a lie . . . right? And as for the rest of the dream . . . well, it didn't matter.

The Oneroi offered no answers. And as more and more dreams came to me, the fate they'd foretold began to come true: I could no longer tell what was real and what wasn't. Often, I tried to tell myself that it was all a lie. That was easier than living with the doubt. No matter how hard I tried, though, I couldn't shake the feel of truth that some had. So, I was always questioning everything, and it grew maddening after a while. It was made worse by the fact that the Oneroi were always feeding off of those dreams, which consequently sucked up my energy. A succubus needed that energy to function. It gave me the ability to move in the world, to think clearly, to shape-shift. Draining me of it wouldn't kill me—I was still immortal, after all—but it made me useless. Not that it mattered in my prison. I still had the sensation of being crammed inside a box in the dark, and what little awareness of my body I had left was simply showing me pain and weakness. Had I been released, I would have had trouble walking. I would also likely be in my true shape.

Since I was mostly suspended consciousness now, the physical aspects became irrelevant. My mind became the true liability, as both the lack of energy and torture from the dreams began to rip me apart. I was more coherent and analytical during the dreams themselves, but when they ended and the emotions hit me, my rational thought began fracturing. My banter with the Oneroi became primal insults and screams. Most of the time I couldn't think at all. I was just pain and despair. And rage. It seemed impossible, yet underneath the agony that smothered me, a small spark of anger just barely managed to stay alive, fueled every time I saw the Oneroi. I think holding on to that fury was the only thing that kept my shattered mind from completely giving in to insanity.

I lost all sense of time, but that had more to do with the strange nature of dreams and not so much my brain. I actually think little time passed in the real world because every time the Oneroi showed me a glimpse of it, no progress seemed to have been made in finding me—something I believed the Oneroi hoped would break me further.

"Why do you keep asking us?"

The question came from Cody. I was now watching him, Peter, and Hugh being interrogated by Jerome. Carter sat in a far corner, smoking in spite of Peter's no-cigarettes-in-the-apartment rule. Roman was there too, invisible in body and aura. That meant I shouldn't have been able to see him, yet something—maybe because he was my target in this dream—allowed me to know he was there, despite what my senses told me. My friends knew about him. He had no need to hide his physical appearance, unless Jerome feared there might be demonic eyes watching Seattle—which wasn't that unreasonable. My disappearance had probably made him extra suspicious.

Cody's question had been directed toward Jerome, and I had never in my life seen such fury on the young vampire's face. He was the mildest of us all, newest to Seattle's immortal circle. He still jumped when Jerome said jump and spent more time watching and learning than taking an active role. Seeing him like this was a shock.

"We don't know anything!" Cody continued. "Our powers are limited. *You're* the one who's supposed to be almighty and powerful. Doesn't Hell control half the universe?"

"'There are more things in heaven and earth, Horatio, than are dreamt of in your philosophy,'" quoted Carter solemnly.

"Shut up, both of you," snapped Jerome. He glared at the angel. "I've already heard you use that one before."

Carter shrugged. "You've heard me use all of them before. Many, many times."

Jerome turned back to my three friends. "Nothing. You're absolutely certain you noticed nothing about her before this happened?"

"She was down," said Peter.

"She's always down," said Hugh.

"She didn't tell any of us about this thing she kept feeling," growled Cody. "She only told Roman. Why aren't you questioning him?"

"I have," said Jerome. He took a step near the young vampire and leaned his face in close. "And watch your tone. You're lucky I'm feeling kindly right now."

"What's Mei doing?" asked Peter. His tone was proper and polite as he cast an uneasy glance at Cody. Half of Peter's question was probably a ploy to save his protégé from being smote then and there.

Jerome sighed and stepped back. "Questioning others. Finding any trace—any at all—of another of our immortals who might have felt something."

Hugh, who was sitting on the couch and keeping his distance from our angry boss, cleared his throat nervously. "I don't want to bring this up . . . but, you're already kind of on probation after the, um, summoning."

Jerome's smoldering gaze fell on the imp, who flinched. "Don't you think I know that? Why is everyone here giving me useless information?"

"All I'm saying," said Hugh, "is that if someone wanted to take advantage of the situation, making you lose one of your immortals would be a good way. Someone who, say, maybe wanted a job promotion."

"Mei couldn't do this," said Jerome, catching on. He'd already had one lieutenant demoness turn, so Hugh's hypothesis wasn't that bad. "She couldn't hide Georgina like this . . . even if she was working with someone who could, she'd find a better way to get to me." There was almost a proud note in his voice.

"What about Simone?" demanded Cody. "She's out there impersonating Georgina, you know."

Both Peter and Hugh stared in astonishment. "She's what?" exclaimed the imp.

The attention from his friends seemed to fluster Cody more than Jerome's wrath. "Yeah, I was, um, visiting Gabrielle at the bookstore, and I saw Simone. She had Georgina's shape, but I could feel it was her."

"You saw Gabrielle?" asked Carter with interest, like my disappearance from the universe had now lessened in comparison to Cody's romance.

Cody flushed. "We . . . had a date. But I canceled it when I heard about Georgina. It's no big deal."

No big deal? My kidnapping was now ruining Cody's chances with the woman of his dreams.

"This is more useless information," growled Jerome. "And, yes, I know about Simone."

"Maybe you should be talking to her," said Cody.

"She didn't do it," said Jerome. The way he spoke implied that it was a closed case.

Peter was still treading cautiously around Jerome. "If you say she didn't . . . then she didn't. But why is she impersonating Georgina if she's innocent in all this?"

"She has her reasons," said Jerome vaguely.

Cody was outraged. "And you're just going to let her do it! How can you?"

"Because I don't care!" roared Jerome. A wave of power

flared out from him like a shock wave. Everyone except Carter was blown back by it. The china in Peter's cabinet rattled. "I don't care what that other succubus does. I don't care about Georgina's human friends or what they think. If anything, you should be grateful. Simone's act is keeping the others from noticing what happened."

None of my friends had anything to say to that. With an exasperated snarl, Jerome turned toward the door. "I've had enough of this. I need real answers."

He stormed out into the hall, leaving the door open. Presumably, he did it as an act of angry defiance, but I knew it was so Roman could follow him. Normally, the demon would have simply teleported out, but for whatever reason, father and son were investigating together today. Once alone on the stairwell, Jerome muttered, "Hold on."

Roman must have because Jerome disappeared. He reappeared—and me along with him—in a new setting: Erik's store. It was evening, and Erik had shut down for the night. The fountains were off. The music had stopped playing. Yet, near the back of the store, a few notes of humming could be heard. They cut off almost immediately, and footsteps sounded as someone approached.

Jerome stayed where he was, not deigning to move. He knew his presence would have been promptly felt. He knew Erik would come to him.

And sure enough, gait still unsteady from being sick recently, Erik made his way to the store's front. He radiated wariness as he moved. For me, he always had a kindly smile and cup of tea. Even Carter, the most powerful immortal in Seattle, would earn a respectful smile. But Erik was on his guard now—which really wasn't that weird, considering who stood in his store.

Erik came to a stop a few feet from Jerome and straightened himself up as well as he could to his full height. He gave Jerome the smallest nod of greeting.

"Mr. Hanan'el," said Erik. "An unexpected visit."

Jerome had just taken a cigarette out of his coat, and it fell from his fingers. The look he gave Erik was a hundred times more terrifying than anything I'd ever seen. I expected another flare-up of power, one that would blow the entire building apart.

"Do not," said Jerome, "ever let that name cross your lips again, or I will rip them off." His voice was low and even, simmering with the rage and power he was holding back.

Had I been there, I would have gasped. Jerome's true name. Erik knew Jerome's true name. I used fake names to blend in and forget my identity. But for angels and demons, names were power. In the right hands, a name could be used to summon or control a greater immortal. In fact, for Dante to have summoned Jerome in the spring, Grace must have revealed that name.

Erik didn't flinch at Jerome being in smite mode. "I assume," said Erik, "you are seeking something."

"Yes," said Jerome, slightly mimicking Erik's tone. "I am 'seeking' my succubus."

Erik's eyebrows rose slightly. "Miss Kincaid?"

"Of course! Who else?" Jerome did technically have another succubus, Tawny. But maybe he wouldn't have gone hunting for her if she disappeared. He took out another cigarette and lit it without a lighter. "Do you know where she is? And don't lie to me. If you're keeping her from me, I will rip you apart, leaving your tongue for last."

"Ripping body parts appears to be a theme tonight," replied Erik, clasping his hands behind his back. "But no, I don't know where Miss Kincaid is. I didn't know she was missing."

Jerome took a step forward, eyes narrowed. "I told you, do *not* lie to me."

"I have no reason to lie. I like Miss Kincaid. I would never wish her harm. If I can help her, I will." Erik's wording was careful. It was me he was offering to help—not Jerome.

"She spoke to you about some force—some 'siren song' that kept coming to her," said Jerome. He gave a curt report of what Roman had observed when I disappeared. "What do you know about this thing? What kind of creature was it? It was feeding off her depression."

From the moment this dream had started, Jerome had displayed nothing but rage and terror. Yet . . . as he shot off questions, it was almost like he was rambling. There was desperation under all that anger. Desperation and frustration because he was in a situation with no answers and felt powerless. Demons, as a general rule, do not like feeling powerless. Resorting to human help—a human who knew his name, no less—must have been excruciatingly painful for my boss.

Erik, classy as always, remained calm and formal. "There are creatures who do that, yes, but I don't believe it was one of those. I believe it chose those times because she was weakest. It was simply a lure—probably not the creature or culprit itself."

"Then what creature is it?"

Erik spread his hands wide. "It could be any number of things."

"God-fucking-damn-it," said Jerome, dropping his cigarette onto Erik's floor and stomping on it hard.

"You're no longer connected to her?"

"Correct."

"You have no awareness of her—one of your kind isn't masking her?"

"Correct."

"And you know she's not dead?"

"Correct."

Erik's brown eyes were thoughtful. "Then the creature is likely one outside of your scope."

"Why," asked Jerome wearily, "does everyone keep telling me things I already know?" The question could have been directed to Erik, Roman, or the air. The demon took out another cigarette.

"You need to figure out who would take her and why. She has enemies. Nyx was not pleased with the resolution of her last visit."

"Nyx is locked up." Jerome spoke as though he had stated

that a hundred times. I was pretty sure he'd been asked all those questions about me a hundred times too.

"Your summoner, Mr. Moriarty, was not overly pleased with her either." Although Erik remained professional, his lips twisted ever so slightly, like he'd tasted something bitter. Regardless of his feelings for the demon, both Erik and Jerome shared a mutual hatred of Dante.

This gave Jerome pause. "I doubt this was human magic, though I suppose he could have had help—he's sought allies before. I'll look into it." He dropped this new cigarette and stepped on it too. "Regardless, I still can't believe I'd have no sense of her in the world."

"Maybe she's not in this world."

Erik's words hung between them for several seconds.

"No," said Jerome at last. "Many have interest in her—but none who would do that."

I saw in Erik's face that the words "Many have interest in her" had caught his notice. He stayed silent, however, and waited for Jerome's next profound statement. Which wasn't that profound.

"Time to go," said the demon, probably so Roman could grab hold again.

Jerome teleported, off to wherever it was he had to go.

And me? I returned to my prison.

Chapter 15

It was 1942, and I was in France.

I didn't want to be in France. I hadn't wanted to be there for the last fifty years, yet somehow, Bastien kept talking me into staying. There was also the small fact that our supervising archdemon didn't want us to go. He liked the way we worked together. Incubus-succubus teams were hit or miss sometimes, but we were exceptional, and our superiors had taken note. It was good for our hellish careers but not for my morale.

Bastien didn't see what my problem was. "Hell doesn't even need us here," he told me one day, after I'd complained for like the thousandth time. "Think of it as a vacation. Hordes of souls are being damned here every day."

I walked over to the window of our shop and peered out onto the busy road, pressing my hands against the glass. Bicyclists and pedestrians moved past, everyone needing to get somewhere and get there fast. It could have been any ordinary weekday in Paris, but this was no ordinary day. Nothing had been ordinary since the Germans had occupied France, and the scattered soldiers in the street stood out to me like candles in the night.

Bad simile, I thought. Candles implied some kind of hope or light. And while Paris had fared better than most people realized under Nazi rule, something in the city had changed. The energy, the spirit . . . whatever you wanted to call it, it had a taint to me. Bastien said I was crazy. Most people were still living their daily lives. The food shortages weren't as bad here as in other places. And after shape-shifting into Aryan nation poster children with blond hair and blue eyes, we were more or less left alone.

Bastien was still going on about my glum mood while he moved about and straightened hat displays in my periphery. He'd chosen millinery as his profession for this identity, one that worked well for meeting well-to-do Parisian women. I played the role of his sister—as I so often did in other scenarios—helping with the store and keeping house for him. It was better than dance halls or brothels, which had been our previous occupations in France.

"What about your friend?" Bastien asked me slyly. "Young Monsieur Luc?"

At the mention of Luc, I paused in my dejected assessment of the world outside the hat shop. If I was going to talk about candles in the night, then Luc was mine. A real one. He was a human I'd met recently, working with his father—a violin maker. Their trade had suffered even more than ours, as the market for luxury items shriveled in these lean times.

But Luc never seemed to let their financial woes affect him. Whenever I saw him, he was always cheerful, always full of hope. The weight of so many centuries of sin and darkness were starting to take their toll on me, and being in Paris only made it worse. Yet, Luc was a wonder to me. Being able to look at the world with such optimism, with such conviction that good would prevail . . . well, it was a foreign concept. One I was intrigued by. I couldn't stay away from it.

"Luc's different," I admitted, finally turning from the window. "He's not part of this."

Bastien snorted and leaned against the wall. "They're *all* part of this, Fleur." Fleur was his long-time nickname for me over the years, no matter what identity I assumed. "I don't suppose you've slept with him yet?"

My answer was to turn away again and remain silent. No, I hadn't slept with Luc. I wanted to, though. I wanted to with the instincts of a woman who had fallen for a man, as well as the craving of a succubus to consume the energy and taste the soul of someone so good. I had never hesitated before. This was the kind of thing I'd always sought out. It was even my job. But something inside of me was changing. Maybe it was these bleak times, but whenever I looked at Luc and saw that purity radiating from him—*and* his growing love and trust in me—I just couldn't do it.

"He's coming by tonight," I said at last, dodging the question. "We're going for a walk."

"Oh," said Bastien. "I see. A walk. That's certain to impress Theodosia." Theodosia was our archdemoness.

I turned back around sharply, glaring at Bastien. "It's none of your business what I do!" I exclaimed. "Besides, if this is the 'vacation' you claim it is, I shouldn't need to secure a good soul."

"Souls are falling left and right around here," he agreed. "But you've still got to turn one in every once in a while. You can't spend the rest of your existence only going after bad ones."

I didn't speak to him for the rest of the day, and fortunately, business picked up quite a bit in the afternoon. It kept us both busy, though I counted down the minutes until Luc showed up that evening. He gave polite greetings to my "brother," and then I hustled us out of there so that I wouldn't have to see the knowing look in Bastien's eyes.

Luc could have passed for my brother too with his sunny golden hair. He always smiled when he looked at me, making small crinkle lines around the blue eyes I fancifully likened to sapphires. He held my arm as we passed through the evening crowd, filled with those going home after work or possibly seeking nighttime entertainment. He told me I looked beautiful, and we talked of other inconsequential things: the weather, neighborhood gossip, day-to-day affairs . . .

We ended up at a small city park that was a popular spot for others seeking evening strolls before curfew. We found a relatively secluded area among some trees and settled onto the grass. Luc had been carrying a small basket the entire time and revealed its contents: pastries and a bottle of wine. He didn't have extra money to throw around for that kind of thing, but I knew better than to protest. It was already done. Whatever else he'd had to sacrifice in return would be well worth it, as far as he was concerned.

He had another surprise for me as well: a book. He and I were always trading novels back and forth, and as I lay down against the grass, skimming through the pages, a strange yet warm peace blossomed within me.

"Next time you should bring your violin," I said, setting the book down. "I want to hear you play again."

He stretched out beside me, his hand finding mine. We laced our fingers together and watched the sky grow purple. "Not out here," he said. "I don't want a public concert."

"You'd charm them all," I said. "The whole city would line up and dance at your command, just like the pied piper."

He laughed, the sound as golden as his hair or even the sun itself. "And then what would I do with them?"

"Line them up and send them all away so that we can be alone."

"We are alone," he said, laughing again. "Sort of."

I rolled to my side and leaned over him. Shadows from the surrounding trees enclosed us. "Alone enough."

I brought my lips down and kissed him, surprising both of us. I hadn't meant to do it. We'd never kissed before. I'd held myself back from him, earning all that chastising from Bastien. I could never bring myself to take Luc's energy and shorten his life. Yet, something came over me just then. It might have been my earlier gray mood or the feelings that were eerily like love within me. Whatever it was, being a succubus didn't matter just then.

Well, it didn't until his energy started flowing into me. Our kissing grew more intense, our lips full of demand. His soul shone so brightly that even that one kiss was enough to taste his energy. It was glorious. My whole body thrilled to both it and his touch.

He wrapped his arm around my waist, and without conscious thought, I began unbuttoning his shirt. He rolled me over so that I was the one on my back now and moved his mouth down to my neck. The knee-length skirts of this time gave him easy access to run his hand up my leg, and I pressed myself closer to him, pulling at his clothes while his hungry lips moved farther and farther down. All the while, that beautiful life filled me. I was drowning in it.

When his lips reached the spot between my breasts, something seemed to jolt him to reality. He pulled up from me, running his hand over my hair as he looked down into my eyes.

"Oh God," he said. "We can't do this. Not now." The mantra of moral men everywhere.

"We can," I said, surprised at the pleading in my own voice. It was the affection I felt for him speaking, not any agenda of Hell's. I wanted—needed—him to be closer to me.

He sighed. "Suzette, Suzette. I want to. But I want us to get married. I can't do this—can't do this to you—unless I know you'll be my wife. It isn't right otherwise."

I stared up at him, uncertainty interfering with my desire. "Are you . . . are you proposing to me?"

Luc thought about it for a moment and then grinned again, giving me another of those radiant smiles that never failed to make my heart race. "Yes. I guess I am. We'd have to wait a little bit—wait until I had more money. But when the war's over, things will get better."

This war's never going to be over, some gloomy part of me thought. But just now, that wasn't the real issue. His wanting to marry me was. It was impossible, of course. I could theoretically shape-shift so that I aged with him, all the while getting succubus sex on the side. Some succubi did that, having countless husbands over the centuries. Most didn't even stick around. They just disappeared. Their marital vows meant nothing.

Looking at him now, at that burning love in his eyes, I felt my heart torn in two. If I said yes, he would wrap me up again and make love to me. If I said no, he wouldn't—not out of spite, but because of what was honorable. This could be so easy. Say yes. Promise I'd marry him and take him now. I could fulfill my heart's longing, my body's longing, and keep my good standing with Hell. I could leave after we were married. Or, easier still, break off the engagement.

All I had to do was give him a dishonest "yes." Sex to him wasn't right without that. Really, it was a wonder he didn't insist on waiting until marriage. The commitment was apparently enough. He believed in me. He believed I was a good, honest person. If I said I loved him and would be true to him forever, then he would accept that. *Just say yes.*

But the words stuck in my throat. I couldn't lie to him. I couldn't let him find out how base I really was. And as his lingering life energy burned inside me, I realized I couldn't steal more from him. The guilt of what I'd done already was hitting me hard. It had only been the barest taste, but it had clipped time off of his life. And if I did back out of marriage after we'd had sex, he'd think what we'd done had been wrong. A sin. A black mark on his soul.

I slid out from under him and sat up. "No," I said. "I can't marry you."

His happy face remained unchanged. "It doesn't have to be now. And it doesn't even have to be . . . about this." He gestured to where I'd just been lying in the grass. "Like I said, we couldn't get married for a while anyway."

"No," I repeated, my heart sinking. "I can't . . . I can't marry you. Ever." *I can't hurt you. I care about you too much. I can't take your light from the world.*

He must have seen something in my face, something that drove home the truth of my words. That smile faded. The sun disappeared behind clouds. My heart broke. I hastily stood up, suddenly unable to look at him. What was wrong with me? I didn't know. All I knew was that I couldn't stay there. I couldn't stay there and see him hurting. If I did, I would start sobbing. As it was, I could feel tears starting to sting my eyes.

"Suzette, wait!"

I hurried away but soon heard him coming behind me. Even after my rejection, he didn't sound angry. He was concerned, worried about me. I hated that even more. I wish I'd driven him into a rage. But, no, even something like this . . . it would hurt him, yet he would respect both me and my choice.

Which was why I had to stay away from him. Not just now, but always. I knew now that I couldn't be around someone I cared about. I couldn't stand the thought of causing pain to a loved one. I couldn't stand the thought of damning a good soul. Somewhere, somehow, after centuries of blithely harming others, I had gone horribly awry as a succubus. How? When? With Niccolò? Was it just the gradual sum of all the lives and souls I'd harmed finally taking a toll on me?

I was headed back for the hat shop. Bastien and I lived above it. I could still hear Luc following me, calling out to me that everything was okay. I knew if I made it inside, he wouldn't come barging in after me. He'd probably knock politely at the door but would go away if Bastien told him to.

I took a shortcut, cutting behind some buildings off the main road. I knew the way well, but it was dark now, limiting my vision enough that I didn't see the soldier until I ran straight into him. He was standing so still and so solidly that it was like I'd accidentally run into one of the building's walls. I bounced back, and he caught me by the shoulder.

"Easy there," he said. His French had a heavy German accent but was articulated well. "You'll hurt yourself."

He was a giant of a man, young and not unattractive. I couldn't quite tell in the fading light, but his uniform made me think he was an officer of some sort. He was smiling down at me and hadn't let go of my shoulder.

"Thank you," I said demurely. I tried to step back gracefully, but his grip was strong.

"You shouldn't be out here at all," he added. "It's dangerous. Especially with curfew coming." Curfew was nowhere near coming, despite the darkening sky. He looked me over as he spoke. My skirt had fallen back into place while running, but several buttons on my blouse had come undone with Luc and hadn't been fixed. It provided a pretty good vantage on my bra and cleavage.

"My house is just over there," I said. "I'll just—I'll just go now."

The hand on my shoulder stayed locked where it was, but his other hand had slipped through the opening in my blouse and was tracing the shape of my breast. Great. After all the deep and traumatic revelations I'd had tonight about the cursed life of a succubus, the last thing I needed was a Nazi feeling me up.

Scratch that. There was something worse.

"Let her go."

Luc's voice rang out behind me, and I winced. I'd hoped I'd lost him in the chase, but if he had seen me coming in this direction, he could have made a pretty good guess about which path I was taking home.

"Walk away," said the officer. "This has nothing to do with you."

Luc's fists were balled up. "Let her go," he repeated. "I won't tell you again."

The officer laughed, but it was a harsh, terrible sound. "You won't tell me anything."

I tried my best to peer at Luc while still in that hard grip. "Go," I told him. "It'll be all right. I'll be okay."

"Smart girl," said the German.

Luc lunged at him, and I was shoved out of the way as the two men grappled with each other. I stared in horror. Everything happened so quickly that my brain barely had time to even register what I was seeing. Luc was strong and fast, but the other guy was huge—and had a knife. I saw it flash briefly in what light was left, and then Luc's body went rigid. The officer stepped back, jerking the blade out of Luc's stomach as he did.

I shrieked and tried to run toward him, but the Nazi's arm stopped me, grabbing hold of me once more. Luc's hands clutched at his stomach as blood flowed from it. He looked down at it in disbelief, like he was waiting for a punch line to reveal itself, and then he collapsed to the ground. I tried again to break free of my captor but couldn't. Luc's eyes gazed up at me, though his lips couldn't form any words as he lay there in that terrible agony, the life pouring out of his body.

"There," said the German officer, pulling me so that I was pressed against his chest. His knife had disappeared to wherever it had come from, and the hand that had held it—the hand that had stabbed Luc—was reaching under my shirt again. "Now there are no more distractions."

I heard Luc make a strangled sound as the officer ripped open the last of my buttons. Enough of my numbed shock wore off that I remembered I could fight back here. I could shape-shift to twice this guy's size and—

Thunk. The Nazi's head lurched forward as something struck him from behind. His hold on me released, and he fell to the ground unconscious. Bastien stood behind him holding a hat block: a heavy, rounded wooden object used for constructing hats.

"I'd know your scream anywhere," he said.

I had no time for his joking or to offer thanks. I dropped to my knees beside Luc and pulled off my blazer, frantically trying to use it to stop the bleeding. He was still conscious, and his eyes were on my face, still full of that hope and love that was so characteristic of him. Bastien knelt beside me, face solemn.

"No human medicine can fix this, Fleur," he said quietly.

"I know." I'd known as soon as I'd seen Luc fall. It was why I hadn't sent Bastien to get help. "Oh God. This can't be happening."

"It's . . . all right." Luc's words were barely audible, and I had a feeling he was choking on blood. "You're safe . . . all that matters . . ." He coughed again, and this time I did see blood near his lips.

"No, no," I said. "It wasn't worth it. It wasn't worth it. None of this should have happened!"

It was my fault. All my fault. Luc had come to save me

from the German. I'd run into the German because I'd fled from Luc. And I'd fled from Luc because I'd suddenly latched on to a moral high ground and refused to have sex with him. If I'd just given in . . . if I'd just said I'd marry him and taken him like a succubus should have, this never would have happened. We would have been lying in the grass right now, naked in each other's arms. Instead, he'd died in this alley because of me, because of my weakness. I was a succubus who'd tried to act human—and I'd done a shitty job at both.

Luc was beyond speech now. Everything was said with his eyes as he gazed at me, like I was some angel sent to carry him home. Bastien nudged me.

"Fleur, he's going to stay alive a little while. You know how long stomach wounds take. It's agony."

"I know," I growled, choking off a sob. "You don't need to tell me."

Bastien's voice was grave. "You can stop it. Ease his suffering."

I stared at Bastien incredulously. "What do you expect me to do? Go get that knife and finish him?"

He shook his head. "He's only got a little life left, Fleur. Only a little. You won't need to do much."

I didn't get it right away. When I did, I felt my eyes go wide. "No . . . I can't . . ."

"He dies regardless," said Bastien. "You can make it faster . . . sweeter . . ."

I was still shaking my head, but Bastien's words had penetrated. He was right. He was right, and I hated him because he was right. Turning from Bastien, I looked back at Luc, whose brow I'd been stroking with my hand. His gaze was still turned upward, still at me. A drop of water fell on his cheek, and I realized it was one of my tears.

"Good-bye, Luc," I said softly. It seemed like I should say a million other things to him, but I couldn't form the words. So, instead, I leaned down and brought my lips to his. I pressed against them, making full contact, though it had none of the animal passion from before. This was gentler. A whisper of a kiss.

But as Bastien had said, it didn't take much. The beautiful, silvery sweetness of his life energy flowed into me. It was just as pure and perfect as before—and it was gone quickly. I took it into me and sat up, just as Luc exhaled his last breath. The eyes that had watched me so adoringly saw nothing now. I sat up and leaned against Bastien.

"I killed him," I said, no longer holding the tears back.

"You brought him peace. You were his angel." It was an eerie echo of my earlier sentiments.

"No, this . . . I mean, before. He shouldn't have been out here. He's here because . . . because of me. If I'd slept with him, this wouldn't have happened. But I couldn't. I didn't want to hurt him . . . didn't want to taint him . . . and then this happened. . . ."

Bastien put his arm around me. "If it makes you feel better, his soul won't be going to our people."

I buried my face in his shoulder. "This is my fault. My fault . . . I should have done what I was supposed to do. I was ready to—then he asked me to marry him and—damn it. I should have done it. I should have lied. It would have been better for everyone. I don't know how this happened. . . ."

"It happened because you get too close to them," said Bastien. He was stern but trying hard to be gentle. "Men like this . . . anyone like this . . . they enchant you, Fleur. You get attached and then you get hurt."

"Or I hurt them," I murmured.

"You need to stay indifferent."

"It's getting worse," I said. "Every time, it's harder on me. I don't understand. What's happening to me? What's wrong with me?"

"Immortality," he said wisely. "Too many years."

"What do you know? You're younger than me."

Bastien helped me stand, though I was reluctant to let Luc go. "I know that you can't keep doing this. Listen to what I said: don't get attached to these good ones. No matter what you do, it won't end well."

"I won't go near the good ones at all," I said in a small voice. "No more. I'm staying away from them altogether."

Bastien's kindly mien dropped. "That's ridiculous," he scoffed. "Weren't you listening to me earlier? You can't go after immoral men for eternity. You'd get no energy. You'd have to do it every other day."

I looked down at Luc, Luc who had loved me and gotten killed for me. My fault. All my fault.

"Never again," I said. "I won't ever hurt anyone like that again."

When I returned to the box in the dark, I didn't need the Oneroi to enlighten me. All of that dream had been true—except for the last part. It had been a lie. I had continued to hurt people, over and over.

Chapter 16

Really, when you thought about it, what I was going through wasn't that much different from dying after all. They always said you saw your life flash before your eyes, and that's how it was for me. Dream after dream. I relived the most painful moments of my life, true dreams where I'd done terrible things and seen terrible things done to those I loved. More "realities" that had never happened were shown to me as well. In one, Roman's recent display of affection turned out to be a scam. It was a front to punish me for my role in the death of his sister. Only, he didn't go after me directly. He went after all my friends, mortal and immortal. I watched him kill them one by one as he ignored my pleas to just finish me off instead.

The Oneroi latched onto how I was bothered more by the suffering of those I loved than of myself. They mocked me, claiming that Roman's rampage was a vision of the future that had come through the gate of horn. I didn't believe it . . . at least, I didn't think I did. Nyx could see the future. Could they? Or were they maybe in contact with her, despite her imprisonment? My higher reasoning was giving way to paranoia as I was stripped further and further of my essence. I even began to dread the true dreams from the mortal world, the ones that showed me my friends. They were no longer a comfort; they only plunged me further into darkness. Because as the Oneroi had predicted, there seemed to be no hope of rescue in sight.

Still, I kept dreaming. . . .

* * *

Roman, Hugh, and the vampires were in a van. Peter was driving, and the clock on the dashboard read two o'clock in the morning. No one spoke in the small space, giving me no clue as to what was transpiring. Their headlights illuminated a sign along the freeway that indicated an exit for Idaho State Route 41. Idaho?

"Can you change the station?" asked Hugh. "I hate talk radio."

"Because you might learn something?" asked Peter.

"Because I'm trying to stay awake."

"It's a rule of the road: driver controls the radio."

"What rule book says that?"

"Enough," said Roman. His voice was weary, his face more so. He looked like he hadn't been sleeping much, but considering the time of night, that wasn't a surprise. He unfolded a map and then checked a piece of paper with some notes scrawled on it. "It should be the next exit."

"How'd Carter even find this guy?" asked Cody.

"Because Carter moves in mysterious ways," said Hugh. "Hard-drinking, hard-smoking mysterious ways."

"Yeah, but if he knew, why didn't he tell Jerome?"

"Because Jerome would go into blasting mode if he found out. I guess Carter was keeping it on the down-low as some sort of compassionate act. He's an angel and all."

"Oh, right." Cody seemed to have forgotten about that. It was an easy mistake.

"Jerome'll blast us too if he knows what we're doing," warned Peter.

"He's too distracted. He thinks we're just following a vampire lead."

"That's the point," said Peter. "If he finds out we lied to him—"

"He won't," interrupted Roman impatiently. "Not if we just get what we need from this guy and get out of here. This is it—take that exit."

Hugh veered off onto what hardly seemed like a road at

all. It had no businesses and only one streetlight to illuminate an intersection, just before darkness swallowed everything. Roman continued giving directions, steering them farther and farther into the countryside.

"You can't do anything to him," said Hugh, craning his head to look at Roman in the backseat. "Show any flare of power in another demon's territory, and you're dead—probably along with the rest of us."

"Do you think I'm stupid?" demanded Roman.

"Not exactly. But I do think you're short-tempered, have poor impulse control, and would do anything for Georgina."

I expected Roman to deny all of that—or at least the last part—but he said nothing. Silence fell again until Roman at last pointed to a narrow gravel driveway. It was so hard to see that Peter drove past it, squealed the brakes, and backed up. They parked near the driveway's end and began walking up it. I saw then that the back of the van had blacked-out windows, and it was a safe bet that the vampires' coffins were likely back there in case daytime travel was required. Out here in the middle of nowhere, stars clustered the sky, and night insects rained down a symphony of chatter. The faint outline of a house appeared. No lights were on within.

"Can we do it SWAT team style?" asked Cody eagerly. "Surround the house and swoop in?"

"I don't think that's necessary," said Roman. He gave the door a sharp kick. It shuddered but didn't come close to breaking apart action-movie style. Keeping his nephilim powers in check meant he had the same abilities as a human.

Peter sighed. "Let me." He took Roman's place, repeated the kick, and this time the door did burst in and break apart. With their goofy attitudes, it was easy to forget sometimes that both Cody and Peter had super fast reflexes and enhanced strength. Peter stepped back, brushing splinters off his pants.

The foursome entered, and a light turned on in the back of the house.

"What the hell?" a voice demanded.

What the hell, indeed. Dante entered the room.

He took one look at my friends and said, "Oh, shit."

Then he bolted back toward the room he'd come from, no doubt heading for a window. He was too slow, though. In a flash, Cody had Dante by the scruff of his shirt and dragged him back to the living room, shoving my ex-boyfriend into a chair. Dante immediately started to rise, noticed how my friends had closed rank around him, and then thought better of it.

Dante sighed. "Well, I knew this had to happen some day. Why didn't your boss come himself?" He peered at Roman. "And haven't I seen you somewhere?" Dante had seen Roman on a beach when we rescued Jerome from the summoning. There'd been a fair amount of chaos, so I wasn't surprised Dante's memory was sketchy—especially since he'd been beaten up by a demon.

"We're not here because of Jerome," snapped Hugh. Then, he reconsidered. "Well, we are, but not for the reasons you think."

"Answer our questions, and you might live another day," said Peter. Apparently, the action-movie theme was still going strong.

"Where's Georgina?" demanded Roman. It was interesting that every time my immortal posse interrogated someone, they phrased the question that way first, instead of, "Do you know where Georgina is?" When you worked for Hell, everyone was guilty until proven innocent.

Dante's face lost some of its fear and took on its usual cynical look. He tossed messy black hair out of his face. "In Seattle, sleeping with that fucking writer."

"No," said Roman. "She's not."

"She's not what? In Seattle or sleeping with the writer?" Dante arched an eyebrow. "And who *are* you exactly?"

"The muscle," said Hugh dryly. "Georgina's gone. Vanished. And if anyone's got reason to make her disappear"— he paused and glanced uneasily at Roman—"it's you."

"I'm not the kind of magician that pulls rabbits out of my

hat. Or makes them disappear." Dante was growing more and more confident, now that he knew Jerome wasn't going to send him to the torture pits of Hell. "If you can't find her, ask your archdemon. Unless he's been summoned again, he'll know."

"He doesn't," said Cody. "But maybe you already knew that."

Dante rolled his eyes. "You think I'm going to go anywhere near Seattle when there's a price on my head? Do you think I'm hiding out in the fucking sticks because I want to? The best I can do is sell charms and fake fortunes to tourists in Coeur d'Alene."

"Carter should have come with us," said Hugh in exasperation. "He should have known that too after sending us here."

Dante stiffened, his arrogance faltering. "That angel knows where I am? Then Jerome has to know."

"He's keeping it from Jerome. For now." Peter was still using that melodramatic voice. "That can change if you don't help us."

"I don't know where she fucking is, okay? I told you: I can't make a succubus disappear."

Roman's hand closed around Dante's neck in a fair approximation of Jerome. Even without supernatural abilities, Roman was still strong. "You've worked with immortals before. You could do it again and have them do the dirty work."

"I show my face to any immortal, and I'm a dead man," choked Dante. Roman fixed Dante with a dark glare that reminded me of the time Roman had tried to kill me. And when he *had* killed me in a recent Oneroi dream. At last, Roman let go. Rubbing his neck, a puzzled Dante asked again, "Who *are* you?"

Cody glanced at the others. "Do you think he's lying?"

"Wouldn't surprise me," said Hugh. He crossed his arms across his broad chest. "But maybe you can be useful. What *could* make a succubus disappear?"

"What'll you give me for helping you?" asked Dante slyly. Yes, that was my ex. Always looking for an advantage.

"We won't call Jerome," growled Peter. This time, the anger in his voice was not faux movie style. It was real, again a reminder that at the end of the day, he really was a vampire who could break necks easily.

This sobered Dante up. "Fine. Not that I care what the fuck happens to her. How did she disappear?"

Again, the story was recounted, something that was beginning to depress me—largely because everyone seemed to emphasize just how depressed and miserable my life was.

"It's a lure," said Dante with certainty.

"We know that," said Roman. "Erik told us."

Dante scowled at the mention of his nemesis. "Of course he did. It's a wonder you need me with his almighty wisdom at your disposal."

"What would lure her?" said Peter, no doubt interrupting Dante from asking again who Roman was.

"All sorts of things," said Dante. "Anything could create a lure, but visions like that would most likely be tied to dreams. Did you guys lose Nyx again?"

"No," said Hugh.

Dante shrugged. "Then look for something else that can control dreams, maybe try a—"

I stood in the village I'd grown up in.

The transition was so abrupt that I was dizzy for a moment. There hadn't been a transition, no fragmenting of the image or a fade to black. It had been a quick movie cut. A bad editing job.

I stared around, seeing again the place that had caused me so much torment. I wondered what else the Oneroi had to show me here and why I'd come here so suddenly. I'd already relived the false wedding accusations. At one point, they'd even had me dream the true story of how my infidelity had led to me selling my soul. I was probably now in store for some new contrived horror. The world spun around me, the buildings and people moving around in rough-spun clothes dizzying me.

"Are you all right?" a voice asked.

Turning around, the scenery settled a bit and I found myself looking into the face of an ancient man. Bushy eyebrows stretched across a heavily lined brow, nearly obscuring dark brown eyes.

"Yes . . . I'm fine." I frowned and did a double take. "Gaius?"

Those eyebrows rose. "Have we met?"

I stared, unable to speak for a moment. I'd known Gaius since the time I could walk. He was a blacksmith, the brawniness of his arms proving as much. But he'd been young the last time I'd seen him, a man in his prime. With no control, words spilled off my lips, words I'd spoken before when I'd lived this event the first time. This was a true memory. So far.

"We met a very long time ago," I said.

He chuckled. "Girl, I'd remember you. And 'a very long time ago' could only have been a few years for you."

I became aware of my body, knowing what I looked like even without a mirror. I had shape-shifted just before entering the village, taking on a form I had sworn I would never, ever wear again. And, in fact, after this day, I never would wear it again. I was in my original body: fifteen-year-old Letha, too tall with thick, tangled black hair. I'd come here to find out something. Something I had to know.

I gave Gaius a weak nod. My old self had been as shocked as my current self at what time had done to him. How long since I'd become a succubus and left my village? Thirty years ago?

"Can you tell me . . . is there a man here—a fisherman—named Marthanes? Does his family still live here?"

"Sure," he said. "Same house they've always been in, out past the—"

"I know where it is," I said quickly.

He shrugged, not minding my interruption. "He's probably down at the bay, though. He's too old to still be working but swears his sons-in-law can't get by without him."

Sons-in-law. Of course. My sisters would have gotten married long ago.

"Thanks," I said. I began to walk away. "It was nice seeing you again." He gave me a puzzled look but said nothing more.

I walked toward the bay, where the water glowed with such a vivid, teal-tinged blue that it seemed to be some Technicolor vision. Surely nothing in nature could produce such beauty. Longing and nostalgia welled up within my watching self.

The town was busy at midday, and I recognized more faces than I expected. Children I'd known grown to adulthood, adults I'd known now in their golden years. The waterfront was just as busy, with ships loading and unloading goods that made commerce in the Mediterranean boom. It took me a while to find my father, and here, I earned more looks than I had in the village. Women were rare in this district, choosing to avoid the rough sailors and workers. I located my father largely because of his voice, shouting orders just as he had in my youth.

"Are you trying to cost me a fortune? What do you do out there all day? My granddaughter could catch this many fish wading by the beach!"

He was yelling at a man I didn't know, his face sheepish and cowed as he displayed what must have been today's meager catch. I wondered if this was one of my sisters' husbands. The man promised to do better and then scurried away.

"Fa—Marthanes?"

My father turned at my approach, and I tried not to gasp. Like Gaius, the years had carved away Marthanes the fisherman as well. How old would he be now? Sixties? Seventies? Time had grown blurred since I became immortal.

"What do you want?" he snapped. "I've got no use for prostitutes anymore. Go down to Claudius if you're looking for business. He hasn't slept with his own wife in ten years. Not that I blame him. That woman's a harpy."

Age might have grayed and thinned out his hair, lines might have creased his face . . . but my father's tongue was still the same.

"N-no. That's not why I'm here. I met you . . . a few years ago."

He frowned, looking me up and down. "Never seen you in my life. Pretty sure I'd remember someone as tall as you."

As a succubus, I could change into any man's fantasy, taking on the shape of a woman whose beauty transcended words. Yet, even with that ability, the old remarks about my height still stung.

"Well, I remember you." Seeing his eyes shift impatiently to his workers, I asked, "Do you know a musician named Kyriakos? He'd be my age—er, about thirty years older than me. He used to live south of town."

My father snorted. "*That* Kyriakos? He's no musician. He took over his father's business when he died. Does okay with it, even though the rates he demands for my fish are ridiculous."

"Does he still live in his same house?"

"You mean his father's house? Yes. Like you said, in the south." My father's restlessness was palpable now. He didn't know me. He had no use for me.

"Thank you," I said. I was about to tell him it was nice to see him, as I had Gaius, but my father was gone before I could.

With a heavy heart, I walked back through town but instead of heading south, I took a detour to my old home, wondering what I'd discover. What I found was my mother, hanging clothing outside, humming as she did. Off to the house's side a middle-aged woman dug herbs out of the ground. It took me a few moments to recognize her as my younger sister.

My mother's face was different, but her kind eyes were still the same as she gave me directions to a place I already knew. My sister glanced up and watched a moment, then returned to her work. Neither recognized me. Just like with my father, I was a brief interruption to their day.

I'd known this would happen. It was what I'd sold my soul for. My contract with Hell had erased all memories of me from everyone who had ever known me. The Oneroi had shown me a lie on my wedding day. I'd been a virgin, faithful to Kyriakos. But a couple years later, weakness had struck me. I'd betrayed him, and it had devastated him more than anyone could have imagined. He'd wanted to kill himself over the heartache, and only my bargain had saved him. That was the truth.

Still . . . some part of me had thought maybe, just *maybe* someone might recognize me. Just the faintest spark of remembrance.

Kyriakos could have been down near my father, overseeing his fleet, but something told me he'd be doing administrative tasks, not manual labor. My hunch was correct. Before I'd become a succubus, Kyriakos and I had had our own house. He must have moved back to his family's home after Hell erased his memories.

I braced myself to meet the lady of the house, the woman Kyriakos must have undoubtedly married. But when he came out to see who was visiting him, I found him alone. Seeing him made my heart stop. He too had been touched by age, but he was still young enough that the lines were few. Only the faintest of gray graced his hair, and like my mother, his eyes were the same. Dark and wonderful and full of goodness.

"Do you need help?" he asked, voice friendly and curious.

For a moment, I couldn't speak. I was drunk from seeing him, filled with a mix of love and pain. I wished so badly that I had stayed with him, that I had never committed such sins. I wished I didn't wear this youthful face. I should have grown old with him. My ability to conceive children had seemed sketchy at the time, but maybe we would have eventually had a family.

Just like with everyone else, I claimed to need directions, stammering out the first random place I could think of. He described the way in detail, though I already knew it.

"Do you want me to escort you there? This is a safe area . . . but you never know."

I smiled but felt no joy. The same Kyriakos. Infinitely kind to others, even a stranger. "I'll be fine. I don't want to take you from your work." I hesitated. "We met . . . a few years ago."

"Did we?"

He studied me, apparently searching for the memory. His eyes remained blank, though. No trace of recognition. I was a stranger. I had never existed for him. I wondered if he'd even remember me when I left here.

He shook his head, sounding sincerely apologetic. "I'm sorry. I don't recall it. . . ." He was waiting for my name.

"Letha." The word burned on my lips. Like this shape, the name was dead to me. Only Hell ever used it.

"I'm sorry," he said again.

"It's okay. Maybe I'm wrong. I thought . . . I thought you were a musician." When we'd been married, he worked for his father but had hopes of giving that up and playing music full-time.

Kyriakos chuckled. "Only as a hobby. Most of my days are hunched over numbers."

The loss of his ambition made me almost as sad as his lack of memory. "Well . . . your wife must be glad to have you home."

"Not married, I'm afraid." He was still smiling. "My sister keeps house for me when she's around."

"Not married?" I asked incredulously. "But why? At your age . . ." I blushed, realizing how rude I sounded. "I'm sorry."

He wasn't offended. "At *your* age, marriage is all girls think about, huh? You probably have a dozen suitors with as pretty as you are." Typical. Few had found me pretty while mortal; he had always believed me beautiful. "I just never found the right woman. I'd rather be alone than spend my life with the wrong person." A dreamy, sad look filled his features, and then he shook his head and laughed. It was an uneasy laugh. "Anyway, you don't want to hear some old man babbling about romantic nonsense. Are you sure you don't want me to show you the way?"

"No, no . . . I think I know where it's at now. Thank you."
I started to turn away and then paused. "Kyriakos . . . are
you . . . are you happy?"

This question from someone less than half his age caught
him by surprise. And I was surprised he answered. "Happy?
Well . . . content, I guess. I have a good life. Better than most.
A very good life, really. Sometimes I wonder . . ."

My breath caught. "Wonder what?"

"Nothing," he said, giving me another good-natured smile.
"More nonsense. Yes, Letha. I'm happy. Why do you want to
know?"

"Nonsense of my own," I murmured. "And you're sure
you don't remember me?"

I had my answer before I spoke. No. Those eyes had never
laid sight on me before. I was just an odd, passing girl. I was
no one.

"I'm sorry, I don't." He winked. "But I'll remember you
now."

Somehow, I doubted it. Leaving him, I felt my heart break.
Really, my heart was breaking all the time. You'd think it
could only happen once. This was what I'd wanted. What I'd
gambled eternity for. Kyriakos was happy. I'd saved him
and should be happy in return. Yet, I felt unhappier than I
had since becoming a succubus. I decided at that moment I'd
never use Letha's shape or name again. I wanted to wipe her
from my mind too. . . .

"It's so easy with you," hissed the Oneroi. It was Two, I
thought. I was back in the box. "We don't even need the
ivory gate."

I was so scarred from that memory of Kyriakos, by the
truth of what it really meant to be erased from someone's
life, that I was inclined to agree with Two. Then, a tiny spark
within me glimmered just a bit. I studied the two Oneroi
carefully.

"What was the other dream?" I asked. "Before the one
about my husband? Why didn't you let it finish?"

"It did finish," said One. Their blue, blue eyes were the same, revealing nothing.

"It didn't," I argued. "You cut it off. It didn't go the way you planned, did it? My friends found out something from Dante—something you didn't want them to know."

"They found nothing," Two replied. "It was a lie. We gave you false hope, hope that will turn to ashes when you find yourself spending the rest of eternity here."

"You're the lie," I said. The spark within my ragged, worn body flared just a little more. "The dream was true."

One continued the denial. "The only truth is that you can't tell the difference. And that there is no hope."

"You're lying," I said, but as those cold sets of eyes surveyed me, my spark wavered. Uncertainty spread within me. I'd been through so much, a mental rape of sorts, that I questioned once more if I trusted myself. My words were bold, but I no longer knew if I could believe them.

Two smiled, able to see into my mind. "Dream," he said.

Chapter 17

My initial time with the Oneroi had been a mix of true and false dreams. As time went on—and I really had no way of saying how much of it did go on—the majority of them seemed to be true ones. They were either visitations of awful memories or more glimpses into my current life, meant to demoralize me and make me homesick.

I was still torn apart, still feeling more animal than human or succubus or . . . whatever. Yet, the fleeting pieces of rationality within me wondered at the sudden lack of handcrafted visions. One might argue the Oneroi were being lazy. They were just giving me recycled material, and whenever I did see my friends in the world, I got the impression that it was less a dream and more like the Oneroi flipping me onto a TV channel to make sure I stayed distracted and gave them something to feed off of. It almost felt like they were trying to keep me busy because . . . well, *they* were busy. But why? What had happened? What had Dante been about to tell Roman and the others? Was it enough to make the Oneroi pull some of their attention from me? Or were these simply more mind games meant to leave me in turmoil?

I kept hoping I'd see a follow-up to what had happened with Dante, but the Oneroi had other parts of the life I'd left behind to show me. Or, well, parts I hadn't left behind. Simone was still impersonating me, and the Oneroi wanted me to know.

Adding insult to injury, she was helping Maddie and Seth

with the wedding. The three of them were out cake shopping, and honestly, I was almost more surprised to find Seth there than I was Simone in her disguise. He'd pretty much kept away from the wedding planning as much as possible, using the pretense that he was no good at decisions and was happy to let Maddie run things the way she wanted.

I didn't doubt the first part of what he said but wondered about the second. In my heart of hearts, the one that believed he was still in love with me, I secretly hoped he was passing it to Maddie just because he was indifferent to it all. I wanted to believe that he really didn't care about the planning because he didn't care about the wedding.

It was clear, however, that I cared. Or rather—Simone cared. Considering my reluctance at dress shopping, you would have thought Maddie might notice the sudden increase in zeal. Nope. Maddie was too caught up in her own bubble of happiness and welcomed "my" assistance.

So, the three of them set off on a cake adventure, visiting all the bakeries Maddie had compiled and ranked on a list pulled from hours of Internet research.

"You want it creamy," said Simone, licking icing off her fingers at a bakery in Belltown. Actually, it was more like sucking. "This is a little too sugary." The threesome sat at a table where they had been provided with a plate of samples.

"That's the point," said Maddie. She was eating a bite-size piece of chocolate cake in a much less pornographic way. "Mega sugar rush."

"Yeah, but if you get too much sugar, it just tastes grainy. You want it to slide right over your lips." She turned to Seth. "Don't you think so?"

Seth had taken a bite out of a piece of marble cake. "It *is* kind of grainy."

Simone gave him a knowing smile, one that seemed to say, *See? I know you better than anyone else in the world.*

Seth held her eyes for a moment, but his expression was unreadable. He turned toward Maddie. "But we can do whatever you want."

"No, no," she said, not sounding too disappointed. "This is for both of us. I want it to be something you like too."

Seth gave her a mischievous smile. "Does it matter? It all gets shoved in the face anyway."

Maddie's eyes went wide. "No, it doesn't! Don't even think about doing that."

"Guess you won't know until the time comes, huh?" His smile had grown.

Seeing him play with her made me (figuratively) squirm, but I took comfort in seeing a flash of annoyance in Simone's eyes. Maddie was succeeding where Simone couldn't. That was how it should be . . . or was it? Maddie's unwitting triumph over Simone meant she had . . . well, triumphed over *me*. Or had she? Simone looked like me but wasn't truly me. Damn. This was all so confusing.

"Seth wouldn't do that," said Simone, resting her hand on his shoulder in what was supposed to be a friendly way. Maddie couldn't see it from her vantage, but Simone's fingers lightly brushed the back of his neck. "Not if he wants a good honeymoon."

She spoke lightly, but there was a sly undertone there. Having her sex life brought up in public made Maddie blush. Seth had shifted uncomfortably, but the reason was unclear. Simone's fingers? The mention of sex? Maybe both. Simone removed her hand, seeming innocent to all the world, except Seth and me.

Maddie seemed eager to change the subject from the romantic goings-on of a honeymoon. "I think you should at least pick the cake flavor," she said. "I'm choosing so much else."

"I don't know," said Seth. He still seemed uncomfortable. "I don't care if you do it."

"Yeah, but she wants you to," said Simone. "Come on, make one firm decision here. You can't go wrong. Maddie'll eat anything you pick."

Loaded statement. Neither Seth nor Maddie acted as though

they read anything into it, but I had a feeling Simone had intended it as a reference to Maddie's very buxom figure.

"Exactly," said Maddie. "What's your favorite flavor?"

"I bet I can guess," said Simone. "Chocolate."

"Strawberry," said Maddie.

Losers. It was vanilla.

"Vanilla," said Seth.

Maddie groaned. "Naturally. Well, there's one decision made." She rose from the table. "Let's try a few other places and get the rest of this taken care of. Not much left after this." They reached the door, and Maddie stopped to glance at Simone. "Oh, hey. Will you do me a favor? Will you take Seth tux shopping?"

"What?" asked Seth. No neutral face now. He was shocked.

Maddie grinned. "If you don't have a keeper, you'll show up at the church in a Billy Idol T-shirt. And it's bad luck if I go with you."

"I thought that was just for the bride," said Seth.

"I want to be surprised," Maddie countered.

"Of course I'll go," said Simone, putting her arm around Seth again in that "friendly" way.

Maddie beamed, and the bakery faded away . . .

. . . transforming into Erik's store.

Erik sat at a small table with Jerome and Roman, and—so help me—they were drinking tea. Even Jerome. Roman was visible, which made me think Jerome must have decided they no longer needed to fear the eyes of higher powers who might wonder why my "human" roommate kept tagging along with Seattle's archdemon.

Erik was tapping his tea cup thoughtfully. "If your theory is right, it would explain a lot." These words were directed at Roman. "The dream quality of the visions. Mr. Jerome's complete inability to find her."

Jerome's slightly arched eyebrow was the only indication of his displeasure over the word "inability."

Erik continued, eyes on his cup as he pondered it all. "And

you're right . . . of all the creatures you suggested, Oneroi or Morphean demons make the most sense."

Oh! I thought in triumph to the Oneroi. *How do you like that, bitches? My friends are on to you.* No response came. No dissolving of the dream, as I would have expected.

"But why her?" asked Roman irritably. I had a feeling he'd taken credit for the dream idea, shielding Dante from Jerome's wrath. "Why a succubus? Don't they only care about human dreams?"

"They're tied to Nyx," pointed out Erik. Oh, yes. My friends were smart. Smarter than Nancy Drew and the Hardy Boys put together. Maybe even Matlock too.

"The 'why' is irrelevant," said Jerome, speaking at last. "Whether it's Oneroi or Morpheans is also irrelevant. If something's taken her to the world of dreams, she's completely inaccessible."

Roman frowned. "Why? Can't you just go in there and pull her out now that you know?"

Jerome gave his son a smile that almost, *almost* seemed genuinely amused. "You're half-human, and it shows. Greater immortals can't go there. We don't dream. Only humans do. The way is barred to us."

"Because you have no hopes or imaginings of what might be," said Erik. His manner and tone clearly indicated he believed such a thing to be a failing for angels and demons. "You need a soul to dream."

"Well, if I'm half-human, then I'll go there," said Roman obstinately, cutting off any retort Jerome might have given. "I dream. So I can enter, right? And I can take on whatever's there." There was so much determination in his voice that I half believed he could take on an army of Oneroi right now.

"You have no idea what you're talking about," said Jerome. "Clearly. Do you have any idea what the dream world is like?"

"Do *you?*" asked Roman dryly. "I thought you couldn't go there."

"Dreams are what fuel human existence. Dreams of power, love, revenge, redemption . . . the dreams of mankind are vast, uncountable. Humans dream both waking and asleep. Those hopes and fears are what put them at risk—they gamble their lives and souls on dreams. You go into the world of dreams, and it's like stepping into a blizzard. Every snowflake is some human imagining flitting by so quickly, you can't even see it. All you see is a blur, a tangle of longings and chaos. If Georgina is there, she is one of those snowflakes. You would never find her soul."

Heavy silence fell.

Finally, Roman said, "That was like poetry, Dad."

"But he's correct," Erik told Roman.

More silence.

Roman glanced between the two of them incredulously. "So that's it? It's hopeless? You're giving up without even trying to find her?"

"Trying is hopeless," said Jerome. Demons might not dream the way humans did, but I suspected even he could picture what his superiors would do when they found out he'd lost a succubus. "Human magic could access the world of dreams, but it'd do no good." He glanced at Erik, who nodded.

"Someone lost among all that couldn't be called back. Not even the strongest ritual could do it. Her soul would never hear anything we could muster."

Roman's face was a mixture of emotions. Anger. Disbelief. And . . . resignation. That didn't surprise me. Jerome's face did, however. He had stiffened at Erik's words, a spark of insight flashing in those cold, dark eyes.

"But you *could* do the ritual, correct?" he asked Erik. "You're human. You're strong enough to open the way."

Erik eyed him warily. "Yes . . . but by your own admission, it would achieve nothing. The connection you had to her was theoretically strong enough to possibly summon her back, but you can't enter. All we'd have is a useless doorway."

Jerome stood up abruptly. He glanced at Roman. "Find your own way home." The demon vanished with a showy poof of smoke.

* * *

And I vanished back into the Oneroi's prison. They stood there in the dark, glowing from what they'd taken from me. In dreams, though I suffered, I never felt the horrific effects they caused until I returned from them. That was when the agony, energy loss, and confusion hit me. Yet, this time, I wasn't completely lost to despair.

"You were wrong," I said. I tried to put some smugness in my voice, but it came out hoarse from my exhaustion. Good God. I was so, so tired. I guess dreaming didn't necessarily mean sleeping. "My friends have figured it out. They know where I am."

As always, One and Two were nearly impossible to read. "What makes you think that was a true dream?"

Excellent question. "Gut instinct," I said.

"You believe you can trust it?" asked One. "After all this time? After so many dreams? How can you tell what's real and unreal?"

I couldn't. I knew when the memories were true—for now—but the "real world" scenes were harder. Maybe it wasn't my gut so much as my blind optimism that believed what I'd just seen was real.

Two guessed my thoughts. "You hope. And we've fed that hope, making you think you have a chance. So you will wait. And wait. And wait."

"It was real," I said firmly, as though that would make it so.

"Even if it was," said One, "it meant nothing. You saw for yourself. There is no way to bring you back."

"Maybe that was the lie," I said. "Maybe the rest was true. You mixed it. They figured out where I was, but you didn't show me the part where they learned how to rescue me. They're going to do that ritual."

"They will fail. Nothing can pull your soul from here."

"You're wrong." I didn't even really know what I was saying. My essence felt like it was tearing apart, and really, the only thing I knew to do was to keep contradicting them.

"And you are naive. You always have been. Lesser immortals carry that weakness over from their human days, and you're one of the worst. Our mother nearly used your weakness to free herself from the angels. Now it will be your downfall."

"What do you mean Nyx almost used it?"

The Oneroi exchanged glances—very, very pleased ones. "Your dream. Your fantasy," explained Two. "The one she promised to show you if you freed her. You wanted so badly to believe it was possible, that you nearly gave in."

For a moment, I didn't see them or that perpetual blackness. I was in a dream of my own creation, not theirs. The dream Nyx had sent to me over and over had been one of my future, with a home and a child—and a man. A man I loved whose identity remained a mystery. Nyx had never shown me the ending. Never shown me the man in the dream.

"You are so full of shit," I said. "You claim Nyx shows the truth—the future. But how could that vision have been true if I'm also supposed to be locked here for all eternity? They can't both be true."

"The future is always changing," said One. "That was true when she showed it to you. Your path shifted."

"Oh, come on! What's the point of having a vision of the future if it can change at any moment? That's not a truth or a lie. That's a guess. And I never believed her anyway. What she showed me was impossible—even if I wasn't here with you two assholes."

"You will never know if it was," said Two. Then, he reconsidered. "Actually it *was* possible, but you will live with the knowledge that it's a future that's been taken from you."

"You can't take what I never had," I growled. "Succubi can't have children. I could never have that kind of life."

What I didn't add was that one startling thing had come from the dream. In it, I'd had two cats. At the time, I'd only had one—Aubrey. Not long after, I'd found Godiva, who was the other cat in the dream. Coincidence? Or had I truly been on the path to that future, only to have it ripped from me now? As always, the Oneroi could see into my heart and knew what I was thinking.

"Do you want to see?" asked One.

"See what?"

"The man," said Two. "The man in the dream."

Chapter 18

It started before I could stop it.

I stood in a kitchen, in one of those dreams where I was both watching me and feeling me. The kitchen was bright and modern, far larger than anything I could imagine a non-cook like me needing. My dream-self stood at the sink, arms elbow deep in sudsy water that smelled like oranges. I was hand-washing dishes and kind of doing a half-ass job at it but was too happy to notice. On the floor, an actual dish-washer lay in pieces, thus explaining the need for manual labor.

From another room, the sounds of "Sweet Home Alabama" carried to my ears. I hummed along as I washed. I was content, filled with a joy so utterly perfect, I could barely grasp it after everything else that had happened in my life—particularly after this imprisonment with the Oneroi. After humming a few more bars, I set a wet cup on the counter and turned around to peek into the living room beyond me.

A little girl sat in there, about two years old. She was on a blanket, surrounded by stuffed animals and other toys. She clutched a plush giraffe in her hands. It rattled when she shook it. As though sensing my gaze, she looked up.

She had plump cheeks that hadn't quite lost their baby fat. Wispy, light brown curls covered her head, and her hazel eyes were large and framed with dark lashes. She was adorable. Behind her on the couch, Aubrey lay curled up in a tight little ball. Godiva lay beside her.

A delighted smile spread over the little girl's face, creating a dimple in one cheek. A powerful wave of love and joy spread through me, emotions that my raw and aching real self barely allowed to come through. Just like the first time I'd dreamed this dream, I knew with certainty—*absolute certainty*—that this girl was my daughter.

After a few more moments, I returned to my dishes, though I wanted nothing more than to go back to the living room. Damned manual labor. Neither my dream self nor my waking self could get enough of the girl. I wanted to drink her in. I could have watched her forever, taking in those long-lashed eyes and wispy curls.

Unable to resist—and bored with washing dishes—I finally gave in and glanced back again. The girl was gone. I pulled my hands out of the water, just in time to hear a thump and a crash. The sound of crying followed.

I sprinted out of the kitchen. Aubrey and Godiva jerked their heads up, surprised at my sudden movement. On the other side of the living room, my daughter sat on the floor beside an end table with sharp corners, a small hand pressed to her forehead. Tears streamed down her checks as she wailed.

In a flash, I was on my knees, wrapping her up in a tight embrace. Watching and feeling this dream, I wanted to weep as well over the feel of that soft, warm body in my arms. I rocked the girl, murmuring soothing, nonsensical words as I brushed my lips against the silken hair. Eventually, her sobs stopped, and she rested her head against my chest, content to simply be loved and rocked. We sat like that for another happy minute or so, and then, distantly, I heard the sound of a car's engine. I lifted my head.

"You hear that?" I asked. "Daddy's home."

Mirrored excitement showed on the girl's face as I stood up, still holding her and balancing her on my hip. It was an act of some coordination, considering how small I was.

We walked to the front door and stepped outside onto a porch. It was nighttime, all quiet darkness save for a small light hanging overhead. It shone onto a long stretch of unbroken white snow on the lawn and the driveway. All around, more snow fell in a steady stream. I didn't recognize the place, but it certainly wasn't Seattle. That much snow would have sent the city into a panic, putting everyone on Armageddon alert. My daughter and I were perfectly at ease, barely noticing the snow. Wherever we were, this weather was a common occurrence.

Down the driveway, the car I had heard had already parked. My heart swelled with happiness. A man stood behind it, a nondescript dark figure in the faint lighting. He took out a rolling suitcase and slammed the trunk shut. The little girl clasped her hands in excitement, and I waved my own hand in greeting. The man returned the wave as he walked toward the house. It was too dark, and I couldn't see him yet.

His face. I *had* to see his face. We were so close. This was where the dream had stopped before, denying me its conclusion. Some part of me was certain this was a trick too—that the Oneroi were going to do what Nyx had done and end the dream.

They didn't.

The man continued walking toward us, and at last, the porch light illuminated his features.

It was Seth.

Lacy snowflakes rested in his messy hair, and I could make out some wacky T-shirt underneath his heavy woolen trench coat. He left the suitcase by the stairs and sprinted up them to get to us that much more quickly.

His arms encircled us, and both my daughter and I snuggled against him. It might have been freezing elsewhere, but our little circle held all the warmth in the world.

"My girls," he murmured. He took one of his gloves off and ran his hand over the fine silk of our daughter's hair. He brushed a kiss against her forehead and then leaned toward me. Our lips met in a soft kiss, and when we pulled away, I could see mist in the air from the warmth of his mouth. He hugged us tighter.

I sighed happily. "Don't leave anymore," I said. "Don't do any more traveling."

He laughed quietly and gave me another kiss, this time on my cheek. "I'll see what I can do. If it was up to me, I'd never leave."

But the dream left, shattering like pieces of glass that were then swept away by a broom. Whereas before I'd counted the seconds for these dreams to go away, this time I wanted to cling to it. The hands I didn't have in this insubstantial form longed to grasp those shards, bloodying my flesh, if only to have a few more moments of that perfect, content bliss my dream-self had held.

But it was gone. I was empty.

For a long time, I simply couldn't get over the dream's loss. I was a tangle of emotions: hurt and anger and longing and incompleteness. It was all feeling, no thought. When coherency began to return, even it was a jumble. Seth. Seth was the man in the dream? Of course he was. Hadn't I felt it from almost the first time we met? Hadn't I often said he was like a piece of my soul? Hadn't I felt like something was missing when we'd split up?

Then, all the doubt that the Oneroi had been so good at instilling in me began to descend. It couldn't be Seth. I couldn't be with a mortal, not in any real capacity. I certainly couldn't have a child with one, and anyway, Seth was marrying someone else. This was a trick. Another lie. Everything here was a lie, meant to continue the torment the Oneroi thought I deserved.

"That can't happen," I said. The words were hard. And hadn't I already said them earlier? Circles, circles. My life was repeating itself over and over. "None of that could ever happen."

"No," agreed Two. "Not anymore. Your future shifted."

"That was *never* my future. You lie. Nyx lied. There's no truth anywhere."

"*This* is truth," said One.

Another dream. A true dream? *No, no.* The part of me

that was starting to lose it swore up and down that it couldn't be true. *There's no truth anywhere.*

I was in the mundane human world again, with Seth and Simone-as-Georgina. They were at a tuxedo shop, browsing suits, and I futilely racked my brain to figure this out. Maddie had requested they go shopping . . . yet, surely it hadn't happened that day. Or had it? Was this another day? How much time had passed? I couldn't tell if these dreams lasted a second or a lifetime. The sky outside was deepening to twilight, so maybe it was the same day.

"You don't have to wear a bow tie," said Simone, studying a well-dressed mannequin. She herself was dressed magnificently, in a tight dress that was an orange reminiscent of autumn leaves. It was short, of course, and emphasized my breasts as much as was decently possible—maybe more so. Bronze high heels completed the look. It was too fancy for tux shopping, but it looked great on her. Me. Us. Whatever.

Seth wandered over to stand beside her, studying the suit. If there hadn't been a salesman straightening a display near the door, I had a feeling Seth would have made a run for it.

"It's more traditional," said Seth. "I think that's what Maddie wants."

Simone scoffed. "So? What about what you want?" She took a step toward him. "You can't just sit by and let others tell you what to do! You have your own needs. Your own wants. You can't be passive here."

There was passion in her words, a conviction that even I couldn't help but admire. It was the kind of speech that rallied people to your cause—but like everything else she'd said lately, there was this sexual subtext laced within it. He stared at her for a few seconds, as impressed as I was, but finally looked away. He also took a step back.

"Maybe. But I don't really feel like my life currently hinges on whether I choose a bow tie or a regular tie. I think I should save my heroic moments for something a little bigger." He wandered off to look at another suit and didn't see the scowl on her face that I did.

Soon, she had that sweet smile on again and was back by his side—very close to his side—while they examined cuts, colors, and all the myriad details that went into planning a lifelong commitment. The salesman couldn't stay away, of course, and finally swooped in to offer his assistance.

"This jacket would be very flattering with your build," he told Seth. "It comes in black and gray, as well as a few others—so it would definitely complement your dress." That last part was directed to Simone. She laughed merrily. It was nails on a chalkboard to me.

"Oh, we're not getting married." She patted Seth's arm. "We're just good friends. I'm helping out."

Seth moved away, escaping the arm, and suddenly seemed very interested in trying on the jacket. The salesman found Seth's size, gushed with compliments, and then left the two of them to mull it over.

"It looks great," said Simone, coming to stand right in front of him. I couldn't see any space between them. She casually straightened the jacket's lapel, not that it needed it. "Fits you like a glove."

Seth grabbed hold of her hands, pushed them away, and then backed off himself. "You need to stop this," he said, lowering his voice so others wouldn't hear.

"Stop what?" asked Simone.

"You know what! The innuendoes. The touching. All of it. You can't keep doing it."

Simone took a step closer, putting her hands on her hips. Her voice was soft as well, but it was more of a purr. What made it especially irritating was that, really, it was *my* voice. "Why? Because you don't like it? Come on, Seth. How much longer are you going to keep fooling yourself? You know you still want me. This scam of a wedding isn't going to change that. What we had . . . what we *have* is too powerful. I see the way you look at me—and you don't look at *her* that way. You say I've got to stop? No. You're the one that needs to stop this wedding. End it with her. Or if you don't have the guts, then let us be together again. At the very least—just one more night. I want to feel you again, feel you in me. And I know you do too."

I was aghast at the boldness. I couldn't believe what that bitch had tried to do. Impersonating me was bad enough, but now blatantly trying to lure Seth into her bed? Unforgiveable. I expected Seth to be outraged as well, but his face was the picture of calm.

He took off the jacket and set it on a counter. "I don't know who you are, but stay away from me. Do not speak to me again—or Maddie." There was a stern, warning tone in his words, that anger I rarely ever heard from him.

For once, Simone faltered. "What are you talking about?"

"You aren't Georgina," he said. "I should've listened when my niece first told me. Georgina would never do this, no matter how she felt. Georgina wouldn't openly try to break up her friend's wedding. She wouldn't betray Maddie."

Simone's eyes flashed with anger. "Really? Then how exactly would you classify your little spring fling?" I wasn't surprised she knew about that. Everyone in my hellish circle had figured it out when Seth's soul darkened.

His smile was both sad and cold. "Georgina did that . . . inadvertently. She was aware of what she was doing, but the motivations . . . well, they were different."

"Stop trying to justify infidelity. And stop talking about me in the third person!"

"You aren't her," said Seth again. "I know her. I would know her in almost any form. And although you look like her, you—obviously—do *not* know her."

He turned around to leave—and ran into Jerome.

Seth hadn't seen Jerome enter or teleport into the shop. Neither had I. Yet, even if the demon had strolled in openly, I think Seth would have had the same astonished and deeply disturbed reaction. The cool attitude he'd shown with Simone vanished.

"Sorry," said Seth, stepping back. He glanced uneasily at Simone, who was just as surprised. "I'll—I'll leave you two alone."

"I'm not here for her," growled Jerome.

"What?" she exclaimed, seeming deeply offended.

Jerome's dark eyes bored into Seth's. "I'm here for you. You need to come with me. Now."

When a demon tells you to do something, it's pretty hard to refuse it. My friends and I might joke about the silliness of Jerome's John Cusack guise, but underneath all that, Jerome was fucking scary. And when he turned his demonic wrath on a human, it was outright terrifying.

Yet, with a remarkable show of bravery, Seth asked: "Why?"

Jerome looked displeased that Seth hadn't instantly jumped to obey. "To get Georgie back."

"Back?" repeated Simone. "But if she comes back—"

Jerome lifted his eyes from Seth and glared at her. "Yes, yes, I know. But you might as well give it up. You failed."

"But I can—"

"Clearly, you can't." Jerome strode over to her, leaning close to her face. He pitched his voice low, but I could hear it from my observer's view. "This is not the way. I know why you're here now, but tell Niphon that every time he tries to fix things, he ends up fucking up more. It's too late. I'll deal with this. It doesn't involve you."

"But—"

"Enough." The word boomed through the store. The salesman looked up, startled, but kept his distance. "I didn't question your presence before, but now you can go."

Ostensibly, it sounded as though he were giving her permission to leave. But both she and I could hear the underlying meaning: if she didn't go on her own, he would "assist" her. She made no more protests.

Jerome returned to Seth. "Georgina's been taken. We're going to get her back. And you are going to play a role in that."

Seth couldn't speak for a moment, and when he did, it was to utter the most obvious response: "How?"

"To start with, you can stop wasting time here with stupid questions. Come with me, and you'll find out." Jerome then made a masterful play. "Every moment you delay, she's in more danger."

Nothing else could have spurred Seth into such action. He flinched at the words, and his face ran through a kaleidoscope of emotions. "Okay," he said to Jerome. "Let's go."

Chapter 19

"Real," I gasped out. "That was . . . real. Seth didn't give in to temptation. Seth stayed with Maddie."

"Maybe," said One.

The instinct to claw his eyes out rose within me, strong and sudden. It was animal and rash—and impossible since I had no form here. It was an urge I'd had on more than one occasion with the Oneroi.

"True. It was true." This was like a child's game with them, over and over. Or maybe the true/false section on the SAT. Circles. Circles. My life was a circle. "And Jerome . . ." The end of the dream came to me where my boss had spirited Seth away. "He's coming for me. He took Seth. They're going to do that ritual. Erik's going to set it up."

"Yes. And he's going to fail."

"No, he won't," I cried. Every ounce of me had become desperation: voice, mind, soul. "Jerome will come for me. He'll save me."

"No one is coming for you," said Two. "They will try, but they will fail."

Again, they sent me back to my world, and as much as I yearned for familiar faces, the doubt and uncertainty the Oneroi kept bringing up filled me with a despairing kind of confusion.

I was at Erik's. And apparently, so was everyone else.

His store had a large back room used for storage that I'd only once caught a glimpse of. It reminded me of a garage, with unfinished cement floors and plain drywall on the sides. A small table held a bowl of burning incense that made the air hazy. The edges of the room were stacked with boxes and crates that appeared to have been shoved to create an empty space around the edge of the room. Also along the edges was the Seattle immortal club: Hugh, Cody, Peter, Carter, and even Mei. Roman was probably there too, hidden because of Mei. In the center of the room, Erik was drawing chalk patterns on the floor. Jerome stood nearby, and Seth hovered uneasily between them and my friends along the wall. I think he was having a hard time deciding who was safest. If not for Mei, he probably would have chosen my friends.

Mei watched Erik and Jerome with disapproval, her nearly black eyes narrowed and brick-red lips pursed. At last, she uncrossed her arms and strode toward the center, her stiletto heels clicking loudly against the cement. Seth scurried out of her way, retreating to the safety of my friends.

"This is ridiculous," Mei said. "You're wasting everyone's time. Even with all of them"—she gestured to the wall gang— "it's not enough to bring her back. You need to report it and get another succubus."

"I report it, and there'll be another archdemon here too." Jerome cut her a look. "I'm kind of surprised you haven't done that already."

Good point. As his underling, Mei obeyed him, but she was ambitious. If Jerome got in trouble for losing me, it could be to her advantage.

"I don't need to," she said flatly. "You'll be telling them yourself soon. Why do I have to be here? I have no connection to her."

"Because I told you to! Stop arguing." Jerome glared at her, and the two demons locked gazes. At last, Mei gave a sharp nod, but it didn't seem like she gave in because of his authority. It was more like he'd communicated something, and she was acknowledging it. She returned to the side of the room, opposite my friends now.

Erik had to lean and get on his knees for a lot of his chalk work, something that had to be agony on his back. With a sigh, he finally stood up and examined his design. It showed two large concentric circles, filled and surrounded with a number of arcane symbols. Some I knew; some I didn't. Jerome studied the pattern too, and for the first time ever, my boss looked . . . nervous.

"Is it ready?" he demanded.

Erik nodded, one hand absentmindedly rubbing his back. "Barring the spell itself, yes."

Jerome's eyes fell on Seth, who flinched. "You," said the demon. "Come here."

Seth eyed the pattern almost as uneasily as Jerome had. "What will happen to me?"

"It won't kill you, if that's what you're worried about. And *you* can leave the circle whenever you want. Now stop wasting time."

I didn't like hearing Jerome boss Seth around. It stirred up those coals of rage that had been burning within me lately. I even grew angry seeing Seth obey; I kind of wanted him to defy Jerome. A moment later, I tried to banish such thoughts. I needed to save my fury for the Oneroi, not this group. Surely Jerome wasn't lying. Carter, who'd remained quiet throughout all of this, would have called Jerome on it. I hoped.

Seth walked over to Jerome's side, careful not to step on any of the chalk lines—like how superstitious people avoid cracks on sidewalks. Erik gave Seth a small smile.

"He's right, Mr. Mortensen. This won't hurt you. Though it will be . . . strange."

Mei suddenly went rigid again. "*Him?* That's all you're using? Jerome, one person can't—"

"Enough!" roared Jerome. "I'm tired of listening to everyone backtalk me. Can we get on with this?"

Erik nodded and walked over to the table with the incense. There was also a small bowl of water and a long, roughly hewn piece of stone. *Smoky quartz*, I thought. Erik picked it up carefully, reverently. He pushed the tip of the wand into the smoldering incense, and then held it up so the smoke could swathe it. A couple seconds later, he dipped the wand's end into the water. When that was completed, he began carrying the wand to the circle.

"Wait," Carter suddenly said. He straightened up from where he'd been slouching against some boxes. "I'm going in too."

"You're all crazy," muttered Mei.

"She has a point," said Jerome. "If you're in here—"

"I know, I know," said Carter, stepping over the lines to join Jerome. "And I also know what might come out." The two of them looked at each other, more silent messages passing, and then neither spoke again.

Erik returned to the circle's center, holding the wand up high. Both Carter and Jerome had moved as far from the humans as possible without crossing the inner circle. As Erik's arms reached heavenward, he suddenly didn't seem like a weak old man. True, his body was frail and growing gaunter every day, but as he stood there and began chanting, he became so much more than human. Dante was a better magician when it came down to it, but Erik wasn't without his own power, even if rarely used. If I'd been there in the flesh, I would have felt the magic he was summoning. Knowing it was there almost made me believe I could see it.

He finished his chant, spoken in words I only knew a little of, and then walked around the circle. He touched it in four spots with the wand, all equidistant from each other. The instant his wand touched the fourth spot, every immortal in the room suddenly flinched and looked uncomfortable—even the greater ones. Seth mostly looked confused.

As a disconnected observer, my view was like Seth's. I saw nothing happen either. But I realized then that if I'd been there, I would have felt what all the other immortals had as well. Erik had locked the circle, slamming invisible walls into place. All magical circles were different, but he'd told Seth that he could cross out—meaning this was a circle to keep only immortals in. It wasn't exactly like a summoning. Summonings required massive amounts of magic because they were enslaving an immortal against his or her will. This circle was a prison too, but it required less magic because the immortals had entered it by choice. Jerome and Carter had just knowingly allowed themselves to be entrapped.

This was why he wanted Mei around. For an unscrupulous magic user—say, like Dante—this was a golden opportunity. Two imprisoned greater immortals? It had infinite possibilities for a magician. Whatever Erik was doing here, I didn't believe he'd abuse this situation. But Jerome, being a demon, didn't trust anyone. Jerome had wanted Mei on hand to do some smiting if Erik wouldn't release his prisoners. Of course, she would be powerless to do anything until Erik left the circle—which he'd have to do eventually.

If they were all trying to rescue me, though, Erik couldn't have created this circle with the intent of trapping Jerome and Carter specifically. The angel's words came back to me: *I also know what might come out.*

Erik stood in front of Seth, who was growing more nervous by the second. The strain in Erik's face showed the power he was keeping in check. He couldn't play kindly old man right now, but he did what he could.

"Do you care about Miss Kincaid?" he asked Seth. "Do you want to save her?"

"Yes," answered Seth swiftly.

"Then you must think about her. Focus every ounce of your being on her. Imagine her. Cry out for her. There must be no other thoughts in your head—only her."

Seth looked puzzled but nodded. Erik turned to Jerome and Carter. "And *you* must stop him from going in entirely. You can't enter yourselves, but you can keep him here. You have to, or you'll lose both of them."

Erik waited for no acknowledgment from the angel and demon. He held up his wand again and touched Seth on his forehead, both cheeks, and chin. Seth shivered.

"Remember," said Erik. "When the gate opens, think of her. Only her. Reach for her. And when you find her, *do not let go.*"

"Gate?" asked Seth. "What—"

But Erik was chanting again, and a wind emerged out of nowhere, ruffling the hair of those in the circles. His voice grew more and more powerful, and then—

I was back with the Oneroi.

"What happened?" I exclaimed. For the millionth time, I wished I could beat on the walls of my prison. I wanted to claw their eyes out again. I wanted to choke them. "Show me what happens!"

"Failure," said One.

"They won't succeed," added Two. "The demoness was correct. A dozen humans who loved you couldn't reach you, let alone—"

He stopped speaking. His eyes met One's, and then both glanced around as though searching for something. I tried to see what they saw or heard, but there was nothing for me. Only blackness and silence.

Then, I felt the stirring of another dream coming over me. The dark world started to go blurry, and both Oneroi jerked their heads toward me.

"No!" exclaimed Two, extending his hand.

Everything grew clear again. I didn't dream. I stayed where I was.

Georgina.

My name. For the first time in—well, I had no idea how many days—I heard something that wasn't the Oneroi. It was so faint, a whisper lost on the wind. My name. One of them, at least.

I couldn't tell where it came from, but every part of me tried to focus on it, to figure out its origin.

Georgina.

"Yes?" I said aloud. "I'm here!"

The world grew blurry again. I didn't hear my name, but it was like the siren song all over again. Music without sound, colors without description.

"Stop this!" cried One. I had never heard the Oneroi raise their voices. They always spoke in those low, sly tones. But they were pretty upset now.

"Fight it!" This was Two, speaking to One. "Join me! Don't let it—"

I left them for another dream. Or, well, more like another place. No, it wasn't even a place. It was like I was floating in space, in a nebula. Perhaps a hurricane was a more accurate way to describe it because things were swirling around me and blowing past. Wisps of smoke. Bits of colors. Brilliant stars. Some touched me. Some went through me. And every time I made contact, I felt an emotion—an emotion that wasn't my own. Happiness. Terror. With that emotion came a brief flash of an image. A green field. An airplane. A monster. It was a snowstorm of stimuli.

I was lost and adrift, almost more scared than in my prison with the Oneroi. At least that had had some substance, no matter how insignificant. But this . . . what was this? Every once in a while, it would start to dissolve to black, like I might be returning to the box. . . . Then, the darkness would fade, again leaving me helpless in this mad riot of sensation.

Georgina.

My name again. And with it, that pull. That pull of familiarity. Though I technically had no body here either, I searched for that voice and that pull, looking through the riotous color.

Georgina.

It was stronger. That sense of summoning. I burned with the need to get to it. It was part of me. It was home. And then, in all that chaos, one light shone brighter than all the others. It was white, pure and pristine amidst the kaleidoscope raining down upon me. I stared at it, reached for it in as much as I could. The world started to fracture to black once again, but it was the last time. I wouldn't return to the box. Not with this light before me. It's hard to say if it became brighter and brighter or if it just grew closer and closer, but suddenly it was before me. It was around me. I *was* it.

Just like when I'd brushed against those other dreams, I had a flash of vision that snapped me briefly from the whirlwind. I was in Seth's arms. Or was I? As he held me, his face seemed to shift over and over to different forms. No, it was him. I would know him anywhere. He was so familiar, and now this close to me, I couldn't let go of him. He was home.

Georgina. The voice came again, and it was his. *Georgina, don't let go.*

No. I wasn't letting go. I was never letting go again. . . .

That brief moment of human contact gave way to the starry field of dreams, but this time, I had an anchor. I was with the light. I was the light. I felt it pulling me, but I needed no urging. I would go wherever it took me. I released all control. I had the sensation of floating, of being stretched and reaching forward. Behind me, something tugged at me, but it wasn't strong enough. I was moving forward. Forward and forward and—

The sound of screaming filled the room. My screaming. Screaming over the pain of being torn apart and reassembled. Pain from being stripped of all energy within me. I was weak. Raw. Nothing.

What room was this? I saw faces. Faces near me, faces along the room's wall. They looked at me like they knew me. Did they? Did I know them? My legs buckled underneath me, weak like a colt's. One of the men standing near me reached out, but I scrambled backward, needing to escape. I couldn't let him touch me. Of that, I was certain. My mind had been shredded and ripped open. I didn't want to be touched in any other way. The floor was cold and smooth as I scurried over it, but I was stopped by a wall. At least, it felt like one. I saw nothing there, only a blue line upon the floor. The invisible wall was familiar and triggered fear. It reminded me of the box. I drew my knees up to me, trying to make myself small as I trembled.

The men near me—four of them—were speaking in a language I didn't know. They were arguing. One kept trying to come to me, but another stopped him. That one was terrifying. His features were nothing extraordinary—tall, with dark brown eyes and hair—but there was something about him that made me cold all over. There was power in him, power all around him. I could feel it and see it. It reminded me of sulfur. His eyes fell on me as he spoke harshly to the others, and I cringed further. I felt certain I knew him, but he still scared me.

Suddenly, another of the men exclaimed something and touched the dark-haired one's arm. This man was blond. I sensed power around him too, but it felt different. It was clean and crystalline. All four turned around, putting their backs to me as they stared at something. Nothing was there at first, then I began to see and feel it. A glowing purple orb appeared before them, becoming larger and larger. As it did, I saw it was more of a spiral, its arms whirling as it grew. The two men who didn't radiate power stepped back. If the unseen wall had let me, I too would have moved away.

Out of the purple light, two black forms suddenly materialized and stepped forward. Two black figures who were somehow luminescent at the same time and had brilliant blue eyes. My own eyes widened. I might not know anything else that was going on around me, but I knew them. I knew them, and I was going to kill them.

I'm not sure how I did it since there seemed to be no spark of life left within me, yet somehow, I mustered the strength to spring up and run toward them. My shrieked words were incoherent, but it didn't matter. Only their destruction did. I would rip them apart. I would make them suffer the way they'd—

Strong arms grabbed me, stopping me as surely as the wall had. It was the blond man, and his grip was like iron. "Let me go!" I screamed. "Let me go! I'll kill them! I'll kill them both!"

The dark-haired man glanced back toward us. "Do *not* let her go," he said mildly, this time in a language I understood. I fought in vain against the arms but made no progress.

The dark-haired man turned to the Oneroi. "This isn't your world," he said.

"We've come for what's ours," said one of the Oneroi. "You took her."

"I took back what was mine," the dark-haired man countered. "You stole her."

"We won her. She came to us of her own free will."

The dark-haired man snorted. Jerome, I suddenly remembered. His name was Jerome. "We have different definitions of 'free will,'" he said.

"We want her back," protested the Oneroi.

"You're taking nothing back," countered Jerome, voice hard. "Go before I change my mind."

I'd gone slack while they spoke, but now my fury was renewed. I struggled again. "Let me kill them!" I screamed. "Jerome, it's my right! Let me destroy them!"

Jerome turned back, maybe surprised I'd used his name. "I don't think you're in any shape to kill anything."

"It's my right," I said. "After what they did—they'll suffer like I did. I will shred them. I'll rip their souls out!"

"They don't have souls," he said dryly. "But I like your enthusiasm." He turned back to the Oneroi. "So, you stole my succubus *and* tortured her." His voice carried that reptilian chill. It froze my blood. It made the air crackle with tension. The Oneroi shifted uncomfortably. They weren't unaffected.

"Because of her, our mother was recaptured," one of them said. But he didn't sound as confident or outraged as before. "We are entitled to revenge."

"You believe insult to another justifies revenge?" asked Jerome. Oh, that voice. That voice made the air grow still.

"Yes," said the Oneroi as one.

"Me too," replied Jerome.

He didn't even move, but I felt the power flare out from him, like a torch thrown into dry tinder. It exploded—and so did the Oneroi. Well, it was more like they imploded. That power hit them, and then—they were no more. Just like that.

"Oh, Jerome," said the man holding me. "Do you know what you've done?"

Jerome glanced back at us and shrugged. "I don't like people taking my things."

The swirling purple gate had never left, and now it began to grow brighter and rotate faster.

"Shit," said Jerome. "I was hoping no one would notice."

The man holding me sighed. He looked down at me, and silvery gray eyes pierced my soul. "Listen to me. Do not move. Do you understand? Stay right here." When I didn't answer, he sighed again. "Do you know me?"

Did I? Yes. The eyes. I knew the eyes. "Carter." The word came out strangely on my tongue.

"Yes," he said. "You know me. Trust me. Do *not* move."

He let go of me, waited to see what I'd do, and then walked up to join Jerome when I stayed in place. Nothing could have made me move anyway, not when I saw what came through the gate.

It was monstrous. Literally. Yellow-eyed and scaly, mottled purple and gray. It had what looked like a pig's snout, and seven horns ran over its head like points on a crown. It towered over Jerome and Carter as it emerged from the gate, but the two of them stood where they were, regarding it defiantly.

"You destroyed my subjects," the creature growled. Its voice came from deep within its throat and made the floor vibrate. "You broke the laws."

"Your subjects were in our realm," said Jerome. He was perfectly calm. "They stole one of my people and abused her. *They* broke the rules."

"That doesn't give you the right to do what you did," came the response.

"They would have destroyed her if they were capable of it. Next time, keep a better watch on your employees so that they don't go causing trouble where they shouldn't."

The monster's nostrils flared. "I could destroy *you* for this."

"Try," said Jerome. "Try taking on both of us."

Those yellow eyes flicked over to Carter. A few teeth showed in the creature's mouth. I think he was smiling. "An angel and a demon fighting together. It would almost be worth seeing."

Heavy silence fell as everyone sized each other up. I had no sense of the monster's strength. Physical size was not proportional to power. Jerome and Carter, however, were burning like small suns, ready to burst at any moment.

At last, the monster shrugged. Or did his equivalent of it. "But it's been enough just to see you defend each other's honor. I will not destroy you ... today. There will be no more assaults on my people. If there are, I won't be so forgiving."

"And if your people don't leave mine alone," said Jerome smoothly, "I won't be as forgiving either."

The creature snarled, and for a moment, I thought he might very well change his mind. He didn't. Instead, he stepped backward toward the purple light. He merged into it, vanishing to our eyes, and then the gate itself disappeared as well.

"He is such a fucking liar," said Jerome. "'Forgiving' indeed. He knew we'd blast his scaly ass out of here."

"Yeah, well, I hope we never find if that's true or not," said Carter. "Fighting a Morphean demon would generate paperwork even on *my* side."

Jerome's lips twitched into a smile. "Now that would be worth seeing."

I looked between both of them, my fear from the near-confrontation fading. With the last of my energy, I lunged for Jerome, beating my fists against his chest. He caught them and stopped me as easily as Carter had.

"You should have let me do it! You should have let *me* destroy them! It was my right!"

"That's what you're pissed off about? Georgie, I'm not even sure how you're still standing."

"It was my right," I repeated. "You don't know what they did."

"I can make some good guesses."

I stopped in my struggles, and at last, the full force of

everything that had happened descended on me. My being's full depletion hit me. I sagged in his arms, and he caught me. The sights and people around me were still a little muddled, but lots of things were starting to come back.

"You were supposed to keep me safe," I said in a small voice. I felt my eyes grow wet. "You shouldn't have let that happen—let them take me. You're supposed to protect me."

Jerome looked truly surprised and didn't respond to me immediately. I was afraid he'd get angry, but instead, he said quietly, "Yes. I am. I did in the end, but—I was late."

"Great apology," said Carter.

Now Jerome's anger returned. "I have nothing to apologize for!" He turned back to me, and again, his voice was calm and patient. Almost gentle. I knew this was uncharacteristic for him. "I brought you back. You're safe now. They will never harm you again. Do you understand?"

I nodded.

"Good. Now it's time to finish this."

Jerome turned toward the humans. One of them was old, very old—with dark brown skin and graying hair. His eyes were compassionate. The other man was younger, with messy hair and brown eyes that turned honey-amber when the light caught them. He was staring at me like he knew me, which wasn't a surprise because I knew him too. I didn't know how, but I did. In fact, I was beginning to realize I knew everyone in this room. Other names were coming back to me. This one man's name eluded me, though, largely because several kept popping into my head. He studied me intently, like he was trying to figure something out, and I found myself falling into those golden brown eyes.

Jerome said something to the gray-haired man in that other language. I still couldn't understand it, but there was something familiar about its sounds. The old man didn't answer or move right away, and palpable tension fell over the entire room. At last the old man took a wand he was holding and began touching points on the circle upon the floor, murmuring softly as he did. When he touched the circle a fourth time, it was as though a great pressure—one I hadn't even known was there—was released from the room.

Jerome exchanged a few curt words with the man and then turned to me. "As I was saying, how you're conscious is beyond me—but considering all the other absurd things you do, I shouldn't be surprised."

He stepped toward me and pressed his fingers to my forehead. I gasped as a jolt of . . . something . . . raced through me. At first, it was shocking and prickly. Then, it transformed into something sweeter and more wonderful. The most wonderful thing on earth. It filled me up, energizing me, making me whole. Until this moment, how could I have thought I was alive?

The world came into greater focus, the sights grew more familiar. I staggered, not from weakness this time, but from the pure bliss of life Jerome had gifted me with. He said something to me in that other language, and I frowned, not understanding.

He spoke again in my own words. "Change back, Georgina. Time to go."

"Change to what?"

"Whatever you want. Your current favorite, I'd imagine. Not this." His hand gestured toward my body.

I examined myself for the first time. I wasn't quite as tall as him, a few inches shorter, maybe. My legs and arms were long and lean, my skin tanned from the sun. A plain ivory dress covered me, and I could see the tips of black hair falling onto my chest. I frowned. This was me . . . and yet not me.

"Change back, Georgina," he repeated.

"That's not my name," I said.

"Shake off what they've done," he said, clearly impatient. "It's over. They've fogged your mind, but you can clear it. Change back, Georgina. Come back to this time." His next words were in that other language, and I shook my head angrily.

"I don't understand. I shouldn't be here. This is my body, but this isn't my time."

He gave another command that I still didn't comprehend, and I uttered the same response. Three times we went through this, and then on the fourth, his words came through to me, perfectly understandable. I knew what he was speaking. The English language exploded in my mind, and with it, much more.

I held out my hands before me, staring long and hard as though seeing them for the first time. "This *is* my time," I murmured in English. I looked down at my long legs. A strange sense of revulsion ran through me. "This is not my body." Yet . . . it was. It was, and it wasn't. With no energy, it was what I had reverted to.

"What's your name?" he demanded.

Letha. My name is Letha.

"Georgina," I said. And with that, I summoned the power to make my body's shape change. Slim and short, with light brown hair, and golden green eyes. The off-white homespun shift became a blue cotton dress. A moment later, I changed it to jeans and a blue shirt.

Jerome glanced at Carter. "See? No harm done."

Carter didn't acknowledge that. Instead, he asked, "So now what?"

"Now?" Jerome's gaze fell on me again. "Now Georgina sleeps."

"What?" I cried. "No! Not after . . . no. I'm never sleeping again."

Jerome almost smiled before touching my forehead again. I slept.

Chapter 20

I woke up in my own bed and found Mei sitting beside it. Not even Nurse Ratched could have startled me that much.

Mei was flipping through a magazine and glanced up, appearing bored. "Oh. You're awake. Finally." She stood up.

"What . . . what happened?" I asked, blinking at the light pouring in through my window. I was kind of surprised she hadn't shut the curtains. She didn't really strike me as a fun-in-the-sun person.

"You don't remember?" Her disinterested expression sharpened. "Jerome said it would all come back to you. If it hasn't . . ."

I sat up, drawing my knees to my body. "No, no. I remember . . . I remember what happened at Erik's. I remember . . . the Oneroi." Saying the word made me shudder. "But what happened after that? How long have I been asleep?"

"Three days," she said flatly.

"What?" I stared at her, my mouth agape. If Mei was the joking type, I would have expected the punch line now. "I don't . . . I mean, it went so fast. And I didn't dream."

She crooked me a smile. "Seems like you'd want that. And heavy sleep heals you faster." The smile changed to a grimace. "Not that waiting by your bedside for three days has really felt that fast. Jerome made me keep all your friends away. *That* was fun."

"Did you just use sarcasm?"

"I'm leaving," she said, back to her all business self. "I've done what Jerome asked."

"Wait! What happened to Seth and Erik? Are they okay?"

"Fine," she said. I waited for her to vanish, but it didn't come. She peered at me curiously. "It shouldn't have worked, you know."

"What shouldn't have?"

"That ritual. There is *no way* that human could have found you. Not among all those other souls."

The Oneroi had said the same thing, and thinking back to the storm of color and disorder, I could understand their reasoning. "We . . . we love each other." I wasn't sure I had the right to those words, but they came out anyway.

Mei rolled her eyes. "That means nothing. Human love—no matter what all your songs and chick flicks tell you—isn't enough. It shouldn't have worked."

I didn't know what to say. "Well . . . I guess it did."

"Jerome knew it would too," she mused, a small frown wrinkling her brow. Her gaze hardened on me. "Did you? Do you know how it happened?"

"What?" I squeaked. "No! I don't understand any of this."

I expected her to deny this and question me further. Instead her frown only deepened, and I realized I was no longer of use in solving this dilemma to her. She vanished.

The instant she disappeared, Roman came bursting into my room. "She's gone?" he asked. If he was nearby, he would have felt her signature go away.

"Have you been hanging out the whole time?" I asked.

He sat down in the chair she'd been in. "Jerome ordered her not to let anyone come near you."

"You could have taken her," I said, attempting a joke.

"Not without causing a whole lot of trouble." He frowned, eyes troubled with thought. "Although, I would have revealed myself if I'd needed to if that . . . thing that came out of the gate had tried to take on Carter and Jerome."

I shuddered at the memory. "I didn't even know there were monsters like that in the—wait. How could you have helped them? Were you . . . were you in the circle?" I'd assumed he'd been watching from the sides.

"Of course." He said no more, and the way he spoke implied that it had been a ridiculous question for me to ask in the first place.

"Are you crazy?" I exclaimed. "You weren't just letting yourself get trapped. If you were discovered by Mei—even any of the dream creatures—you'd be fucked. They would have turned you in too."

"There was no choice," Roman said. "I had to be there, in case you needed me."

"It was too big a risk," I countered, my voice faltering this time. "If there'd been a fight, Jerome and Carter would have had no reason to defend you. And while that Morphean might have been afraid to hurt them, you would have been fair game."

"I told you, it doesn't matter. I had to be there for you."

His eyes, those eyes that were so like the sea I'd grown up with, held such earnestness and affection that I had to look away. I couldn't believe he'd risked what he had for me. Why? He had no reason to care about me after what I'd done to him, yet it was clear he still wanted me. The night I'd been captured seemed like a lifetime ago, but its events came back to me in perfect detail: his lips, his hands . . .

"I wish you wanted to kill me again," I muttered. "It was easier."

He rested his hand on mine, its warmth spreading through me. "Nothing about your life is ever easy."

I looked back up at him. "That's for damn sure. But I don't know . . . I don't know if I can do this . . . by which I mean, well, you know."

"You don't have to do anything," he said. "We'll just keep going on like we have. Roommates. We'll see where things go. If they change, they change. If not . . ." He shrugged. "So it goes."

"Did I mention that it was easier when you wanted to kill me? I'm not sure how I feel about you being so reasonable."

"Yeah, well, maybe I just feel sorry for you right now after everything that happened. Maybe I'll change my mind in a little while." He squeezed my hand. "Was it . . . was it awful?"

I looked away again. "Yes. Beyond awful. It's hard to explain. They showed me every nightmare I could have, every fear made flesh. Some of the things they showed me had already happened—and were almost as bad as the nightmares. I couldn't tell what was reality anymore. They showed me you guys . . . but it wasn't always real. I doubted everything: who I was, what I felt . . ." I swallowed back tears, glad I had averted my eyes.

"Hey," he said softly, reaching out to tip my chin and make me look back at him. "It's over. You're safe. We'll help you get better—I'll help. I won't let anything happen to you."

Again, his feelings for me made me uncomfortable and confused. Was it a lingering effect of the Oneroi? No, I decided a moment later. This was the kind of situation that would confuse anyone. My heart was still tangled up in Seth, someone I knew I should let go, but who had found me against impossible odds. And here was Roman, someone I could be with a bit more easily—well, kind of—and who had risked his life for me. Could I move on with him? I didn't know. But I could try.

I found his hand again and squeezed it. "Thank you."

He leaned toward me, and I think we might have kissed, but the ringing of my cell phone jolted us out of any romantic spell. I pulled my hand from his and grabbed the phone from my side table.

"Hello?"

"Miss Kincaid," came the kind, familiar voice. "It is a pleasure to speak with you again."

"Erik! Oh, I'm so happy it's you. I wanted to thank you—"

"There's nothing to thank me for. I would gladly do it again."

"Well, then, I'm still thanking you anyway." Roman, realizing this had nothing to do with him, got up and wandered off—but not before giving me one more fond look.

"As you wish," said Erik. "Are you feeling better?"

"More or less. Certainly better in body. And I think the rest will come." I wished that with my body's healing, I could also forget all the horrible things I'd seen. That wouldn't happen, though, and I felt no need to trouble him with my problems.

"I'm glad," he said. "Very glad."

Silence fell, and a suspicious feeling nudged its way into my brain. I'd assumed he was simply calling to check up on me, but something now told me there was more.

"Miss Kincaid," he said at last. "I'm sure you don't want to talk about what happened. . . ."

"I—well." I hesitated. I knew Erik. He wouldn't bring this up without a good reason. "Is there something we *should* talk about?"

Now it was his turn to hesitate. "You thank me . . . but to be truthful, what we did shouldn't have worked. I didn't expect it to."

Mei's comments came back to me, as did the other conversations I'd witnessed via the dreams. "Nobody seemed to."

"Mr. Jerome did."

"Where is this going?"

"I don't know how it worked. Mr. Mortensen should not have found your soul."

I loved Erik and hated the irritation in my voice. "I keep hearing that over and over, but obviously he did. Maybe it should have been impossible, but after what I went through? I don't care how it happened."

"I would imagine not, but still . . . still, I can't help but wonder at this. Would you mind telling me what it was like when he found you?"

That was one part of the ordeal I didn't mind recounting, largely because it had had a happy ending. Of course, the logistics of explaining it weren't so easy. I did my best to describe what it was like being adrift in the dream world and how Seth had seemed to call to me. Erik listened patiently and then asked if I'd tell him about my contract with Hell and how I'd sold my soul.

That was a little harder to tell, not to mention a bizarre question. The Oneroi had shown me so many versions of what had happened with Kyriakos and me, and while some had been true and some false, they'd all been horrible. Still, sensing something big might be going on here, I haltingly recounted the whole experience: how I'd cheated on Kyriakos with his best friend, infidelity that was later discovered. It was the sorrow from that that had driven Kyriakos into suicidal grief, which in turn drove me to sign a contract with Hell. I'd sold my soul and become a succubus, in exchange for everyone I knew—including Kyriakos—to forget me and the awful things I'd done.

"Tell me the terms one more time," said Erik.

"It was that everyone I knew back then would forget me and forget what happened—family, friends, and especially my husband." My voice choked a little. "It worked. I came back later, and no one knew me. Not even a glimmer of familiarity."

"There was nothing else in the contract?"

"No. An imp I know looked it over recently and verified it."

"Oh?" This caught Erik's interest. "Why would he do that?"

"She. As a favor. The imp who'd brokered my sale was the one who worked with Nyx and kept messing with Seth. Hugh said when an imp shows that much interest, there's something wrong with a contract. So Kristin—this other imp—looked at my contract." She hadn't been very happy about doing that. If she'd been caught snooping in Hell's records, there would have been some very, very bad consequences. Her gratitude over me hooking her up with her boss had overpowered her fear. "She told me it was airtight. Everything was like it was supposed to be. No errors."

More silence. This conversation was starting to make me uneasy. "Did this imp—Niphon?—end up doing anything to Mr. Mortensen?"

"Not so much . . . I mean, it was part of what led us to

breaking up. . . ." I paused to collect myself. "But there were a lot of other factors that caused that too."

"Has Niphon been back?"

"No, but there has been this succubus." With everything else, I'd forgotten about Simone. "She was impersonating me. Kept trying to seduce Seth . . . but it didn't work. I *think* Jerome sent her packing, but I'm not sure."

Again, Erik took a long time in responding. Finally, he sighed. "Thank you, Miss Kincaid. You've given me much to think about. I apologize if I've brought up painful memories. And I'm very happy you're feeling better."

"Thanks," I said. "And thanks again for your help."

We disconnected, and I wandered out to the living room. Roman was in the kitchen, plating up some grilled cheese sandwiches. "Hungry?" he asked.

"Starving," I said. He handed me a plate, along with a cup of coffee, and I smiled. "Thanks. Not sure what I did to deserve this."

"You don't have to do anything. Besides, I had extra. Wanted a big meal before going to work."

"Before—what?"

The grin he gave me indicated he'd been dying to deliver this news. "I got a job."

"You did not."

"I did. Went back to the school I used to teach at. They had a couple openings, so I'm doing a few classes."

I was dumbfounded. After all my badgering, Roman had sought gainful employment—in his specialty, no less: linguistics.

"Does this mean you're going to pay rent now?"

"Let's not get carried away, love."

He grabbed a plate of his own, and we ate in the living room while the cats watched hopefully for leftovers. Seeing Godiva, I felt a frown coming on. The dream. The man in the dream. The Oneroi had said it was Seth . . . but that was impossible. I lifted my eyes up to Roman, wondering if I could rekindle the love I'd once had. If there was any man in any dream, he would be a better candidate.

"You talked to Erik for a while," Roman said, noting my scrutiny.

"He's weirded out by my rescue. He says it shouldn't have worked."

"Yeah, I heard that too."

Between bites, I recounted the conversation, including Erik's interest in Seth and my contract. "I don't see what the big deal is," I concluded. "Seth and I still have feelings for each other—feelings we're trying to get past." In that moment when our souls had met, though, separating from him had been the last thing I wanted. "Maybe that was enough. Maybe people don't have faith in the power of love."

"Maybe," said Roman. But he looked thoughtful now too.

A knock at the door interrupted further conversation. I felt no immortal signature and hoped it wasn't my neighbor trolling for more sex. He'd mercifully left me alone so far.

But no, it wasn't Gavin. It was Maddie.

And she was crying.

I asked no questions. When friends are in trouble, you take care of them first. I pulled her right inside and led her to the couch, immediately putting my arms around her. "What's wrong?" I asked finally. "What happened?"

She couldn't speak right away. Her sobs were too great, and she was choking on her own tears. Something nudged my arm. It was Roman handing me a box of tissues. I shot him a grateful look and gave some to Maddie.

At long last, she gasped out, "It's Seth."

My heart stopped. For a moment, a hundred awful scenarios flew through my mind. Seth hit by a car. Seth struck by some deadly disease. I clutched her arm, so tightly that I realized my nails were digging into her. I relaxed my grip as best I could.

"What happened?" I demanded. "Is he okay?"

"He ended it." Her crying renewed. "He broke the engagement and told me it was over." She buried her face against my shoulder, and I stroked her absentmindedly as my brain tried hard to really comprehend her words. I must have misheard.

"He couldn't have," I said, my voice as cracked as hers. "He . . . he loves you."

She lifted her head and looked at me with mournful, glittering eyes. "He said he didn't love me the way he should—that he didn't love me the way I deserved. He said it'd be wrong to make me marry him, that we weren't meant to spend our lives together." She took a tissue and wiped her nose, then her eyes grew wide with desperation. "What does that mean, Georgina? Why would he say he's making me marry him? I *want* to. I don't understand."

I looked over her and met Roman's eyes. We couldn't speak the way greater immortals could, but enough messages passed between us. Seth hadn't forced her to get engaged, no, but he'd done it out of guilt, guilt for cheating on her and continually being drawn to me when he believed it was better for us to stay apart.

"He said he loved me," Maddie continued. "But that I needed someone who loved me more—someone I was the world to. He said he'd only hurt me worse if we went on. How could it hurt worse?" The tears grew worse. She pulled away and buried her face in her hands. "It can't hurt worse than this. I want to die."

"No!" I said, drawing her back to me. "Don't say that. *Don't ever say that!*"

"Georgina," warned Roman softly. I realized I was shaking Maddie and immediately stopped.

"Listen to me," I said, turning her face toward mine. "You are an amazing person. You are one of the best people I know. You'll get over this . . . I swear it. I won't let you go through it alone, okay? And you deserve the best. If it's not him, then you'll get someone better." The next words were hard for me. I should have rejoiced at this news. I wouldn't have to watch them together. I also had a feeling that I was somehow involved in this. What had she said? That Seth said she deserved to be someone's world? He'd told me I was his. In one of the dreams, he'd said that to her, but I now knew that was a lie. Still, I couldn't help it when I said, "And maybe . . . maybe if you guys talk more, you'll understand . . ."

The sobs abated—just a little—as she gave me a puzzled look. "That's the thing. I can't."

"It may seem that way, but he's not totally unreasonable." Why the hell was I playing devil's advocate here? Because Maddie was my friend, and I couldn't stand to see her hurting—and because I had also had my heart broken too many times. "Wait a couple days, then find him and see if you can have a, I don't know, productive dialogue. Maybe you can fix things." Ugh. "Maybe you'll at least understand . . . understand his decision."

She shook her head. "But I *can't* find him. No one can. Georgina, he's disappeared."

Chapter 21

Maddie claimed that even Seth's family didn't know where he was. According to her, he'd really just . . . vanished. He wasn't answering his phone. He wasn't showing up at the bookstore. When people disappeared, I immediately jumped to supernatural conclusions, but Maddie then added—through more tears—that she used her key to get her belongings from Seth's place and found a suitcase and some clothing missing. Feeling guilty about having the key anymore, she then shoved it into my hand and told me to return it. Or throw it away.

I did my best to comfort her some more and then offered to take her over to Doug's. Roman shot me a warning look as we were about to leave.

"Don't do anything stupid," he said out of Maddie's hearing.

"I knew your nice bedside manner wouldn't last," I returned.

Despite Doug's slacker rocker-boy lifestyle, I knew Maddie'd be in good hands with him. I dropped her off there and found Doug a mixture of personas. To Maddie, he was astonishingly kind and gentle—the caring brother as opposed to the usual teasing brother. Once she was lying down in the other room, he made sure I knew exactly what he thought of Seth in very explicit detail. There wasn't much I could say to that except that they should call me if they needed anything. I left.

In spite of Maddie's words, I drove to Terry and Andrea's anyway. Seth ending things with Maddie so abruptly was crazy—almost crazier than him proposing to her in the first place. But him disappearing without telling his family? No. He wouldn't do that. He was too responsible. Most likely he'd told them not to tell Maddie where he was.

Kendall opened the door when I arrived, her face lighting up like Christmas morning. "Georgina! Georgina's here!" Morgan and McKenna, who had been watching cartoons, came tearing over and each wrapped themselves around a leg.

"Nice to see you guys too," I laughed.

Terry had been sitting on the couch near the twins and came over to me with a little less zeal. "Hey, Georgina," he said, face typically friendly. He was shorter than Seth and a few years older, but overall, they bore a notable resemblance. "Sorry for the mass assault."

"No problem." I unwound Morgan from me, but McKenna proved a little more resistant. Glancing back at Terry, I said hesitantly, "I was wondering if I could talk to you, uh, about something."

Terry wasn't stupid. None of the Mortensens were. "Sure," he said. "Girls, let go of Georgina and go back to the cartoons. We're going to go into the kitchen."

"But we want her to watch TV with us!"

"Can we come?"

Terry laid down firm but friendly fatherly law, and with great reluctance, the girls returned to the couch. I was impressed. I wasn't sure I could have refused that group anything. He led me to the kitchen, but before either of us could say anything, Andrea came in from down the hall, smiling in surprise when she saw me. I smiled in surprise right back at her, but it was more from her appearance than anything else. It was the middle of the day, but she wore a robe over pajamas. Her mussed blond hair and dark eye circles suggested she'd been sleeping.

Terry had been leaning against the counter but jumped up when he saw her. "Oh, honey, you should go back to bed."

She shrugged him off. "I wanted to see who's here. How's it going?"

"Fine," I said. Then, unable to resist: "Are you feeling okay?"

"A little under the weather. Fortunately, Terry's manning up today. He does *almost* as good a job as me with the girls."

I laughed politely at the joke, but it soon faded. We stood awkwardly for a moment, everyone knowing why I was here but no one doing anything about it. Finally, I took a deep breath.

"I've come to ask you where Seth is."

"Funny," said Andrea. "We were going to ask you the same thing."

I was taken aback. "How would I know?"

They both just stared.

"I don't!"

"When this happened a couple days ago . . . this thing with Maddie . . ." Terry glanced uneasily at his wife before continuing. "We just assumed, well, that it was because of you."

"Why would it be because of me? I just found out about this today."

"It's always been because of you," said Andrea gently. "There was never anyone else. We like Maddie. *He* likes her. But that's the problem. Throughout it all, we could just tell that you were always the one. Now, whatever happened between you guys to make it go bad isn't any of our business. We're just not that surprised to see this new development."

"We would, however, like to know where he is," said Terry more pragmatically.

"I don't know," I said helplessly, still a little stunned by Andrea's words. "Maddie said he'd packed up, and I figured you guys were keeping his location a secret from her." I eyed them suspiciously. "And me?"

"No," said Terry. "We really don't know." I didn't have an angel's talent, but I believed he was telling the truth.

Andrea nodded in agreement. "He just called us a couple days ago and said he'd ended things. Didn't give any explanation—but well, you know how he is. He doesn't explain much anyway. Then, when Maddie and no one else had seen him, we started to get worried."

A couple days ago. Seth had ended things with her a couple days ago—when the whole soul retrieval gig had gone down.

"We actually tried calling you," added Terry. "But never got an answer."

"Ah, yeah. I've been sick this week too." Eyeing Andrea—who looked exhausted—I suddenly felt bad for taking up any more of their time. "Look, I should go. Thanks for the info. Will you ... let me know if you hear from him?"

Andrea smiled again. "Something tells me you'll hear from him before we do."

I wasn't as confident. Leaving the house was a little tricky since the other girls didn't want me to go, but I managed to escape their adorable clutches at last and make a break for it. I was walking toward my car when a voice said, "She's sick, you know."

I turned, startled, and saw Brandy standing near a gate that led to their backyard. She had the same sullen look about her she'd had for so long. "Hey," I said in greeting. "Where'd you come from?"

"I was around. I heard you talking to Mom and Dad."

I replayed Brandy's initial words. "Your mom ... you mean she's sick, right? I could tell."

"No, I mean she's *really* sick. She's really sick, and they won't talk about it." Brandy gave a nod toward the front door. "No one else knows. Not even Uncle Seth knows just how sick she is."

A chilly breeze stirred dried leaves around my feet, but it was nothing compared to the cold starting to fill me. "Just how sick are we talking, Brandy?"

Brandy scuffed her feet against the driveway, eyes averted. "She has ovarian cancer. It's bad ... but they're still trying to figure out just how bad it is."

"She was going to the doctor that day I was here," I recalled aloud. Andrea had been so bright and cheery, I'd assumed something routine was going on. I also realized I hadn't technically been here; I'd seen it in a dream. Fortunately, Brandy was too distracted to notice my slip.

"She's been at the doctor a lot. Dad's missing tons of work. Uncle Seth's helped out sometimes, and I've been babysitting all the time."

I suddenly felt incredibly selfish. I'd been assuming Brandy's moodiness was all over me and Seth breaking up. But that was only a symptom of the larger problem. Her mother was dangerously ill, and every part of her world was destabilizing. Her own life was probably being put on hold to watch her sisters, and even something like her uncle's romantic life could ripple what she'd regarded as the norm. All the constants in her world were disappearing.

"Brandy, I—"

"I have to go," she interrupted, heading back toward the gate, face stony. "Kayla'll be up from her nap soon. I'm supposed to keep an eye on her today."

Brandy disappeared around the corner before I could say anything. I stood there, feeling lost. I didn't know who I felt worse for: Brandy and Terry for knowing what was going on or the little girls for being oblivious. I felt bad enough for myself because there was nothing I could do. There was never anything I could do. I had powers beyond human imaginings, but they were nothing that could actually help humans.

I drove downtown with a heavy heart, trying hard—and failing—not to overreact. Brandy herself had said things were bad but that they were still learning the extent of it. Surely there were more tests, tests that would give some hope. And surely there was treatment. Humans could do that much on their own.

Jerome was where I'd hoped he'd be. Really, I decided, the Cellar was nearly as good as him having an office. Carter was by his side at the back table, both of them doing shots from a bottle of Jägermeister. Those two didn't discriminate among their liquor. I wondered if they were drinking away the hardships of the other day or toasting their success over it.

It must have been the latter because Jerome almost smiled when he saw me. "Georgie, out among the living and back to your petite self. Yet . . . so blue. Blue like always."

Yes, they'd been drinking. Angels and demons could sober up at will, and he was apparently indulging in the full effects.

"I got some bad news," I said, sitting opposite them.

"What, about losing Mortensen?" asked Jerome.

"How do you know about that?"

"I talked to Roman. He recapped your day—the old man checking in, you comforting your romantic rival . . . it was quite moving."

I scowled. "Great. You have Roman spying on me."

"It's not spying. I just demand answers from him. If it makes you feel better, he's never very happy to give up those answers."

"How often do you do it?" I asked incredulously.

"Not that often." A waiter set down a new bottle. "Mostly I wanted to see how you were recovering post-dream."

"Fine. I'm fine." I glanced at Carter. "No comments from you today?"

"Leave me out of this," he replied. "I'm just drinking." So he said, but he was also watching and listening very carefully. He was not letting the alcohol affect him.

I turned back to Jerome. "I've come to call in my favor."

The dark amusement in his eyes turned to suspicion. "What favor?"

"The one you promised me for helping save you from Grace, remember?"

Yes, no amusement at all anymore. "I just rescued you from another plane of existence from creatures who were torturing your mind."

I flinched but pushed on with my words. "You *promised* a favor, and I didn't call it in for that. Besides, you would have done it anyway so that you wouldn't get in trouble."

"That favor offer was brought on by the drama at the time," he countered. "I probably said all sorts of things."

"You *promised*," I repeated.

"I can understand you just fine without putting italics in your voice, Georgie," he snapped.

"You did, though," pointed out Carter. Demons could lie—and did—but certain deals they were bound to. Jerome had said he'd grant me a favor out on the beach, and it had been a true promise.

"Fine," he said irritably, gesturing for another shot. "What is it you want? And I don't have to grant it if it's something totally unreasonable."

"I want to know—"

"Careful," interrupted Carter.

I paused, and Jerome glared at the angel. Carter offered no other insight, but those gray eyes were still watchful—and cautious. Which was what I needed to be. Jerome had promised me a favor, and like all demons, he would try to find as many loopholes in it as possible. I had been about to ask where Seth was, but that wouldn't necessarily do me any good. I wouldn't be able to *get* to Seth.

"I want you to send me to Seth so I can spend a few days with him."

Jerome studied me, expression shrewd. "There's a couple problems. One is that you've kind of asked for two things. The other is that I'm not omniscient. I don't know where he is."

"You can find out," I said. "At least, if he's flown anywhere, you can find out."

Seth packing indicated serious travel. Maddie had said his car was still at the house, meaning he hadn't driven somewhere. If he had, he'd be harder to track. But airports had records, and Hell had its hand in that kind of thing. Jerome could easily get an imp or lesser demon to access Sea-Tac's records this week and see where Seth had gone. I probably could have asked Hugh to do it, but that wouldn't have gotten me leave to actually go to Seth, hence my wording.

"And we both know it'd be stupid for you to send me right there and right back. Asking for a few days makes it worthwhile or else it's a shitty favor."

"Debatable," Jerome replied.

"It could be worse," said Carter. "She didn't ask for world peace or anything."

"Stay out of this," returned the demon. "I know what you want."

Carter shrugged and ordered another drink.

"Fine," said Jerome at last. "I'll have Hugh check travel records. You know there might not be a paper trail."

"I know. But if you find him?"

"Then you can go to him. For now, go home. You're ruining my good mood. I'll find you if there's news."

I didn't need to be told twice. "Soon," I said. "You have to search soon."

Jerome's lips quirked. "You didn't put that into the wording."

Carter elbowed him, and I had to take it on faith that Jerome would act in a timely manner. My words had implied that I wanted to be where Seth was *now*. One could argue that waiting meant Seth would change locations, meaning I couldn't have what I wanted. I also had to believe that Carter had a point in saying this was a relatively easy favor. I could have demanded more.

Simple or not, it was hard to wait to hear back. Roman was gone when I returned to my condo, and I had nothing to do but ruminate. I'd given myself a leave of absence at work and didn't regret it. Still, being alone with my thoughts was never a good thing, and I had far too many to trouble me: the Oneroi, Seth, Andrea . . .

"Okay, Georgie."

It was four hours later when Jerome appeared in my living room with a *pop*.

I sagged in relief. "You found him?"

"I did."

"And you'll send me to him—for a worthwhile amount of time?"

"Three days," the demon said. He sounded irritable and impatient. I'd wondered if he'd been drinking this entire time and was angry at the interruption. "I want you back here in seventy-two hours, and you're on your own as to how you do it. Do you understand?"

"Yes," I said eagerly. "Just send me to him." I had to talk to him. I had to find out exactly what had happened. I had to make sure he was okay.

"And that settles the favor. Agreed?"

"Agreed," I said. There was power in that word, just as there had been in Jerome's initial promise. I could ask for nothing else.

"Then go," he said.

I vanished from my living room . . .

. . . and reappeared on a busy sidewalk. People swarmed around me, none of them seeming to notice I'd appeared out of thin air. The sun was on its way down, but the sky was bright and clear—and hot. Very hot. The masses around me were dressed in beach clothes and had the feel of tourists. I stepped out of their path and found myself standing in front of a large, resort-type hotel.

The abrupt change in location—and discomfort of tele-portation—had left me disoriented, and I needed to get my bearings. Taking in more of my surroundings, I could hear people speaking in both Spanish and English. I turned to the closest person near me, a short, deeply tanned man in a hotel uniform who was directing taxis around the building's drive-way.

I started to ask where I was and decided that would be a little too stupid sounding. I pointed at the hotel and asked him what its name was. I knew tons of languages perfectly, and Spanish rolled off my lips easily.

"*El Grande Mazatlán, señorita,*" he replied.

Mazatlán? This time, I did ask a stupid question: *"¿Estoy in México?"*

He nodded, giving me the are-you-crazy look I'd expected. It was probably made worse by my jaw dropping.

Well, I supposed if you were going to run away, you should run away somewhere warm.

Chapter 22

I wandered into the hotel, still a bit stunned by the situation I found myself in. Seth was . . . in Mexico. Presuming Jerome was holding true to his bargain, of course. I had to believe he was, but the question was if he'd actually sent me near Seth. That was a wording in my request that could be blurred a little. Glancing up at the hotel, I hoped Jerome's minions had gone as far as to search local hotels for Seth's name when they tracked the plane ticket. With a quick smile to the man who'd helped me, I headed toward the hotel's entrance.

In a place that catered to so many tourists, plenty of the staff spoke English, not that it mattered much to me. I went to the front desk, asking if they had a guest named Seth Mortensen. The woman working there looked it up, and when she found him in their computer, I caught my breath. He was here. I'd really found him.

Well, kind of. When I asked her for his room number, she told me the hotel couldn't disclose that information. She could, however, connect me to his room. I hesitated before accepting. If Seth truly didn't want to be found, he might change his hotel or even city once he knew I'd located him. Still, I didn't necessarily have any other way to get in touch, so I let the woman connect me. It did no good. There was no answer.

Thanking her, I headed out to the back of the resort, figuring I'd walk off my frustration and hopefully clear my thoughts as I determined my next course of action. The pool and beach stretching out behind the building were intended for guests only, but it was easy enough to slip past security. I even took the opportunity, when briefly alone in a hall, to shape-shift into more appropriate clothing: a red bikini and sarong.

Outside, the heat hit me once again, and I paused, letting the sun soak into me. The time zone wasn't far off from Seattle's here, but even in early evening, the temperature was intense—which I loved. Beyond the pool and its bars, I could see a stretch of soft golden sand curving around blue, blue water. Still not as vivid as what I'd grown up with, but beautiful nonetheless. Lounge chairs and cabanas were scattered along the beach as sunseekers tried to grasp the last of the day's rays.

I walked toward it, hoping to find a chair of my own and maybe a mai tai. If I wasn't going to find Seth right away, I might as well—

There he was.

I came to an abrupt halt, nearly causing a young, giggling couple to walk into me and spill their drinks. I couldn't believe it. God might work in mysterious ways, but Hell worked in efficient ones.

I murmured apologies to the couple and started toward Seth, stopping again after a few more steps. What would I do? What would I say? Seth had broken an engagement and fled from everyone he knew. Now, here I was, intruding on his escape. I'd run through a few mental scenarios but hadn't decided on anything concrete. With a deep breath, I decided to just push forward and wing it.

I came up behind his chair, my shadow falling over him as I grew closer. He lay sprawled out in shorts and a Tootsie Pops T-shirt. A drink that looked suspiciously alcoholic sat by his side, and he was reading a book whose cover I couldn't see from this angle. Once more, I halted, confused over how I felt.

"The perfume," he said without warning. "Even out here, I can smell it. I'd know you anywhere. Tuberose and incense."

I walked around, coming to stand off to his right side. I put my hands on my hips. "You don't seem surprised to see me."

He took off his sunglasses and studied me, one of those small, amused smiles on his face. "I am . . . and I'm not. I thought I did a good job of disappearing. But I knew if anyone did find me, it would be you."

"Because I'm well connected?"

"Because you're you."

Searching for a clear spot of sand, I lowered myself to sit, but Seth scooted over on his lounge chair and indicated the space beside him. Hesitating only a moment, I sat next to where he lay, looking over him as our legs touched. He reached for his drink—a peach-colored monstrosity with enough sliced fruit for a salad in it—and took a sip.

"What's that?" I asked.

"They call it el Chupacabra."

"They do not."

"They do. I think it's got about fifty kinds of vodka in it. You'd like it."

"I'm surprised you like it."

"If you're going to become a villain, you might as well go the whole way," he replied, gesturing for a waiter to bring another drink.

"You're not a villain," I said softly.

"Yeah? Is that what they're saying back home?"

I glanced away and watched small waves break on the shore. "I haven't really talked to that many people. Mostly your family is worried."

"You've neatly dodged the question."

"Do you want to talk about it?" I turned back to him.

He gave a small shrug. "What's there to say? I broke her heart. I broke your heart. I don't think someone like me is meant to be in relationships."

"That's ridiculous. You're not the one who sucks people's souls away."

"Depends how literally you take the metaphor."

"Seth, stop. Stop making a joke out of this. Why'd you do it?"

"You have to ask?" The new drink arrived remarkably fast, and he handed it to me. He was right. It did taste like it had fifty kinds of vodka. "I didn't feel it. Not the way I should. You know that."

I did, and I was surprised at the frank and honest nature of our conversation. We hadn't had anything like this . . . well, not since we were dating. It had all been awkwardness and guarded feelings since things fell apart.

"But why now?"

It was his turn to look away, gazing off at the postcard view without seeing it. The sunlight hadn't quite turned orange yet, but it was bringing out the copper in his hair and amber of his eyes. I stared at him, taking it all in, hardly noticing how long it took him to answer.

"Georgina," he said at last, eyes still elsewhere. "When I ended things with us at Christmas . . . I did it so I wouldn't hurt you someday. And, I suppose, so you didn't hurt me. I went to Maddie for the wrong reasons then, but it didn't seem so bad since I actually cared about her—I mean, aside from the fact you had to live with it in front of you every day. I never meant for that part to happen."

"It's okay," I said automatically, hating the sadness in his voice. "I don't—"

"Shh," he said, holding up a hand. "I'll actually talk for once, so you better let me before I lose the nerve."

I smiled—though none of this was all that funny—and nodded.

"Anyway, I wish I'd chosen someone I didn't like or respect. It would have made things simpler. But as time went on, I found myself growing closer to her—but not farther from you. My plan wasn't working. I was only hurting the two of us more and more. Maybe I should have disappeared then."

I bit my lip on any comments.

"The only one who wasn't hurting was Maddie—because we were keeping her in the dark. And after you and me . . .

well, you know. After we were together, I felt so horrible . . . so guilty . . . I hated myself for what I'd done to her. I wanted desperately for one person to come out of this happy. I wanted her to stay in blissful ignorance. I wanted to make it up to her."

I'd deduced as much. And I also knew about the guilt . . . the guilt from the sin that had left a stain on his soul. Seth didn't know about that part and probably shouldn't ever.

"But whatever happiness I could give her wasn't real," he continued. "And I realized that the other day when we were at Erik's, and I . . . hell, Georgina. I don't really know what happened or even what I saw. There are only two things I'm sure about. One was that when Jerome came and said he needed me to come with him to help you, I did. If he'd said he had to take me to Hell itself, I would have."

I closed my eyes. "Seth—"

"And when I was there and Erik sent me wherever he did, I felt . . . well, it was beyond anything I'd experienced. At first, I was so confused and disoriented. I didn't get what they were saying about finding you. It seemed surreal. Then, it was the easiest thing in the world. I just looked for you, and there you were. In all that space and all that chaos, reaching you was like looking into myself. We were so close . . . it defied physics and every rule of nature I knew. It didn't seem real that I could be together with anyone like that.

"And when it was over, it's like I said—I wasn't sure what I'd just been a part of. But I knew that I had never experienced any bond like that with any other woman. Maybe you're the only one, maybe there's another . . . but regardless, I didn't have it with Maddie. She's amazing. I do love her. But in that situation again? I would never find her. And I knew it wasn't fair to lead her into a life without that connection. You and I . . . I don't understand what's between us, but I'd rather spend my life alone than with someone who isn't you."

He fell silent, and it was one of those weird times where I had no quick response. Instead, I linked my hand with his and stretched alongside him in the place he'd made on the chair, resting my head on his chest. He placed his hand on my shoulder, his fingers pressing into my skin to make sure I stayed. His heart beat against my ear.

"How's this going to end?" I asked bleakly.

"I . . . don't know, any more than I know how Cady and O'Neill are going to end." He sighed. "I have a feeling I *will* be alone. In spite of everything that's changed between us, nothing's actually changed."

"I . . . I don't know."

Again, my clever words were gone, but he was right. A lifetime seemed to have passed since we had split up, but all the same problems were still there. I might wax poetic about the universal connection of our souls, but it could never be matched physically, not so long as I refused him that. And mortality . . . always there was mortality beating down upon us. Seth wouldn't live forever, and that knowledge—figuratively speaking—killed me.

Which reminded me of something. I lifted my head and propped myself onto him so that my hair hung around us as I looked down at his face. "When are you coming home?"

He brushed some of the hair away, tucking it behind my ear. It came loose again. "Who said I'm coming home?"

"Don't joke. You have to."

"I'm not joking. Do you think I can go back there? I can't see Maddie. . . . I can't stand to see what I've done to her."

"You don't have to see her," I said. "Don't go to the store. People break up all the time and don't have to move."

Seth shook his head. "Yeah, but with my luck, we'd still run into each other. At a movie. A restaurant. Something. I'm a coward, Georgina. I don't want to see her . . . not after . . . well, you didn't see her face when I told her."

"I saw her face afterward," I said. "It was probably close enough. I can't believe you're seriously saying you'd never come back to Seattle just to avoid her."

"She's not the only one I'd be avoiding." Again, he tried to tuck the unruly hair back. When he failed again, he simply slid his hand down my arm, tracing its curves with his finger-tips. "I don't think I can handle seeing you either. Even being with you now . . . it's like the best thing in the world and the worst. Seeing you all the time would just drive home how we can't be together—and we *would* see each other all the time, you know. If I've learned anything, it's that fate doesn't let you and me stay apart for long."

Seth's words were such an odd contradiction. On one side, they were all filled with love and romantic sentiment about how agonizing his life was without me. Yet . . . there was more than just that. There was a defeatist attitude through-out it all, one I'd never seen in him before. Somewhere in all of this, Seth had gained a new bitterness, and I had the un-easy thought that if I could see his soul like Hugh could, the stain of sin would be even darker than before. I made one more attempt.

"Pull me out of the equation. You have to go back for your family. They need you. Andrea's sick."

"Everyone gets sick. That's not a convincing argument."

"No . . . you don't understand. They didn't tell you. She doesn't have the flu . . . she's got cancer."

That got a reaction. His expression went rigid. "No, she doesn't."

"She does. Brandy told me."

"She must have been confused," he said adamantly. "They would have told me."

"I don't think she'd mistake 'cold' for 'ovarian cancer.' And do you think she'd make something like that up?"

He considered a moment. "No, no, she wouldn't. But why didn't they say anything?"

"I guess they didn't tell anyone so they could find out more. Don't you see?" I leaned closer, hoping to drive home my plea. "They need you. You have to go home for them."

For a moment, I thought I had him, and then he slowly shook his head. "They'll be fine without me. And you said yourself they're waiting to find out more. It might not be that bad."

"Seth! It's cancer. It's going to be some level of bad, regardless. How can you abandon them?"

"Damn it," he said, about as angry as I ever saw him—which always came off pretty mild. "I don't need a moral angel on my shoulder right now. Just let me . . . just let me be selfish for once. I want to just be away from it all. I want to hide from my problems for once, instead of always being the responsible one. If you're just here to torment me with what can or can't be, then you should just . . . you should just go. Let me hide out and be free. Let me write the new series and forget about everything else."

It was almost a mirror of what I'd done so long ago. Only, instead of trying to forget my problems, I made everyone forget me. Sometimes, I kind of wished I added that last part to the bargain. Consequently, I could understand where he was coming from. I could understand that longing to just make all the bad things disappear. I'd wanted it too. I'd *made* it happen. The thing was, I'd expected more from him than from me. Sensing my hesitation, he cupped my face between his hands and drew me down into a small kiss. I drew back and stared in astonishment.

"What was that?" I asked.

"I might ultimately be trying to avoid you, but if I've got you now, I might as well enjoy it for the moment." There was a wicked gleam in his eyes, one I couldn't help but smile at, despite all the misgivings within me.

"You're a hypocrite," I said.

"An opportunist," he countered. "What are you really doing here, Georgina? What do *you* want?"

I lowered my gaze. I didn't know. I didn't know why I was here. I'd come to make sure he was okay . . . but then what? I was always going back and forth. I loved him. I had to forget him. Back and forth.

"I don't know," I admitted. "That's the best I've got."

And with no more deliberation, I kissed him again, longer this time, surprised at how easy it was to fall back into the kinds of kisses we used to do—the ones that just pushed the envelope of when I started to take his energy. He seemed like he was ready to go further, so I was the one who stopped him and returned to lying against him as we watched the sun sink down and paint the sky with brilliant colors. He gave no protest, seeming content just to have me close.

We ate dinner inside one of the resort's restaurants, my lack of packing not being a problem with shape-shifting. I pulled out a sexy v-cut evening dress whose violet shade reminded me of our first meeting. And as we talked and drank over dinner, our conversation slipped into the funny, comfortable manner we'd always shared. With Maddie removed from the equation, it was exactly as he'd said: so much had changed yet not changed. The rapport, the connection . . . it all burned between us—as did the sexual tension while we studied each other intently through the effortless conversation. He came alive more than I'd seen him in a while, but whether that was from the drinks or his freedom, I couldn't say.

Though my heart sang at finally being with him again, I was still battered with a million doubts. He'd told me to push them aside, but it was hard. Maddie. His underlying pessimism. His desire for escape. His family. My own selfishness.

But when we finished dinner, all such worries fled. As soon as we were back in his room—a wide and spacious suite that looked out to the now-dark water—we were all over each other. The longing that had built up between us exploded. His hands undid the zipper of my dress, peeling it from my body. We fell onto the bed, and I tore at his shorts, reason and responsibility nonexistent. His hands ran the length of my body, down the sides of my hips while his mouth moved from my collarbone to the spot between my breasts and then finally onto one of the breasts and its hardened nipple.

I was prying off his pants when I felt the glow of life energy start to creep into me. For a few moments, I was able to ignore its implications. I just wanted him. I wanted to feel what I'd felt months ago when his body had been in mine and I'd had that sense of perfect union. The life energy was an aphrodisiac, enhancing the desire my physical body felt.

Maybe it was a kneejerk reaction from the days of dating, but once more, I was the one who had to stop it all. I put some distance between us, though we were still intertwined.

"Okay," I said, my heart pounding in my chest. "We're about to cross the line."

There was lust in Seth's eyes. Lust and love and that same burning need I had to reach ultimate completion. "We crossed it a little, didn't we?" he asked breathlessly. "I felt it."

"Yeah," I admitted. "Not much." *Not much is too much.*

He frowned a little, his hand still running over my leg. So, so dangerous. A little more and we would teeter over the edge again.

"I've felt it before," he said. "When you started to take some of me. Just a vague sense, but it was there. Somehow . . . somehow, it didn't seem *quite* as bad this time."

He was right, and that was because of that slight darkening on his soul. Sure, he was nowhere near as bad as a lot of Hell-bound people, but even that slight mark made a difference. I could feel it. Before, he'd been pristine and pure, all sparking silver and undiluted life. Most of it was still there . . . save that slight shadow, a shadow that I suspected was increasing the more he decided to turn his back on the people in his life. And the darker a soul was, the less of it I took.

"You're right." I didn't bother getting into the technicalities. "But it'd still be bad."

"Too bad to risk just one time?"

An old argument. "What happened to you giving me up?"

"I will if I have to. I was ready to. But that was before you came here . . . you still haven't told me why, what you want. I'd do it again. I'd be together again, but no more physical boundaries." He cut off my protests. "I know, I know the risks. And I know—as should you—that what's between us is about more than sex. But that was still a thorn, no matter how much we knew it shouldn't be. I don't want anything like that happening again. I'll take the risk. It's my choice."

"I—I don't know. I just don't . . ."

"Well, that's better than 'I can't.'" He chuckled. He moved closer, his lips just brushing mine. "And if you decide no, then that's how it'll be. But maybe . . . maybe just this once we could . . . maybe just once you could give in. . . ."

I closed my eyes as his lips pressed against mine once more, harder this time, and our bodies moved back together. Again, he was right. I could almost give in this time. I'd been through too much recently, so much emotional and spiritual upheaval. Being with him felt like the most natural thing in the world right now . . . but my warning alarms were still going off. If I shortened his life with a dark soul, he'd be that much closer to Hell.

"No," I said at last. It was growing more difficult to keep pulling back. "I still can't. Not yet. I'm not saying never . . . I just. I'm so confused. I'm sorry."

He looked disappointed, but to my relief, he didn't push the issue again. I might not have been able to resist if he did. "But you'll stay? You'll stay the night with me at least?"

I nodded. "I can stay for three days."

"Three days. That's perfect. I can handle that. Three more days to think about it all. If we can stay together . . . then we will. If we can't, then I'll be alone until there's another Georgina." His wry tone indicated his doubts about that. "For now, this is enough."

We lounged in each other's arms naked after that, miraculously managing to keep things from escalating. Of course, it was a skill we'd perfected while dating, so we fell into it naturally—though also reluctantly. We stayed up talking for a long time, as though we hadn't seen each other for years and had a lifetime to catch up on. Which really wasn't that far from the truth.

At last, he slept, but I was restless. I watched his peaceful breathing in the darkness, his sleep heavy from the drinks. His skin was warm against mine, and I felt safer than I had in a while.

Three days. We'd have these three days, and for a little

longer, I could pretend he was mine again, just like he used to be. If I chose, I could even make this permanent. I'd told him I'd think about it. The one problem with it all was that things *weren't* like they used to be. The dream replayed in my head, the dream that might have been a lie. Seth had been the man in the dream, the one I could have been with if what the Oneroi had showed me was true. But was this Seth lying in my arms the man in the dream? The one I'd dreamed of had been infinitely kind and good—the one I'd fallen in love with. The real Seth had changed—gradually, yes . . . but the change was there.

It was wrong of me to judge, seeing as part of the change over the last year had been a result of me in his life. Yet, once more, that selfish part inside me thought he should have resisted. I'd fallen for Seth because of his moral character, something that always attracted me to a man. Ironic and possibly hypocritical for a servant of Hell. I still loved Seth, still felt that connection, but things were off now. This bitterness, this attitude that made him want to lock himself away in easy, selfish retreat was not what I'd expected of him. I'd expected more.

I didn't want to lose him. I wanted these last few days with him. I wanted forever with him, but if I stayed, I'd be furthering this attitude I hated. I'd encourage the darkness to build within him. I didn't want to see it. And as much as I loved him and yearned to cling to a few more moments with him, I realized staying with this Seth who disappointed me so much was a bad idea. Seth had said he'd rather be alone than be with the wrong woman. I'd rather be apart from him than see him like this. I wanted my memories of him to stay pure.

And so, though it broke my heart, I untangled myself from him. In his heavy sleep, he didn't stir. Again, the hypocrisy wasn't lost on me. I'd tried so many times to coax him into one drink, and now I looked down on him for using cocktails as a way to dull the pain. How stupid, I thought, that his darkened soul made it easier for us to finally be together . . . and yet, for my heart, it made it impossible.

I shape-shifted into jeans and a light tank top and found some hotel stationery. On it, I scrawled:

> Seth,
> I'm sorry—but I have to leave. I told you I'd con-
> sider everything, but I was wrong. I love you too
> much to stay.

Cryptic much? A meager way to express all those feelings, but somehow, I suspected he'd understand. He knew me. I left it on the bedside table and then watched him for a few moments, admiring the man I loved and always would. Finally, my eyes wet, I turned away and left the room to catch a taxi to the airport.

Chapter 23

"Where've you been?" asked Roman.

I hadn't landed in Seattle until later the next day. Turns out getting flights from Mexico to the Pacific Northwest can take a little longer than immortal teleportation, particularly on short notice.

"To the edge of the known world and back," I said, falling onto the couch. Both cats came to me, which I took with some smugness, seeing as they usually fawned all over Roman.

"So, what, South Dakota?"

I made a face and covered my eyes with one arm. My trip to locate Seth had only taken twenty-four hours, but really, that was a lot to endure in so short a time. "I found Seth."

"Oh." Roman's enthusiasm dimmed considerably. "I guess his disappearance wasn't as milk carton–worthy as Maddie made it sound."

"Well, I had to—literally—call in a demonic favor to hunt him down."

"And? Are you guys running into the sunset together now that he's free?"

The mention of sunset made me flinch, recalling how Seth and I had held each other on the beach. "Not quite. I . . . left him."

"What's that mean exactly?"

I tried to explain all that had gone down with Seth, but it wasn't easy. It was almost too much for my brain to wade through, let alone articulate to someone else. When I finished, I felt even more exhausted than before.

"So that's it? You're never going to see each other again?" Roman's voice was skeptical.

"He said he's not coming back, and I didn't stick around. So, yeah."

"I have a hard time believing that. Is he just going to live at that hotel permanently? Even he can't make that much money."

"No, he mentioned at dinner that he'd be settling down somewhere else. He just hasn't decided where."

All was quiet between us for a minute or so. The only sounds were the traffic outside and Aubrey purring near my ear. At last, Roman asked, "Are you okay?"

I glanced over at him in surprise. "What do you mean?"

"Exactly what I said. This can't be easy on you. I mean, you haven't even had any downtime since the Oneroi."

I don't know why his words caught me by surprise. I guess it was because amidst all the woes that were always going on in my life, few people ever asked if I was okay. Maybe they'd given up asking because depressing things were so commonplace for me. How weird, I thought, that Roman had swung from sociopathic to compassionate while Seth had fallen down a darker path. Of course, I had no hard evidence that Roman wasn't actually a compassionate sociopath. Still, I gave him a smile of gratitude.

"I am okay—or will be eventually. Thanks."

There must have been something in my smile that gave him hope or just made him feel inspired because his own smile grew radiant. I'd forgotten just how beautiful it was, the way it could light up his face. We left dangerous topics alone after that but spent the rest of the night hanging out together. I wasn't totally okay by any means, but it was nice to simply be ordinary for a while and free of drama. I wondered if that's what my life would be like now—and what role Roman would play.

*   *   *

Still, adjusting to a world without Seth wasn't easy over the next few days. Even when he'd been with Maddie, even when the sight of him had caused me pain, he'd still been *there*. And I'd known he was there. Now, the knowledge that he was gone and that he wasn't coming back left a strange emptiness in my heart, even as the rest of my life began to stabilize.

I returned to work, a good thing for the store because Maddie had taken some much-needed time off. I checked on her via Doug and offered to go to her if needed, despite knowing I wouldn't enjoy listening to her mourn for Seth. Of course, since I was doing the same thing, maybe I shouldn't have been so quick to turn down commiseration.

"She just wants to be alone right now," Doug said, leaning in my doorway. He had no joke today, none of his usual wackiness. "Still upset—but she's a trouper. I'll let you know when she's ready to see anyone."

"Okay." My heart went out to her. "Keep me posted."

It was nearing closing time, and I went out to the store's main part to help with some of the evening tasks. A few of the staff members were already going home. One of them was Gabrielle. And she was leaving with Cody.

"What's going on?" I whispered to him while she went to get her purse. He wasn't even wearing black.

"We've gone out a couple times since . . . well, while you've been distracted." He sounded apologetic for his happiness.

"That's fantastic," I said. Love was managing to survive somewhere in this world. "What changed her mind? The concert?"

"A little. I think that opened the door. She's really excited that I'll only hang out at night. And that I can show her real vampires."

"What? You managed to convince her Peter was a vampire?" To the average human, that would be even less likely than Cody being a vampire.

"No, of course not." His lovesick expression hardened a little. "But Milton—you know that vampire from Eugene?—

he's been in town this week. Claims he's visiting friends."
Vampires were very territorial about their hunting grounds,
even ones like Peter and Cody who rarely took victims and
didn't kill when they did. "He hasn't caused any trouble, but
I don't buy that vacation thing. It's as ridiculous as Simone
just visiting."

"She *is* gone, right?" That had been the rumor, and seeing
as there'd been no wacky mishaps with two Georginas, I had
to believe it was true. I'd never know what her motivation
had been.

"Yup, as far as I know. Anyway. Milton. He sure does
look like a vampire. Have you seen him? He's like a modern-
day Nosferatu. I took Gabrielle when I went to spy on him at
a dance club, and she got really excited. She thinks I have
some special knack for finding vampires—at least wannabe
ones."

"Huh," I said. "That's somehow bizarre, funny, and cute
all at the same time. Maybe a little disturbing." He grinned at
that, showing his fangs. "What's she think of the teeth? You
can't hide those if you're up close and personal all the time."

"Told her I had them cosmetically done." He looked very
pleased. "She thinks it's hot."

His new romance left me in a good mood when I finally
took off. I stepped outside into the chilly night, surprised I
didn't mind it so much. Something about the clean, brisk air
seemed refreshing to me, and for the first time in a while, I regretted moving out of Queen Anne. It would have been nice
to walk home on this early winter evening, instead of climbing into the plastic and metal of my car.

There was nothing to be done for it, though. I turned the
ignition and checked my cell phone before heading out of the
parking lot. I often left the ringer off while working, and
three calls had come in for me. I had a voice mail for each.
The first was from a few hours ago, from Erik. He spoke in
his usual genteel tones, but I could hear some urgency underneath. He told me he'd come up with some theories about my
contract and wanted to talk to me soon.

The next message was from Roman, from about an hour ago. He knew my work schedule perfectly and was calling to see what kind of takeout I wanted. If I called as I was leaving, he said, he'd probably have food by the time I walked in. I felt my lips turn into a smile at that—one that promptly dropped when I heard the last message. It had come in five minutes ago and was from Erik again.

"Georgina—"

That was it. Just my name, tense and strangled. After that came static, what sounded like the phone dropping, and then the voice mail ended. I stared at my phone as though it were a totally foreign object.

I had never, ever heard Erik call me by my first name.

My car was already headed toward his store when I dialed him back. It was too late for the store to be open, but that was the number my cell phone had logged. No answer came. I tried his home number, just to be safe, and received no answer there either. My fear increased, as did my speed. Easy traffic moved me along, but I still felt like his store might as well be hundreds of miles away.

I made it there in fifteen minutes, which was actually pretty remarkable. The store's lights were on, though everything else in the strip mall and its lot was dark. I parked right in front, in a handicapped spot, and tore out of my car, nearly coming to a halt at what I found.

The glass of the door and window were smashed, with glittering shards covering the sidewalk. Even if the door had been locked, I could have reached right in to open it. I pushed through, stepping inside to find more destruction. Fountains still tinkled, music still played, but everything else was in shambles. Bookshelves knocked over. Statuary in pieces. Jewelry cases broken—and empty.

"Erik?" I called, hurrying through the store. There was no answer. I passed the register, saw the drawer hanging open, and suspected I'd find it as empty as the cases.

I was heading for the store's back room when I heard a

small noise. Turning, I peered around wildly and caught a glimpse of a hand, behind the checkout counter. There, I found Erik sprawled on the floor, pale despite his dusky skin. A hand lay over his stomach, which was a pool of dark blood. His eyes were glassy, and for a moment, I thought he was dead. Then the lids twitched, and his eyes focused on me.

"Miss Kincaid . . ."

I dialed 911 while simultaneously trying to rip my coat off. I screamed at them to send an ambulance and pressed the light fabric of the trench coat into his stomach. The effort was futile. A red strain promptly began spreading through the cloth.

"Don't say anything," I pleaded when I saw his lips move. They were blue-tinged. "Someone's coming. You'll be okay."

I wanted to ask a hundred questions: what had happened, who had done this. None mattered. Only saving him did— and besides, the scenario seemed painfully clear. A break-in, one in which he must have interfered. Two bullet holes on the wall revealed what had happened to his stomach. The third shot had hit.

"Miss Kincaid . . ." His voice was so small, barely a croak.

"Shh. We'll talk later, after the paramedics come. Save your strength."

"There won't be a later," he gasped. I swear, he tried to smile. "Not . . . for . . . me . . ."

"They'll be here in, like, five minutes," I countered.

"Doesn't matter. Too weak. Too much blood."

"No," I said desperately. "No." Even as I begged, my hysteria growing, I knew he was right. He had lost too much blood. He was only alive now because this was a slow-killing wound. Even if paramedics walked in right now, they wouldn't get him away in time to save him. With his age and recent illness, he wouldn't come back from this. Still, I denied it. "You'll be okay. Listen—"

"You listen." There was no real force behind the command, but I shut up. One of his hands clung to me. "It's not . . . your contract."

I was confused, my mind still on his condition and the store. Then, I caught the context. "Let the contract go. We'll worry about it later."

His grip tightened. "There must be another. Two contracts."

"There . . . what? No. That's not how it works. I know that for sure. One contract per soul. I signed one. Now, please. Don't say anything else."

"Find it," he coughed. There was blood on his lips. "Find . . . it."

"I will, I will." I would have agreed to anything, though what he was saying made no sense. My words must have comforted him because he relaxed ever so slightly. There was still no question that he must be in agonizing pain, though. I glanced up at the front of the store, willing myself to hear sirens. "They'll be here," I said.

"Too . . . late. You . . . you can stop the pain."

He was so hard to hear now, I had to lean close. Even then, I didn't fully parse his words until a few moments later. "I'm trying." I shifted the coat a little, which was proving totally ineffectual.

"A kiss . . . one kiss . . ."

"I . . ." My eyes went wide. "No. No. It'll kill you . . ." Even as I said the words, I realized how stupid they were. This gunshot was already going to kill him. He was going to die. *One kiss.* He wanted a kiss to speed his dying, just as I'd given Luc. I'd never performed that deed again, nor had I wanted to. Maybe it had been mercy, but I'd felt like a killer. And yet, just like I had then, I knew it would ease the passing. . . .

I shook my head. "No."

"Nyx . . . showed me. Showed me my death: you."

He coughed again and could speak no more. Still, he clung to life, with pain on his face and pleading in his eyes.

Nyx? Nyx had shown him his death. . . .

In the far reaches of my mind, I remembered finding him one day, right after Nyx had visited him and shown him a vision. He'd recoiled from me at first and then later shrugged it off, laughing it away as the remnants of a nightmare. But I understood now. He'd seen his death—seen me causing it. He'd been afraid of me in those moments. My man in the dream had been a lie, but all the other visions she'd shown had been true. My role in Erik's death had been destined . . . just not in any malicious way. That was how her dreams often worked. Never quite what you expected.

And so, for the second time, I became an angel of mercy . . . an angel of death . . . whatever. I hunched down and kissed him, ignoring the blood on his mouth. Just like with Luc, there was only a breath of life left. Five more minutes, and Erik would have been gone without me. That tiny bit of life was as pure and good as I'd known it would be. Erik would be rewarded in the afterlife.

As I lifted my head and watched peace settle over his features, faint feelings flitted through me, as sometimes happened when I took energy. There was affection for me. It wasn't romantic love. More like fatherly love. Friendship. Fondness. And underneath it was a warning, a warning for me he never got to convey. I was so caught up in those last bursts of life, that I was only distantly aware when the lights and sirens came.

Someone lifted me away, and I saw people huddling around him—too late. I stared at the commotion that followed—paramedics, police. I saw it without seeing it, answered questions without even knowing what I said. A policeman with kind eyes took it all down and spoke to me gently, often repeating himself. I don't know how long it all took. Maybe an hour, maybe more. I only remember assuring them over and over that I was okay, that I was going home, and that I would answer any other questions that came up.

But when I drove away, still in shock, still barely grasping what had happened, I didn't go to West Seattle. I went to Pioneer Square, parking in a lucky street spot and then winding my way through the partying crowds. A few people gave me curious looks when I walked into the Cellar, looks I gave no heed to as I honed in on Jerome's table. He drank alone tonight, his dark eyes watching me intently as I approached.

"Georgie," he said when I came to a stop in front of him, "what's the point of shape-shifting if you're going to walk around with blood on you?"

I looked down, only then registering the stains on my shirt. I turned back to him, ignoring the shape-shifting suggestion.

"Erik's dead," I told him, my voice flat.

Jerome's face displayed no reaction. "How?"

"A break-in. Somebody shot him."

Jerome sipped his bourbon and remained silent.

"Well? Don't you have anything to say?"

He scowled. "What do you expect me to say? Should I cry? Put on sackcloth and ashes? Humans die all the time, Georgie. You're the one who mourns them—not me. I have no sentiment for any of them. You know that. And certainly not for him."

I did know that. When Duane—one of Jerome's former employees—had been killed, the demon's only reaction had been annoyance.

"What's weird . . ." I paused, putting to words what had been coalescing in the back of my mind this whole time. "What's weird is that someone would break into a New Age store at all. It's not a good place for a robbery."

"If it has money, it's a good place for a robbery. If it's in a deserted strip mall, with only an old man there, it's even a better place for a robbery. Were the valuables gone?"

"Yes," I admitted.

"Then why are you here wasting my time?"

"The glass."

"The glass?"

"The glass was broken from the inside," I said. "The pieces were scattered on the sidewalk. Whoever did it didn't break the glass to get in. It just looked that way."

Jerome sighed irritably. "After everything you've seen, can you honestly question the behaviors of humans?"

"It just seems strange that someone like Erik—someone

who deals in the supernatural and who had—" I hesitated, about to say that he'd been pondering my contract. Instead, I said, "Who had just been involved with a big immortal blowout would be the victim of this by coincidence."

"Coincidences happen."

"I don't believe in coincidences anymore."

"Then replay your own words. Your 'big immortal blowout' is the answer. They might not live in our world, but do you think dream creatures don't have connections here?"

I frowned. "What are you saying?"

"That I thought it was too convenient for the Oneroi's overlord to walk away. He knew he couldn't touch me or any other immortal. But a human? One who had been actively involved with thwarting him?" Jerome shrugged. "It's revenge. He could arrange for that. We can't prove it—and *we can't do anything.* Make sure you understand that. I'm not going to avenge your friend, if that's what you're asking for."

I hadn't expected him to. In fact, I really wasn't sure what I'd expected of him at all. Why had I come here? Because I was in shock. Because what had happened to Erik didn't make sense. Because Jerome often had answers for me.

This time, he did too . . . but I wasn't sure that I believed them. The old adage came back: *How do you know if a demon is lying? His lips are moving.*

"Okay," I said with a small nod. His eyes narrowed a little. I think he was surprised I'd given in so quickly. Glancing down, I shape-shifted the blood away. "I'm going to go home and . . . I don't know. I don't know what I'm going to do."

My confusion wasn't faked, and I hoped it would be enough to clear any suspicion. And really, what did he have to be suspicious of? I didn't even know. *Two contracts.*

Jerome didn't try to stop me. I drove home with almost no realization of what I was doing until I pulled into the parking lot under my building. As soon as I opened my condo's door, I caught the faint smell of Chinese food. It smelled delicious, yet at the same time, it had that slight twinge of food that had been sitting around for a while. Roman sprawled on the couch, staring at nothing as far as I could tell. The TV was off. The cats remained unpetted.

"I'm sorry I didn't call," I said. "You won't believe what—"

"I've got something for you," he said. "Two somethings, actually."

The odd tone of his voice was about the only thing that could have stopped me from gushing about what had gone down at Erik's tonight. Even now, the events in the store were so surreal that it hardly seemed like something that had happened to me. Surely it was something I'd seen in a movie. I sat down in the armchair near Roman, the queasy feeling in my stomach growing as I wondered what else could possibly happen tonight.

"What is it?"

He handed me a piece of paper. "This was under the door when I got back with the food. I didn't mean to read it, but . . . well, it wasn't in an envelope or anything."

I took it wordlessly, immediately recognizing the scrawled writing. Seth's. To a lot of people it would be undecipherable, but I'd had a lot of practice in decoding his sloppy penmanship.

> *Georgina,*
>
> *When I woke up without you in Mazatlán, I was so angry. I felt betrayed and abandoned and wondered if you'd been playing me the entire time. Then, the more I thought about your words, the more my life began to come into focus. I still don't want to deal with the mess here in Seattle. I don't want to face Maddie. I don't want to face myself. But, I realized, I do want you to be proud of me.*
>
> *Maybe "proud" isn't the right word. Respect? Like? Love? I'm not sure, but the events at Erik's have still left an impression. Really, lying in your arms has left an impression. I meant what I said: I'd rather be alone than not be with you. Even apart, though, I can't stand the thought of you being*

disappointed in me. To regain your good opinion, I would risk almost anything. I'd even come back here to face my demons.

And I have come back here, despite how much I wish I could run away. Disappearing won't erase the bad things around me, however. Maybe you're a messenger of some sort, some agent of destiny. If not for you, I almost certainly wouldn't have returned, but it turns out I needed to. Terry and Andrea received their results yesterday. She only has months to live, something that I'd almost swear was the doctor's joke. Only a few weeks ago, she seemed perfectly fine. I don't want to face that, any more than I want to face everything else. But they need me more than ever now, and I love them. I love them so much that I realize my own life and wants don't matter. As soon as I finish this book, I'm putting everything else—even the new series—on hold. None of it matters. Only they do. They'll need me in the next few months. They'll need me more in the months after that.

I don't know when we'll see each other again—though you'll notice I say "when" and not "if." Like I mentioned in Mexico, I know better than to think the universe will keep us apart. Regardless, I want you to be happy wherever your life takes you—and I hope someday I can be worthy of your respect again.

I also want you to know that in returning, I don't expect anything from you. I just wanted to make sure you understood what I did . . . and how you've affected me.
—Seth

I looked up at Roman, who had been studying me while I read. I didn't know what astonished me more: Seth returning—because of me—or the god-awful news about Andrea.

Both were monumental in their own ways. One was a tragedy of epic proportions.

I swallowed, afraid if I fully processed it all, I'd start crying. "I'm not sure how much more I can handle tonight," I said in a small voice.

Roman's face was a mixture of sympathy and cynicism. "Well, you've got one more thing."

He handed me a magazine. It was a trashy celebrity gossip one that was a popular source of mockery over at the bookstore. I couldn't imagine why he was giving something so trivial to me, in light of everything else that had gone on. One page was marked with a Post-it, and I flipped to it.

It was a spread of assorted celebrity shots, the kind of candids that paparazzi delighted in: actors out with their children, pop stars spotted in Las Vegas nightclubs. I skimmed over the two pages, feeling a frown grow on my face as I tried to figure out why on earth I'd care about this right now.

Then, I found it. It was a small picture, shoved off to the side between much more interesting and larger ones of badly dressed actors. The caption read: *Best-selling author Seth Mortensen enjoys some natural beauty in Mazatlán.*

And it showed Seth and me kissing on the beach.

Chapter 24

"This . . . isn't possible," I said.

"I don't know," said Roman dryly. "Looks pretty possible to me."

"But Seth's an author. These kinds of magazines don't care about people like him."

"He's so commonplace for you that you don't realize how famous he is. And, hey, if it's a slow week, they probably take what they can get. Sex sells—and that's pretty sexy."

I looked down at it again. It *was* pretty sexy. They'd taken it when I'd been lying on top of Seth, and the sarong had slipped enough that I was showing an awful lot of skin. Nausea rolled through me.

"Maybe no one will see this." Yet, even as the words left my lips, I knew that was wishful thinking on my part. As I'd noted before, this magazine was a favorite at the store, largely because of its outrageously ridiculous articles. Someone, somewhere was going to see this picture. And while the articles might be fabrications, a photo like this—which clearly showed our faces—could hardly lie.

I let the magazine fall to the floor. "I can't . . . I can't deal with this. Not after everything else."

Roman frowned, legitimate concern filling his features. I don't think he was happy about either the picture or Seth's new resolve, but it had to be obvious that more than these bits of news were plaguing me.

"Georgina, what else is—"

I held a hand up. "Not now. Tomorrow. We'll talk tomorrow. Too much . . . too much has happened tonight." Erik's lifeless eyes flashed in my mind. "It makes this seem like nothing."

He hesitated, then nodded. "Okay. You want to set aside some time for tomorrow night? I don't mean a date. Just, I don't know. Get dinner, talk about all this so it doesn't eat you up. I really am worried about you."

I started to say he shouldn't worry, that I'd be okay, but I backed off. I really didn't know if I was. "I'd like that," I said honestly. "If my damage control doesn't conflict, then sure. I'll tell you all about it." I stood up wearily. "But now—bed."

He let me retreat to my bedroom, his heart in his eyes. It made me feel worse, largely because of what a low priority his feelings were for me right now. Obviously, they were important to him, and I appreciated his ardor. And his feelings *did* mean something to me. There was something very sweet and comforting in his offer to breathe and just talk. But in light of everything else going on? I couldn't allow myself to process anything too deep with our relationship right now.

Particularly when I had to face the gauntlet at the bookstore the next day. I'd had a number of past times entering Emerald City where I'd been met with curious and covert looks. More often than not, it had been over something ridiculous, and I'd had no clue until later. Today, I knew exactly what was going on. There was no question that the damned magazine had gotten around.

And the looks this time weren't inquisitive or smug. They were accusatory. Disdainful. I couldn't face them. Not yet. I hurried through the store as quickly as I could, seeking my office—which I vowed not to leave for the rest of my shift. It was pretty hypocritical, considering my judgment on Seth avoiding his problems. Only, I didn't have as much luck getting away from mine.

Maddie was sitting at my desk.

I hadn't seen her in a week, not since she'd come to my condo. I'd told her then she could have indefinite leave from work and hadn't expected to see her back anytime soon. Now she stopped me dead in my tracks.

Her face was much calmer than I would have expected. No, it was more than calm. It was still. Perfectly, eerily still. Like a sculpture. And when she looked up at me, it was like looking into the eyes of the dead. Cold. Emotionless. Nonetheless, I shut the door, fearing what was to come.

"I had a million theories, you know." Her voice was as flat as her expression. "Never, ever did I consider this one. I mean, I wondered if there could have been another woman. But I never thought it'd be you."

It took an impossibly long time for my lips to move. "No . . . it wasn't that. It wasn't like that at all. That's not why he did it. . . ." I couldn't finish and suddenly questioned my words. Wasn't *that*—by which I meant, me—exactly the reason he'd left her? Maybe our beach interlude hadn't been the direct cause, but I had certainly been the catalyst.

The magazine lay on my desk, open to the guilty page. She picked it up, studying it with a calculating look. "So what then? You were just comforting him after the fact?"

"Actually . . . well, actually, yeah. That shot was taken afterward."

It still sounded lame, and we both knew it. She threw the magazine down, and finally, the emotion came to her face. "What, and that makes it okay?" she cried. "You—one of my best friends—running off with my fiancé the day after he dumps me?"

"It wasn't like that," I repeated. "I went to find him . . . to see if he was okay."

"And then you made sure he was okay?" she demanded. Her words were sarcastic, but tears glittered in her eyes.

"No . . . I didn't expect anything like that to happen. And really, nothing much did happen. The thing is . . ." I took a deep breath. "We used to date. Before you guys were together. We never told anyone. Things ended . . . well, pretty much just before you started going out." Like, almost the day before.

That caught her off guard. Her eyes went wide. "*What? You had a past . . . you went out with *my* boyfriend and never told me? *He* never told me?"

"We thought it'd be easier."

"Easier? Easier?" She pointed at the magazine again. "You think seeing you guys back together in full color was easier?"

"We aren't back together," I said quickly. "He didn't end things because he was cheating—" Again, I had to admit the truth to myself. He hadn't been cheating on her when he broke the engagement, but we'd slept together earlier in the relationship. "I was as surprised as you were. And I was worried. I told you, I went to find him, but we didn't sleep together. Then I left. That's it."

The tears were on her cheeks now. "It wouldn't have mattered if you had slept together. You guys keeping that past from me—you guys *lying* is worse. I trusted you! I trusted both of you! How could you do this? What kind of person does this to their friend?"

A damned soul, I thought. But I didn't say that. I didn't say anything.

Maddie shot up from the desk, futilely trying to wipe away the tears that were still coming. "Doug warned me once, you know. He said there was this way you guys always looked at each other that made him wonder. I told him he was crazy. I told him he was imagining it—that it was impossible. That you guys would never do that to me."

"Maddie, I'm sorry—"

She hurried to the door, pushing past me. "Not as sorry as I am for putting my trust in you. For putting my trust in both of you. I'm quitting. Right now. Don't expect to see me again." She jerked the door open. "I don't know how you can live with yourself. You two deserve each other!"

The door slammed loudly, rattling my ears. I stayed where I was, staring blankly at the desk, unable to move. Unable to think or react or do anything useful. *I don't know how you can live with yourself.* Me either.

"Boy, things are pretty screwed up for you."

Carter materialized beside me, his angelic signature filling the room. Dressed as ratty as always—except for his hat—he strolled casually to the desk and picked up the magazine. "That's a good shot of you, though."

"Shut up," I said. The agony I'd tried to keep locked up with Maddie began to burst out. "Just shut up! I can't handle your commentary right now, okay? Not with everything else. Certainly not with this . . ." I sank to the floor, leaning against the door and raking my hands through my hair. When I looked up at Carter, I expected one of his laconic smiles, but his face was all seriousness.

"I wasn't being sarcastic," he said. "Things *are* screwed up."

I suddenly wished I had a cigarette. "Yes. They certainly are. Erik's dead, you know."

"I know."

I closed my eyes for a moment, allowing myself to feel the full grief over that. With so much going on, it didn't seem like I'd really allowed any of these problems to have the full mourning they deserved. Someone, I realized, would have to do the proper things for Erik now. Did he have family somewhere? Dante of all people might know. Otherwise, I was willing to take on any funeral arrangements—no matter the cost or work. I owed Erik that much. I owed him so much more.

"It wasn't a coincidence," I said softly. "It couldn't have been. Jerome says it was some revenge from the Oneroi's master . . . but I don't believe that. Erik had been trying to figure out my contract. Before he died . . . before he . . ." My voice caught as I recalled how *I* had been the one to take that last breath. "He told me there were two contracts. That it wasn't mine that was the problem. I don't know what that means."

Carter still said nothing, but his eyes were fixed so intently on me that they might as well have been pinning me to the wall.

"But you know, don't you?" I asked him. "You've always

known. And Simone . . ." I frowned. "Before Jerome sent her away, he mentioned something about her knowing Niphon and 'fucking up things even more.' That's a piece of all this too, isn't it?"

Carter still remained silent. I gave a harsh laugh.

"But, of course, you can't say anything. You can't do anything. Hell's always got its hands in mortal affairs—or even lesser immortal affairs—but you guys? Nothing. How can you be a force for good in this world? You don't help bring it about! You just wait and hope it happens on its own."

"Most of the good in this world happens without any of our help," he said evasively.

"Oh good God. What a lovely answer from you. And you know what? I don't believe there *is* any good in this world. All this time . . . ever since I sold my soul, I've been clinging to this idea that there is something pure and decent out there. That there was something to give me hope that even if I was a lost cause, at least there was something bright and good in the world. But there isn't. If there was, Seth wouldn't have fallen. Erik wouldn't have died. Andrea Mortensen wouldn't be dying."

"Good can still exist when bad things happen, just as evil persists when good things happen."

"What good comes from Andrea dying? What good comes from leaving five little girls alone and motherless in the world?" I was choking on my own sobs. "If you—if any of you—could really affect the world, you wouldn't let that happen."

"I can't change fate. I'm not God." He was still so fucking calm that I wanted to punch him. Yet, what could I expect? Jerome had no attachment to humans, and at the end of the day, angels and demons weren't so different.

I buried my face in my hands. "You can't change anything. None of us can change anything. We're resigned to our fates, just like Nyx showed."

"Humans change their fates all the time. Even lesser immortals do. It starts small, but it happens."

I was suddenly tired. So, so tired. I shouldn't have come

here today. I should never have left my bed. I no longer had the energy to argue with him or berate his frustratingly useless attitude.

"Can Seth change?" I asked at last. "Are good intentions enough to redeem a soul?"

"All things are possible. And I don't mean that as a cliché," he added, no doubt seeing the scowl on my face. "It's true. Mortals and mortals-turned-immortals don't always believe that—which is why Hell has such a foothold in the world. And I'm not saying that if you believe it, it *will* happen. Things don't always turn out for the best, but miracles are real, Georgina. You've just got to lift yourself out of the muck to make them. You've got to take the chance."

Yes, I was definitely getting a cigarette after this. Carter probably had one on him. I gave him as much of a smile as I could muster. "Easy for you to say. Can *you* make miracles?"

"I try," he said. "I try. Will you?"

And with that, he vanished before I could bum a cigarette. Fucking angels.

But his words stayed with me when I went home that night, maybe because even as depressing as they seemed, they were still more cheerful than enduring that shift. My managerial mandates were still obeyed, but otherwise, I could see the seething disapproval and condemnation in the eyes of my colleagues. It was a startling reminder of my village's reaction when everyone had found out I'd cheated on Kyriakos. Only this time, I had no way to blot it from these people's minds. I had nothing more to bargain with Hell.

At the condo, I found a note from Roman, saying he'd be staying at the school for a while that evening to finish up some setup. If I wanted, though, he'd be happy to take me out for dinner as he'd promised. That gave me time to stretch out on the couch, seeing as I was still exhausted from the emotional miasma I'd been wading through this last week. No sleep came, just a kind of bleak malaise as I stared at the ceiling. Probably just as well. God only knew what I'd dream.

Dream.

I sighed. The man in the dream. It had been bugging me over and over in my subconscious, and without even mentioning it, Carter had somehow brought it back to the forefront of my mind. The Oneroi had claimed Seth was the man in the dream. I told myself for the hundredth time that it was a ridiculous fantasy. I couldn't have any real relationship with a mortal. Seth had fallen from grace, and I'd refused him. It was all impossible now.

All things are possible.

Erik and Mei had said it was impossible for Seth to find my soul across the vastness of the dream world—yet he had.

Kristin had told me my contract was airtight—yet Erik had sworn there was a flaw somewhere. He'd died for that knowledge, I was certain.

Seth had claimed nothing could bring him back to Seattle—yet *I* had.

Everyone who worked for Hell had told me darkened souls almost never redeemed themselves—yet Seth was striving to regain my good opinion. He was also sacrificing what he loved—his writing—to help the family he loved more. Would that be enough? Could he be saved?

All things are possible.

I sat up from the couch, my gaze falling on the spot where Aubrey and Godiva slept next to each other. Godiva had come to me after I'd dreamed her. The dream I still maintained was impossible.

Miracles are real, Georgina. You've just got to lift yourself out of the muck to make them. You've got to take the chance.

Could I? Would I? Was there a miracle somewhere in the muck of this despair, heartache, death, and betrayal? I couldn't see through it. I didn't know where to start. Carter had said change happened through small acts. All I had to do was pick something. Anything. Take the chance.

Again, I focused on Godiva. The man in the dream. Maybe it was Seth. Maybe it wasn't. Maybe I could make it him. His love had been great enough to rescue me and then try to rescue himself. I realized now what had been bothering me. He was doing all of this—how could I do any less? All my life, I'd hidden from hard choices. I'd always found some compromise to avoid bad things, the results of which never really turned out that great. If anything, they'd become worse. My love for Seth was no less than his for me, but I hadn't been willing to do the things that might hurt.

He'd told me there was no way the universe would let us stay apart. He was right—and this time, *I* would be the one who made sure we came together again. I wouldn't abandon him.

I was moving toward the door, my coat and purse in hand, when Roman came home, carrying flowers. He took one look at me and offered a small bitter laugh that carried all the woe and resignation in the world. The bouquet sagged in his hands.

"You're going to Seth."

"How did you know?"

"Because . . . because you're shining. Because you look like you've found all the answers in the universe."

"I don't know about that," I said. "But I've found some kind of answer. He's risked so much for me. . . . We found each other across all the other souls in the world. . . ." I trailed off, feeling horrible. My decision about Seth burned brightly in me, but Roman's face . . . there seemed to be nothing in this world that didn't end up causing someone pain. "I was wrong to abandon him. Especially now."

"Sounds like you better go to him," said Roman at last.

"Roman—"

He shook his head. "Go."

I went.

I hadn't been to Seth's condo in so long, not in the flesh. Walking up to the door, a barrage of memories flooded me, particularly that first night I'd stayed over when he had taken care of me. . . .

It wasn't that late, but when he opened the door, there was a scattered, mussed look to him that made me think he'd been sleeping. Or maybe he'd just been too consumed by writing to properly groom. It happened sometimes when he got caught up with the worlds in his mind.

From the look on his face, it was clear he was in this world now. I don't think he'd believed he'd see me for a very long time. I wondered if I was still shining the way Roman had claimed I was because Seth's eyes regarded me with more than just surprise. There was wonder and awe there. I'd only driven across town, made one impulse decision to come here, but we might as well have been meeting across time and space again.

"Georgina," he breathed. "What are you—"

I didn't let him finish. I threw myself into his arms and kissed him.

And this time, I didn't pull back.

Chapter 25

Not even when I felt his life energy come into me. I kept going.

He pulled me into his condo, deftly kicking the door shut with his foot. His arms gripped me close, and we never broke the kiss as we stumbled through the living room and into his bedroom. We fell onto the bed, removing each other's clothing with practiced ease, almost like Mexico had just been the warm-up. My hands ran over the lean muscles of his chest, the scent of his skin drowning me. Letting down all restraint made me feel that much giddier—as did the sweet, glorious taste of his soul wrapping around me.

Was it my imagination, or was it a *little* purer than it had been in Mexico? Had one decision to come back and face his fears cleaned that darkness even a little? I didn't know for sure, and even if it wasn't perfect, the energy still felt amazing.

"Why?" he asked at last. His thoughts and feelings were coming through with the energy, and I'd wondered when he'd bring up the question warring with his desire. His hands continued touching me the whole time, one sliding up between my thighs. "Why now?"

I arched my hips against his, crying out softly as his fingers slid into me. His mouth crushed mine, killing off my response for a moment. "Because I'm tired of fighting it. You're right. We're going to keep coming back to each other over and over. . . ." My eloquent speech was put on hold again when his mouth moved down to my breast, letting his tongue toy with my nipple. "You've said before you'll risk the shortening of your life. . . . I'll risk your mortality. I'll risk it all to be with you . . . to help you. If you still want it . . ."

"Yes," he breathed against my flesh. "Yes."

"I won't leave you alone through this," I murmured. "And I don't want to be alone either. . . ."

Those were my last coherent words. He gently rolled himself onto me and slid his hands up my arms so that they could hold my wrists against the bed. I spread my legs, welcoming his body as it pushed into mine. Just like the first time we'd had sex, there was one perfect moment—one moment of astonishing, total completion. Like we'd found something we'd lost and were afraid we'd lose it again if we moved.

Then, the metaphysical sentiment was gone, replaced by the driving desire of our bodies. He thrust into me, gently at first, then steadily increased the strength. I stared at him wide-eyed, taking in every feature, refusing to miss one instant of this experience. And believe me, I was getting quite the experience. Aside from the ecstasy of our bodies moving together, I still had his energy and feelings coming in. Knowing what he was thinking as we made love added a whole new dimension to it all. Sometimes with men it would be coherent thoughts. With him, it was just pure emotion. Love and trust and longing . . . feelings so strong that he was willing to risk anything for them, anything to be with me. Even his life.

My body burned against his, growing increasingly turned on by the rapture and love on his face juxtaposed with the fierceness of the way he held me and kept pushing into me. Everything grew more intense—both physically and spiritually—and my body finally reached its breaking point. I came with a loud cry and thrashed against him, wanting to free my arms and wrap them around him. He continued holding me until he came, which didn't take much longer. The full burst of his soul's energy flooded me with his orgasm, and I heard myself moaning again at the joy of it. He thrust in a few more times, the motions growing slower and longer as his body took its release. The grip on my wrists loosened, and he shifted over to his side, taking me with him. I pressed against his chest, feeling the racing of his heart and sweat on his skin.

My own heart was pounding too as my body reveled in its own satiation. Every part of me still tingled, and though there was really no way to get closer, I tried anyway. I wanted as much skin to touch as possible. I wanted as much of him blending into me as possible. He brushed the hair from my face and rained kisses down upon my forehead.

"So that's the full succubus effect, huh?"

"Yup."

"Worth it," he murmured. Already, I could see the loss of energy taking its toll. "Whatever the cost, worth it."

I refused to allow myself to ponder that cost. Making love in the full throes of my succubus abilities might have added a powerful element, but it had undoubtedly taken years off his life. It wasn't for me to decide if it had been worth it, though. He'd made this choice.

Said choice was exhausting him, and I knew he'd soon sleep for a very long time as his body and soul recovered their losses. I shifted so that we changed positions, bringing his head to lie against my breasts.

"Rest," I said, wrapping my arms around him.

He tilted his head, looking up at me with warm, sleepy eyes. "Don't want to sleep yet . . . I want to stay with you. Will you be here in the morning this time?"

"Yes," I said, kissing the top of his head. "I promise. I won't leave you again."

A small smile played over his lips, and he allowed his lids to close. He snuggled against me, body relaxing. "The world . . ." he said softly, as sleep began taking him. "You are the world, Letha. . . ."

I stiffened.

"What did you say?"

My voice was too loud, jarring enough to momentarily startle him out of the slumber his body now longed for. "Hmm? I said you were the world, Georgina." He gave a small yawn.

"That's not what you called me," I said, trying to keep my voice calm.

"What did I call you? Thetis?" Oh, if only. If only it had been his nickname for me.

"You called me . . . Letha."

He fought to keep his eyes open and yawned again. "Why would I have said that?"

"I . . . don't know. Where did you hear it?"

Yes, indeed. Where *would* he have heard my name? Hardly anyone knew it. Greater immortals knew it, and that was pretty much it. The only lesser immortals who did were Niphon and Kristin, who'd had access to my records. I was pretty sure they'd never told my other immortal friends. I was confident they'd never told Seth.

Seth's brow furrowed a little, then smoothed as he closed his eyes again. "Don't know. Greek myths, I guess. The River Lethe, where the dead go to wash away the memories from their souls . . . to forget the past. Isn't that right?"

"Yes," I said, scarcely breathing. *Where did he pull that name from?*

"Letha, Lethe . . ." I could barely hear him now. "Almost the same."

"Almost," I agreed. My voice was nearly as inaudible as his. My name. He shouldn't have known my name. A panic I couldn't explain began fluttering within me.

Something about my mood must have still penetrated his haze because he stirred slightly, though his eyes remained closed. There was worry in his drowsy words.

"What's wrong?"

"Nothing. Get some rest."

Where had he heard my name? Minutes ago I'd been on fire. Now I felt cold.

"You sure?" he murmured. "Everything's okay?" He exhaled deeply, and I felt him succumb to sleep with those last words.

"Fine," I said, staring off into the night. "Everything's fine."

RICHELLE MEAD

If you love Richelle's sensational 'Succubus' series, why not try her fast and fun 'Dark Swan' novels, featuring shaman-for-hire Eugenie Markham who's got her hands full binding and banishing creatures from the Othwerworld . . .

Storm Born and *Thorn Queen* are both out in paperback and over the page you'll find the opening chapter to each of these stories.

And the good news is that there's more great reading to come from this bestselling writer.

STORM BORN

Chapter 1

I'd seen weirder things than a haunted shoe, but not many.

The Nike Pegasus sat on the office's desk, inoffensive, colored in shades of gray, white, and orange. Some of the laces were loosened, and a bit of dirt clung around the soles. It was the left shoe.

As for me, well . . . underneath my knee-length coat, I had a Glock .22 loaded with bullets carrying a higher-than-legal steel content. A cartridge of silver ones rested in the coat's pocket. Two athames lay sheathed on my other hip, one silver-bladed and one iron. Stuck into my belt near them was a wand, hand-carved oak and loaded with enough charmed gems to probably blow up the desk in the corner if I wanted to.

To say I felt overdressed was something of an understatement.

"So," I said, keeping my voice as neutral as possible, "what makes you think your shoe is . . . uh, possessed?"

Brian Montgomery, late thirties with a receding

hairline in serious denial, eyed the shoe nervously and moistened his lips. "It always trips me up when I'm out running. Every time. And it's always moving around. I mean, I never actually see it, but . . . like, I'll take them off near the door, then I come back and find this one under the bed or something. And sometimes . . . sometimes I touch it, and it feels cold . . . really cold . . . like . . ." He groped for similes and finally picked the tritest one. "Like ice."

I nodded and glanced back at the shoe, not saying anything.

"Look, Miss . . . Odile . . . or whatever. I'm not crazy. That shoe is haunted. It's evil. You've gotta do something, okay? I've got a marathon coming up, and until this started happening, these were my lucky shoes. And they're not cheap, you know. They're an investment."

It sounded crazy to me—which was saying something—but there was no harm in checking, seeing as I was already out here. I reached into my coat pocket, the one without ammunition, and pulled out my pendulum. It was a simple one, a thin silver chain with a small quartz crystal hanging from it.

I laced the chain's end through my fingers and held my flattened hand over the shoe, clearing my mind and letting the crystal hang freely. A moment later, it began to slowly rotate of its own accord.

"Well, I'll be damned," I muttered, stuffing the pendulum back in my pocket. There was something there. I turned to Montgomery, attempting some sort of badass face, because that was what customers always expected. "It might be best if you stepped out of the room, sir. For your own safety."

That was only half-true. Mostly I just found lingering clients annoying. They asked stupid questions and could do stupider things, which actually put me at more risk than them.

He had no qualms about getting out of there. As soon as the door closed, I found a jar of salt in my satchel and poured a large ring on the office's floor. I tossed the shoe into the middle of it and invoked the four cardinal directions with the silver athame. Ostensibly the circle didn't change, but I felt a slight flaring of power, indicating it had sealed us in.

Trying not to yawn, I pulled out my wand and kept holding the silver athame. It had taken four hours to drive to Las Cruces, and doing that on so little sleep had made the distance seem twice as long. Sending some of my will into the wand, I tapped it against the shoe and spoke in a sing-song voice.

"Come out, come out, whoever you are."

There was a moment's silence, then a high-pitched male voice snapped, "Go away, bitch."

Great. A shoe with attitude. "Why? You got something better to do?"

"Better things to do than waste my time with a mortal."

I smiled. "Better things to do in a shoe? Come

287

on. I mean, I've heard of slumming it, but don't you think you're kind of pushing the envelope here? This shoe isn't even new. You could have done so much better."

The voice kept its annoyed tone, not threatening but simply irritated at the interruption. "*I'm* slumming it? Do you think I don't know who you are, Eugenie Markham? Dark-Swan-Called-Odile. A blood traitor. A mongrel. An assassin. A murderer." He practically spit out the last word. "You are alone among your kind and mine. A bloodthirsty shadow. You do anything for anyone who can pay you enough for it. That makes you more than a mercenary. That makes you a whore."

I affected a bored stance. I'd been called most of those names before. Well, except for my own name. That was new—and a little disconcerting. Not that I'd let him know that.

"Are you done whining? Because I don't have time to listen while you stall."

"Aren't you being paid by the hour?" he asked nastily.

"I charge a flat fee."

"Oh."

I rolled my eyes and touched the wand to the shoe again. This time, I thrust the full force of my will into it, drawing upon my own body's physical stamina as well as some of the power of the world around me. "No more games. If you leave on your own, I won't have to hurt you. *Come out.*"

He couldn't stand against that command and the power within it. The shoe trembled, and smoke poured out of it. Oh, Jesus. I hoped the shoe didn't get incinerated during this. Montgomery wouldn't be able to handle that.

The smoke bellowed out, coalescing into a large, dark form about two feet taller than me. With all his wisecracks, I'd sort of expected a saucy version of one of Santa's elves. Instead, the being before me had the upper body of a well-muscled man, while his lower portion resembled a small cyclone. The smoke solidified into leathery gray-black skin, and I had only a moment to act as I assessed this new development. I swapped the wand for the gun, ejecting the clip as I pulled it out. By then, he was lunging for me, and I had to roll out of his way, confined by the circle's boundaries.

A keres. A male keres—most unusual. I'd anticipated something fey, which required silver bullets; or a spectre, which required no bullets. Keres were ancient death spirits originally confined to canopic jars. When the jars wore down over time, keres tended to seek out new homes. There weren't too many of them left in this world, and soon there'd be one less.

He bore down on me, and I took a nice chunk out of him with the silver blade. I used my right hand, the one I wore an onyx and obsidian bracelet on. Those stones alone would take a toll on a death spirit like him without the blade's help.

Sure enough, he hissed in pain and hesitated a moment. I used that delay, scrambling to load the silver cartridge.

I didn't quite make it, because soon he was on me again. He hit me with one of those massive arms, slamming me against the walls of the circle. They might be transparent, but they felt as solid as bricks. One of the downsides of trapping a spirit in a circle was that I got trapped too. My head and left shoulder took the brunt of that impact, and pain shot through me in small starbursts. He seemed pretty pleased with himself over this, as overconfident villains so often are.

"You're as strong as they say, but you were a fool to try to cast me out. You should have left me in peace." His voice was deeper now, almost gravelly.

I shook my head, both to disagree and to get rid of the dizziness. "It isn't your shoe."

I still couldn't swap that goddamned cartridge. Not with him ready to attack again, not with both hands full. Yet I couldn't risk dropping either weapon.

He reached for me, and I cut him again. The wounds were small, but the athame was like poison. It would wear him down over time—if I could stay alive that long. I moved to strike at him once more, but he anticipated me and seized hold of my wrist. He squeezed it, bending it in an unnatural position and forcing me to drop the athame and cry out. I hoped he hadn't broken any bones.

Smug, he grabbed me by the shoulders with both hands and lifted me up so that I hung face to face with him. His eyes were yellow with slits for pupils, much like some sort of snake's. His breath was hot and reeked of decay as he spoke.

"You are small, Eugenie Markham, but you are lovely and your flesh is warm. Perhaps I should beat the rush and take you myself. I'd enjoy hearing you scream beneath me."

Ew. Had that thing just propositioned me? And there was my name again. How in the world did he know that? None of them knew that. I was only Odile to them, named after the dark swan in *Swan Lake*, a name coined by my stepfather because of the form my spirit preferred to travel in while visiting the Otherworld. The name—though not particularly terrifying—had stuck, though I doubted any of the creatures I fought knew the reference. They didn't really get out to the ballet much.

The keres had my upper arms pinned—I would have bruises tomorrow—but my hands and forearms were free. He was so sure of himself, so overly arrogant and confident, that he paid no attention to my struggling hands. He probably just perceived the motion as a futile effort to free myself. In seconds, I had the clip out and in the gun. I managed one clumsy shot and he dropped me—not gently. I stumbled to regain my balance again. Bullets probably couldn't kill him, but a silver one in the center of his chest would certainly hurt.

He stumbled back, half-surprised, and I wondered if he'd ever even encountered a gun before. It fired again, then again and again and again. The reports were loud; hopefully Montgomery wouldn't do something foolish and come running in. The keres roared in outrage and pain, each shot making him stagger backward until he was all the way against the circle's boundary. I advanced on him, retrieved athame flashing in my hand. In a few quick motions, I carved the death symbol on the part of his chest that wasn't bloodied from bullets. An electric charge immediately ran through the air of the circle. Hairs stood up on the back of my neck, and I could smell ozone, like just before a storm.

He screamed and leapt forward, renewed by rage or adrenaline or whatever else these creatures ran on. But it was too late for him. He was marked and wounded. I was ready. In another mood, I might have simply banished him to the Otherworld; I tried not to kill if I didn't have to. But that sexual suggestion had just been out of line. I was pissed off now. He'd go to the world of death, straight to Persephone's gate.

I fired again to slow him, my aim a bit off with the left hand but still good enough to hit him. I had already traded the athame for the wand. This time, I didn't draw on the power from this plane. With well-practiced ease, I let part of my consciousness slip this world. In moments, I reached the crossroads to the Otherworld. That was an easy transition; I did it all the time. The next crossover was a little harder, especially with me being weakened from the fight, but still nothing I couldn't do automatically. I kept my own spirit well outside of the land of death, but I touched it and sent that connection through the wand. It sucked him in, and his face twisted with fear.

"This is not your world," I said in a low voice, feeling the power burn through me and around me. "This is not your world, and I cast you out. I send you to the black gate, to the lands of death where you can either be reborn or fade to oblivion or burn in the flames of hell. I really don't give a shit. *Go.*"

He screamed, but the magic caught him. There was a trembling in the air, a build-up of pressure, and then it ended abruptly, like a deflated balloon. The keres was gone too, leaving only a shower of gray sparkles that soon faded to nothing.

Silence. I sank to my knees, exhaling deeply. My eyes closed a moment, as my body relaxed and my consciousness returned to this world. I was exhausted but exultant too. Killing him had felt good. Heady, even. He'd gotten what he deserved, and I had been the one to deal it out.

Minutes later, some of my strength returned. I stood and opened the circle, suddenly feeling stifled by it. I put my tools and weapons away and went to find Montgomery.

"Your shoe's been exorcised," I told him flatly. "I killed the ghost." No point in explaining the difference between a keres and a true ghost; he wouldn't understand.

He entered the room with slow steps, picking up the shoe gingerly. "I heard gunshots. How do you use bullets on a ghost?"

I shrugged. It hurt from where the keres had slammed my shoulder to the wall. "It was a strong ghost."

He cradled the shoe like one might a child and then glanced down with disapproval. "There's blood on the carpet."

"Read the paperwork you signed. I assume no responsibility for damage incurred to personal property."

With a few grumbles, he paid up—in cash—and I left. Really, though, he was so stoked about the shoe, I probably could have decimated the office.

In my car, I dug out a Milky Way from the stash in my glove box. Battles like that required immediate sugar and calories. As I practically shoved the candy bar into my mouth, I turned on my cell phone. I had a missed call from Lara.

Once I'd consumed a second bar and was on I-10 back to Tucson, I dialed her.

"Yo," I said.

"Hey. Did you finish the Montgomery job?"

"Yup."

"Was the shoe really possessed?"

"Yup."

"Huh. Who knew? That's kind of funny too.

Like, you know, lost souls and soles in shoes . . ."

"Bad, very bad," I chastised. Lara might be a good secretary, but there was only so much I could be expected to put up with. "So what's up? Or were you just checking in?"

"No. I just got a weird job offer. Some guy— well, honestly, I thought he sounded kind of schizo. But he claims his sister was abducted by fairies, er, gentry. He wants you to go get her."

I fell silent at that, staring at the highway and clear blue sky ahead without consciously seeing either one. Some objective part of me attempted to process what she had just said. I didn't get that kind of request very often. Okay, never. A retrieval like that required me to cross over physically into the Otherworld. "I don't really do that."

"That's what I told him." But there was uncertainty in Lara's voice.

"Okay. What aren't you telling me?"

"Nothing, I guess. I don't know. It's just . . . he said she's been gone almost a year and a half now. She was fourteen when she disappeared."

My stomach sank a little at that. God. What an awful fate for someone so young. It made the keres' lewd comments to me downright trivial.

"He sounded pretty frantic."

"Does he have proof she was actually taken?"

"I don't know. He wouldn't get into it. He was kind of paranoid. Seemed to think his phone was being tapped."

I laughed at that. "By who? The gentry?" "Gentry" was what I called the beings that most of Western culture referred to as fairies or sidhe. They looked just like humans but embraced magic instead of technology. They found "fairy" a derogatory term, so I respected that—sort of—by using the term old English peasants used to use. *Gentry.* Good folk. Good neighbors. A questionable designation, at best. The gentry actually preferred the term "shining ones," but that was just silly. I wouldn't give them that much credit.

"I don't know," Lara told me. "Like I said, he seemed a little schizo."

Silence fell as I held onto the phone and passed a car driving 45 in the left lane.

"Eugenie! You aren't really thinking of doing this."

"Fourteen, huh?"

"You always said that was dangerous."

"Adolescence?"

"Stop it. You know what I mean. Crossing over."

"Yeah. I know what you mean."

It was dangerous—super dangerous. Traveling in spirit form could still get you killed, but your odds of fleeing back to your earthbound body were better. Take your own body over, and all the rules changed.

"This is crazy."

"Set it up," I told her. "It can't hurt to talk to him."

I could practically see her biting her lip to hold

back protests. But at the end of the day, I was the one who signed her paychecks, and she respected that. After a few moments, she filled the silence with info about a few other jobs and then drifted on to more casual topics: some sale at the mall, a mysterious scratch on her car . . .

Something about Lara's cheery gossip always made me smile, but it also disturbed me that most of my social contact came via someone I never actually saw. Lately the majority of my face-to-face interactions came from spirits and gentry.

It was after dinnertime when I arrived home, and my housemate, Tim, appeared to be out for the night, probably at a poetry reading. Despite a Polish background, genes had inexplicably given him a strong Native American appearance. In fact, he looked more Indian than some of the locals. Deciding this was his claim to fame, Tim had grown his hair out and taken on the name Timothy Red Horse. He made his living by reading faux-Native poetry at local dives and wooing naive tourist women by using expressions like, "my people" and "the Great Spirit" a lot. It was despicable, to say the least, but it got him laid pretty often. What it did not do was bring in a lot of money, so I'd let him live with me in exchange for housework and cleaning. It was a pretty good deal as far as I was concerned. After battling the undead all day, scrubbing the bathtub just seemed like asking too much.

Scrubbing my athames, unfortunately, was a task I had to do myself. Keres blood could stain.

I ate dinner afterward, then stripped and sat in my sauna for a long time. I liked a lot of things about my little house out in the foothills, but the sauna was one of my favorites. It might seem kind of pointless in the desert, but Arizona had mostly dry heat, and I liked the feel of humidity and moisture on my skin. I leaned back against the wooden wall, enjoying the sensation of sweating out the stress. My body ached—some parts more fiercely than others—and the heat let some of the muscles loosen up.

The solitude also soothed me. Pathetic as it was, I probably had no one to blame for my lack of sociability except myself. I spent a lot of time alone and didn't mind. When my stepfather, Roland, had first trained me as a shaman, he'd told me that in a lot of cultures, shamans essentially lived outside of normal society. The idea had seemed crazy to me at the time, being in junior high, but it made more sense now that I was older.

I wasn't a complete socialphobe, but I found I often had a hard time interacting with other people. Talking in front of groups was murder. Even talking one-on-one had its issues. I had no pets or children to ramble on about, and I couldn't exactly talk about things like the incident in Las Cruces. *Yeah, I had kind of a long day. Drove four hours, fought an ancient minion of evil.*

298

After a few bullets and knife wounds, I obliterated him and sent him on to the world of death. God, I swear I'm not getting paid enough for this crap, you know? Cue polite laughter.

When I left the sauna, I had another message from Lara telling me the appointment with the distraught brother had been arranged for tomorrow. I made a note in my day planner, took a shower, and retired to my room, where I threw on black silk pajamas. For whatever reason, nice pajamas were the one indulgence I allowed myself in an otherwise dirty and bloody lifestyle. Tonight's selection had a cami top that showed serious cleavage, had anyone been there to see it. I always wore a ratty robe around Tim.

Sitting at my desk, I emptied out a new jigsaw puzzle I'd just bought. It depicted a kitten on its back clutching a ball of yarn. My love of puzzles ranked up there with the pajama thing for weird-ness, but they eased my mind. Maybe it was the fact that they were so tangible. You could hold the pieces in your hand and make them fit together, as opposed to the insubstantial stuff I usually worked with.

While my hands moved the pieces around, I kept trying to shake the knowledge that the keres had known my name. What did that mean? I'd made a lot of enemies in the Otherworld. I didn't like the thought of them being able to track me personally. I preferred to stay Odile. Anonymous. Safe. Probably not much point worrying about it, I supposed. The keres was dead. He wouldn't be telling any tales.

Two hours later, I finished the puzzle and admired it. The kitten had brown tabby fur, its eyes an almost azure blue. The yarn was red. I took out my digital camera, snapped a picture, and then broke up the puzzle, dumping it back into its box. Easy come, easy go.

Yawning, I slipped into bed. Tim had done laundry today; the sheets felt crisp and clean. Nothing like that fresh-sheets smell. Despite my exhaustion, however, I couldn't fall asleep. It was one of life's ironies. While awake, I could slide into a trance with the snap of a finger. My spirit could leave my body and travel to other worlds. Yet, for whatever reason, sleep was more elusive. Doctors had recommended a number of sedatives, but I hated to use them. Drugs and alcohol bound the spirit to this world, and while I did indulge occasionally, I generally liked being ready to slip over at a moment's notice.

Tonight I suspected my insomnia had something to do with a teenage girl . . . . But no. I couldn't think about that, not yet. Not until I spoke with the brother.

Sighing, needing something else to ponder, I rolled over and stared at my ceiling, at the plastic glow-in-the-dark stars. I started counting them, as I had so many other restless nights. There were exactly thirty-three of them, just like last time. Still, it never hurt to check.

THORN QUEEN

Chapter One

Sad fact: lots of kids know how to use knives and guns.

I'd been one of them, but instead of pursuing a life of crime, I'd trained to be a shamanic mercenary. This meant that while my friends were at dances and football games, I'd been out banishing spirits and wrestling down monsters with my stepfather. On the upside, I grew up never fearing muggers or any other assailants. On the downside, an adolescence like that really screws with your social development.

It meant I'd never really been like other kids. I'd had some friends, but compared to their world, mine had been terribly stark and terribly deadly. Their dramas and concerns had seemed so petty next to mine, and I could never fully relate. As an adult now, I still couldn't really connect to kids because I had no shared experiences to draw on.

Which made my job today that much more difficult.

"Go ahead, Polly," crooned the girl's mother,

smiling with overplump lips. Too much collagen, I suspected. "Tell her about the ghost."

Polly Hall was thirteen but wore enough makeup to rival a forty-year-old whore. She sat slouched against the back of a couch in her family's perfectly decorated house, chewing gum loudly, looking everywhere but at us. The more I studied her, the more I decided she probably did have problems. I suspected they had less to do with supernatural influences and more with having a mother who had named her Polly and let her wear thongs. It was an unfortunate side effect of Polly's low-cut jeans that I could see the afore-mentioned thong.

After a minute of silence, Mrs. Hall sighed loudly. "Polly, dear, we've been over this. If you aren't going to help us, we can't help you."

Smiling, I knelt down in front of the couch so I could look the girl in the eyes. "It's all right," I told her, hoping I sounded sincere and not like an after-school special. "I'll believe whatever you tell me. We'll get it taken care of."

Polly sighed just as loudly as her mother had a moment ago and still refused to look at me. She reminded me of my unstable teenage half sister who was currently MIA and wanted to conquer the world. "Mom," she said, "can I go to my room now?"

"Not until you've talked to this nice lady." Glancing back to me, Mrs. Hall explained. "We

302

hear strange noises all night: bangs, cracks, bumps. Things fall over for no reason. I've even . . ." She hesitated. "I've even seen things fly around the room. But it's always when Polly's around. Whatever this ghost is, it seems to like her . . . or be obsessed with her."

I turned my attention back to Polly, again taking in the sullen mood and thinly veiled frustration. "You got a lot on your mind, Polly?" I asked gently. "Problems at school or something? Problems around here?"

Her blue eyes flicked to me ever so briefly.

"What about any electrical issues?" This I directed to her mother. "Things shorting out? Stereos or appliances not working right?"

Mrs. Hall blinked. "How'd you know that?"

I stood up and stretched the kinks out of my body. I'd fought a wraith last night, and he hadn't been gentle.

"You don't have a ghost. You have a poltergeist."

Both of them stared at me.

"Isn't that a ghost?" asked Mrs. Hall.

"Not really. It's a manifestation of telekinetic powers, often brought on by rage and other strong emotions during teenage years." I'd evaded after-school special mode, only to slip into infomercial mode.

"I . . . wait. Are you saying Polly's causing this?"

"Not consciously, but yeah. In cases like this, the subject—Polly—lashes out without realizing it, venting her emotions in physical ways. She probably won't stay telekinetic. It'll fade as she gets older and settles down a bit."

Her mother still looked skeptical. "It sure seems like a ghost."

I shrugged. "Trust me. I've seen this lots of times."

"So . . . isn't there anything you can do? Anything we can do?"

"Therapy," I suggested. "Maybe get a psychic to come out."

I gave Mrs. Hall the contact information for a psychic I trusted. Waiving my banishing fee, I simply charged her for the house call. Once I'd double-checked the cash she gave me—I *never* took checks—I stashed it away and made moves toward the living-room door.

"Sorry I couldn't be of more help."

"No, I mean, I guess this helps. It's just so strange." She eyed her daughter with perplexity. "Are you sure it's not a ghost?"

"Positive. These are classic symp—"

An invisible force slammed into me, pushing me into the wall. I yelped, threw out a hand to keep my balance, and shot daggers at that little bitch Polly. Eyes wide, she looked just as astonished as I felt.

"Polly!" exclaimed Mrs. Hall. "You are grounded, young lady. No phone, no IM, no . . ." Her mouth dropped open as she stared at something across the room. "What's that?"

I followed her gaze to the large, pale blue shape materializing before us.

"Um, well," I said, "that's a ghost."

It swooped toward me, mouth open in a terrible screech. I yelled for the others to get down and jerked a silver-bladed athame out of my belt. A knife might seem useless against spirits, but they needed to take on a substantial form to inflict any real damage. Once solid, they were susceptible to silver.

This spirit bore a female shape—a very young female shape, actually. Long pale hair trailed in her wake like a cloak, and her eyes were large and empty. Whether it was a lack of experience or simply some inherent trait of hers, her attack proved floundering and uncoordinated. Even as she screamed at the first bites of the athame, I had my crystal-studded wand out in my other hand.

Now that I'd regained my bearings, I could do a banishing like this in my sleep. Speaking the usual words, I drew from my internal strength and sent my own spirit beyond the boundaries of this world. Touching the gates of the Underworld, I ensnared the female spirit and sent her over. Monsters and gentry I tended to send back to the Otherworld, the limbo they lived in. A ghost like this needed to move on to the land of death. She disappeared.

Mrs. Hall and Polly stared at me. Suddenly, in her first show of emotion, the girl leapt up and glared at me.

"You just killed my best friend!"

I opened my mouth to respond and decided nothing I had to say would be adequate.

"Good heavens, what are you talking about?" exclaimed her mother.

Polly's face twisted with anger, her eyes bright with tears. "Trixie. She was my best friend. We told each other everything."

"Trixie?" Mrs. Hall and I asked in unison.

"I can't believe you did that. She was so cool." Polly's voice turned a little wistful. "I just wish we could have gone shopping together, but she couldn't leave the house. So I just had to bring her *Vogue* and *Glamour*."

I turned to Mrs. Hall. "My original advice still stands. Therapy. Lots of it."

I headed home after that, wondering for the hundredth time why I'd chosen this mercenary shaman profession. Surely there were other jobs that were a lot less trouble than interacting with evil supernatural beings. Accounting. Advertising. Law. Well, maybe not that last one.

About an hour later, I arrived back home and was immediately assaulted by two medium-sized dogs when I cleared the door. They were mutts, one solid black and one solid white. Their names were Yin and Yang, but I could never remember who was who.

"Back off," I warned as they sniffed me, tails wagging frantically. The white one tried to lick my hand. Pushing past them, I entered my kitchen and nearly tripped over a tabby cat sprawled on the floor in a patch of sun. Grumbling, I tossed my bag onto the kitchen table. "Tim? Are you here?"

My housemate, Tim Warkoski, stuck his head into the kitchen. He wore a T-shirt with silhouettes of Native Americans that said *Homeland Security: Fighting Terrorism since 1492.* I appreciated the cleverness, but it lost something since Tim wasn't actually an American Indian. He merely played one on TV, or rather, he played one in local bars and tourist circles, using his tanned skin and black hair to elude his Polish heritage. It had gotten him into trouble with a lot of the local tribes.

With a garbage bag in one hand and a cat scoop in the other, he gave me a dark look. "Do you know how many fucking boxes of litter I've had to change today?"

I poured a glass of milk and sat down at the table. "Kiyo says we need one box for every cat and then an extra one."

"Yeah, I can count, Eugenie. That's six boxes. Six boxes in a house with fifteen hundred square feet. You think your deadbeat boyfriend's ever going to show back up and help out with this?"

I shifted uncomfortably. It was a good question. After three months of dating between Tucson and Phoenix, my boyfriend Kiyo had decided to take a job here to save the hour and a half commute. We'd had a long discussion and decided we were ready to have him simply move in with me. Unfortunately, with Kiyo came his menagerie: five cats and two dogs. It was one of the woes of dating a veterinarian. He couldn't help but adopt every animal he found. I couldn't remember the cats' names any better than the dogs'. Four of them were named after the Horsemen of the Apocalypse, and all I could really recall was that Famine ironically weighed about thirty pounds.

Another problem was that Kiyo was a fox— both literally and figuratively. His mother was a kitsune, a sort of Japanese fox spirit. He'd inherited all of her traits, including amazing strength and speed, as well as the ability to transform into an actual fox. As a result, he frequently got "the call of the wild," making him yearn to run around in his animal form. Since he had downtime between jobs now, he'd left me to take a kind of wild vacation. I accepted this, but after a week of not seeing him, I was starting to get restless.

"He'll be back soon," I said vaguely, not meeting Tim's eyes. "Besides, you can get out of chores if you want to start paying rent." That was our deal. Free lodging in exchange for food and housework.

He wasn't deterred. "Your choice in men is questionable. You know that, right?"

I didn't really want to ponder that too much. I abandoned him for my room, seeking the comfort of a jigsaw puzzle depicting a photograph of Zurich. It sat on my desk, as did one of the cats. I think he was Mr. Whiskers, the non-Apocalyptic one. I shooed him off the puzzle. He took about half the pieces with him.

"Fucking cat," I muttered.

Love, I decided, was a hard thing. Well aware of my grumpy mood, I knew part of my anxiety over Kiyo stemmed from the fact that he was also passing part of his sabbatical in the Otherworld, spending time with his ex-girlfriend who just happened to be a devastatingly beautiful fairy queen. Fairies, sidhe, shining ones . . . whatever you wanted to call them, they were the tall, long-lived rulers of the Otherworld. I and most shamans referred to them as gentry, an antique term. Maiwenn, Kiyo's ex, was almost nine months pregnant, and although they'd broken up, he was still a part of her life.

I sighed. Tim might have been right about my questionable taste in men.

Night wore on. I finished the puzzle while blasting Def Leppard, making me feel better. I was just shutting off the music when I heard Tim yell, "Yo, Eug. Kujo's here."

Breathless, I ran to my bedroom door and flung it open. A red fox the size of a wolf trotted down the hall toward me. Relief burned through me, and I felt my heart soar as I let him in and watched him pace around in restless circles.

"About time," I said.

He had a sleek orange-red coat and a fluffy tail tipped in white. His eyes were golden and sometimes bore a very human glint. I saw nothing like that tonight. A purely animal wariness peered out at me, and I realized it'd be a while before he changed back. He had the ability to transform to a wide range of foxes, everything from a small, normal-sized red fox to the powerful shape before me. When he spent awhile in this bigger form, turning human again took more effort and time.

Still, hoping he'd transform soon, I dumped another puzzle on my desk and worked it as I waited. Two hours later, nothing had changed. He curled up in a corner, wrapping his body in a tight ball. His eyes continued to watch me. Exhausted, I gave up on him and put on a red nightgown. Turning off the lights, I finally slipped into my bed, falling asleep instantly for a change.

As I slept, I dreamed about the Otherworld, particularly a piece of it that bore a striking resemblance to Tucson and the Sonora Desert surrounding us. Only, the Otherworldly version was better. An almost heavenly Tucson, warmed by bright sunshine and ablaze with flowering cacti. This was a common dream for me, one that often left me yearning for that land in the morning. I always tried my best to ignore the impulse.

A couple hours later, I woke up. A warm, muscled body had slid into bed with me, pressing against my back. Strong arms wrapped around my waist, and Kiyo's scent, dark and musky, washed over me. A liquid feeling burned inside of me at his touch. Roughly, he turned me toward him. His lips consumed me in a crushing kiss, blazing with intensity and need.

"Eugenie," he growled, once he'd paused long enough to remove his lips—just barely—from mine. "I've missed you. Oh God, I've missed you. I've needed you."

He kissed me again, conveying that need as his hands ravaged my body. My own hands slid along the smooth perfection of his bare skin, awakening my desire. There was no gentleness between us tonight, only a feral passion as he moved on top of me, his body pushing into mine with a need fueled as much by animal instinct as by love. He had not, I realized, completely regained his human senses, no matter his shape.

When I woke up in the morning, my bed was empty. Across the room, Kiyo pulled on jeans, meeting my eyes as though he had some sixth sense that I was awake. I rolled over on my side, the sheets gliding against my naked skin. Watching him with a lazy, satisfied languor, I admired his body and the sexy features gifted to him by Japanese and Hispanic heritage. His tanned body and black hair stood in stark contrast to the light skin and reddish hair my northern European ancestors had given me.

"Are you leaving?" I asked. My heart, having leapt at his presence last night, suddenly sank.

"I have to go back," he said, straightening out a dark green T-shirt. He ran an absent-minded hand through his chin-length hair. "You know I do."

"Yeah," I said, my voice sharper than I'd intended. "Of course you do."

His eyes narrowed. "Please don't start that," he said quietly. "I have to do this."

"Sorry. Somehow I just can't get all that excited about another woman having your baby."

There it was. The issue that always hung over us.

He sat down beside me on the bed, dark eyes serious and level. "Well, I'm excited. I'd like to think you could support me in that and be happy for me."

Troubled, I looked away. "I am happy for you. I want you to be happy . . . it's just, you know, it's hard."

"I know." He leaned over me, sliding his hand

up the back of my neck, twining his fingers in my hair.

"You've spent more time with her in the last week than with me."

"It's a necessity. It's almost time."

"I know," I repeated. I knew my jealousy was unwarranted. Petty, even. I wanted to share his happiness at having a child, but something in me prevented it.

"Eugenie, I love you. It's that simple. That's all there is to it."

"You love her too."

"Yes, but not in the way I love you."

He kissed me with a gentleness very different from the roughness of last night. I melted against him. The kiss grew stronger, filling with ardor. With great reluctance, he finally pulled away. I could see the longing in his eyes. He wanted to have sex again. That said something for my charms, I guessed.

His responsible inclinations winning out, he straightened and stood up. I stayed where I was.

"Will I see you there?" he asked, voice even and neutral.

I sighed. "Yeah. I'll be there."

He smiled. "Thank you. That means a lot to me."

I nodded.

He went to the door and looked back at me. "I

love you." The heat in his voice told me he truly meant it. I smiled back.

"I love you too."

He left, and I pulled the sheets more tightly against me and made no motions to get up. I couldn't stay in bed all day, unfortunately. Other things—like my promise to Kiyo—demanded my attention today. There was a trip to the Otherworld ahead of me, one that would take me to a kingdom I'd reluctantly inherited. You see, Maiwenn wasn't the only Otherworldly queen in Kiyo's life.

Yet, astonishingly, that wasn't the problem for me today. That was easy compared to what else lay in store for me.

I had to go to a gentry baby shower.